WINGS OF STEELE
The Series

EPIC SCIENCE FICTION ACTION-ADVENTURE NOVELS

"I don't know how he does it but each book just keeps getting better... The dialogue between Jack and Lisa is worth the price of the book. A really good story, well written. Keep it going Mr. Burger, I am already anxious for Book 4." Robert H.

"I just finished reading Revenge and Retribution and loved it. It is very fast paced and flows well. I loved your assessment of the world situation and in particular what is happening here in the U.S. I realize that this is a work of fiction but I think you are right-on with what occurs with the alphabet agencies. I look forward to reading the further adventures..." K. S. P.

"All I can say is... WHAT A RIDE!!! This was definitely an edge of the seater... It's going to be hard to wait for the next book. I'm going to read it again and savor it. Thanks for another WOWZER of a story." Jolene E.

"Book three kept up the high standards of the preceding volumes in the series. The cliffhanger ending left me wanting more." Gary K. R.

"I could have read this in one sitting... I wanted to read this in one sitting... but my wife had other plans. All through dinner with our friends, all I could think of was getting back to this book!" Mark W.

"Intense. Relentless. Fun. Exciting. Couldn't put it down and loved every minute of it. Jack Steele is the character you want to be, but I'd be happy just being on his crew." Bobby, R

"The universe unfolds before my eyes and it feels so real, like I get to actually be a part of it, living it. Mr. Burger switches from space to current events on Earth and back again, weaving reality and science fiction together so naturally it's almost frightening. Love the tidbits of history! I really look forward to the continuation of the series." Tony S.

WINGS of STEELE
REVENGE and RETRIBUTION

A NOVEL BY
JEFFREY J. BURGER

Books in the series...

www.wingsofsteele.com

First Print Edition September 2014

Published in the United States by Templar Press. Templar Press and the mounted Templar Knight colophon are registered trademarks and may not be reproduced.

TEMPLAR PRESS

Wings of Steele – Revenge and Retribution
Copyright © 2014 Jeffrey J. Burger

Registered with the Library of Congress
ISBN-13: 978-0692258750 (Templar Press)
ISBN-10: 0692258752

Cover artwork, copyright © 2014 Jeffrey J. Burger
WINGS of STEELE logo, copyright © 2014 Jeffrey J. Burger
www.wingsofsteele.com

DEDICATION

I want to thank all my readers who have enjoyed the Wings of Steele Series of adventures and offered their support, enthusiasm, and interest in the continuation of the story. You will be happy to know that as promised, this projected trilogy has progressed into a true series with a total of five books planned so far. Book 4, Wings of Steele - Dark Cover is the next planned edition.

A huge thanks to Cheryl Stepp, for her expert care and effort in editing the series, she's done a wonderful job.

To Fritz... my buddy, who is turning 10 this summer but never seems to grow up, entertaining me with his skillful silliness and affection.

To my friend Mike, who has had an exceptionally tough year, losing lifelong friends; Bobby, Mark, John and Tony... all while having to fight his own medical issues. I've known you for 35 years, you've never been a quitter, keep going.

To Leslie, for all the things you do, for everyone but yourself, your strength and endless energy never ceases to amaze me... thank you. For all of it.

TABLE OF CONTENTS

PROLOGUE

CARILOON SYSTEM, FREERANGER – DD217 : *FOLLOW THE GOLD*

The DD217, a Miro Class Destroyer cruising under the FreeRanger banner, had cleared the gate from Zender's Trek into Cariloon, en-route to Velora Prime to join the FreeRanger flotilla. Her captain, Commander T. B. Yafuscko, was taking a little time to update his command logs in his ready room, paging though his notes on his e-Pad, enjoying a moment of peace and quiet with a cup of dark tea. Reviewing the profit and loss statements for their current set of missions sent from Council Dispatch, Tibby was still hoping to cash in on part of the bounty offered on the Freedom to push them a little further into the black. Granted, the 217's accounts were out of the red, but even a portion of the bounty would be a juicy addition. And a little action would be nice... Ever since they had left Raefer Station he'd felt like a glorified taxi driver. He sighed and leaned back against the arm of the sofa to close his eyes for a moment...

"Red Alert! All hands to battle stations! All hands to battle stations!"

Lights flashed red and the alarm klaxon blared, launching the Commander out of his comfortable recline, his e-Pad clattering to the floor as he hustled out onto the bridge. "Report!" he shouted, sliding into his command chair.

"A cruiser just dropped out of a GOD jump, sir." *Gate on Demand.*

Yafuscko initiated his command and control screens, trying to retrieve data on the target. "What do you mean *dropped out* of GOD, how is that possible?"

"She's heavily damaged, sir, I'm guessing her GOD systems failed and it dumped her here..."

The Commander glanced up at the big screen, "All stop! Whose is she?"

"Ours..." replied the tactical officer. "It's... it's the CC64."

Yafuscko felt a sudden rush of heat across his body, the CC64 had been in Velora Prime... *By the Gods, she is absolutely shredded...* "Open communications!"

"She's not responding, sir, her comms are down..."

Ensign Grinah appeared at the Commander's side, her hand resting on his shoulder, "What's going on Tibby?" she whispered.

"It's the CC64, it just dropped out of GOD in front of us..."

"Hellion, she looks horrible... She was in..."

"Velora Prime..." said the Commander with a wince, finishing her sentence.

The tactical officer looked back over his shoulder, "Sir, she's got a runaway core... she's launching E-pods."

"Dammit! Helm, pull us back, get us clear."

"Aye, sir. Full reverse thrusters."

He pointed at the empty First Mate's seat, "Grinah, get the boys ready to run the shuttles on emergency pod recoveries..."

"Think any of those pods will survive?" she asked, dropping herself into the seat.

"Depends on how long that core holds out..."

"About thirty seconds," called the science officer.

Streaks of light extended out on both sides of the stricken cruiser's hull, the pods racing away, invisible in the darkness except for the brilliant tails of their engines.

"Tracking pods..." Small green markers winked into view, drifting across the big screen, showing the location of each pod as it raced across the void.

"We're reaching clear radius, sir."

"Fine. All stop at clear radius." He rose from his seat and walked toward the big screen, watching the emergency pods jet across space, his hands resting on his hips. "C'mon people," he breathed, "hurry up, there's not much time..."

Even on the view screen, the flash lit up the bridge as clearly as if it had been viewed first-hand and the Commander scrunched his eyes shut, the crew momentarily shielded their faces. T.B. Yafuscko blinked away the white, watching the sphere of energy, debris and light, grow outward, dissipating as the shock wave did its best to catch the retreating escape pods. "How many did we lose?" he asked grimly.

"About half of them."

"Dammit." He took a deep breath and held it for a moment, letting it out slowly, as the weakening wave passed over the DD217, barely affecting it, the deck rolling gently underneath his feet. "Launch the shuttles for recovery," he said quietly.

"Aye," replied Grinah, "launching shuttles."

9

"Sir! We have another ship entering the system... It's coming in from the gate to Velora Prime."

"Identify."

"Stand by." The science officer narrowed the sensors, his fingers dancing across the glass keyboard. "She's one of ours... It's the DD158, sir. She's damaged but mostly intact. Looks like she's operating on one engine."

What the Hellion went on in Velora Prime? "Hail, please." The Commander was still standing in the middle of the bridge facing the screen, his arms now folded across his chest.

"This is Commander Boxxe, FreeRanger DD158..."

Tibby looked over his shoulder, "Where's the picture?"

"Audio only, sir."

He nodded and turned back, staring at the mess of debris littering the center of the system. "Commander T. B. Yafuscko, FreeRanger DD217. Can we be of assistance?"

"I think we'll make it, Commander... can't say as much for some of our other ships..."

"What happened out there, Commander Boxxe?"

"Damned if I know. We had them by the numbers, but they knew we were coming, they jumped us coming through the gate. We went through with DD99 and we both got hit from behind. She got hit first, shields down, and it took her stern clean off. It cracked her core and she went almost immediately. We deployed countermeasures so I'm not sure if we were hit or were damaged by the 99 when she went nova, it took one of our engines off and destroyed shields and turrets on that side. We turned right around and headed back into the gate..."

Tibby frowned, "You said you were hit from behind?"

"That's right. There was a Halceón Class Missile Frigate behind us most of the way through the transition from Cariloon to Velora Prime. She pinged FreeRanger, we didn't think anything of it."

"So we have a rogue Ranger out there?"

"Or a spy..."

Tibby dropped his head and let it hang, rolling his neck. "This is not good."

"Sir! Fighters coming through the gate!"

"Relax," called Commander Boxxe over the comm, "they're ours. They had no choice but to try to follow us through, they lost their carrier."

Yafuscko blinked hard, *"We lost a carrier?"*

"Yeah, it went nova right after we jumped in. We never did see what hit it..."

Tibby turned around and headed back to his seat, having a difficult time fathoming the loss of one of their carriers. "By the Gods..." He dropped into his seat. "Did they get the Freedom?"

"I honestly don't know, Commander. When we jumped, she was still in the fight as far as we could tell, and there was a fresh UFW battleship *and carrier* entering the engagement... we counted almost a hundred fighters coming from that carrier..."

"Hellion. Where did these new ships come from?"

"No idea. And we weren't in any shape to stick around."

Tibby leaned back in his command chair. "Understood. Where are you headed?"

"Raefer Station for some initial repairs. Enough to get us to the rear for major repairs."

"Safe travels, Mr. Boxxe."

"Thank you. Will you be able to pick up these pilots? They are most certainly out of fuel, many of them barely coasted through the gate. We lost several in transition, dropping out into null space when they fell below transition speed protocols. Poor bastards."

"Of course, we won't leave any of them behind." Yafuscko motioned to Ensign Grinah and she nodded her understanding, relaying the orders to the rescue shuttles.

"Thank you. One piece of advice..."

"Yes?"

"Good hunting. But stay out of Velora Prime, Commander. It's ugly. Very ugly. DD158, out."

■ ■ ■

Retreating to the relative quiet of his office, T. B. Yafuscko paused at the e-Pad laying on the floor, staring down at it, having a severe desire to stomp on it or kick it across the floor in his frustration. He took a deep breath, letting it out slowly, and bent over to pick it up instead.

What was it about this ship, the Freedom, that made it so indestructible? She was becoming a phenom, not only to the UFW but to the FreeRangers... revered by one, detested by the other. It was nothing more than a ship, but Tibby was concerned that it was somehow becoming bigger than life, a

11

mystical Messiah of sorts. And when it was finally destroyed, the ship and crew were going to take on some kind of ethereal martyr status. This whole bounty plan could very well backfire on the FreeRanger Council. In a big way. It may already have...

He dropped himself down on the sofa, extending his legs and leaned back against the armrest. When the door chimed, he resisted the urge to throw the e-Pad against it. "Come..." he called.

Ensign Grinah entered, slightly apprehensive, but she relaxed some when he offered her up a warm smile, the corners of his pale blue eyes crinkling up at the corners. "The senior pilot would like a moment of your time, if you have a minute, Tibby."

"Sure," he replied. "How are the recoveries going?"

"Good progress, but we'll be another few hours..."

The Commander nodded, "S'okay. We're in no hurry. After seeing what's coming out of the meat grinder in Velora Prime, we're not going near that system..."

"It's not worth it."

"No, it's not," he sighed. "Though I think I'd like to meet the Captain of that ship some day... have a drink with him..."

"By the Gods," she breathed, "why would you ever..."

"To ask him how he does it..."

WINGS of STEELE – REVENGE and RETRIBUTION
CHAPTER ONE

VELORA PRIME, VELORIA, AIR AND SPACE PORT: *NEW BEGINNINGS*

Rear Admiral Jack Steele stood at the fourth-floor windows of the ASP main-terminal in the executive conference room, arms crossed, overlooking the runways. Long morning shadows stretched across the tarmac from the terminal buildings and control tower, the sky a clear turquoise blue, not a cloud in sight. His sleek, black, UFW frigate, *Revenge* sitting over on the landing pad on the far side of the facility, closest to the tree line, looked small in comparison to the cargo ship unloading on the pad just north of the control tower. Hover trucks unloaded supplies and equipment for the facility and for the Velorian recovery efforts, courtesy of the UFW Directorate. Steele wondered how much of that new-found love and attention being showered on the planet was guilt and how much was self-serving... probably about 50-50, he figured.

The UFW had been terribly slow in responding to the events on Veloria, only thinking to dispatch the task force to investigate months after the planet had fallen off the UFW communications network, their orbital station destroyed, the planet heavily embedded with pirate infiltrators, the Velorian citizens enslaved by a criminally-run mining consortium, a total planetary socio-economic breakdown... The place was a mess, plain and simple.

But then the UFW found out how valuable the mines were, and suddenly aid and assistance was immediate and plentiful. Shameful pandering. But there it was. If the Queen and the Prime Minister could maintain a handle on the situation, they'd be able to manipulate the UFW Directorate and get whatever they needed, whenever they wished.

With the assistance from the Prime Minister, Veloria's Peacekeepers were making a comeback, the UFW Army Engineers at the ASP, supplying weapons, ammunition and equipment to get them back into operation. So far, the Peacekeepers had been making pretty fair progress, rounding up infiltrators on the list found at Mine 02. It was too bad that Mine 01 had been sanitized so well before it was abandoned, Steele was sure there were additional people on their list as well. It meant interrogations were going to be critical in finding out who was on the missing list. Prime Minister Nitram Marconus had his own techniques and talents for that... a little out of the ordinary, but effective.

Professor Walt Edgars stepped out of the terminal onto the concrete apron below in the shade of the building. He paused, turned and looked up, waving at the fourth floor executive conference room, unable to see through the gold reflective glass. No matter, Jack waved back. "Goodbye Commander," he muttered, watching him get into a waiting hovercar. He understood Walt's desire to retire and move on. The destruction of the Freedom hadn't been his fault and everyone told him as much, but he took it personally and carried it with him anyway. His heart was heavier for it. *If you can't let us forgive you, then forgive yourself,* Jack had told him. The Professor had been a great officer, a good friend and everyone was going to miss him.

Jack wondered how they would get along without Walt's unique brand of wisdom and insight. He had the distinct feeling that because they no longer had the Freedom, that Walt no longer saw a need to stay. The carrier, Conquest, had a full crew, there was no place for him there. It simply wasn't so, Jack had fully intended to put him on the bridge of the cruiser that would later be added to their task force.

But the Professor decided to stay on Veloria. He saw it's unexplored history as an unpainted canvas, a place where he could go back to being a paleontologist, chiseling away at rocks and fossils, discovering ancient history. It's what he loved. He even discussed teaching again if Veloria added a school of higher learning. Jack was sure Alité would create the school just for him if he wanted it.

Jack was happy to see Walt's nephew, Commander Derrik Brighton, had seen fit to stay on with the Conquest... The Conquest, that was going to take a while to get used to.

No more Freedom. She was gone now... it felt like a part of him had been ripped away, torn from his heart when they sent her into the Velorian sun... He was fairly sure there was some psychobabble, mumbo-jumbo about assigning human properties to inanimate objects or machines, but the Freedom *did* seem to have a personality and a soul.

They had pulled her from the ashes, figuratively, when she was in desperate disrepair and gave her new life. She had been restored, reborn, given new purpose and been a home. He had always looked forward to returning to her... He hated being away from her when duty took him off the ship... And now they had returned her to the fire, back to molten slag, back to the base elements she was born from. It only seemed fitting; a Viking's funeral. There would remain no trace of her existence or her death – only the stories of her exploits. The pirates would forever chase a ghost, a phantom. She would haunt them... He would find a way to see to that.

Task Force Vice Admiral... my God. Steele was having his doubts. Did he bite off more than he could chew? He wondered if he should have taken Fleet Admiral Higdenberger's offer for a new Freedom jump carrier. Maintain the status quo. It would have been a simpler life.

Simpler, that was almost laughable. There was nothing simple about life in space, or on the Freedom. On the surface it all looked easy enough, but nothing could be farther from the truth. In comparison, the existence he left behind, his life on the beach shuttling planes around; schedules, travel, business, taxes, friends, relationships... something that had felt so complex, now seemed so mundane. So ordinary. He decided simple was a matter of perspective.

So, by that reasoning, difficulty or complexity would be a matter of perspective as well. That was one of his core strengths, being able to see things from more than one perspective. He wished he'd had that time to reflect before answering the call to becoming a Vice Admiral... But all things happen for a reason and he had to believe this was his intended course, like it or not.

Staring out the window at nothing in particular, he blinked away the dryness when the conference room door opened, turning to meet the guest. "Lieutenant Commander Walrick..." he smiled.

"Admiral." The pilot stuck out his hand and Jack took it, shaking briefly.

"Are you all squared away?" Steele asked, motioning to chairs at the conference table.

"Yes sir," replied the pilot, taking a seat.

"Y'know, we're going miss you... you're a good pilot..."

"Thank you sir, but as a Velorian, I felt it was my duty to stay with the Queen."

"No need to explain, I understand completely," waved Steele. "In fact, I feel better knowing you're here. I wish we had some other pilots for you though..."

Walrick nodded. "I wish we hadn't lost LaNareef, he was such a good pilot..." His expression reflected some distress, "I don't think I ever apologized for that..."

Steele lifted an eyebrow, "Why would you feel the need to apologize for that? *He* tried to kill me and Alité, *not you.* I never held his actions against you..."

"And I thank you for that, sir. But there is something you might not know..."

"What's that?"

Walrick had struggled with this decision for some time and it showed in his face. "He was... my brother..."

Steele's eyes widened with surprise.

"I was the one who told your security officers something was wrong... I only wish I'd been able to catch it sooner. I'm not really sure what happened inside his mind. He had been such a dedicated pilot."

The only thing Steele could think of was radicalization. At least that's what it sounded like when LaNareef had confronted him and Alité on the beach at the Tonturin Spindle Spaceport. The pilot had expressed a fierce hatred for the then-Captain, and the perceived affront to the Velorian people for engaging in a relationship with Princess Alité and damaging her purity... That encounter was more than two years ago but the conversation was still fresh in his mind. Like it was yesterday. But retelling it would serve no purpose now. "I really don't know, Commander. He really didn't say much. I'm sorry, I wish there was something I could add, something more I could tell you... But thank you for doing the right thing, I can only imagine how difficult it must have been."

"Sometimes duty is difficult," replied the pilot.

"And command doesn't make it any easier..." added Steele. "Are you up for this?"

The Lieutenant Commander nodded. "Yes, sir. Thank you for the promotion and the chance to prove to you that I could do it."

Steele smirked, "Let's see if you can still say that a year from now..."

"I guess it doesn't get any easier..."

"You guessed right," chuckled Jack, leaning back. "I find myself making decisions every day that I never imagined I'd be forced to make. And they seem to get tougher and tougher."

"Well when you put it that way..."

"You'll do fine, Walrick," said the Admiral, rising from his seat. "Just don't let the base commander push you around. The Major's a stickler for protocol and this is his base, but this is *your* squadron. And you still work for me."

"Understood," said Walrick, rising, shaking hands with Jack.

"If he gives you any problems, or you need anything... don't hesitate to let me know."

"Thank you, Admiral. It was an honor flying with you..."

■ ■ ■

Back at the conference room's fourth-floor windows, Steele was reviewing his notes for the new Velorian squadron, or more precisely, the equipment for it. With the addition of the Freedom's fighters, the Conquest was a little overcrowded, so Jack decided to reassign twelve of her Warthogs to the ASP for a much-needed defensive squadron. Or the start of one at the very least. Now they needed pilots. There was a small handful coming in on a transport at the end of the week, new graduates from the Flight Academy on Phi Lanka that were all as green as could be. But it was a start. And Walrick had proved himself a good tutor and instructor with the new cadet graduates the Freedom had received. That young man had a hefty responsibility handed him... Steele almost felt sorry for him. Until he reflected on his own new duties. *Ugh.*

The Conquest was nothing like the Freedom, she was a behemoth in comparison, and it would be Jack's turn to feel like a freshman in a new school, wandering her corridors. The difference being, it was good to be an Admiral. Absolutely no one was going to give him a ration of shit for getting lost.

The conference room door opened again, Lieutenant Commander Brian Carter came strolling casually in. "What's up, big guy?" he grinned, glancing around to make sure they were alone.

"Hey, Bri. Listen I've been going over our roster... are you OK on the Revenge?"

Brian froze with apprehension mid stride. "Yeah," he replied slowly... "why?" *Please don't take it away,* he thought.

"I was just wondering," replied Steele. "Wanted to make sure you were comfortable. Make sure you wouldn't rather be in a cockpit or something..."

"No way," waved Brian, relieved. "The Revenge is awesome!"

"Alright, good to hear. You'll have a full crew now... though I might rearrange a few people when we pick the Archer or Bowman back up. Not sure how much crew they'll send along with it when we get it back."

"Who are you going to assign as her Captain?"

Jack turned away from the window and laid the e-Pad on the table, leaning his elbow on the back of one of the table's high-back chairs. "I don't know... I guess we'll have to cross that bridge when we come to it."

"Maybe you should take it," offered Brian.

"Nah, I want to be able to fly, can't do that from a cruiser."

Brian frowned, "That's kinda risky ain't it? Flying I mean? For an Admiral..." He cracked a goofy smile, "Dude, you're a freaking Admiral," he laughed.

"What's so funny? You think because I'm an Admiral I suddenly forgot how to fly? I fucking fly better than you do!"

"No, it's just weird... an Admiral... I never woulda' thought..." Brian's face broke into a frown, "Wait, you think you fly better than me?"

"Uhhh, *yeah.*"

"In your dreams, Jack."

"Who's dreams are doing what now?" asked Paul Smiley, strolling into the room. Mike Warren was right behind him.

"Captain Smiley," began Steele, "please remind our deluded friend here, that I am a better pilot than he is..."

"Would if I could, Skipper," shrugged Paul, "but I can't..."

"You are so full of shit, Pappy," snapped Jack.

"They are actually pretty well matched," volunteered Mike, trying to help.

"We are not," interrupted Steele. "Hell, I'm almost as good as Pappy..."

"Oh now you *are* dreamin'..." countered Mike.

The four men broke into simultaneous laughter.

"Sounds like a party in here," announced Maria, walking in. Members of the Freedom's command staff and pilots filed through the door, mixed with members of the Revenge crew.

"The Skipper was just entertaining us with a few jokes," offered Pappy.

"Anything you can repeat in mixed company?" asked Maria.

"Not really," replied Steele, shooting Pappy, Mike and Brian a *shut the hell up,* look. "Coffee, juice and pastries are along the far wall," he announced, pointing across the room. "Everyone find a seat, we have a lot to cover..."

Lisa made her way through the crowd to her brother in a fresh UFW uniform, cadet pips on her collar. "Admiral," she saluted.

Steele returned the salute and pulled her close, "No formalities in these meetings, kiddo..." He motioned to the refreshments, "Grab us some breakfast?"

"Sure," she nodded, heading across the room. Jack decided it best to give her an official position as his aide, allowing her full access, removing the restrictions imposed on her as a civilian. So far she had been studying hard, learning as much as she could about the ships, fighters, shuttles, ranks and protocols.

It was a Cadet crash-course of sorts. As she was showing a real interest in flying, he gave her free rein to use the simulators or do ride-alongs in the shuttles. Twice she rode second seat, once with Maria who handed her control for a while. Two days later and Lisa was still talking about that... He wondered if her intense focus had anything to do with the loss of Nina Redwolf, they had become quite close. Nina's body had never been recovered. Like many others who perished on the Freedom, she was probably lost when the area she was in suffered a hull breach, simply disappearing out into space.

As people found their seats and the banter calmed down, they held a moment of silence for all the friends they had lost, Steele standing at the front of the room, leading them in a short prayer.

As he completed the prayer, the group rose to their feet, holding up their cups and glasses, *"Remember the Freedom..."* they toasted.

■ ■ ■

Two hours into the meeting and it became obvious that the absence of the Professor had not gone unnoticed.

At the head of the table, Jack eyed the room. "And as you all know, Walt Edgars won't be going with us," he announced. "He has elected to stay here on Veloria to study and take a break from command life..."

"Will we be seeing him before we leave?" asked someone from the group.

"No," replied Jack, "he thought it best to let me say goodbye for him..."

There was a murmur that swept through the group before Walt's nephew, Derrik Brighton, rose from his seat at the table. "Maybe I can clarify?"

"Feel free, Commander," prompted Jack.

"Uncle, er, Commander Edgars, thought it would be less disruptive this way. He wishes each and every one of you good health and long life. He is very fond of everyone he's served with over these last two years and holds you all in the highest regard. But he is a man who is not comfortable with long goodbyes or outward shows of emotion. He thought this would be easiest for everyone..."

19

"I hope he understands how much we all love him and how much we'll miss him," said Maria, choking up a little. She looked like she was fighting back her emotions.

"He does," replied Derrik. "And that is the reason he felt comfortable parting in this manner. Let's not forget if someone feels the need to contact him - for whatever reason," he eyed Maria, "he will only be a GalNet call away..."

"As soon as they get Veloria back on the network," added Steele.

"Of course," nodded Derrik, sitting back down.

Steele ran his fingers through his hair. "Ok then. Does everyone understand their assignments and duties....?" There were a lot of faces exchanging wordless glances. "Is anyone unhappy with their assignments or promotions?" He watched the same actions mirrored about the room. "Because now is the time to speak up, before it becomes official. While I can still make changes. Anyone feel shortchanged?" Silence. "Well alrighty then," he grinned, rubbing his hands together. "Time for a new beginning! Paul, as we discussed, you are our new CAG." *Commander Air Group.* "You will also, with Mike and Derrik as your lead instructors, initiate our very own Top Gun program. As soon as we get back to the Conquest, get it started. Some of the Conquest pilots showed solid talent, but they've been rather oppressed by past leadership... which shall remain nameless."

There was a light wave of chuckles that passed over the group.

"So we have to fix the morale problem." he continued. "The current CAG is due for retirement, we're going to initiate that early, he may be part of the problem."

"What about the Captain?" asked Paul.

"Captain Anthony Ryan... I've talked to him at length," replied Jack. "He seems solid and capable enough. But I think past circumstances held him back from doing his job effectively. He knows the Conquest like the back of his hand, so I'm pretty much going to give him the reins and let him do his job for once." He looked around the room. "I'm relying on all of you to keep your eyes open. Low morale can cause all sorts of behavioral problems. If we have someone who is broken I need to know about it. ASAP. We will do our best to fix them, but we don't have unlimited time. We saw what the Pirates are capable of, we need our crews with their heads screwed on straight. Anyone who can't cut it gets bounced."

"Does that include us?" asked someone from the back of the room.

20

Steele wasn't sure if the inquiry was an attempt at lightening the mood or serious. "That includes anyone who insists on being a screwup," he replied. A few laughs rippled across the group. He looked down at the new data device strapped around his wrist like an oversized watch, called an eGo. Its curved two inch by four inch screen was basically a miniaturized e-Pad. "Ok folks, if there's nothing else..." he looked up at the faces around the room.

"The Freedom..." he stopped mid sentence, catching his momentary lapse. "The *Revenge,* is due off-surface in one hour. So get yourselves together and get going." Chairs shuffled as people rose from their seats. "Who's my ride back to the Conquest?"

"Me," said Maria raising her hand.

"We lift off in four hours," he pointed at her. "I have a few other things to take care of before we go. Anyone heading to the Conquest can lift off the same time as the Revenge. If you're short on seats, we have room on Maria's ship. Lisa, you're with me." Lisa nodded silently.

Steele raised his half-empty glass of juice, "Remember the Freedom."

"Remember the Freedom..." they replied in unison.

The double doors to the conference room opened, framing his wife, Alité Galaýa Steele, Queen of Veloria, in the doorway. She was flanked by the Prime Minister, Nitram Marconus, on one side and several Peacekeeper Officers on the other. She was dressed in a gauzy-white suit with flowing sleeves and pants, resembling a tuxedo with tails, albeit with a very feminine flair.

Steele glanced over his shoulder to find out who had entered and was a little surprised to see her at the meeting. She wore her royal sword in its sheath slung over her shoulder against her back, and by the hang of her jacket he could tell she was sporting a sidearm.

He smiled at her. He couldn't help it, it was a natural reaction every time he saw her glowing face. "I was just getting ready to come see you..." But there was something odd about the group's appearance that he just couldn't nail down.

She stepped forward, her entourage staying put, silently blocking the doorway, standing stoically.

Steele raised an eyebrow, "What's going on, Alité?" he asked, forcing his voice soft and low, suddenly aware of the abundant audience.

"Admiral," she announced firmly, but without emotion. "Please kneel."

"Excuse me?" he said, taken aback.

"Kneel."

"What? Kneel?" *Kneel?* For some reason the word held no meaning for him in the present context.

"Kneel, Admiral."

"What are we doing here?" he whispered, shifting his eyes to his left and right, nervously aware of the crowd.

Her hand reached back, grasping the hilt of her sword, "Kneel," she repeated again. *"Take a knee,"* she hissed quietly.

Her face softened momentarily and as he focused on her eyes, he realized they were brown... Alité's eyes changed color with her mood. He had come to understand those colors and what they meant. Brown was akin to neutral. Now black, that would be another story. One with a bad ending... He let out a low breath and looked around, the faces around him watching with a mixture of curiosity and concern. He dropped to a knee and watched as she drew the sword from its sheath, making a spike of adrenalin shoot up from between his shoulder blades into the base of his skull. He looked up into her eyes. Still brown. Maybe a twinge of deep purple. He took a measured breath to calm his heartbeat. Purple was love, passion, desire... *Odd.* None of this was making any sense.

But it was more the way she moved that calmed him. She was slow, methodical, smooth. With both hands on the handle she held the gently curved samurai-like blade vertical and brought it to her lips, kissing the flat of the blade near the guard, on the detailed engraving of an angel in a flowing gown. She dropped the tip toward him and rested the flat of the blade atop his head and prayed softly, her eyes closed. Her supplication complete, she gently tapped him on each shoulder with the blade, crossing over his head each time to the opposite side. "My love. My husband. My guardian. My King..." She touched the top of his head one last time before swinging the blade back over her shoulder and sheathing the blade with one motion without looking or guiding it into the narrow slot. She extended her hand. "Kiss my hand," she whispered.

Her eyes had shifted to a deeper purple, staring down at him, unblinking, shining. He took her hand in his and kissed it, still totally clueless as to what was going on. He hoped this was not some elaborate joke at his expense. But the little voice in his head was chattering excitedly away in his ear without really saying much. He wished it would slow down so he could understand it.

The Queen pulled on his hand, "Arise my husband. Stand with me, my King..."

He rose slowly. *King? Did she just say King? No, couldn't be... She must be speaking figuratively... Please let it be figuratively.*

She pulled him closer, facing him, removing an oversized gold ring from her finger, obviously made for a man's hand and slid it onto his left ring finger. It fit perfectly. Gazing from her eyes to the ring, he realized the top of the ring had the winged horse, Pegasus standing rampant against the red rising sun like the logo they had used on the Freedom. Like the one on the Medieval shield hanging on the wall in his home back on Earth. The sides of the ring had surprising details. On one side two knights rode tandem on a single horse, the other side had a religious cross passing through a crown, suspended over a Maltese cross. "How did you know…?"

She touched his lips with her index finger. "Later," she whispered. She drew him to her side, facing the silent, anxious group in the conference room. "I present to you," she announced loudly, "my *witnesses* of this event... My husband, *King of Veloria.*"

What? Steele swallowed hard. *Oh hell...*

CHAPTER TWO

UFW CARRIER CONQUEST: *UNEASY LIES THE HEAD THAT WEARS A CROWN*

The Conquest had completely different ambient sounds than the Freedom and Jack was having difficulty getting used to her unfamiliar rhythms. Her heartbeat was different, her energy felt foreign. It made him restless, longing for the comfort he felt on his beloved Freedom. He supposed he would get used to it. Eventually. Even Fritz had been listless at first. He'd finally settled down and fallen asleep on the sofa.

Designed to be a fleet flagship, the bridge of the Conquest had two ready rooms, one on each side, so the ship's Captain and the fleet commander, in this case, Jack, could have private areas to conduct ship and fleet business simultaneously without having to split time or share amenities.

He was sitting at his desk, semi-reclined, feet up, contemplating the comfort of the sofa, but he didn't feel like disturbing the dog who was stretched out across two-thirds of it. Steele rolled the gold Pegasus ring around in his hand, examining the engravings, still amazed at the quality, detail and remarkable similarities the symbols had to his life's background. Alité didn't get a chance to explain to him before he left how she knew, how she did it...

He looked up when the door chimed. "Come in."

Lisa strolled in, an e-Pad tucked under her arm, accompanied by her German Shorthaired Pointer, Gus. She took a quick glance around making sure they were alone, "Playing with your man-candy, huh?"

Gus, rarely short on energy, bounced over to Fritz, and jumped up on the sofa initiating a play fight, the two dogs tumbling off the furniture onto the floor, rolling around, canines bared, huffing and snorting.

Steele slid the ring back onto his ring finger, lifting one eyebrow. *"Man candy?"*

Lisa plopped herself onto the now vacant couch, "King... are you freaking *kidding me?* Like your ego isn't big enough already... I'm surprised that you could even fit your head through the door." She was one out of a very small handful of people in the universe who could speak to him like that without getting bitch-slapped.

"Hey look," he objected, "it wasn't my idea..."

"Please," she waved dismissively, "I know how your mind works, you probably had this planned out from the very beginning..."

Jack sighed. "Did you come up here for a *real* reason, or just to give me crap?"

Lisa shrugged with an evil grin, "Can't it be both?" She got up off the couch, slid her e-Pad across his desk and dropped back down on the couch again. "Paul wanted me to..."

"You mean *Captain* Smiley?" he interrupted, slightly annoyed.

"Yeah, is there another Paul?"

Jack closed his eyes for a moment and took a deep breath. "To you, he is not *Paul,* he is *Captain.*" Aggravation crept into his voice. *"Do not* expect that your relation to me will cut you any slack with the members of this crew..."

"But..."

"No," he said holding up his hand. "Don't fuck with this... it's a respect thing. If someone requests that you call him by his first name or in a friendly manner, that's one thing, but you can never make the mistake of doing it out there," he pointed in the direction of the bridge.

"OK, OK, I get it. We are alone, though..." she muttered. She studied her brother for a moment and realized there was more on his mind than just this. He wasn't someone who sweated the small stuff. Petty wasn't his style. Gus and Fritz took a break from their wrestling match and Gus backed up, leaning against Lisa's leg, looking for a friendly hand. Which he got. "What's bothering you, Jack?" she asked. "Is it the whole King thing? Because I didn't mean anything by it..."

"Oh I know," he waved, sounding apologetic.

"So what's going on? You miss her? Because, y'know we've only been gone a *couple of days..."*

He leaned forward pinching his lower lip in trepidation. "Yeah I do... Miss her I mean. Colton too, he's growing up so fast. But that's not it. I'm worried about her safety." He leaned back, "I originally thought the whole *King* arrangement was primarily a figure for the people..." He shrugged, "To show a royal family unit... I was hoping it was just a title..."

"Like a trophy wife in reverse...?"

Jack smirked briefly, "Yeah, sort of."

"But..." prompted Lisa.

Jack rubbed his chin. "It's in case something happens to her..." his voice was low, dropping off. "There would still be a leader for Veloria."

"You?"

"Me," he said flatly. "A real King. With all the responsibilities it entails. For a whole damn planet," he sighed. "I didn't sign up for *that...*"

"Woah..." she breathed, wide-eyed.

He pointed at his sister, "Uh-huh, yep," he nodded. "Now you're at where I was twenty-four hours ago when she told me. Let that run around in your head for awhile," he said, wiggling his fingers over his head, "and you *might* be where I am now."

"Wow that's... umm..."

"No shit, right? Like I'm not hip-deep in enough crap already..."

Lisa leaned forward, "What are you going to do?"

"I don't know," he groaned. "What the hell can I do? It's not like I can quit..." He stared down at the ring, twisting it around his finger. "I'm just going to have to come to grips with it somehow..."

"There's a lot of military support there... do you really think she's in danger?"

Jack took a deep breath, letting it out slowly. "Yeah I do..."

"Gut feeling?"

He nodded. *"And* the little voice..."

Lisa had long known about Jack's little voice, the insights and precognitive ideas it fed him. Heck she had her own. The whole family had this uncanny knack for knowing something was out of whack before it was obvious. Almost telepathic to some degree. Jack's little voice was probing, deductive, and alerted him to danger. Her knack was similar though a bit more empathetic; she didn't so much hear a little voice as she could sense and feel things. If Jack's little voice had warned him of danger, she was inclined to believe it. It was right more often than not.

■ ▦ ■

Jack Steele took the steps at the back of the bridge down a half level to the flight tower overlooking the flight bay. With his back to the upper deck of the bridge, Captain Paul Smiley was examining the system on a holo-chart, including the ships in the task force, a training flight and the fighters on patrol.

"I hate to bother you Pappy..."

Paul straightened up looking over his shoulder, "C'mon in, Skipper, what can I do you for?"

"You got a spare bird? Maybe I can do a patrol? I need to clear my head."

"Sure your Lordship," he joked, "whatever you need..."

"Don't," said Jack, raising an eyebrow, his ire raising. "Just don't."

"Sorry. Too soon?"

"Yeah. Too soon. Indefinitely too soon..."

Paul nodded, "Copy that. OK, let's change the subject, what do you want to fly?"

"Whatever you've got, doesn't matter."

"You want a wingman?"

Steele shrugged, "Probably wise. Got someone who's not chatty?"

Paul chuckled, "Sure. Suit-up and head on down to the flight deck. I'll have one of the Chiefs fix you up with a couple of birds."

"Thanks Pappy."

"No sweat."

■ ■ ■

The crew of the Freedom had lost so much, not just their ship - their home. They lost all the little things, like their personal effects. It was hard to calculate how much until you noticed you needed something and realized it was gone. Like Jack's flight suit, helmet and gloves. It sounded like something so small and insignificant, but things like that made him feel a little melancholy. Everything and anything that connected him to home was gone. Civilian clothes, pictures, wallet, his original 1911, favorite leather jacket...

"How does that fit, sir?" asked the crewman fitting his flight suit.

Jack snapped back into his head. "Feels just right." He flexed his arms and legs to test for room and movement.

"Good, then the measurements I got from your crew were just right."

"You made this new?"

"Everything is new, Admiral," replied the man, handing him gloves and a helmet. "I'm sorry we didn't get your call sign on your helmet, but I didn't get that information."

Jack glanced down at the glossy, plain white helmet as he walked out onto the flight deck from the pilot's ready room. "It's *Stainless,* but that's OK, don't worry about it..."

"Stainless Steele..." smiled the crewman, "I like that, Admiral. Have a good flight." He saluted and pointed Jack across the deck to the port side of the bay.

The bay was so much larger than the Freedom's bay, probably nearly three times the square footage. But then again she carried more than three times the craft that the Freedom did. The walk across the bay was almost worthy of a transport cart ride. At a total length of 1,987 feet in length, the Conquest was a big girl. Of course she wasn't all flight deck, but it was close. Sixteen launch racks lined each side of the bay. It was impressive that she could field anywhere from one, to thirty-two birds simultaneously. Each rack had an independent door that would open and close as needed for launch, sealing in the atmosphere with a stasis field.

"Admiral..." The Line Chief stuck out a ham-sized gloved hand. He was wearing an IAS *Independent Atmosphere Suit,* something very few of the crew on the Freedom ever wore.

"Chief..." they shook hands.

"A couple Lancias suit you OK?" he asked, guiding Jack around to the left side of a Lancia sitting in a rack, the hull door in front of it still closed.

"Sure, Chief."

"Good, then we're all set. Up you go," he pointed at the ladder.

Jack snugged his gloves and headed for the ladder, suddenly realizing the Chief was tethered to an anchor ring on the floor between the racks. "Chief, why are you roped to the floor?"

"Ah, this?" he tugged on the long strap. "Just a precaution. Occasionally we get a blowout when one of the stasis emitters hiccups..."

Jack paused on the ladder, the Chief below him. "Hiccups?"

"Sure Admiral. Look, the old gal is nearly a hundred years old, she's not perfect. It's no big deal, it almost never happens..."

"How often is almost never?"

"Once in a while..."

Steele frowned at him.

"About once a month..."

"And then what?"

28

"Well, sir, we lock down the outer door, pull the unit, rebuild it and pop it back in. The rack is usually only down for a day. Sometimes less if we have a rebuilt or two in reserve."

"Why haven't we just replaced them all, Chief?"

"Well we did... about twenty-five years ago."

"And how long did they last before they started to *hiccup?*"

The Chief shrugged in his suit. "About twenty years I guess."

Steele rolled his eyes. "And in the last five years, how many people did we lose during these *hiccups?*"

"A few..."

Jack almost bit down on his tongue. "Why didn't the emitters get replaced again?" he asked disdainfully.

"I guess the old man didn't want to take us out of service..."

"Pottsdorn?"

"Yes, sir. The Admiral wasn't exactly... um..."

"Sane?" said Jack flippantly.

"Uh yes, sir."

Steele stepped back down off the ladder. "How long would we be out of service to do the whole repair job? Replace all of the emitters?"

"Well for just the emitters, probably about a week. But if you're going to do the emitters, you should actually replace the reflectors, sensors and cabling to avoid any other issues..."

"How long?"

"Two weeks. Maybe a little more."

"Could you do them one at a time while we were under way?"

"Theoretically, yes. It would take us a lot longer though."

"Theoretically?"

"Well we'd actually have to lock down three doors at a time, one on either side of the one we're working on to pull and replace the cabling."

Steel took a deep breath, rubbing his forehead through his open visor. "OK, Chief. Tell you what... Make a list of all the parts and supplies you guys are going to need... tools, anything. I'll make sure you get it. If we can't find the time to sit in a station, we'll do it under way. Either way we'll get it done..."

"I'll need to get the engineers involved too..."

"Do whatever you need to do, Chief," interrupted Jack. "Your job is dangerous enough without having to worry about worn out equipment blowing you out into space." He began climbing back up the ladder to the fighter's cockpit, "Good freaking grief," he muttered.

■ ■ ■

While the Freedom's launch tubes shot a launching fighter through about half the length of the ship, the launch run in the Conquest was barely longer than the length of the fighter. Staring at the door in front of the nose of his Lancia, Steele checked the seal on his canopy and initiated his systems. Going through his flight check, a wash of cool air surrounded him as the climate control system kicked on. Glancing to his left, he exchanged nods with his wingman sitting in a Lancia in the neighboring launch rack, who had already been prepared to launch before he arrived in the bay. He listened to the tower's comm traffic as he waited for the launch.

The Chief retreated twenty feet behind the racks, crouched down and latched a short strap to the ring on the deck that his long strap was tethered to. He could now only move about five feet. "Nine and ten, all systems ready, drivers ready," he looked left and right, "deck clear, ready for launch."

The red lights above the launch doors flicked to green and the blue stasis fields wavered into existence, the outer doors splitting horizontally like some toothy grin, opening wide. The door panels disappeared quickly into the ceiling and floor.

"Tower – Nine and Ten... have a good flight, gentlemen. Launching...."

The electro-magnetic launch sled flung Jack's Lancia out into the space of New Vanus, bouncing his helmet against the headrest, the instantaneous 4G acceleration making him grunt. It felt more violent than the Freedom, but he guessed it would have to, the rails being only marginally longer than the fighter itself. Thankfully, it was only momentary. He reached forward toggling his engine power, feeling the familiar bump of the thrusters. Swinging the Lancia to the right in a gentle, lazy arc, he took up the heading of the task force toward the gate to Irujen. Greeted by the motionless waves and swirls of iridescent blue dust spread across the system, the stunning abstract beauty was enough to catch his breath and make him smile to himself. Enough to elicit a chill that raced up his back and caused the hair on the back of his neck to bristle. Having described it to Lisa, he hoped she would get a chance to see it before the task force got to the gate. He made a mental note to take her out in a shuttle at the very least before they left the system.

Looking over his left shoulder Steele could see his wingman's Lancia catching up and wondered who Pappy had paired him up with. Whoever it was hadn't made a peep so far, keeping with the protocol he'd requested. Curiosity was gnawing at him. *Who was it....?* Pappy hadn't given him any clue as to whom he might have chosen. It was probably one of their own people from the Freedom. He supposed it didn't really matter, he wasn't up for conversation anyway...

Steele sighed to himself. "White One to White Two... call sign?"

"Redline, sir."

"Redline, huh?" *Who the hell is Redline?* "That's a pretty interesting call sign, how'd you get it?"

Like most pilots, Commander Dar Sloane was used to multitasking, adjusting his sensors as they chatted on a local channel. "I got it when I was racing. Early on, I had a bad habit of pushing my engines too far and burning them up... I didn't finish my first couple of races. It took me a while before I got better at conserving them. Of course by then the name was already permanent."

"Yeah..." began Jack, thinking back on the damage he inflicted on the Zulu engines. "I've burned a few, it's not hard to do. So what type of racing were you doing?"

"Canyon racing in Drifters..."

"What's a Drifter?" Jack glanced out over his port wing at the Lancia off his wingtip, the fighter silhouetted against streaks of iridescent blue dust.

"A thruster-powered air racer. They've got about a twenty-five foot wingspan, closed cockpit... They'll do about a thousand, flat-out. Not that you get to do that too often in a canyon race."

"Is this a professional thing?" Jack was trying to imagine a combination of America's favorite racing league, the dedicated fans filling the grandstands, the carnival atmosphere, the food, the announcers and sponsors, all transplanted to a place like the Grand Canyon, watching air racing between the rugged canyon walls. *Where would you make a pit stop?*

"Oh yeah. There's a whole racing circuit for this sport. When I was competing there were about fifteen courses... there's gotta be at least twenty-five by now."

"Not all on one planet..."

"No, of course not. They're spread all over the universe. I can't think of any planet that had more than one course. At least not while I was racing."

"Wow, that's got to be a ton of traveling."

Dar Sloane nodded inside his helmet, "Constantly." He shrugged, "But there can be a lot of money in racing... the victory purses, sponsors, betting... I did OK, I won a few races, but it's nonstop, bone-weary exhausting... If you weren't racing, you were traveling, promoting, schmoozing sponsors, practicing, testing, tuning the equipment, fixing the Drifter... it was never-ending."

"So, how did you end up in the military?"

The Commander smirked to himself. "Are you kidding? Bigger, faster, cooler equipment... and you get to blow shit up. It's like racing, *cubed* – with explosions added for fun. And somebody else takes care of the equipment. It doesn't get much better than that."

"No it doesn't," laughed Jack.

They might as well have had a couple beers and a bowl of pretzels between them. It was just two guys with a common interest passing the time with a topic that seemed to translate across the massive divide of their differences. It mattered not that they came from opposite ends of the universe and different cultures, that they were sitting in a couple of heavily armed star fighters cruising across deep space so far from home it was difficult to comprehend... *That* simple fact was never lost on Jack, the sheer expanse of space, its seeming infinite reaches, its supreme desolation, its intense spectrum of colors, its moments of terror, its unexplored territories, its boundless and surprising beauty.

Most importantly the diversion was cathartic, taking Jack's mind off the complexities of recent events and the overwhelming expectations of his responsibilities. In comparison to the universe around them, his responsibilities seemed miniscule and insignificant. It was what he needed, a perspective that clearly illustrated how small his problems were in comparison to the big picture. A picture so infinite... Well, they were all just self-conscious, self-aware specs of dust racing though space. He wondered what Voorlak might say about that.

The conversation had dropped off and it had been quiet for a while when they reached the farthest waypoint on the scheduled patrol route. "Outside waypoint, Admiral. Want to keep going?"

"Nah, I'm good. Let's head back..."

The Commander followed the Admiral's lead as the two Lancias pulled a tight arc, looping back toward the Conquest, their scanners finding nothing ahead or behind them.

"So, Admiral... scuttlebutt is that..."

Jack inhaled sharply. *Please don't ask me about Veloria...*

"We're headed to your home system... Terran is it?"

Jack exhaled, relieved. "Oh yeah... My home planet is Earth. We're going to head there via Ossomon..."

"That's not exactly a direct route..."

"No it's not. It's part of a patrol we missed when Fleet rerouted us to Velora Prime. Probably won't be anything there now though."

"Mmm," acknowledged the Commander. "You never can tell, maybe we'll get lucky."

"We can hope," joked Steele.

■ ■ ■

There was something familiar about landing on the Conquest although Jack had never done it before, sort of like dèjá vu. Perhaps it was the familiarity of landing on the Freedom that made it feel like that... it was the same, yet different. Landing tandem – two abreast, on the Conquest was a fairly easy matter due to her width and depth, something that required a steady hand and rather precise flying when attempted on the Freedom. He speculated it might be possible to land three wide here.

Having followed the directions from the deck crew to the port side of the flight deck, Steele shut down his systems in a marked parking area, pulling the handle on the canopy release. It popped with a hiss of air rushing in from the flight bay, bringing with it the smells of fuel, lubricants, electronics and hot metal. He sucked it in, almost tasting it, the mixture oddly enjoyable. The hydraulics hissed until the canopy reached its full extension, allowing him to stand up after unbelting. He stretched before plucking the comm and power umbilicals from his suit, allowing him to freely climb down the ladder to the deck.

After setting his helmet on the wing root of his Lancia, Steele was removing his gloves when Commander Sloane ducked under the nose of his own fighter to greet the Admiral.

"Good flying with you, sir," he said, offering his hand. "I'm Commander Dar Sloane."

They shook hands briefly. "Good to meet you, Mr. Sloane."

"Can I buy you a drink in the lounge, Admiral?"

Steele checked the curved screen of the new eGo wrapped around his wrist. Seeing nothing pressing, he saw no reason not to. "Sure, I can go for a cold one."

■ ■ ■

Lisa picked her eGo up off the desk and activated the screen, "Hello?" Her brother's face appeared in video form.

"Come meet me in the lounge, will you?"

"Sure," she replied, "see you in about five minutes." The video winked out, replaced by the welcome screen. She slid the eGo onto her wrist, grabbed her e-Pad and headed for the door from the Admiral's office to the bridge. Pausing at the door as it slid open, disappearing into the wall, she pointed back at Fritz and Gus, "You guys stay here and be good." She did a double take as she caught Fritz making a silly face at her. Lisa shook her head and passed out onto the bridge, heading for the main corridor. "Damn dog is too smart for his own good," she muttered, hustling past the Marine sentry who flicked a glance in her direction.

The eGo on her wrist was a great tool for finding her way around the ship, the screen displaying a live, active floor plan, plotting her location. She could input her destination and the eGo would display routes much like a GPS. If there was an area of the ship that was compromised, blocked or damaged, it would tell her that too and route her around it in real time. Like the Admiral and the Captain's eGos, hers was tied into the ship's systems, communications and sensors, allowing her access to nearly everything the senior staff had access to. This allowed her to fulfill her position as aide to the Admiral, but her position and responsibilities were not indicative of her rank as a mere officer cadet.

When Lisa got to the lounge she was stopped inside the entry by the hostess, "I'm sorry Cadet, this is the *Officers* Lounge," the woman said politely, stalling her with a wave, "you're not an officer... Not yet anyway. You can't go in."

"Oh," smiled Lisa, "I'm the Admiral's aide, he asked me to meet him here..."

The hostess looked her up and down slyly, not sure whether to believe her or not. "Well he is here, let me check with him..."

"Oh, no need," said Lisa pulling up the sleeve of her uniform blouse to reveal the screen of her eGo. "I'll just let him know I'm here..."

The hostess knew they didn't hand those devices out to just anybody. "Follow me, Cadet... welcome to the Officers Lounge."

Well appointed, the lounge wasn't extravagant but it was very nice, decorated with rich wood trim, polished brass, stainless steel, glass and crystal. Winding their way between the tables, Lisa inhaled deeply, drawing in the scent of finely grilled steaks, reminding her she'd skipped lunch. She glanced at the food on the tables she passed, this was *much* nicer than the galley food. Not that the galley food was bad, but this was like a fine restaurant.

The Hostess paused and pointed the rest of the way, "Last booth on the right," she said politely.

"Ah, there she is," waved Jack, "sit... sit." Lisa slid into the booth next to her brother, a bowl of munchies sitting between the two men, drinks on the table. "Lisa, this is Commander Dar Sloane," he waved. "Dar, this is my aide, Lisa Steele..."

Dar reached across the table to shake her hand, "Nice to meet you." He glanced at Jack, "Is *this* your sister?"

Jack nodded, popping a chip into his mouth, "Yep."

Dar grinned in Lisa's direction, "I heard you're a tough gal. Survived a punch out, survived in the wilderness and made friends with locals... is that all true?"

"And then some," she boasted. "Fought some Volkens too..."

The Commander cocked his head to one side, "What's a Volken?"

Jack raised his index finger, "Think very large, hairy, fast, cat-wolf-bear thing, with a *really* bad attitude and saber teeth..."

Dar Sloane snorted a chuckle, "You're kidding, right?"

"Totally serious," said Lisa. "Insanely vicious. And they hunt in packs. Scariest things I've ever seen..." She glanced at her brother, "Four hundred pounds?"

Jack nodded. "I'd have to say that was probably the average... some had to be closer to six or seven hundred pounds though."

"That's a monster," blurted Dar.

"You have no idea," waved Jack, "until one is standing over you, looking down at you like you're lunch..."

"Speaking of which," interjected Lisa, "Can we order food? I'm starving..."

CHAPTER THREE

UFW CARRIER CONQUEST, IRUJEN SYSTEM

Dar Sloane had taken Lisa out for a flight in one of the Conquest's two-seat fighter trainers to see the spectacle of New Vanus before the task force reached the gate to Irujen. That little jaunt continued to be a topic of conversation... along with Dar Sloane. Jack wasn't sure if she was more excited about flying a fighter-trainer, the celestial display of New Vanus or Commander Sloane. In retrospect, Jack supposed it didn't really matter... what mattered was that she was adjusting well, coping, not only to her new surroundings and situation, but to the loss of her friend, Nina Redwolf.

Jack was standing at the chart table in his office, making notes on the 3D hologram when Lisa strolled in from the bridge, the door hissing closed behind her. Gus bounced up off the floor and trotted over to greet her.

"Our delivery from Resurrection Station just landed in the bay."

"Good, did we get all the parts we ordered?"

She shook her head, "I don't know, I haven't seen the manifest yet, it just touched down."

"Ok, so let's go take a look..."

Lisa pointed at her eGo, "We'll - get - the - manifest - here..." she said slowly. "Or here..." she added, indicating her e-Pad.

"Well, *I'd* like to get out of my office, take a walk and *go see,* if you don't mind."

She waggled her finger at her brother, "You want to make sure the old CAG gets off the ship, don't you..." It was more a statement than a question.

Jack made a face of distaste. "Mmm, sue me, there's something about him I don't trust." Jack slid his eGo onto his wrist. "I got Dayle Alaroot to put a couple of our Marines on our friend... keep an eye on him."

"Dar said he was a real hardass... kind of an asshole," Lisa volunteered. Jack shot her a glance. "Yeah, I know, I know," she waved. "Respect. For your information he wants me to call him Dar... and yes, I know I have to make sure not to do it *out there."*

Jack didn't reply, just smirked, waving her out the door, the halves disappearing into the wall. Pausing in the doorway he looked back, "You coming?" Fritz nodded and sliding off the sofa, stretched leisurely as Gus trotted past him. "Don't let me rush you or anything..." said Steele, sarcastically.

"OK," replied the dog with a toothy grin. He sauntered out past his human, onto the bridge. Having gotten used to their presence, the bridge crew paid no attention to the two dogs. "Where we go?" asked Fritz.

"Flight bay," offered Lisa. "We're going to spend an hour doing what we could have done comfortably in the office in five minutes..."

"Why?" he asked looking up at her as they walked down the corridor, Jack and Gus trailing behind.

"You got me," she shrugged, nodding slyly towards her brother, "it wasn't *my* idea..."

"Funny," said Jack, "but you know, he doesn't always understand when you're kidding..."

"Yes I do," muttered the dog. "It just not funny..."

"Oh, damn!" laughed Jack, *"Burn!"*

■ ■ ■

The freight shuttle was parked off to the right of the traffic and landing lanes, crew members loading and unloading hoverdollies from the shuttle to the deck and to the large cargo movers. The pilot was leaning against the boarding ladder to the cockpit chatting with a deckhand from the Conquest.

"Coming to see me off, Admiral?" asked the retiring CAG sarcastically. "I'm flattered."

Ignoring the frosty reception, Steele passed him a data chip. "The UFW Directorate would like me to extend their sincere gratitude for your service, Commander. There is a nice little early retirement bonus included in your pension documents... it's on page ten, I believe..."

"Save it, Admiral," he waved. "You're taking away a whole year of service and I'm getting a little bonus. That sucks and you know it. I'm getting screwed..."

"On the contrary," countered Jack. "Your bonus is a full year and you're getting a full pension... Do yourself a favor Commander, take a vacation, you deserve one. Go see your family. Go..."

"Screw that, Admiral," he waved, "this is all I know. I've got nobody out there..."

Steele remained stoic. "Then move to the private sector, Commander. There are hundreds of companies who could put a man with your experience to good use. And the pay is certainly..."

"Maybe I'll go sign on with the FreeRangers..." the Commander said with an evil grin. "I hear their pay is pretty good..."

Steele's jaw set and he exuded calm, though the Commander didn't know it was the calm before the storm if he continued to push. "You could do that. But it would be a mistake. A big one. At a minimum, you can kiss your pension goodbye. On the other hand, it could be seen as treason. I'm sure you're well aware of the military punishment for treason..."

"I'm not military anymore," he waved the data chip. "I'm a civilian..."

Dar Sloane strolled up and nudged Lisa who was standing next to Marine Warrant Officer, Dayle Alaroot, "Hey, what's going on?" he nodded toward the conversation between the Admiral and the retiring Commander.

"Hello Commander," Lisa said sweetly. "The Admiral just gave the CAG his walking papers and the CAG is *not* happy."

"Oh," nodded Dar, knowingly. "He's being himself... a total asshole."

"He's doing it to the wrong person," interjected Dayle. He exchanged glances with Corporal Dunnom on the far side of the shuttle's cargo ramp, the two Marines communicating wordlessly. "He's about to have a very bad day if he's not careful."

"Think the Admiral would toss him in the brig?" asked Dar.

Dayle Alaroot smirked wickedly, "I'm more worried the CAG is going to push too far and the Admiral's going to permanently rearrange his face... and a few choice body parts."

"You're joking..."

"Nope," replied Lisa. "He is not someone to be fucked with."

Dar Sloan's eyes widened. "Really... because the CAG is a scrapper... every time we had leave, we were pulling him out of a bar fight..."

"He's in over his head..." said Dayle, not taking his eyes off the two men. "Trust me..."

Fritz was keeping an eye on the altercation as well, circling slowly to a flank position, reading their body language and testing the air with his nose for the chemical changes that telegraphed a physical confrontation. The air was thick with testosterone and the CAG looked agitated. Agitated but unfocused, indecisive, nervous. Jack was calm but guarded, his hands open and ready.

Dar was trying to listen but couldn't hear the words. "I can't hear them, can you?"

Lisa shook her head, "No, too much noise." She glanced around at the heavy cargo units moving past.

The CAG was pointing now, poking at the Admiral without touching him. Dayle Alaroot nodded over at Corporal Dunnom. "We've decided if he touches the Admiral, we take him down."

"Might be best for him," commented Lisa. They watched Jack rest his hand on the top of the CAG's shoulder, it appeared to be a friendly, comforting gesture. "OK, I wasn't expecting that..."

"Nope," confirmed Dayle, "went a completely different way than I thought it..." The CAG shuddered once, like a small convulsion, his arms flopping to his side before he went completely limp and collapsed to the deck like a bowl of spilled spaghetti. "OK, wasn't expecting that either," said Dayle, stepping quickly to the Admiral's side.

"You OK, Admiral?"

Jack took a deep cleansing breath, "I'm fine Dayle." He looked down at the unconscious CAG, a circle of people appearing to all take a look. "He just would *not* shut the hell up..."

Dayle Alaroot looked over at the Admiral, "You'll have to show me how you did that sometime, sir."

"Sure thing, Dayle."

"What do you want us to do with him? Brig? Medical?"

"No, no, he'll be fine in about a half hour. He'll probably have a headache though... Just find a seat and strap him in. Let him be someone else's problem." Steele shook his head as the two Marines lifted the unconscious man off the deck. "He's got some serious anger issues..." Steele turned back as the two Marines dragged the former CAG's limp form up the cargo ramp. "Oh, and scan his gear. I want to be sure whatever he's taking is rightfully his..."

■ ■ ■

The Officer's Club was full. But when the Admiral shows up with the ship's Captain, you find them a table. Period. Even when there's a dog in the mix. No arguments. The hostess had no problem finding them a booth, and the officers she moved offered no complaint, moving to the bar with their food and drinks.

Jack laid his e-Pad on the table as they seated themselves, ordering their dinner and drinks. He found himself biting the inside of his cheek to keep from breaking into laughter when Fritz ordered his own steak, meduim-rare of course. The waitress' stunned expression was priceless as she stared wide-eyed at the dog sitting like a gentleman at the back of the booth.

Jack waited until she was out of earshot. "So, Mr. Ryan..." he said leaning in, "we've got quite a stash of parts that came in for the work on the flight bay's stasis field emitters. Not enough to do every launch bay, but a little more than half. We cleaned Resurrection Station out of their entire stock. Any ideas where we can pick up a few more along the way?"

"We can detour to Blackmount..."

Jack looked down at the blank e-Pad screen, thinking. "That's quite a detour. I'd rather not..." His eyes flicked up and he leaned back against the booth.

Captain Ryan rubbed his chin in thought, "We can order the parts from Tanzia, Phi Lanka or Yarwa Station... they might be able to get them into our next resupply."

"Might, hmmm..." Steele pinched his lower lip. "When's our next resupply?"

The Captain paged through several screens on his eGo. "A resupply ship is due to meet us in forty-six days."

"And if our parts miss that transport?"

Ryan shrugged, "If they send it direct through a parts shipper, maybe the same time frame. If not, it could be more than three months."

Jack shook his head, "I don't want to wait that long. Are there any places on our patrol route that might have some of what we need?"

Anthony Ryan had been around the proverbial block a few times, if the block was the galaxy... He closed his eyes and bowed his head, reviewing the chart in his mind which he found easier than trying to see it on the small screen of the eGo. He suddenly looked up, "Rikovik's Reef..."

"Is that a system or a planet?" interrupted Steele.

"A system. There's not much there, except the rock in the middle of the system where it get's it's name. It's what's left of a mined-out asteroid field. A guy named Rikovik crash-landed on the rock about a hundred years ago and since they couldn't get back off, started a station. The mine offices and equipment were abandoned there so he had the tools... It's expanded into a trade hub of sorts. The station sits on it and runs through it."

"Must be a pretty big rock..."

40

The Captain nodded, "About fifteen or sixteen miles across."

"That *is* a pretty big rock," mused Jack, "gotta be about fifty miles around, then..."

"Well it's not exactly round," countered the Ryan. "It's more oblong with a flat side. They say he was trying to land on the flat side to salvage the equipment and went in a little hot. Wasn't even close to his landing zone..."

"Bad planning?"

"Drinking," smirked the Captain. "He was hammered at the time."

"I'll bet the crew was thrilled..."

"They were all drunk, as I heard it," he waved. "Sat on that rock for a month until the alcohol was all gone. When they sobered up, they went to work. The thing now spans across to another rock and they've fastened the two together. "

"So this is more than a station, it's a small inhabited planetoid..."

"Oh yeah. It's not pretty, but it's got its charms I guess. They have manufacturing, agriculture, warehousing... The population wavers, but I hear it's about a hundred-thousand people. It's got a healthy black market too. And because of its relative remoteness, there's usually an abundance of parts..."

Steele sipped his drink. "Sounds worthy of a look."

"Of course we might have a little problem there..."

"What's that?"

"They're fairly neutral," explained Ryan, "but let's just say their clientele isn't totally enamored with the UFW."

"Pirates?"

"They preferred to be called FreeRangers, but yes. Pirates, freelancers, traders, shippers, smugglers, corporations..."

"Wonderful. Interesting mix."

"Yes, it is. So in light of their favored clientele, they might refuse to deal with us."

"Hmm," nodded Jack, "I can be pretty convincing." "

"I've noticed that..." smirked Ryan, sipping his drink.

"I'm sure we can come to some agreement that will make everyone happy."

The Captain leaned back so the waitress could put the plates of food on the table, the steaks still sizzling, fresh off the grill. "It's sure to ruffle a few feathers but I expect we'll get what we need if they have it."

41

Steele glanced at Fritz as a little string of drool left the corner of his mouth. "You're drooling..." Jack began cutting up the dog's steak for him.

"Sorry," mumbled the dog, licking his chops. "Smells good."

Annoyed, not too understanding of the *animals as friends* thing, Anthony Ryan tried not to look, instead concentrating on his own meal. "Umm, so, where were we?"

Jack sipped his wine. "You were going to tell me why you let some of these things go, why you hadn't taken care of these issues earlier..."

"Permission to speak freely, Admiral?"

"Sure."

"I did not have operational control of the Conquest. Admiral Pottsdorn..."

"Was nuts. I understand," interrupted Jack. "There was no way of circumventing him to get things done and ensure the safety of your crew?"

The Captain stopped mid-chew, sighing pensively. "In many respects I was powerless to do anything without his approval. He had six aides. One was always present on the bridge, another with him round the clock. On shifts. They kept track of everything whether he was present or not. It was maddening." He tried not to watch the dog eating off the plate on the table but it was difficult to ignore. He looked away.

"So you gave up then?" asked Jack, sampling his vegetables.

"No, I did what I could under the confines of the restraints put upon me."

"Did you ever inform the Fleet Admiral or the Directorate of what was going on?" Steele stabbed a piece of steak with his fork.

"No sir. That would not have succeeded, I don't have the same kind of status or recognition..." he paused awkwardly, *"you* seem to have garnered. Anything coming from my position would have fallen on deaf ears."

"I understand," waved Steele. "I'll tell you what I need from you Anthony..." he said, pointing an empty fork in the officer's direction. "Honesty and open communication. I've read your record, you've got quite a distinguished career. Before Pottsdorn. You've been living under a glass for the last five years. But Pottsdorn's gone, that's over now. So I need you to be the officer you were *before* the crazy years. Can you do that?"

"Of course." He eyed the young Admiral sitting across the table from him.

"OK, Captain, I can see your mind working... out with it."

Ryans' eyes shifted to the dog and back to Steele. "With all due respect, sir, I'm wondering if I've traded one type of crazy for another."

Steele took no offense to the comment, ready with an immediate reply. "I suppose that depends on how you look at things, Anthony." He slid his drink to the center of the table. "Is this glass half full or half empty?" he gestured at the glass, not waiting for a reply. "Some might say half full, some might say half empty depending on their view. If you're thirsty, it's half empty. If you're satiated, it's half full." He retrieved the glass and took a sip.

"What is it now?" asked the Ryan, thinking there was another point.

"That was nothing, I was thirsty."

"Oh."

"So for five years," continued Steele, "you've been running on empty, with little or no control. Now, you have nearly complete control. Is that crazy or smart? From Pottsdorn's viewpoint, that would be crazy. From my viewpoint, you know your ship and people, which makes it smart."

"Viewpoint..." nodded Ryan.

"And of course," added Jack, flippantly, "there's good crazy - which is smart, and there's bad crazy - which is, well, just plain wackadoodle. I'm the kind you *want.*"

"Good crazy," confirmed the Captain.

"Exactly."

"Good, because we've had our fill of the other kind, what did you call it...?"

"Wackadoodle."

"Right, wackadoodle."

"Just remember this, Mr. Ryan - we may do things that wander outside the lines of what the Admiralty and Directorate consider *normal operations*, but we get things *done.*"

Captain Ryan thought about Steele's actions and results against the Pirate carrier in the battle of Velora Prime. "I've seen that."

"I'm not a real big fan of red tape," said Steele, "or the bureaucratic cesspool people call politics... My best assessment is someone goes into politics because they can't get a real job, so they make a place for themselves telling other people how to do things they themselves have never done before."

"Or tell people how to live on planets they've never been to before..." volunteered the Captain. "It *is* shameful..."

Jack let it be quiet for a moment, just eating. "So we understand each other then?"

"Yes sir."

43

"OK, good. I think our first order of business, is to take care of our ships. I want to categorize all the mechanical issues with the Conquest... and the battleship Westwind if *she* has any problems. We will do our best to get whatever is needed to bring both of these ships back to one-hundred percent readiness... this includes mechanical, operational *or personnel.* If we have anyone like the CAG who is gravel in our gears, let's pull em out. We need to communicate openly on these issues but they need to be handled so they don't cause bigger issues for us later."

"Understood." Captain Ryan eyed Fritz finishing off his meal, licking the plate clean. "So, completely open communications between us, but I get to handle most things as I see fit...?"

"Yes, Captain. This is your ship..."

"Thank you, sir." He eyed the dog, who was casually monitoring the conversation. "I'm not really comfortable with him on the bridge," he said, indicating Fritz. "Or having him in the Officer's Club much less eating at the table..."

"Except that," said Steele slyly.

Ryan pursed his lips, nodding. "Duly noted."

■ ■ ■

"Jack, check this out!" blurted Lisa as she entered the Admiral's office, her arms laden with small boxes. The bridge door swished closed behind her with a hiss and she unceremoniously dumped the boxes in a pile on the sofa. She spun around and slid a small device across his deck that looked like any number of flat modern cell phones from Earth.

"You found my cell phone?" he frowned, puzzled.

"That's your new e-Pad. It's called the h-Pad mini. Touch the screen," she pointed, grinning. The glass screen was 2 ½ inches wide and 5 inches long, the whole thing less than a half inch thick.

He touched the screen and a little blue diode lit up, projecting a full color holo-screen above it, positioned like a tactical monitor. "Holy crap..."

"Touch the screen..." she prompted. "You can actually *feel it.*"

Jack reached out and tested the screen with his fingertips actually feeling resistance in the form of an electronic buzz. "That's amazing..."

Lisa moved around to his side of the desk and reached out. "Watch this," she said, grabbing the corner of the screen and pulling it outward, the screen growing in size. She tilted the screen back and forth, then pinched the corner again and moved the edge back in, making it smaller. "You can position it any way you want. It also takes verbal commands and responds verbally..."

"Where did these come from?"

"The transport. The pilot said they came in from Fleet Supply on Tanzia, they'd been trying to deliver them to the Conquest for ages... The delivery courier got tired of chasing the Admiral around and finally just left them at Resurrection."

"Pottsdorn..." muttered Jack in disgust, touching the screen's icons, paging to other information. "Remind me to bitch slap that man if I ever see him again..." He turned the device, realizing the back of the holo-screen was blank, the information only displayed to the viewer of the device. *"Nice..."* He offhandedly wondered how it accomplished that.

"It gets better..." said Lisa, tearing open another box. She dug out the contents, holding up a smaller, more streamlined eGo. "Meet the eGo-h."

"Holographic?"

"Yeppir. And at half the size," she said, tossing it to him.

He caught it and examined it closely. The 2 inch by 3 ½ inch screen was smaller than the curved screen of the older unit but it was more streamlined and much nicer looking. "The screen's a little smaller..."

"That's OK, because you can use the device screen or the holo-screen, just like on the h-Pad mini." She pointed at the eGo on his wrist. "If you'll give me your old one, I'll take care of it." He pulled the old one off and slid it across the desk at her. "Now," she continued, "the new one is more of a personal unit. It's secure. Once you use it, no one else can use it or even activate it..."

"That's *very cool*..." he said, sliding it on his wrist, fitting the clasp. *"Ow..!* What the fuck?" mumbled Jack, taking it back off.

"Yeah, you didn't let me finish," she chuckled. "It samples your blood and DNA when you first put it on. Mine did the same thing..."

Try as he might, he could find no marks on his wrist. He slid it carefully back on, "It won't do it again..."

"No, just once. Stop," she said holding her hand out to stay him from doing anything else. "Before you start her... She's going to ask your name and how you want to be addressed... so give it some thought before you turn her on... OK," she waved, "That didn't come out right, but you get the idea."

"Her?"

"Yeah, her name is TESS. It stands for *Tactical Engine Synthetic Service,* the personality it's assigned is female. I don't think you can turn her off once you... activate her..."

Jack smirked at Lisa's wording.

"Shut up," she warned.

"OK..."

"Remember, it's a computer, it's *very* literal..."

Jack pushed the small button along the eGo's edge, watching the screen come to life and flicker through its startup process. "Something tells me this is more than our other report and communication devices."

Lisa nodded, "Oh yeah. A lot more. And there's *no manual...*"

"What? Why the hell not?"

"How the hell do I know," Lisa shrugged, "I didn't build it." She started gathering the boxes and old equipment. "I'll be back later, I'm going to distribute these things to the senior staff... When I'm done here, I'll be heading over to the Westwind to deliver theirs, then to the Revenge..."

"Super," nodded Jack approvingly, "maybe Maria can give you some more stick time..."

"Stick time? I've been soloing for a couple days now."

"Hello, I'm TESS, Tactical Engine Synthetic Service, who are you?"

Jack's eyes went wide. "You've soloed?"

"Hello, Youve Soloed..."

■ ■ ■

Maria had tears in her eyes and her cheeks hurt from laughing. "So did he finally get it straight?"

"After arguing with it for five minutes..." chortled Lisa. "It was like Abbott and Costello, *who's on first, what's on second..."*

"Shuttle Lightspeed, pattern is free, you are clear for takeoff, lane right. Observe the deck control."

Lisa keyed her mic, "Acknowledged, Conquest Control. Lifting off." She twisted the grip and the anti-gravity lifted the shuttle off the deck as she locked eyes with the deckhand who directed her out of the revetment. "Gear up, please."

"Gear up," repeated Maria, toggling the switches. The landing feet withdrew into the belly, locking in with a metallic thump and Lisa nudged the throttle. They coasted across the deck, through the stasis field, over the ship's fantail and out into space.

Lisa keyed her mic, "Lightspeed is clear."

"I would have loved to have been there for that," said Maria, resuming the conversation.

"It was touch-and-go there for a minute or two," joked Lisa. "I thought he was going to rip it off his arm and throw it against the wall..."

"So what was the final verdict?"

Lisa adjusted her sensors, heading for the Westwind. "*Jack,* if he is alone. *Admiral,* if there are other people present."

Maria tilted her head curiously, "How does it know?"

"TESS has all sorts of sensors, so I guess she can tell. She even has an on-screen face if you want to talk to her that way... It's like video chat."

"Wow, an artificial intelligence..."

"Sort of," confirmed Lisa. "It does learn through its engagements with the person wearing it... she even has the proper facial expressions when she's talking to you..."

"Sounds a little creepy to me..."

"Y'know, I wasn't really sure about it at first," admitted Lisa, "but so far it's been pretty cool. The more you interact, the more her personality develops."

Maria leaned back and pursed her lips in thought. "I wonder if her personality develops differently for each owner with individual nuances, or does it simply mirror the owner...?"

Lisa shook her head inside her helmet, "I don't know... it'll be interesting to see."

CHAPTER FOUR

CAPE CORAL, FLORIDA: *FUN IN THE SUN*

Chase Holt lifted up his sunglasses and looked in the rear view mirror to look at the raccoon eyes he'd gotten from a day on the water playing with his Jet Skis. He slid the glasses back down. *Man, those aren't going away anytime soon.*

It had been a long hectic week and he had needed a break... Firearm classes, security system installations, a few bug sweeps with security assessments for new clients... All in a week's work in paradise. Sometimes the most brutal part was doing his job surrounded by opulent luxury, emerald green water, ice cold drinks and women in bathing suits. Yeah it was tough. He decided Saturday on the water with Penny was a day well spent.

His German Shepherd, Allie, stuck her head between the seats from the back of the extended crew cab, taking a deep whiff and a poke at the big paper bag sitting on the passenger seat - her normal spot to sit. The bag from China Garden was filling the truck with an amazing aroma and Allie was having a hard time containing herself. So was Chase, seriously having to resist the urge to steal one of the egg rolls on the ride back to the house. *Mmm, Chinese food, a cold beer and a little face-time with my sweetie... a good way to close a day in the sun.*

Some people liked living on the beach, Chase preferred living on the canal off Bimini Basin where he could be on the water but actually make use of it. The floating dock at the back of the house was far more convenient than requiring a trailer to get the Jet Skis in and out of the water at a public launch ramp. His deck's floating PWC *Personal Water Craft* ramp made it easy get them in and out of the water even with one person. The canal dumped all the local residents out into Redfish Cove and the Caloosahatchee River. From there you could go literally almost anywhere with the Jet Skis only requiring a few inches of water. There were tons of places to explore including the Gulf of Mexico, the Intracoastal Waterway, Peace River, Myakka River, all the border islands... the possibilities were only limited by fuel range and available fuel stops that Chase had methodically marked on his GPS.

Chase moved over a lane, slowing down to let an ambulance pass, lights flashing, siren wailing, prompting a bark and short howl from Allie. He checked his mirror before pulling back out into traffic. "Damn, he's flying..."

Reaching Tower Drive, Chase pulled off Coronado Parkway into his neighborhood surrounding the Bimini Basin and idled down the street, his heartbeat quickening when he spotted the smoke a couple streets away in the direction of his house. *That was more than someone's over zealous backyard cookout.* His mind raced ahead, connecting the ambulance with the smoke and he punched the accelerator, the big pickup chirping the tires as it leapt ahead, charging down the street. He wheeled it hard, manhandling it around the corner, the big tires howling, Allie sliding across the back seat struggling to stay off the floor and maintain a position as close to upright as possible.

Halfway down the block the street was clogged with emergency vehicles of all kinds, resembling the organized chaos of a Tetris puzzle. Police vehicles parked up on lawns, fire trucks, and the ambulance that had passed him moments before parked curb-to-curb. Three black SUVs and a SWAT vehicle sat on the far side of the fire trucks. Flying down the street, time slowed, his eyes scanning for details, his mind trying to catalog the information and make sense of the movements of neighbors and emergency personnel. It wasn't until he jammed on the brakes that he realized all the action revolved around his house. *"Penny..."*

The tires howled as the truck shuddered to a stop, inducing smoke and the smell of burnt rubber. Throwing the door wide, Chase jumped out shouting Penny's name, a flood of adrenalin pumping through his body. Following closely, the German Shepherd jumped down to the pavement behind him, staying on his heels. Chase cleared the front fender of the truck making a beeline to the front door, his tunnel vision focusing on the form laying on the gurney escorted out of the front door of his house. The person in black body armor, helmet and balaclava that entered his narrow field of vision was pointing at him and he suddenly realized he was being converged upon. Allie raced past to cut them off...

"Dog, dog, dog!"

Chase dove to catch Allie and felt the Tazer darts hit him in the back sending him plank rigid, driving him into the grass face-first arms extended, teeth clenched. *"Nooooo!"* he snarled, watching them shoot at his dog, the rounds kicking up grass and dirt as she weaved past them, running full out and cutting past the paramedics into the house. A neighbor ran past,

49

attempting to catch her only to be blocked by a uniformed police officer. *"Leave her alone!"* grimaced Chase, *"She won't bite...!"*

"Shut up, asshole..." Whomever was holding the Tazer squeezed the trigger again, and Chase felt the fire race through his muscles. Managing to roll on his side he attempted to tear out one of the probes, only to be shot with two more darts in the stomach by someone else with a Tazer. "Where d'you think you're going?"

"Hands behind your back! Hands behind your back!" they screamed at him.

"Gun! Gun, he's got a gun!"

While under juice from both Tazers, Chase had little chance of moving anything. And the armored men that pounced on him, wrestling with his arms, were having little success moving them for him. *"Penny...?!"* he *grunted.* A neighbor tried to get close enough to talk to him and was stiff-armed by an officer, knocking her to the ground. *"Karen? Karen, what's going on, where's Penny?"*

"They shot her Chase, they shot her..."

"Why? *Why...?"* His eyes burned and his vision blurred with tears. Tears of fury. He saw red, he wanted to start killing people. At six-foot-three and two-hundred-thirty pounds, Chase was not a small man, but size doesn't have a lot to do with the effectiveness of the electronic Tazer devices. But to some extent and in some cases, sheer determination and rage can. The combat-hardened soldier in him was calculating the moment and the rage was overwhelming. Finally handcuffed, the assault team stood him up. To do that they had to release their triggers. He spun himself, tearing free from their hands and bolted forward, breaking the connection on one set of darts, colliding with one team member and bulldozing him into the ground with a shoulder to the face. He felt the Tazer fire from the remaining set of darts and he powered through the burn, lashing out and catching another member in the face with his bare foot, sending him sprawling. Tackled bodily, he head butted the agent on top of him, breaking the man's goggles and his nose.

It was a messy free-for-all with witnesses from up and down the block that had gathered to investigate the action in their neighborhood. Covered in grass stains, Chase's next door neighbor, Karen, slid up next to her roommate, Pam, gathered in a group with other neighbors.

"Somebody said he was a national security risk... maybe he's a terrorist."

"Who said, that?" snapped Karen. "I'll kick your fucking ass. Chase is a decorated soldier who fought in Iraq and Afghanistan..."

"Didn't you see him fight with the cops?"

Karen pushed past a few of her neighbors to get closer to the woman from up the block. "They're not cops, they're FBI and they raided his house, *shot* his girlfriend and *tried to kill* his dog. Are you really that damn stupid?"

Pam grabbed Karen by the elbow and drew her back, "Ignore the stupid people, K. Where's Allie?"

"I locked her in our bathroom."

"Is she hurt?"

Karen shook her head, "I don't think so. She has some blood on her but I can't find anything." She stood with her hand on her hips, glaring at the stupid woman in the group as the agents with FBI on the back of their armor, dragged an unconscious Chase Holt across the grass toward the SWAT truck.

"Let's clean Allie up and take her to the vet."

Karen was enraged, she wanted to be able to do more but she had no idea where to start. She couldn't believe this was happening in her neighborhood. To her neighbor, a person she knew to be of high integrity and ethics. Could it be possible he was a risk of some kind? She refused to believe it.

■ ■ ■

Hunched over, speaking on the phone with both elbows on his desk, Sheriff Naywood suddenly leaned back in his chair and tossed his reading glasses on his desk in disgust. "Are you kidding me? So they had a no-knock warrant then... They had *no* warrant? Not in my county, dammit! I want a team of investigators at the house now. Yes, right now, they should be out the door five minutes ago. And send another team to the girl's hospital room. I want someone with her the moment she wakes up. And I want a twenty-four hour guard on her, I don't want her disappearing. Nobody sees her without one of our investigators present, understand? Good." He waved a plain-clothes detective passing his door into his office as he continued his phone conversation. "I'm tired of these federal clowns running their games on our citizens. National security risk? That's a bunch of bull and you know it. If they had *anything* of substance, they would have had a warrant. So where's the guy they picked up? What do you mean you don't know? The PD didn't ask? Oh for the love of Pete..." he slapped his forehead. "Let's see if we can find this guy, shall we?"

51

He dropped the phone into the cradle and rubbed his eyes with the palms of his hands. "Looks like the Feds rode roughshod over the Cape Coral PD that showed up to the scene. Played the national security card and told them they didn't need a warrant.

Any idea where the FBI would drag some poor sap they picked up in a warrantless raid?"

"Tampa," replied the detective. "Probably... Suppose it could be Miami, but I doubt it."

"Why... Why do they want this guy? Who is he?"

"He's a security specialist and an NRA firearm instructor. Ex-military. I heard he's a friend of Detective Dan Murphy..."

■ ■ ■

When Chase Holt came-to he was lying on the concrete floor of a featureless room barely ten foot by ten foot, the only light coming from a small window in the steel door on the other side of the room. Still dressed in the cargo shorts and t-shirt he was abducted in, his entire body ached and he was slow to rise, tasting copper from the blood in his mouth. His lips were swollen and he instinctively knew both of his eyes were black and blue, though he could tell his nose wasn't broken. He felt the puffiness around his eyes and his fat lip. Running his tongue across his teeth he determined that although sensitive to pressure, they were all there. Peering through the door's small window he could only see a small swatch of an empty corridor, a door like the one he was standing behind, on the opposite wall. "What the hell is going on...?" he muttered, pressing his face against the glass, trying to see further down the corridor. Anxiety and hopelessness welled up inside of him when he thought of Penny's form lying motionless on the paramedic's gurney. How bad was it? Was she dead? The thought knotted his gut. What about Allie? He thought he saw her make it into the house but he had no idea if she had been hit or not. His stomach rolled and he pounded on the door. *"What the fuck is going on here...?! Who are you people?!"* He tried to think if he saw any markings on their uniforms but it all happened so fast it was splintered in his mind.

"You don't need to shout," came a voice from a speaker above him, "we can hear you..."

Chase looked around but in the muted light he couldn't see anything. "Can you see me too...?" he asked giving the ceiling the middle finger.

"Nice," came the response. "Very mature."

"Fuck you and all your little friends out there... prick bastards. Fucking cowards."

"You kiss your mother with that mouth...?"

"No, but you can kiss my ass with yours," spat Chase.

"Do you know why you're here, Mr. Holt?"

Chase was doing his best to push their buttons. He wanted to lay hands on someone and getting one of them in the room was the first step. "Because a bunch of dick gobbling bitches..."

"You're a national security risk, Holt..." interrupted the voice.

"You're so full of shit I can smell your breath from here..."

"We needed a little sit-down with you...'

"SO," he shouted, interrupting, "breaking into my house, shooting my girlfriend and trying to kill my dog is acceptable in your World? Ever heard of the *Fourth Amendment*, you sick fucks..." It wasn't really a question, he knew they didn't care about the Bill of Rights they'd trampled on. "You never heard of a phone call or an appointment? Freaking retards..."

"Because you are a dangerous man, Mr. Holt, you have a violent history..."

"What?" snorted Chase. "You mean killing *enemy terrorists?* Yeah that happens in combat..."

"Did you know you put two of my agents in the hospital? You broke one agent's nose..."

"Hospital? For a broken nose?" sputtered Chase, laughing. *"You bunch of pussies.* We used to fix shit like that in the Humvee and go back out on patrol..."

"The other agent has a dislocated jaw and you knocked some of his teeth out."

"Pssh, I'm slipping. It shoulda killed him."

"You're lucky it didn't."

"It occurs to me," said Chase, pacing, "It took five of you... or was it six? In full armor, with me handcuffed *and* Tazed. You are nothing but a bunch of *little bitches...* Shooting innocent women and defenseless animals... Does that make you feel like a badass? Jesus, you must have some really tiny dicks..."

"Sort of like you and your platoon running around Afghanistan killing innocent women and children...?"

Chase knew it was a deliberate dig but he wished for the chance to crush his face in anyway. "Innocents in a war zone are few and far between. If we killed them, they needed killing," he said calmly.

There was no response, only silence.

"C'mon down," urged Chase, "We'll talk, just the two of us. It's what you wanted, right? A sit-down? We'll keep it all neighborly. I'll tear off your arms... stuff one up your ass and the other down your throat so you could shake hands with yourself... Nice and friendly."

There was a measurable silence before the voice returned. "The reason you're here is that you're a national security risk..."

"Yeah you said that already - you're starting to bore me..."

"Where were you the night the craft came down on the beach in front of Jack Steele's house?"

"So the chit-chat's over, we're finally getting to the point?"

"Where were you?"

Chase sat on the floor and leaned back against the wall. "At home, watching TV."

"Have you had any contact with Jack Steele or his family?"

"I taught his sister and her friend how to shoot."

"What about Jack Steele?"

"He already knows how to shoot," quipped Chase.

"Have you been in contact with Steele?"

"We all know that's not possible."

"I don't know any such thing," snapped the voice coming through the speaker. "How do *you* know it's not possible?"

"I saw the videos, I've heard the stories. I don't expect he'll ever be coming back."

"From where? Where did he go, Mr. Holt?"

Alpha Centauri, Proxima Centauri... maybe Andromeda," replied Chase, sarcasm dripping from his voice.

"And how would he do that?"

"Y'know, you guys make it really difficult to have an intelligent conversation... Your agency might want to reexamine their IQ requirements - set their sights a little higher than *absolute moron.*"

"When did you and Steele start thinking about overthrowing the government, Mr. Holt?"

"What?" Chase snorted, laughing. "Kiss my ass. While you were running around terrorizing innocent Americans, I was over in the sandbox doing *real work."*

"If you're cooperative, we're in a position to help you Mr. Holt."

Chase shrugged, "And you'll let me go on my merry way and we can forget this whole thing ever happened..."

"Something like that."

"Uh-huh," grunted Chase, folding his arms across his chest. "Because that's just so believable..."

"We're looking for Deputy Dan Murphy... he seems to be missing."

"Really. Well I wouldn't know anything about that. Haven't seen him in a couple months," said Chase defiantly.

"You see Mr. Holt, you seem to be the nucleus where a lot of information comes together. All the people we're interested in finding have one thing in common..."

"Do tell..."

"Yes, they all know you..."

Chase licked his swollen lip. "So I know a lot of people, so what? When did that become a crime?"

"When those people are all a risk to national security... Like Dan Murphy and Jack Steele..."

"How about I call my lawyer and you can discuss your thoughts with him."

Laughter rang through the speaker, sounding tinny and hollow. *"Lawyer? Funny man. You think you're under arrest? You're not under arrest, you're being detained as a terrorist risk. The Patriot Act says we don't have to let you go... Ever."*

■ ■ ■

It was almost 9pm when the veterinarian came out into the waiting room where Karen and Pam were sitting nervously. "Allie will be just fine. She got hit in the right thigh but it passed right through the muscle tissue. Probably a 9mm. You said the police shot her?"

"FBI," volunteered Karen. "They did a raid on a neighbor's house and they tried to kill the dog..."

"Good Lord, what kind of neighborhood do you live in?"

"Bimini Basin..."

"That's a nice neighborhood," confirmed the vet.

"And our neighbor is a decorated Army vet back from Afghanistan. I've known him since high school, he's one of the best people I know..."

The veterinarian shook his head, "What's this country coming to..." It was more a statement of dismay than a real question.

"Can we take her home?"

"Sure," nodded the vet. "We'll help you get her into your car. Keep her quiet and don't let her fuss with the bandages. I'm going to give you some sedatives and medication, just follow the directions on the bottles..."

■ ■ ■

They weren't short of time but NSA Special Agent Doug Mooreland was getting tired of the game with Chase Holt. "Pete... *Pete,* " he hissed, "wake the fuck up."

Agent Pete Whitman had been reclining on the chair with his feet up. He lifted his head, "Sorry Doug, the pain meds are making me drowsy..." he mumbled, sounding like he had the worst sinus cold in history.

"That's twice in less than a year Pete..." said Mooreland sarcastically, "you *really* ought to learn how to duck."

"Bite me, Doug. He smashed my face with his freaking head." He glanced at the video screen, "Where are we? Any progress?"

"No. These guys that come out of combat are less susceptible to tampering with their daily light cycles. They get conditioned to sleeping anywhere, light or dark, on almost any surface. We'd need more time. Way more than I want to spend. If I wanted to blow a couple of weeks we might be able to do it with sleep deprivation..."

"What about sodium pentobarbital?"

Doug Mooreland dismissed the thought with a wave, "You know we can't do that without medical supervision..."

"Well, we're not exactly running by the book as it is..."

"No," said Doug flatly, "I've never administered. I don't want to run the risk of killing him, we need him. If we change his life circumstances and nudge him in the right direction, we just might get him to do what we need to locate the others."

"What about boarding him... that usually works pretty fast..."

"No..."

"Why not?" waved Whitman. "We could save ourselves a lot of time..."

"Because I'm just not comfortable waterboarding one of our vets... there's something inherently wrong with it..."

"Wow. When did Doug Mooreland suddenly get a conscience?" asked Pete sardonically.

"Don't push it Pete, or I'll add something to that broken nose." He lit a cigarette. "Besides, if we drive him hard he may lead us in the right direction. I'm more inclined to let him go and track him, see who he turns to."

"Well, Wilson said whatever it is, we should to do it soon. The Sheriff stirred the pot over at the Tampa field office and got the Feds all up in arms."

Doug nodded, "We knew that was gonna' happen sooner or later."

■ ■ ■

Consciousness came and went, a cool, steady drizzle falling gently. It was real and it was dreamlike, the only sound the hushed movement of the air and falling rain. Chase's mind struggled to make sense of the mixed realities, wading through the muddy quagmire of an abstract dreamworld. The salt spray from the Jet Ski racing silently across the water soaked his face and body. The water, emerald green like meadow grass, swayed with the breeze like waves of the ocean. The shuffling steps of the cattle through the shimmering, swaying green surf made perfect sense. A ripple of lightning and a low faraway rumble flickered across his eyes, his mind fighting to connect what he was seeing to what his mind was thinking. The two halves refused to mesh into a cohesive interpretation. Was he still dreaming or were his eyes really open?

With a curious snort and a halfhearted moo, the bovine reached down to get a closer look at the man laying in the grass. Munching a mouth full of sweet meadow grass, she stared at him, nearly nose-to-nose, studying him. When he finally stirred, she jumped back, bleating a warning, retreating a few yards with the others. The herd continued to graze, casually monitoring the prostrate man, occasionally raising their heads and pausing their graze, if only for a moment.

Consciousness came rushing forward to Chase, accompanied by a wave of nausea. He rolled to his stomach and raised himself onto all fours, heaving up what little was left in his stomach. Not much. And then again. "Fuck," he groaned. He had a splitting headache to boot and dry-heaving on all fours wasn't helping. The tiny red cylinder sticking out of the puddle caught his blurry vision and he moved it with his finger. "Son of a bitch..." he hissed "they tried to chip me..." He wiped the RFID, *Radio Frequency Identification,* capsule on his soggy cargo shorts, examining it to get a better look, a fine hair-like antenna hanging from one end. "Hmm" he snorted, stuffing it into his pocket. "Bastards."

He plopped himself into a sitting position and looked around, the herd scrutinizing their visitor. "Don't mind me ladies..." he waved, somewhat drunkenly. His mouth felt like it was pasted together. He needed something in his stomach. Something that would calm his nausea and possibly counteract whatever the hell those assholes put in his food to knock him out. There wasn't a house or building in sight, just rolling fields and trees as far as he could see. Chase eyed the full udders on the cows. "Hmm, warm milk..."

■ ■ ■

A transplanted Wisconsin farm boy, patience and persistence paid off for Chase, the Guernsey allowing him to milk her right into his mouth. As empty as his stomach was, he was careful not to drink his fill, fearing another bout of nausea. He'd forgotten how delicious raw milk was... there was nothing in a store that could compare. If people knew the difference they'd probably never want to drink processed milk ever again.

"Thank you mama," he said, stroking her muzzle, finally able to manage being upright. Taking stock of his surroundings, he gave her a final pat and chose a direction, padding barefoot across the meadow... being careful to avoid the cow pies.

Chase still had his wallet, but it was completely empty. No money, no credit cards, no ID, not even a scrap of paper. It was a cruel joke, but of course he expected nothing less. They had even taken his watch and cell phone. He had absolutely nothing of value and could never recall ever being so destitute.

■ ■ ■

It was a good thing Chase was a person who barefooted on a regular basis - Florida was a place you actually could do that... because this excursion was not for a tenderfoot. But even then, there were limitations. "Crap," he mumbled, climbing gingerly over the barbed wire fence, staring at the gravel road. "I hate gravel." He looked up and down the empty road, the overcast sky giving no directional assistance whatsoever. He looked up at the sky and the drizzle drifting down. "A little help? Anything? No? OK I got the milk, thank you for that... but I could use a little more guidance..." Then it dawned on him. Farmers and ranchers build their spreads on high ground. "Oh, thanks!" He turned right and headed uphill, walking carefully in the grass and scrub alongside the road.

Fifteen minutes of walking along the deserted road, a vintage pickup truck approached from behind him going in the same direction, a middle-aged woman alone behind the wheel. She slowed at first but sped away after getting a good look at him. He didn't blame her really; filthy, soaked to the bone, with two black eyes and a fat lip, he could probably take the ugly prize at the county fair.

A short time later the same pickup approached from up the hill, slowing as it neared, its tires crunching on the gravel as it came to a stop, a man behind the wheel, the same woman as before sitting in the passenger seat. "Say mister, are you lost?" asked the man, rolling down the window.

"Completely," admitted Chase.

"Where are you going?"

"I need to get back to Cape Coral..."

"Cape Coral... *Florida?*" The two people said in unison.

"Yes. Why, where am I?"

"Mister, you're in *Georgia...*"

■ ■ ■

The FBI had sent agents from both the Tampa and Miami field offices to meet with Sheriff Naywood. The FBI's *stated* task was to assist the Sheriff's Office with any resources necessary to aid in their investigation. Their *official task* was to catch the impersonators. The FBI was none too happy with the raid conducted under their banner, and they were more than just a little peeved at whomever was impersonating their field operators. If they found Chase Holt in the process, well, that would be a bonus.

Naywood stood at the end of the table in the conference room filled with FBI agents and investigators from his own office. "Tell me about this operation you fellas botched in my county..."

The agents shared glances. "Sheriff, I can assure you the FBI had nothing to do with this raid... In fact, this guy, Chase Holt, wasn't even on our radar for anything."

"You wouldn't bullshit a bullshitter, would you boy...?" To those who didn't know him, the Sheriff might come off as a yokel, and at times that worked to his advantage, having a seasoned background and five years in the bureau himself. He didn't find the work to his liking and went back to the police work he loved, moving up through the ranks to become the elected Sheriff. He didn't dislike the Feds so much as he didn't trust them. While local law enforcement simply did its best to enforce the laws and keep the peace, the government agencies never seemed to do anything that didn't benefit their agenda somehow. Whatever the *agenda du jour* happened to be. "Look, ever since that guy disappeared..." he looked over at his detectives, "what was his name...? Lived on the beach...?"

"Steele?" volunteered one of the FBI agents, jumping in.

"Ever since then," continued the Sheriff, "you government types have been stirring up all sorts of trouble around here... and making a mess of it. Like when that *thing...*"

"UFO," volunteered one of the detectives.

Naywood shot the detective a *shut the hell up* look. "Like when that *thing* landed out on Ft. Myers Beach. You started a war on my beach. I won't stand for that kind of..."

"To be fair, Sheriff," interrupted one of the agents, holding up his hand, "that was the NSA... And maybe a little CIA. We weren't involved in any way in that..."

"Well you damn sure had to know what was going on."

"No sir. Our two agencies don't communicate too often on things like that..."

Sheriff Naywood folded his arms. "Well that right there sounds like a problem to me... Doesn't it sound like a problem to you? Because Steele disappeared and nobody has been able to find him since. Then his sister disappears during a war on the beach with... well, who knows what..." he waved his arms. "A local news personality was murdered after airing a news special I'm sure you've seen, and her husband, one of my Deputies, took a leave of absence and has since disappeared. Now Mr. Holt, who was friends with both Steele and my Deputy, is abducted in broad daylight by a raid you say wasn't one of yours..." He folded his arms again. "And nobody seems to know a damn thing about anything."

"Mistakes happen, Sheriff. The FBI doesn't like it, but like everybody else, we're juggling cases and budgets. Things fall through the cracks. It doesn't help when secretive agencies like the CIA and the NSA who think they're above the need for communication with what they perceive as less important agencies, hold back information. That's been a bone of contention for years."

"I don't want to hear about bones of contention..." waved Naywood. "Falling through the cracks? I know what a turnip truck is... but it doesn't mean I fell off one." He stared at the men in the dark gray suits. "How about you stop blowing smoke up my skirt and tell me what you really know about what's going on here?"

"The Steele case is an open investigation of national security. The topic is not open for discussion..."

"Bullshit!" snapped the Sheriff. "You opened it for discussion when you spilled it all over my goddamn county..."

"We've already told you this wasn't us..."

"There's so many loose ends and unanswered questions... it's got Fed fingerprints all over it." Naywood was watching their posture and each of the FBI agents sat openly and casually.

"My assessment, Sheriff, is that this was an NSA move. Now, you could place an official inquiry with them but I don't think you'll even get so much as an email."

"What do you recommend then?"

"I'm going to put you in touch with an agent who is familiar with the original case... he'll only speak with you off the record, but maybe it will be of some help to you. His name is Phil Cooper. Officially, I will have no involvement in that introduction..."

The Sheriff nodded, "I appreciate the effort."

"In the meantime we will circulate the information about Holt and your missing deputy, maybe we can generate some movement..."

"I noticed you didn't mention locating Steele who seems to be the crux of this whole thing..."

"At this juncture," began one of the agents, "Steele is out of the picture, he's out of reach..."

Nawood saw an opening. "So he's someplace without an extradition treaty... you can't touch him?"

"I cannot tell you anything more."

"He's dead..." guessed the Sheriff.

"Not to our knowledge..."

He's already being held somewhere..."

The lead agent stood up abruptly, smoothing his suit jacket, followed by the other agents. "We're done, this conversation is over. We'll be in touch."

CHAPTER FIVE

UFW CONQUEST, GEDHEPP SYSTEM: *SMOKE AND ASH*

"Jack, you have an incoming communication."

"Thank you, TESS." Steele opened his eyes and swung his legs off the couch in his darkened quarters, rubbing his face. "Source?" It had been a long day and he'd never made it to bed, falling asleep on the couch still in uniform.

"Air and Space Port, Veloria."

Jack stepped over Fritz's sleeping form to get to the desk in his quarters and ran his fingers over the gently lit glass keyboard, the screen winking on, its blue glow illuminating the room around him. The logo of the Velorian Royal family in the middle of the screen matched the gold Pegasus silhouetted against a red rising sun on his ring. He glanced down at the ring on his finger and back up again. The logo sat on a black shield framed by olive branches, flanked by outstretched gold wings. Alité had taken the image he'd used for the Freedom and adopted it for Veloria. He was to say at the very least, floored.

The screen flickered for a moment as the Queen of Veloria's face appeared. "Hello my husband..."

"Hello gorgeous."

"Do you like my little surprise?"

"Which one?" he teased. "The fact that your communications are up, or the new logo?"

"The logo, *of course...*"

"It's beautiful. I'm stunned... but why?"

"I wanted to show the people that the old royal family was gone. This is about rebirth and a new beginning. A new image seemed to be a good way to convey that. I wanted something that would be totally different, something they had never seen before. Something they could not associate with anything past or present. Your winged horse and your flight wings seemed to fit together nicely."

"It looks spectacular, sweetie. I hope it works for your..." he stumbled, "*our* people," he corrected himself. "So how did you get communications up?"

"The UFW Directorate was kind enough to send a comm satellite on one of their transports. Before coming down to land at the ASP, they set it up in synchronous orbit with the base so we have constant signal. How's your reception?"

"Looks pretty good to me."

The small screen on Jack's eGo-h lit up, "Jack, we are entering the Gedhepp System in five minutes."

"Thank you, TESS," he replied.

"Who was that?" asked Alité.

He held up his arm so Alité could see the eGo-h on his wrist. "TESS, large screen..." The holographic screen lit up, hovering above his wrist, her animated face smiling at Alité. "TESS, this is Alité Steele, my wife. Sweetie, this is TESS."

"Hello Alité."

Alité raised one eyebrow, "Hello, TESS," she said slowly. She shifted her eyes to her husband. "What is she... it, whatever..."

"Sort of an electronic assistant," he countered. "She's tied into the ship's systems and can feed me live information and communications..."

"So she's not real, then?"

Jack taped the holographic screen in the corner and it disappeared. "No, she's a computer-generated artificial intelligence."

"Interesting. She looks pretty realistic."

Jack wasn't sure if her expression was wary or unimpressed. "What's wrong...?" he asked.

"You have a girlfriend," she pouted.

It struck him seriously which tore at his heart. But only for a moment. "Ooh, you little minx," he scolded, his eyes narrowing, "you're messing with me."

She smiled wickedly, "Yes, I am." Her expression shifted and her eyes changed to a vivid purple, "Do you want to punish me...? she purred."

It was Jack's turn to smile wickedly. "Lady, if I could climb through this screen, you'd be in big trouble..."

Her head tilted coyly, "What would you do to me, husband...?"

"I um..." Steele looked around in the darkened room, knowing full well he was alone but feeling a pang of nervousness just the same.

"We are on a secure diplomatic channel," she reminded him. "I want to *play...*"

"Woman, you never cease to amaze me."

Alité pointed at him, "But I don't want that *bitch* showing up and ruining things," she hissed in mock anger.

■ ■ ■

Commander Paul Smiley was watching the squadron screens in the flight tower, waiting for the Conquest to clear the gate, the ship at yellow alert - a standard precaution when entering a system not considered strongly-held UFW territory. "Two flights ready to go?"

"Aye, Captain."

Paul listened in on the bridge communications between the ships. "The Westwind is clear..." he announced, checking the roster then glanced up at the vid screen again. "Revenge too. Both ships reporting poor visibility. Tell our flights to take it easy, sensors are impaired..."

"What do we have out there?" asked the launch coordinator.

"Heavy clouds of dust, like smoke. High metallic content," replied Paul. "Ok, we're clear. Go for launch..."

"Launching..." Two flights of four fighters launched simultaneously, one flight on each side of the ship. The *kachunk* of the launch sleds could be heard throughout the ship in rapid succession as they hit the end of their rails, ejecting the fighters out into space.

Pappy keyed his mic, "Bridge, do you have any scan data for us?"

"Our scans are severely hampered Captain, the Revenge is pushing ahead looking for a break in the conditions."

"Copy that." Paul turned back to the tower controller. "Launch a Zulu to escort the Revenge. Inform the flights on patrol to reduce the distance on their routes by half."

"Aye, sir."

"And I want two more flights on standby and two more suited up..."

■ ■ ■

On the bridge of the Revenge, Lieutenant Commander Brian Carter was pacing the bridge watching the big screen. Seeing, well... nothing. "Anything..?"

"Nothing, Skipper."

"Zulu moving up on our Starboard side, sir."

Brian chewed on his lower lip. "Anybody ever seen anything like this before?" He got a few glances but it was obvious this was a unique situation for all of them. "How about any ideas on what could cause something like this..?"

Ragnaar turned in his seat, "There are no notations on UFW records or updates on the charts of any anomalies like this in this system, Commander. It may be something relatively recent. It is not a heavily traveled system... it may have gone unnoticed until now."

"How long to the gate?" Brian squinted and could make out the shape of the Zulu off their starboard side.

"At this pace, Rikovik's Reef gate in about seventy-six hours."

"This is going to be a long seventy-six hours," mumbled Brian.

"Direct communication, coming in Commander," said a decidedly female but artificial voice.

Brian had almost forgotten about the eGo-h on his wrist. "Go ahead, TESS."

Paul Smiley's face appeared on TESS' holographic screen. "How's it going over there, Commander?"

"Blind as a bat, Pappy."

"Yeah, us too. We sent you a Zulu escort and we've got two flights out with two more on standby. You've got the most advanced sensors in our group so press ahead, but don't go beyond the reach of our current sensor sweep. The bridge is forwarding you our numbers."

"We saw the Zulu..."

"Good. It's fitted with the sensor magnapod, so piggyback your sensors - let's see if we can improve our results."

"Will do, Pappy."

■ ■ ■

Commander Dar Sloane looked back and forth, out across his wingtips to see the faint outlines of the rest of his flight as they flew through the smoke and ash drifting through the system... so dense he might as well be blindfolded.

"Say Commander, aren't there supposed to be a couple planets in this system?"

His headset chirped as the comm ended. "Several," he replied. "It'd be nice if our sensors could cut through some of this stuff so we don't fly into one..."

"Am I imagining it, or do I feel buffeting?"

Sloane keyed his mic, "Yeah... seems to be a current of some sort. I can't tell which way it's moving though."

"Oh good, I thought I was losing my mind."

Sloane switched over to SPD, *Scanned Phase Doppler Radar,* and narrowed the beam, slowing the sweep. "I'm getting the best results on SPD, although that's not saying much..."

"Same here," chirped the speaker in his helmet. "MPB," *Magnetic Pulse Beam Radar,* "just shows a wall of white."

"I've got a blob ahea... *WOAH!*" Sloane yanked on the stick and kicked his rudder pedals hard, firing maneuvering thrusters as the chunk of rock the size of a building materialized in front of him. The Cyclone reared up and rolled, the left wing catching a massive outcropping of rock, barely missing the cockpit perspex, the screaming sound of crushed, tortured metal and shattering of composite armor vibrating through the fighter's frame. The Commander slammed hard against his harness, his vision going gray as the mangled wing ripped from the fuselage was flung outward. The engines still under power threw the Cyclone into a wild cartwheel, venting the oxygenated fuel gel with quick blobs of flame flying through space in all directions. The cockpit alarms were screaming at him as the confined space filled with tangy, metallic, electric smoke. His visor shield slammed shut and the wash of pure oxygen in his suit snapped him to his senses.

The rest of the flight, in a delta formation had passed the monster rock on either side and they tried to track their crippled flight leader.

"Stay on him!" screamed Santine. "Don't lose him in this stuff!"

"Commander! Commander! Cut your engines! Cut your engines! You have fire!"

Santine switched channels, "Red Flight to CFC, *mayday, mayday!* We have a midair with debris, we need rescue out here!"

"Conquest Flight Control, copy Red Flight. Launching emergency recovery. Please feed us your flight path numbers..."

■ ■ ■

Captain Smiley was scrutinizing the holo-chart in the flight tower. "Chart, zoom fifty percent." The table obeyed silently, bringing the flights, ships, coordinates and flight paths closer, allowing a more detailed view. "There it is," he pointed, indicating the debris location, fed to the tower from Red Flight. "If Rescue follows their exact path, they should be able to walk her around the debris..." Smiley straightened up and looked down through the glass to the flight deck below. "Tell her to take it easy, no hotdogging. We don't need any additional casualties. And have White flight join up with Red, we're calling them back after this..."

■ ■ ■

Lieutenant Maria Arroyo and her copilot Lieutenant JG Myomerr, were strapping into the cockpit of Rescue Two, running as fast as they could through their preflight checks as the medical and rescue personnel raced across the deck toward the boarding ramp.

"I'm in!" called Lisa, beating the rest of the team.

Maria looked over her shoulder, "No you're not, get out."

"I want to go..."

"No! This is not amateur hour. There's no room for you."

"But..."

Maria keyed her mic, waving and getting the attention of the Marine on the deck at the base of her ramp. "Get her off my bird. *Now!"*

Without saying a word, the Marine grabbed Lisa around the waist and hauled her bodily off the ship's ramp, the ramp retracting and the hull door scissoring together with a clank.

"Goddammit! Put me down!"

Maria looked out her side window at Lisa on the deck and shook her head no. "You'll get your turn kid, just not today," she mumbled.

"Cleared for stern launch," announced Myomerr.

Maria twisted the anti-grav throttle and Rescue Two went buoyant, bouncing off the deck like it was floating on water, a gentle blue glow under its landing feet.

Lisa stood on the deck with her hands on her hips and watched the craft rotate smoothly under direction of the deck controller and sail out through the shimmering blue stasis field with an electric hiss, moving out over the fantail, with her landing legs retracting as she retreated out of sight.

Commander Dar Sloane was wrestling unsuccessfully with his crippled fighter to get her wild cartwheeling under control. Snatching the throttle to zero he toggled off the engines and punched the fire control system button. Fire retardant foam sprayed across her engines and injected into the fuel systems sealing the broken lines and snuffing out the fire. Gobbets of foam and dwindling streams of fuel slung out into space in long ribbons. "C'mon baby," he breathed, "settle down..." He punched an emergency all-stop button which fired all maneuvering thrusters simultaneously for a long blast, the Cyclone shuddered under the force, her damaged frame groaning. "Mayday, Mayday, can anybody out there hear me?" The fighter rolled slowly, still drifting.

"You're signal's weak but we're tracking you Commander. Rescue Two is in route, is your fire out?"

"Fire's out, controls are dead. I've got nothing."

"Just sit tight. We'll find you but these asteroids are all over the place."

Smoke was still pouring out of the vents and Sloane couldn't see a damn thing. "Canopy's gotta go," he breathed, reaching for the release handle. He heaved but it wouldn't budge. Two-handed and it still didn't move.

Santine was weaving carefully through the drifting asteroids, the remainder of the flight waiting safely outside the field. "Commander, I've got you in sight." Smoke and ash drifted through the asteroid field obscuring his view. "Brother, I think you've got a problem..."

"Yeah, my canopy's jammed."

"Then you've got two problems. You're drifting towards a big one, flat up on your Z axis."

A spike of adrenalin shot through Sloan, in the smoke filled cockpit he could barely see the canopy perspex. "How far?"

"You've got about thirty seconds as far as I can tell," replied Santine.

It was either get out, or become an ingredient in a Cyclone pancake. "Ejecting!" He reached back and pulled the ejection loops on either side of his headrest, the canopy's explosive bolts firing slowly, one-by-one...

Santine eased closer, his shields bouncing a gently drifting chunk of rock away from his Cyclone's nose. "Get out Commander! *Get out!*" All he could hear in response was a string of epithets and static.

Maria was probably flying a little faster than she should, following a tracking line on her HUD, fed by the computer and the waypoint tracking calculations received from Red Flight. "I can't see a fucking thing, can you?"

Myomerr's feline features twitched, her eyes locked on the scans and sensor readouts, "Me neither."

Maria keyed her mic, "Rescue Two approaching final waypoint."

"Two birds ahead," said Myomerr taping on the screen, indicating their location.

"Back it down, Rescue Two, you're running hot. This field is a drifting obstacle course and you can't follow a tracking string, so shut it off."

"Copy, tracking off," Maria replied as Myomerr reached forward and typed in the command to end the computerized sequencer.

"Entering Asteroid field," announced Maria. "Keep your eyes peeled, people," she called to the rest of the crew. She nosed the ship down, passing underneath the first of the asteroids.

"Trees," pointed Myomerr.

Maria looked up at the underside of the rock then glanced over at Myomerr before switching back to the task at hand. "What the hell are trees doing on an asteroid..?"

■ ■ ■

Dar Sloane was panicked, swearing, beating on the canopy above him. The bolts had blown but didn't clear the canopy from its rails and the seat didn't fire. He couldn't tell if the radio was still transmitting, because it sure as hell wasn't receiving. Thirty seconds had to be ticking down and he was out of ideas. He couldn't believe he was going to die without being in a fight. If he had to go, that's the way he had wanted it... Fast and furious. He sat back to wait, folding his arms across his chest... *son of a bitch.*

The .45 caliber, 1911 semi-auto, charged particle blaster, like Admiral Steele's, was neatly tucked into his shoulder holster. Its performance was the talk of the ship and the Freedom's Chief Engineer had been producing them in the machine shop for anyone who wanted them. He'd decided to get one on a whim.

■ ■ ■

Santine hadn't been aware that he was screaming at the top of his lungs into his mic, urging the Commander to get out. It was obvious there was something wrong and he was feeling monumentally helpless. He was fifty feet off the fuselage of the crippled Cyclone, staring at the jagged remains of the missing wing, guts hanging out, blackened, trailing fuel and gelatinous white goo. The asteroid was alarmingly close and he was going to have to brake, letting the Commander's crippled fighter go.

The flashes in the cockpit caught his attention, hot streaks of glowing crimson exiting the edge of the canopy, crossing past the nose of his own fighter. "What the hellion..?" One after another in rapid succession, a steady cadence, one or two deflected by his shields as they sailed his way. As abruptly as they began, they stopped, the canopy moving then lifting, floating free.

■ ■ ■

Sloane shoved and the canopy broke free, floating above him. Jamming his new favorite firearm and best friend back into its holster, he unbuckled his harness and ripped his cords free, standing up in the seat. Shoving the canopy out of the way, he climbed out over the fuselage and propelled himself with all his might away from what should have been his coffin. But he wasn't safe yet; his suit would only have enough air for about five minutes, max, if he stayed calm. And he wasn't, his heart was pounding like a jackhammer. But at least he wasn't alone, he could see Santine's fighter through the smoke and floating ash.

■ ■ ■

"Ping me, Red Leader," said the voice in Santine's helmet.

"Copy, pinging. How far out are you Rescue Two?"

"Fifteen minutes. I'd love to tell you it'll be less but I can't, this is like a friggin maze."

"Copy." Santine knew Sloane didn't have that much time. With his engines at zero he crabbed his bird gently sideways with maneuvering thrusters, easing his way toward the Commander who was drifting toward him. He watched in all directions for anything that might be coming in his direction. Convinced there were no immediate collision threats he reached forward and flipped off his shields.

71

■ ■ ■

Sloane watched as Santine's Cyclone approached him sideways, the wingtip facing him, growing slowly larger, clearer. *What the hellion was he doing?* The flash behind him meant what was left of his ship had rammed itself into the asteroid but he couldn't turn far enough to see it. What a stupid way to lose a ship. It would have been a stupid way to die too. He reminded himself that he wasn't home yet.

The wingtip missile poked through the gloom and he grabbed a hold of it as he half-collided with it, climbing over it, arms and legs wrapped around it, holding on. *Now what?* Illuminated by the screens in the cockpit he could see Santine waving him toward the cockpit.

Holding tightly he positioned his feet and pushed off, parallel above the wing, careful not to touch the surface lest he drift free. It wasn't until he leapt that he wondered what he was supposed to grab onto. *Crap.*

Santine closed his visor and grabbed the cockpit lever releasing it, warning lights and a tone chorusing a blast of air venting out into space as he slid the canopy back on its rails all the way back to the lock-open position. Extending his arm, he caught Sloane's free hand and pulled him close, the Commander grabbing onto the canopy and cockpit frame.

The gold coated visors meant they couldn't see each other's faces, but there were always hand signals. Santine nudged the throttle, easing them towards the area where they'd entered the asteroid field. "Red Leader to Rescue Two, about face, we'll meet you in clear space near the final way point."

"What? How..."

"No time to explain, Rescue Two. Just do it. Red Leader will be communications dark for five minutes, starting now." He unplugged his umbilicals from his suit and handed the cords to Sloane outside the cockpit who would be nearly out of air. They would buddy breathe, easing themselves through the asteroid field. Slowly, carefully, without shields, a rescued pilot riding a fighter piggy-back to safety.

CHAPTER SIX

GEORGIA, CHESTER'S TRUCK STOP: *BFE*

The rancher and his wife were nice enough to let Chase get cleaned up, washed his clothes and fed him something solid. But he didn't trust them. It was too easy. Too convenient. Sure, they were nice enough, friendly, welcoming, sympathetic. They seemed genuine. Everything that he needed... and it felt too arranged. They accepted him without asking much about his circumstances – not that he would have told them anything anyway. But at this point he didn't trust anyone as far as he could throw them. Realistically, if you met someone in his condition, wouldn't you ask what happened to him? Where he came from?

If they *were* curious, they didn't say a word and he found that very strange, very controlled. He did consider that maybe they were being sensitive to his predicament, waiting for him to bring it up... but *that* wasn't going to happen. So, a pair of old shoes, a baseball cap and a hundred dollars later, he got a smile, a blessing and a ride to the nearest truck stop on the interstate. He thanked them of course, waving as they pulled away; fully aware that they may just have been good people. Maybe.

"Time to get back in the game," he breathed, watching the traffic flow in and out of the truck stop. He pulled the RFID from his pocket, "And time to put you, my little friend, to use." He had checked his clothes, the hat and the newly acquired shoes for any signs of alteration or tampering but could find none. Hopefully this RFID was the only thing tracking him, they hadn't expected him to throw it up.

Chase went into the mini mart and bought a few things to nibble on and stay hydrated including a pack of bubble gum. I-75 went north and south, reaching from Naples below Ft. Myers all the way up to the top of Michigan. He needed to go south but he was searching for a vehicle going north. Way north.

The rain had stopped and slivers of afternoon sunlight were playing through the breaking clouds. Reddish-brown muddy puddles dotted the gravel truck lot which smelled like diesel, oil and gasoline. This would be a terribly dusty place without the rain, the red Georgia clay dust settling on everything.

Leaning against the outside wall of the mini mart, Chase did his best to be anonymous, watching the traffic, chewing a sizable wad of gum. And there it was, exiting the northbound ramp, a huge RV, a family motor coach the size of a tour bus, rolling up to the gas pumps with Ontario plates.

"Thank you," he breathed, wrapping the RFID in the sticky bubble gum. He passed the family as they filed past him, heading into the mart, checking over his shoulder as he walked toward the RV. Most of the other patrons were busy pumping their gas, oblivious to the rest of the world as he rounded the back of the bus, pausing only momentarily to stick the wad of gum in behind the spare tire carrier. Protected in its cozy little spot, the RFID wasn't likely to fall off on its own and no one was going to find it unless they needed that spare tire. He grinned to himself as he headed for the southbound on-ramp, sliding on the cheap mini-mart sunglasses to hide his eyes, pulling the ball cap down over his forehead. "Time to find a ride home..."

■ ■ ■

Sheriff Naywood was stretched out on the couch at home with his wife watching the end of the ten o'clock news when his cell phone rang. His wife reached over picking it up off the coffee table and handed it to him. "You sure you want to answer it?"

He glanced at the number on the screen and recognized the number. "You know I have to..." He hit *send* with his thumb and placed it against his ear, "Talk to me, Detective."

"We're headed over to a citizen-reported B & E with shots fired..."

Naywood could hear the police unit's siren in the background. "Where?"

"You're gonna love this, boss... our boy, Chase Holt's house. Thought you might like to attend."

"Definitely. On my way."

"Frank, do you really have to go?" pleaded his wife.

He rose from the couch, sliding the cell phone into his jeans pocket, "Sorry Honey, this one's kind of important..."

She watched him sling his duty belt over his jeans. "They're *always* important..." she waved.

"Sorry, Honey..." he grabbed a Sheriff's windbreaker off a chair in the dining room and slid it on over his t-shirt, meeting her at the door. "Don't wait up..." He held her chin and kissed her goodnight, swinging the door open with his free hand. They'd been married better than twenty years and he knew damn well, she'd be up watching television or reading a book when he got home, no matter what time it was. She was a peach.

"You be careful, Frank," she called from the door. She watched him pull his unmarked cruiser out of the driveway, his headlight and tail light strobes coming on halfway down the block. She could tell when he made it to the main street, his siren coming on, fading away in the distance.

■ ■ ■

Cape Coral PD was already on the scene when the Sheriff's detectives got there and by the time Naywood arrived, his detectives were busy taping off the crime scene. The next door neighbor was sitting on her porch wrapped in a Sheriff's jacket and flanked by a German Shepherd.

"What do we have so far?"

A detective with a beard, looking more like a biker than a cop, guided Sheriff Naywood off to the side, out of earshot of the neighbors and Cape Coral policemen. "Karen, that's the neighbor girl," he thumbed over his own shoulder, "saw a black SUV in our boy's driveway. Thinking he had returned, she went over to see how he was and return the guy's dog. Walking across the grass, she catches moving lights in the house through the window and the house is dark. She peeks through the window and there are three guys in black going through the house. They spot her and come running out, the dog attacks and nails one in the arm and leg. They Taze the girl and shoot at the dog but miss her in the dark. Get this, Karen said the guns didn't make much noise..."

"Suppressors..."

"Yeah. Now, they're wearing balaclavas so she can't see their faces - so I'm figuring they don't worry about not killing her. But she seems to think the dog recognized the one that got bit. She said the dog took a real dislike to that one."

The Sheriff smirked, "And people say dogs are just stupid animals..."

"They tossed the house pretty good, made a hell of a mess but the big thing is the safe."

Naywood winced. "Gun safe?"

The detective nodded. "Yep, he's an NRA instructor, remember?"

"Do we know what they got? I hate to think of more stuff on the street..."

"No, boss. I'm thinking these are probably the same guys that scooped him up."

"The black hats? If they have him, why would they bother?"

"I don't know, but they cracked the safe without leaving a mark... It's completely intact."

"What the hell could they be looking for?" Naywood folded his arms across his chest. "Are we sure our boy didn't just forget to lock it?"

The detective shook his head. "No, I thought of that. Karen said she went over and inspected his place after the raid, after the fire department and everybody left. She said she actually checked the safe. Then she had another neighbor come over to repair the door so she could lock up the house. She's got a key. The guys that visited tonight didn't force entry, they picked the locks. And in their haste they left some of their tools behind..."

"Thank God. We could use a clue..."

"Yeah... but I've never seen technology like this, boss. It's some real digital, James Bond, Sci-Fi shit..." They quietly angled over to the detective's unmarked cruiser and he unlocked the trunk, looking around nervously before lifting the lid to reveal the contents, "Check this out..."

Sheriff Naywood stared at it blankly. "That's definitely some government gear."

"If it's not alien," added the detective.

Naywood shot him a glance. "You guys like throwing that possibility around, don't you..."

"I was on the beach that night, boss. That thing wasn't from around here..."

"I saw the films..."

"As God as my witness," said the detective raising his hand in oath, "it turned that Coast Guard chopper into flaming confetti with a goddamn lightning bolt."

Naywood nodded, "I'm not debating you saw something extraordinary, Buck, but you have no idea what they're cooking up at places like Area 51. When I was with the Feds, I saw and heard all sorts of things. Most of them I still can't talk about. And that's one of the reasons I got out, I didn't want to become a nameless casualty of their top secret hush list. So, for now, let's try to focus on what we have at hand, shall we?"

"Sure, boss."

The Sheriff closed the trunk, staring blankly at it for a moment. "Did you call CSI?"

"Yeah," the detective checked his watch. "They should be here any minute."

"Ok, let's not mention the gear," Naywood tapped on the trunk, "to anyone but our team."

"Sure thing, boss."

"And tell 'em all to keep their lips *zipped...*" He pointed to the trunk again, "Do not leave that in your car when you go home, take it in the house with you but don't let anyone see it. This doesn't go into evidence, understand?"

"Yes sir..."

■ ■ ■

When the eighteen-wheeler exited I-75 at Daniels Parkway, Chase felt relieved and nervous at the same time. All the while hoping that RFID was enjoying its ride to Ontario... and still holding the attention of the NSA. It didn't take a genius to figure out who they were. After all, they were the same ones responsible for the Steele's misery, the death of Dan Murphy's wife and the disappearance of Dan himself. He hadn't talked to Dan in a couple of months, now he knew why. He was either dead or hiding so deep they felt the need to focus on someone new to locate him. Parting ways with the trucker, Chase plodded west along Daniels Parkway, not in any particular hurry. It was midday and he couldn't go home in broad daylight. He'd wait till after dark and go knock on Karen's door, hopefully she still had a key to the house. He hoped his tools were still in his truck, he was pretty sure he was going to need to do a bug sweep. *His truck...* he hadn't even thought about that, would it still be there?

■ ■ ■

Chase purposely waited until well after dark to get back to his neighborhood. Walking down his street somehow felt foreign and he was fighting a stomach full of butterflies. He studied every parked car, spied every window, listened to every sound. Nothing but crickets and the smell of freshly mown grass.

Despite the yellow crime scene tape his house didn't look any different, but his truck was nowhere to be seen. Standing at Karen's door, he unscrewed the light bulb from the porch light before knocking on the door. He cringed, it sounded far too loud on the quiet street. He could hear Allie's bark and was relieved she was still alive. There was a moment he didn't think Karen was going to open the door when the light didn't come on. She peered through the window and there was finally a spark of recognition in her face.

■ ■ ■

Allie jumped all over Chase as he knelt on the floor, showering him with affection. "I missed you too, sweetie..." He looked up at Karen and Pam, "Thank you for taking care of her... just let me know what I owe you."

Karen waved it off and Pam stood mute, "What happened to you, Chase? You've been gone a week... and you look terrible."

"It might be better for you two if I didn't tell you... the less you know the better."

"The Sheriff and the FBI are looking for you..."

"What did they do with my truck?" he interrupted.

"Nothing," waved Pam, "we put it in your garage after everybody left..."

"Oh my God, thanks! Was there anything *in the truck?*"

"Your duffel and your laptop? Yes. We thought about leaving it in the truck but at the last minute we decided to bring it home with us. I'm not sure why..."

He grabbed them together and gave them a bear hug. "Oh you beautiful dolls, you are *so awesome!*"

"Whew," Pam pushed him away, "and you are *so stinky.* No offense..."

"Sorry," he chuckled, "it's been a rough road."

"I can tell," Karen replied with a crooked smile.

He stared down at his hands for a moment, not sure what to do with them, Allie's big brown eyes staring up at him. "What about Penny?" he asked, looking back up.

The girls shared a glance then looked back at him, Karen shifting uneasily, "We don't know. Nobody will say. We called around to the hospitals and we couldn't find her anywhere. We didn't know what else to do... None of this was on the news or anything. It's like it never happened. When they came back last night..."

"When *who* came back?" interrupted Chase.

"The guys in black armor. They were in your house. They made a real mess..."

"What did they take?"

Pam shook her head, "We don't know. They Tazered Karen and shot at Allie while I was calling 911..."

Chase was pacing like a caged animal. "They Tazed you... *son of a bitch.* And what's with these assholes shooting at dogs?"

"She bit one pretty good..."

He looked down at Allie who wagged her tail slowly, "Good girl."

"And when the police showed up they were already gone. The Sheriff showed up and then the FBI. They were here till three in the morning."

"I had to give them the key to lock up the house," volunteered Karen, "they didn't want me to go near it. Their forensics van came back again this morning for a couple of hours."

Chase stopped pacing. "Did you get the key back?"

"No..."

"Dammit," he bit his lip out of reflex and winced. Too soon. "I'm gonna have to break in."

"How?"

"As quietly as possible. Got a big screwdriver..?"

■ ■ ■

Approaching his house from the patio facing the water, Chase used the oversized screwdriver as a lever and the head of a carpenter's hammer underneath as a fulcrum to get the sliding glass door to his kitchen to jump it's track. Lifting it carefully, he moved it far enough to squeeze past. "Stay out here and keep Allie with you..." he whispered. "Is Pam watching?"

"Yes," whispered Karen, "she can see the whole street. Why are you cutting off the power?"

Chase opened the breaker panel on the patio side of the house. I have automatic sensors in some of the rooms that'll turn the lights on, I want it to stay dark. I'm also hoping I'm cutting power to any video they might have... video usually needs a power feed."

Leaving Karen and Allie outside, Chase squeezed his bulk through the sliding glass door, picking up the mini flashlight he left on the kitchen counter for walking the dog at night. Making his way silently through the house, the only illumination coming in from the streetlights outside, he was appalled at the condition of his home. *Fucking son of a bitch...* What they didn't open or rummage through, they smashed or destroyed. The house still smelled like smoke from the flash-bang that burned the carpet in the center of the living room.

He gnashed his teeth, his sixty-inch flat screen TV lay face down on the living room floor, a set of boot-prints in the middle of its back. In his office, there were two 9mm bullet holes in the side of the case of his computer tower, another through the monitor. With the mini flashlight in his mouth, he knelt down and unscrewed the twist knobs, removing the side of the computer case. The CPU and motherboard were destroyed but the hard drive was still intact. He unlatched the quick lock and pulled the drive out, unplugging it and heading to his bedroom. He passed the open gun safe in the hall closet without looking or even pausing. He knew it was going to be empty.

Tossing the hard drive on the bed, he hastily stripped naked and redressed with fresh clothes and running shoes. He would have liked to take a shower but he seriously doubted he had the luxury of time for that.

Popping open an air conditioning vent on the wall along the floor, Chase reached inside and by feel, punched numbers into a keypad hidden inside, silently closing the vent again. The back wall of his bedroom closet unlocked with a clank and rolled backward, a battery system operating the door motor. With the mini flashlight back in his mouth, he pushed his hanging clothes aside, stepping into the tiny room, grabbing two backpacks; prepacked emergency go-bags, commonly referred to as bugout bags. He eyed the pair of AR-15 carbines on the wall. It would be nice to take a long gun but he worried about concealment, deciding to leave them behind. He was hoping that wouldn't be a mistake. He tossed the bags on the bedroom floor behind him and cleared the extra cash off the safe-room's shelf to add to the money already in the bags, snagging a dog harness with packed pouches off the wall. He palmed the door button inside the room, backing out as it motored closed and rearranged all the hanging clothes to make the closet look undisturbed. The safe-room door latched with a quiet clank as he gathered the bags and headed for the kitchen, his running shoes squeaking on the tile floor. He paused, stuffing the extra cash and hard drive into his bag.

Chase was trying to decide if he should stay on foot or take the truck, knowing he could cover a lot of ground quickly by vehicle. But the decision had been made for him, three of his tires flat. "Dammit!" he slammed the garage door.

"Chase! *Chase!*" Karen's voice was whispered but strained.

"What?" he asked, running through the house back into the kitchen.

"Someone's coming!"

"Where?" He passed the bags one by one through the open door.

Pam ran around the corner from between the houses, sliding to a stop on the patio. "Two SUVs blocking the street at the end of the block and it's hard to tell, but I think there's four men from each car coming..."

Hmm, they blocked the street. "Doesn't matter, my truck is trashed." He hung the harness over Allie and fastened it around her, the pouches hanging on either side of her body. He stood up slinging his backpack over his shoulder, moving over to snap the house's electrical breakers back on, the house still dark. "We gotta go," he said pointing down the dock and handing Karen the other backpack, "now."

"We?"

"You really think it would be a good idea to stay?" he hissed.

"What did you get us into, Chase? Who are these people?"

"I'm sorry guys, I think you were in this from the start. They'll use you to get to me, just like they're using me to get to someone else..." He moved down the dock dragging her by the hand, Pam trailing behind.

"Why don't we just call the police?" breathed Pam, trying to keep up.

"We'll be dead or gone by the time they get here," replied Chase.

"I don't understand, why..?"

"We don't have time for this discussion..." Chase whispered, slinging the little duffel with his debugging gear and laptop over the handlebars of the first Jet Ski.

The two houses were stormed simultaneously, flash-bangs thumping the night air, the flash illumination seen through the widows. Yelling of voices could be heard and Chase, Pam and Karen flattened themselves on the watercraft ramp between the Jet Skis, doing their best to remain invisible in the darkness. Chase clutched Allie and gently held her muzzle lest she bark. Two figures in black ran between the houses and stopped at the seawall, checking the small yards, patio and water. Seeing nothing, they moved back to the street side.

"Who knows how to drive one of these?" whispered Chase.

"I do," volunteered Karen.

"Pam, you ride with her, Allie will ride with me. Get on but don't start it until mine's in the water. Leave your lights off..."

"Ok." Karen hung the backpack over the handlebars so it sat in her lap, swinging her leg over and sliding up onto the seat. Once they were both on, a couple shoves with his feet and the Jet Ski slid nearly silently into the water.

"They're on the dock two houses down..." hissed Karen.

"Stay still." whispered Chase, frozen in place. He watched, barely able to see their heads as they disappeared between the houses. He tapped the seat and Allie climbed up, laying awkwardly with her rear legs hanging off one side, perched on the foot board. Chase pushed the Jet Ski back, swinging his leg over the seat as it slid into the water, keeping his body low over the German Shepherd. "Go," he whispered, pushing his start button.

The two PWCs puttered once or twice and sputtered to life, idling quietly, Chase pulling up abreast of Karen. He idled slowly down the channel hoping to remain unnoticed but the sound echoed off the backs of the houses on the quiet canal. He caught the bobbing motion of flashlights out of the corner of his eye coming between the houses and the shouts for them to stop as the men ran out onto the docks. More lights ahead of them appeared between the houses.

"GO! GO! GO!" shouted Chase, squeezing the throttle. *"Stay with me!"* The Jet Ski leapt forward, coming up out of the water on plane almost instantly. He checked his mirror and Karen was right behind him. *That a girl!* He couldn't hear over the engine whine but he could see the muzzle flashes and the sprites of water out in front of his Jet Ski. He passed through the sprays of water, docks, boats and mooring posts passing him in a blur. He drifted right to make the left-hand turn into the main channel at speed.

Karen saw the muzzle flashes and the shots hitting the water, weaving, to avoid them, sailing through the spray, slowing down some to maintain control. Pam was holding on with a vice grip with her head buried against Karen's back, screaming. Seeing Chase swing right, Karen thought that's the way they were going, then realizing they were going left. She steered hard and squeezed the throttle, the PWC skidding across the surface of the water before digging in, launching ahead, jetting hard to catch up. The men in black were running around the tip of the block along the seawall, taking shots at them and she did her best to go fast and stay small, crouching as low as she could, docks and houses whizzing past. She weaved hard to avoid a boat sticking out from its dock, missing its exposed outboard motor by inches, the sight of the stainless propeller flashing past her face imprinted in her mind.

Swinging wide through Bimini Basin, Chase felt they were in the clear and slowed down to let Karen catch up. Besides, he didn't know how far they we going to go and they needed to conserve fuel. He knew he could milk a hundred miles out of a tank of gas, but not hot-rodding like that they couldn't.

He flipped on his running lights so she could see him and kept it at a steady thirty miles an hour, well below the sixty to sixty-five miles an hour they were capable of. He checked his mirror to be sure she was staying with him. He couldn't see her face but he was sure she was scared to death. He didn't blame her. He rolled a chart of the islands through his mind's eye but still had no idea where they were going yet.

■ ■ ■

"They're heading for the Casahoochee... Coolahatch... "

"Caloosahatchee River," said the driver of the black SUV, stomping on the accelerator, launching the heavy vehicle down the quiet street. "Yeah, I can see that."

"Turn here! Turn here!" pointed the passenger in the front seat. "Take this all the way to El Dorado!"

The driver wrestled the SUV around the corner, tires wailing, the SUV behind him racing to keep up. At the end of a two block stretch the driver had to brake hard and navigate another corner, smoke coming off the complaining tires. "Fuck it doesn't connect... Gotta cut over another street," he grunted. The black SUV behind them didn't brake hard enough and slid up on the grass of the house at the end of the block, plowing up the lawn, a shower of grass and mud splattering the house as its driver fishtailed the truck across three lawns and the sidewalk to catch up, barely missing the cars parked in the driveways.

"Where the hell are you going?" crackled a voice over the radio.

Sitting in the passenger seat of the first SUV, Doug Mooreland grabbed the mic. "To El Dorado. We can take the parkway all the way to the bridge and cut them off at the bridge..."

"What bridge, Doug?"

Doug keyed the mic, "The bridge from East El Dorado Parkway to West El Dorado Parkway... where it crosses over the canal." He shook his head. "Dumbass," he muttered.

"Doug, there's no bridge."

"Bullshit. What connects East and West then?"

"Nothing..." came the reply. *"They're not connected."*

"Then how the fuck do you get to the other side?" demanded Mooreland.

"You have to take Coronado out to Cape Coral Parkway and go all the way around..."

"Son of a bitch!" Doug threw the mic against the dash, "We passed Coronado a half a mile back."

Mooreland wanted to know how the RFID ended up heading north when Holt had ended up back here. He had been so sure if he stranded Holt, he would reach out, connect with whomever could help him most. Dan Murphy. He wanted to catch the group together. He wanted that equipment, he just didn't know who had it. Maybe the neighbor girls had it. It would make sense considering he came right back here. He knew if he could find that alien transmitter he could lure Steele back to Earth.

■ ■ ■

Running in close formation, Chase felt comfortable turning his running lights back off. Allie was watching over the handle bars as they made the last turn in the canal toward the river. Once they hit the open river nobody would be able to track them. At least not easily. But where to go? There were plenty of marinas, fuel wouldn't be a problem. He wanted something secluded, removed from vehicle traffic. Maybe North Captiva for a few days till things cooled down. Hell there were any number of islands with little or no habitation. He was hoping they might find an empty house, something that wasn't lived in year-round. He was getting ahead of himself... One thing at a time, they needed to get out to the river first. There was little if any moonlight and Chase was staying in the middle of the channel, guided by the lights of the houses and the docks lining the water.

It was the moving shadows along the seawall blocking out those lights that caught his eye. "Hold on Allie!" He squeezed the throttle all the way in, a straight shot to the river. The Jet Ski launched, the engine screaming and when he checked his rear view mirrors all he could see was the giant rooster tail his craft was making. *Cmon, girls!*

The flashes lined the seawall, men running along it, rounds splashing the water around him. He couldn't hear a thing except for the scream of the engine and the gale force wind ripping past his ears. He lay down across the Shepherd, his chin on her head. When he glanced down at the gauges, he was hovering just below seventy on the glassy surface of the canal, dock posts whipping past like fence posts. Dammit, he hadn't thought about them taking El Dorado all the way to the end like that. But in a few short seconds he was clear, the docks, cabanas and moored boats blocking their lines of sight. The opening into Redfish Cove and the Caloosahatchee River never looked so good. He eased off the throttle, looking for Karen, his rooster tail dropping as he slowed down. She wasn't far behind him and he had to speed up to keep her from over-running him. He waved her to the right toward the Gulf of Mexico and they followed the sweeping curve paralleling the shoals of Glover Bight.

Nearly a mile wide at this point, the breeze kicked up a little chop on the river. When Karen waved back at him he slowed down waving her closer. "What's wrong?"

"Where are we going?"

"Some place we can beach these things and rest for the night."

"I think there's something wrong..."

Chase let go of the throttle altogether, steering gently towards Karen's PWC to get closer. "Sounds like it's running OK," he gestured to the other Jet Ski.

"No, *Pam*. She won't answer me."

"She's probably scared to death... Pam!" hollered Chase. *"Pam!"* He shrugged, squinting in the dark, I can't see anything, maybe she fainted. Is she holding on?"

"Yeah," nodded Karen.

"Might be like battlefield shock. I've seen guys freeze up. We'll go over to the back of Captiva and beach over there for the night. You OK?"

"Depends on what you call OK..."

■ ■ ■

Chase coasted in to the beach and let the nose of the Jet Ski nudge the sand. One extra goose on the throttle to push it a little further up and he shut it off. "Ok, Allie," he sat back and took his weight off her. She got up stiffly and jumped off onto the beach, stretching, wandering off to explore. Chase

85

waved Karen in, "Just let it coast." He reached down and caught the nose. "Ok, shut it off." He pulled on it to secure it a little higher on the sand. "Ok climb off..." he said, opening the hatch on the nose. He reached in and pushing other gear aside, pulled out a small anchor with some line.

Karen looked over her shoulder, "Pam, you can let go now, we're safe..." she looked over at Chase in the darkness. "She still won't let go."

Chase dropped the anchor in the sand and sloshed over in the water. Her arms wrapped around Karen's waist, he grabbed Pam's hand and had to pry her fingers off her other wrist, her hands ice cold. It sent a spike of fear up his spine and he touched her face, her skin cold. It was more than eighty degrees outside, she shouldn't be that cold. He dug the small flashlight out of the cargo pocket of his shorts and turned it on, putting it in his mouth so his hands were free. He released Karen from Pam's death grip and picked her lifeless form off the Jet Ski, carrying her to the sand. He could feel the sticky slickness on her back and side as he laid her down, Karen standing there, mute.

Chase examined her closely, she had been hit twice in the lower back and once in the side about three inches below her armpit. She had saved Karen's life. "I'm sorry," was all he could think of to say. "She's... gone..."

Karen wailed and sank to her knees in the sand, burying her face on Pam's prostrate form, sobbing heavily. Allie trotted over and lay down next to her, doing her best to be comforting, nuzzling her hand.

Karen and Pam had been friends since grade school, pretty much inseparable as best friends. Anyone who didn't know them would have assumed they were lovers, when the truth was they were better described as twins from different mothers. Chase had known them for the better part of fifteen years, since high school. Karen was the athletic one, competing on the swim team and running track, while Pam who could have easily passed for a cheerleader, was the bookworm. Chase was heartbroken, he loved them both dearly. Probably even more than Penny... because, well, Penny was new in his life, he had a long -term connection to Karen and Pam. Now he had lost three important people in his life, two within the span of a week. And as far as he could tell, to the same evil.

■ ■ ■

Sheriff Frank Naywood was not a happy man, by any stretch of the imagination. Cape Coral Police and his Sheriffs had missed the carnage by mere minutes as it spread through the neighborhoods between Bimini Basin and Redfish Cove. Property damage was widespread; cars, boats, houses, broken windows... The minor consolation was no injuries were reported. Detectives and CSI teams were combing the entire area for evidence, having a good portion of the block cordoned off with crime tape, from the house where the two girls lived all the way down to the end of the street.

Standing in Chase Holt's driveway, Naywood greeted the man getting out of the black Crown Victoria, his hand out, the two man shaking briefly. Frank Naywood..."

"Phil Cooper, FBI. Looks like you're a little busy tonight..."

"Understatement of the year, Mr. Cooper. We have empty brass casings from the house behind me all the way to the end of the street along the seawall."

"9mm, I'm guessing. Sounds like they were trying to stop a boat?"

"Jet skis, plural. I think the two girls who lived next door got swept into this whole mess..."

Phil Cooper pursed his lips. "My guys briefed me about Holt. I understand you have a Deputy at large somewhere that fell off the radar too?"

Naywood nodded. "Dan Murphy..."

Cooper casually stuffed his hands in his pockets, "Mmm, husband of the dead newscaster, right?"

"That's right."

"How about Holt's girlfriend?" Cooper's head tilted to one side.

"She's OK, we have her in protective custody."

"Does he know that? Holt, I mean."

"No, Holt's been missing for about a week, we've had no contact with him... well until tonight," motioned the Sheriff. "We're guessing he came back. Not sure how it involves the neighbor girls yet."

"Hmm, exponential expansion. Let me tell you a little story Sheriff," began Phil Cooper, leaning in. He reached into his suit jacket and withdrew a pack of cigarettes. "Do you mind?" he motioned.

"No," waved Naywood, "go ahead."

Cooper tapped the pack, and pulled out the tallest one. Lighting it, he inhaled deeply. "I'm trying to quit, but I never know what to do with my hands..."

"The story?" prompted Naywood, a little annoyed.

"This is completely off the record, open to interpretation and may or may not represent the whole truth..." grinned Cooper. "It's not repeatable. Ever. But you need to believe everything I'm going to tell you, understand?"

Naywood sighed, "I get it."

"Once upon a time, the CIA was running guns to Venezuela by way of Brazil. It was a bid to supply weapons to rebels fighting against Chavez in an attempt to destabilize the government. The White House wanted him out. A man named Jack Steele was the pilot flying that transport. Now, Steele didn't work for the CIA and he had no idea he was being used, he was *just a pilot*. Someone tried to steal that plane and bless his heart he wasn't about to let that happen. Cop skills. The Kid's a serious boy scout. Did I mention he used to be a cop? Yeah it runs in his family." Cooper took a draw on the cigarette before continuing, the smoke expelling as he talked. "Well it started a whole incident... especially when his plane disappeared over a corner of the Bermuda Triangle with two navy fighters in hot pursuit. They disappeared too."

Naywood rolled his eyes and Cooper caught him. "It gets better, Sheriff. And I'm telling you, it only gets farther out there. But believe me, you can't make this stuff up. Everybody's looking for this Steele kid; FBI, CIA, Military Intelligence, KGB..."

"KGB?"

Cooper smirked, "Yeah. But that's not important. At least not right now. See, the Steele kid comes back a year after he disappears and I get a call from his folks, I know them pretty well. When he comes back a little hell breaks loose, after which I get to actually meet him." The Agent's face changed to one of contemplation, "Interesting kid. He's definitely got a strong command presence..."

"Did you put him in custody?" asked Naywood, wondering how this all tied together.

"No, that wasn't going to happen. Because we want the technology he has at his disposal and the Bureau figured to make nice to get it..."

"What kind of technology?"

Phil Cooper exhaled a cloud of smoke and looked up at the sky. "The kind that you get from out there..."

Naywood didn't know whether to laugh or take him seriously.

"But the Bureau wanted proof," continued Cooper. "So, the kid showed it to me..."

"What kind of proof?" interrupted Naywood.

"Concrete proof. We'll leave it at that."

"Like what?"

Cooper sighed, "You wouldn't believe me if I told you."

"Try me. What, did you see a ship or something?"

Cooper's jaw muscles flexed while he was deciding how much to tell Naywood. "Nah, I didn't see a ship. I *visited* a ship."

Sheriff Naywood stared at him blankly, looking for deception in the FBI agent's face. He saw none. "You're not kidding..." his voice trailed off to a whisper.

"No I'm not. It was an *angels singing, shaft of light from heaven,* life-changing event." He paused for a moment, neither man speaking. "So... I got the FBI to back off and play nice. The CIA got in hot water, facing a Congressional investigation to explain why they were pursuing an American citizen inside our borders. Basically they got a slap on the wrist for being in a pissing match with the Bureau and not letting us handle it."

"So how did the NSA get involved?"

"They saw the data from NASA and DARPA during his visit and basically went nuts that they hadn't been included in something they'd decided was a national security concern. Well, the Steele kid left a gizmo behind for his family to stay in contact with him and..."

"Because he's... out there..." said Frank Naywood slowly, pointing at the stars.

"Right," nodded Cooper. "Well the signal's encrypted but it's not invisible. SETI saw it, got all excited, thought it was an ET contact. DARPA saw it and suddenly the NSA's all over it. They can't crack the encryption and that scares the crap outta' them. And reportedly, the unit's the size of a laptop. Our equipment requires eighty-foot dish transmitters and hundreds of tons of electronics. Yeah, they want it bad. *Real bad."* Cooper flicked the cigarette butt into the street and took a moment to fish out another, lighting it, taking a draw. "Anyway, they suspect the one with the gizmo is the sister staying at Steele's beach house. At this point the NSA is playing it cool, watching the house, hoping they can catch the gizmo in use and recover it. But the KGB is watching the same house, though to this day, nobody knows why. But the Ruskies make a move first, the shit hits the fan and the KGB team gets themselves offed."

"Jesus Christ," mumbles Frank. "So let me backtrack a moment; the news broadcast reports a year ago about the sightings and the things near the moon..."

"All true. CSS and NSA squashed them for national security. Don't panic the citizenry and all that..."

"Who's CSS?"

"Central Security Service. They're controlled by the DOD. The orders for the NSA guys involved in this are probably coming from the CSS."

"Which is coming from the DOD, then..."

The FBI agent took another drag on his cigarette. "Yep. Some righteously scary people."

"And the incident on the beach..."

Cooper dropped the cigarette butt on the concrete and ground it out with the toe of his shoe. "Yeah. Real. I wasn't here that night but to hear the kid's parents tell it, that wasn't Steele or his ship..."

"Who then?"

"Another member of his fleet," said Cooper casually.

"FLEET?!" That was way louder than Naywood had intended. *"Fleet?"* he whispered.

"Fleet." confirmed Cooper. "So anyone remotely connected to Steele, is going to get a serious rectal exam from the NSA. They want Steele and the technology so bad; I really don't think they give a shit about anything else. In fact, I haven't talked to his folks in a while, I ought to do that. Make sure they're OK. This is starting to give me a seriously bad feeling."

"Exponential expansion," nodded Naywood, understanding a little better. "So all these people are connected to Steele?"

"In one form or another," confirmed Phil Cooper. "Holt, Steele and Murphy are all in the same Masonic Lodge..."

"What about Caroline Murphy? What happened there?"

"That was an enemy asset elimination. She embarrassed them and they wanted her gone for that. They wanted a loud and clear signal this was something not to be fucked with."

Naywood rubbed his face with his hands. "My God. These guys are acting like rabid animals. They're supposed to be protecting the citizens..."

Cooper shook his head, "No, protecting citizens is the job of law enforcement. Your job. These guys are tasked with protecting the country; which means sacrifices by the few for the benefit of the many. They have license to do whatever they need to do. Many levels of collateral damage are anticipated and accepted. "

"I thought these people were supposed to be special..."

"They are special. *Very special.* Most are ex- Rangers, Seals, Special Forces... but there's a lot of internal pressure for results. I'm not making excuses but I certainly understand their frustration."

"Doesn't excuse their behavior," retorted the Sheriff. "This is an unacceptable excess of force." His cell phone rang and he excused himself, answering it.

"Sheriff, this is dispatch. We have a phone call from someone claiming to be Chase Holt."

"Put it through." The Sheriff listened to the tone change, the line switching over. "Hello..?"

"Hello, this is Chase Holt... You won't be able to trace this call, so don't even try."

"You're on my cell phone Mr. Holt. Are you alright?"

"Yes..."

"Do you have the girls with you?" There was a pause and Naywood thought maybe he'd lost the call. "Mr. Holt?"

"Yes sir," his voice wavered. "They killed Pam. She's dead..."

"Goddammit," he breathed. "Is Karen alright?"

"Yes, she's alright."

"Where are you Mr. Holt? We know this wasn't your fault. Let us come and get you, we can help you."

"No you can't Sheriff. Nobody can. We're on our own. I called to let you know where we left Pam, so you can get her..."

"Can I talk to Karen?"

"Maybe later, she's finally asleep now..."

CHAPTER SEVEN

UFW CONQUEST, GEDHEPP SYSTEM: *BIRTH OF JAX MERCURY*

The heat was staggering, a wind blowing across the desolate terrain like an unrelenting blast furnace. Very little grew there save the cactus and the scrub, an occasional rattlesnake or scorpion hiding in what little shade was available in the inhospitable terrain. A range of purple mountains shrouded in heat waves stretched across the backdrop and flat-topped buttes jutted out of the desert floor. Kyle Steele stood next to a barrel cactus in jeans and a loose white t-shirt looking bronzed, nearly sunburned. His t-shirt flapping in the breeze, he scoured the horizon with binoculars, "Lynette... *Lynette!*"

Lisa sat bolt upright, drenched in sweat, her heart pounding. Disoriented and confused, she had to examine her surroundings to determine where she was. It didn't make much sense at first, still feeling the heat of the desert and the hellish wind. In contrast, the climatized air in her quarters felt cool on her damp pajamas.

"Miss Lisa, I detect elevated body temperature and an accelerated heart rate. Are you feeling satisfactory?"

"Not now, TESS," mumbled Lisa throwing off the sheets and running toward the door of her quarters, Gus on her heels.

■ ■ ■

Foggy, half asleep. Jack Steele reached for his robe, "Hold on, hold on..." He shuffled barefoot through his quarters to the incessant pinging of the door chime. Fritz lay on the sofa in the salon, his ears up, eyes open, unmoved.

"OK, OK," said Steele, "enter already..."

The door swished open, disappearing into the bulkhead, his sister stumbling through the door, Gus trotting over to where Fritz lay, sitting quietly next to him. "Something's wrong. Something's wrong..." she chattered.

Sleepily, he waved her in. "Sure, c'mon in. I wasn't sleeping or anything..."

"I had a dream, a *bad dream...*"

"And you just couldn't wait till morning to tell me about it," he said yawning. He opened a small fridge inset into the interior wall, "Juice?"

"Yeah, whatever," she waved, obviously distressed, pacing.

"Look, I get it, you had a bad dream," he said calmly. "It was *just a dream...*"

"No, it was one of *those,*" she countered.

Jack paused mid hand-off, a bottle of juice half-extended towards Lisa. He knew what that meant. She had a *vision.* Much more than a dream, more vivid, more real, almost tangible. His mother had them too.

"About Mom and dad," she continued. "There's something wrong. *Really wrong.*" Lisa took the bottle, her hands a little shaky. "There's something else, I can't put my finger on it. There's other people too..." her voice trailed off as she stared off into the darkness.

"What other people? Who?"

She shook her head as she opened the juice, "I don't know I couldn't see faces."

"Could you tell what's wrong?"Jack dropped wearily onto the sofa next to Fritz.

"It's very abstract, I'm not sure I can understand it all, but I could *feel* it..."

Jack took a swig of juice from his bottle. "Could you be misreading it?"

Lisa stopped pacing for a moment, reflecting, reviewing it in her head like a video playback. "No... they're very alone, it's desolate, unbearably hot, hostile..." she was staring off into the darkness again. And despite the heat in her vision she shivered. "How soon before we get home, Jack?"

Jack the man, her brother, wanted to tell her they would break for home *now,* make a beeline for the Terran system. But Jack the Admiral; knew that was an impossibility. There were pros and cons to being an Admiral, this was definitely in the *con* column. "We're headed that way, but we have a lot to do and a lot of distance to cover..."

"How long?"

"Lisa, we have a job. A big job. Look at the mess we have in this system and how it's slowed us down..."

"How long?"

Jack sighed, "About two-and-a-half months. Maybe more."

"Fine," she waved. "The Revenge is fast. I'll take the Revenge and meet you there."

Jack almost snorted juice through his nose. "You'll do what now?" he sputtered.

"Sure that would work," she started, "you could get task force business done and we could go home..."

"On what planet," interrupted Jack, waving his hand "skip that, in what *universe* did you become a command officer capable of commanding a ship? And where was I when it happened?"

"Don't be an asshole," she snapped.

"Then stop being irrational," he replied calmly. "You're letting your emotions run away with you. Get a grip."

"Give me a shuttle."

Jack couldn't help but laugh out loud at the absurdity of the idea. "That's like asking for an inner tube and a paddle to circumnavigate the globe. It's ridiculous."

"We've got to do *something.*"

"We *are* doing something, Lisa. But everything has its limits. In our fastest ship, in a direct route, we're six to eight weeks away." He stood up and stopped her pacing, his hands on her shoulders, "You know as well as I do..." he felt how damp she was and touched her back. "You're *soaked.* And you're shivering. Go take a hot shower," he pointed at the bathroom. "I'll find you some fresh PJs."

"What were you going to say?" she asked padding through Jack's quarters.

"That those *things* you and mom have are not always present-tense. They're possibilities... what *might* be."

"I wish I could say that makes me feel better," she shouted over the shower's rush of water. The warmth felt good, allowing her tense shivers to melt away as her body relaxed, unclenched. She spent a few minutes just letting the water pound on her muscles.

Stepping out of the shower, pulling a towel off the rack, she wrapping herself up. "Were you able to find something for me to wear? Or do I have to go back to my quarters in a towel?" She patted herself down and threw her wet hair over her shoulder after tucking the oversize towel into a beach wrap. "Jack?" She walked out of the bathroom, through the sleeping area into the salon. "Where'd you go...?"

The old man in the hooded cloak sat on the sofa, legs crossed at the knee, next to Fritz. Gus sat at his feet. "I believe he went to get you some fresh sleepwear my dear," the old man said softly.

Lisa yelped, stumbling backwards, clutching at her towel, meeting the wall behind her. His presence startled her; she had not seen him in the dimly lit room. "Who are you?!" she demanded angrily, her eyes adjusting to the light.

"Friend," said Fritz.

"Yeah... well..." she stammered, searching for words. "A warning would have been nice. Dammit." Strangely, she didn't feel threatened. She wasn't sure what she felt, other than surprised. She tried to slow her heart. "Who are you and what are you doing here?" she said in her sternest voice, forcing calm.

"Aww," he said in mock disappointment, "you don't remember me..." He pulled his hood back, revealing his lined and weathered face.

Lisa's eyes grew wide and her hand shot over her mouth as she inhaled sharply, pointing at him with her free hand. *"You're the man in the forest!* On Veloria," she whispered. "I thought I made you up..."

"No, I'm quite real." he smiled. He sipped from a snifter of brandy she hadn't noticed a moment before.

"But..." there were so many questions running through her head.

He offered his snifter to her. "Here, take a sip."

"I, I Don't drink."

"Just a sip. It's some of the best brandy in the universe. Diterian Brandy. It will calm your nerves. You *will* like it. I promise."

Oddly she trusted him completely. Lisa took the glass offered her and sipped. More than once before handing it back, the rich flavor and substantial body of the thick brandy warming her. "Mmm, that *is* good. Thank you." She felt a calm radiate through her and wondered if it was the brandy or what he had said, some type of hypnotic suggestion. She knelt on the floor, sitting on her feet, Gus moving to her side.

"No my dear, not hypnosis, just really magical brandy." He smiled and her heart warmed.

"You read minds," she observed. "Interesting. I was wondering where you went. On Veloria I mean. I wanted to thank you..."

"I know," he replied, "I heard you."

"Why did you leave me?" she asked. "I was *totally lost.* I had no idea what to do or where to go..."

"You were never alone," he waved. "There are certain things we have to accomplish on our own in order to grow. And you grew a lot that night. I am very proud of you; you are strong like your brother..."

"You know Jack?"

The old man smiled and nodded, "Jack and I are well acquainted." He put his feet flat on the floor and leaned forward, his elbows on his knees. "Which brings me to our topic for tonight. Jack has a difficult job with a tremendous amount of responsibility and pressure on his shoulders." The old man paused to sip the brandy, letting it slide down his throat. "You are his teammate. He needs you, and he needs you to be levelheaded so he can count on you. You cannot let him down. You are one of the very few people in the universe he trusts completely. He respects your opinion, but you need to work *with* him, not against him. Understand?"

"Sure," she replied. "But I'm worried about our parents. Can you tell me..."

"I cannot," he interrupted politely, holding up an open hand. "Anything I tell you could affect any number of decisions you make along the way. The repercussions could cross entire star systems. I assume you understand the *Butterfly Effect?*"

"Yes."

"It is exactly for that reason. It could easily change the course of history and the lives of millions of beings for decades, centuries even. It must be what it must be."

"There are certain things we have to do on our own..." she muttered.

"Exactly right," he confirmed, rising from his seat. "Well, I've taken up enough of your time." He bent down and kissed her on top of her head.

"Wait, what's your name?"

"Voorlak," he replied, pulling the hood back over his head. "Jack likes to call me *Old Man,* when he thinks he's being irreverent."

"Does that bother you?"

"No. It *does* accurately describe me, after all." His form seemed to shift, changing transparency, perhaps changing planes of reality as he passed through the outer wall of the hull, disappearing completely.

"Whoa," she breathed, "that's wicked cool."

The door swished open, Jack carrying fresh pajamas. "Here you go kiddo," he muttered, tossing them to her as he passed, heading back to bed.

"Jack?"

"Yeah?"

"I'm gonna sleep here, OK?"

"D'you snore?" he asked, flopping onto the bed.

"No."

"Fine. Sleep wherever you want."

"Thanks, Jack."

"Mm-hmm."

■ ■ ■

The Conquest's senior staff was huddled around the holo-chart in the Admiral's office, the commanders of the Westwind and Revenge on vid-com, sitting in on the conference from the Captain's ready room of their own ships. A close-up of the Gedhepp System floated over the table, the task force holding station on the far edge of the asteroid field facing the gate to Rikovik's Reef.

It had been a long process, the ships slowly forging ahead through the asteroid field, either nudging aside the smaller chunks with their shields like an ice breaker ship through frozen water, or decimating larger asteroids with ship's guns. A full size version of the asteroid video game Jack remembered playing at the arcade as a kid. Thinking back on that made the corners of his mouth curl a little, almost imperceptibly.

"Between the information fed to us from the patrol and shuttle pilots," began Captain Ryan, "and the information astrometrics and cartography discovered, we have determined that this field of what we've been calling asteroids is actually the remains of a planet in this system. Whether it broke apart on its own or it was impacted by something catastrophic, we don't know. If cartography is right, it is the remains of a planet in the fifth orbit from the sun."

"And we're passing through what would be the fourth, aren't we?" asked Jack.

"Correct. Astrometrics estimates the rock field extends from the fourth orbit to the sixth."

"My God, It's going to affect two other planets..."

"Correct. Fortunately they are uninhabited. It is apparent that their orbits have not carried them through so far. And the field is orbiting as well, but far slower than the orbit of the planet it used to be."

"It's going to be a real mess when they do," said Jack. "Things will be pinballing all over the system."

"Pinballing?"

"Bouncing," clarified Jack. "This stuff is going to scatter all over the place. The UFW may have to close or restrict access to the system. How soon before the closest planet makes contact?"

"About seventy days for the planet in the fourth orbit, about three hundred days for the sixth planet. The fourth planet is rather small, it may not survive its full orbit. The sixth planet will sustain damage but nothing to cause its destruction."

"Is there anything sizable left of the fifth planet?"

"About one-half," volunteered Pappy. "We found that the closer we got to the fifth orbit, the less-dense the field was. The pieces were bigger and easier to navigate. Also, less smoke and ash. The Zulu was able to get closer to take some scans. To me, it looked fairly hollow, sort of honeycombed."

"Could it have been mined out?"

"It's possible," offered the Westwind's Captain. Once they're that fragile, an impact of some kind or instability in her tectonic plates or core and it tears itself apart. If they drilled too deep it may have released some volcanic event... we'll probably never know. Because if it was a mining company, they will *never* admit to this."

Jack folded his arms across his chest. "If this was a mining project, this is huge... hundreds of thousands of people had to be involved. It must have taken decades..."

"Not necessarily, Admiral," countered the Westwind's Captain. "Standard mining, yes. But strip mining can be done on a planetary scale in five or six years by laser dredge ships. As you can see, they don't leave much..."

"You've seen this before, Captain?"

The Captain nodded, "Yes, unfortunately. I was a cruiser commander at the time. We were tasked with clearing the mess out of the system because it threatened an inhabited planet. Our group was there nearly three months blasting what was left into dust. I don't think the inhabited planet was ever the same after that. I remember reading some time later that it had severely affected their seasonal climate because the cosmic dust floated between the planet and their sun."

"Did you ever find out who the mining outfit was?"

"Not to my knowledge, Admiral. Although I remember VirTech Mining being a suspect."

"There's that name again," said Steele, stone faced. "Somebody who knows what goes on in operations like this has to have a conscience. We just need to find that somebody."

"Needle in a haystack," volunteered Brian from the Captain's office on the Revenge.

"A *really big* haystack," offered Paul Smiley.

"Dissension in the ranks," breathed Jack, staring blankly at the holo-chart. "And they won't be alone, there will be others. Scuttlebutt spreads like wildfire; we just need to get it to come to us..."

"I know that look," said Brian. "Whatcha thinking, Ja, er, Admiral?" Brian caught himself, his mind stumbling across Jack, then Skipper, finally spitting out the right title.

"I have an idea..."

Paul looked at Steele across the chart table, only seeing half of him through the holo-chart floating between them. "Do I even dare ask..?"

■ ■ ■

"So let me get this straight," said Lisa, as she and Jack walked down the corridor from the meeting. "The Revenge is now the Raven?"

"Right..."

"And you're not you. You're Jax Mercury?"

"You got it."

"Who the hell am I, then?"

"You're you." he replied.

"What if I don't want to be me?"

Jack stopped mid stride, pausing in the corridor. "Why would you want to be somebody else? I have to because they may know my name; it's connected with the Freedom..."

"And whose *last name* do I have?" she queried.

"Oh. Yeah." *Doh!*

"Yeaaah..." she teased. "And *you're* the Admiral."

Jack rested his hands on his hips. "Ok, so who do you want to be?"

"Princess Sunshine," she joked.

He rolled his eyes and kept walking. "Over my dead body. It needs to be similar," he explained, "something easy to remember." He snapped his fingers, "How about Lisa Stone?"

"Ooh, like Sharon Stone... OK, I like that."

■ ■ ■

Steele belted the holster around his waist, strapping it to his thigh, dropping in the .45 caliber, 1911 semi-auto, charged particle blaster. He tested the release and reholster to be sure it was smooth and secure. It felt good to be in civilian clothes again, something akin to what he used to wear on the Freedom. Dark gray form-fitted pants tucked into high boots, a dark blue, high collar shirt and a leather flight type jacket. All-in-all, comfortable *and* stylish. The ship's tailor had done an extremely nice job of making him look like an entrepreneurial ship's owner... with a slant towards bad boy.

He hefted the duffel off the floor and took one last look around his quarters, "C'mon, dog, time to go." Fritz jumped up with a snort and a quick wag, beating him to the door.

■ ■ ■

Lisa was already at the shuttle, having an animated chat with Dar Sloane, her duffel stowed in the cargo compartment. She was dressed in tall flight boots and a leather and fabric body suit, a 1911 particle blaster like Jack's belted around her waist, strapped to her thigh, having traded her trusty Glock for something with a little more punch.

"Well look at you, *Ms. Stone,*" commented Jack, strolling up. "Slick outfit."

"Looking good, Mr. Mercury," she retorted. "Nice touch," she indicated his unshaven stubble. "My friend, Mr. Sloane here," she patted Dar Sloan's shoulder, "has promised to look after Gus for me while we're gone."

"Good deal." replied Jack, somewhat distracted. He pointed at the open gull-wing doors on the four-person shuttle from the Revenge, Ensign Tusker seated at the controls in the pilot's seat. "Go ahead Fritz." The German Shepherd jumped up over the door threshold into the seat next to Tusker. When Jack turned back, Lisa and Dar were lip-locked like two horny teenagers tongue-wrestling under the high school bleachers. *"Aww, crap, I didn't want to see that,* groaned Steele. "Eww..." He grabbed his sister by the collar and pulled her away, dragging them apart. "Time to go, Barbie," he said sarcastically. "Tell Ken you'll see him again at the sock-hop."

Buckled in, gull wing doors closed and secure, Lisa waved and Dar looked on sheepishly, smiling back. Jack glared at him through the canopy perspex. He didn't dislike or even hold it against the pilot, he knew the two had been spending a lot of time together... it was just seeing it. It was, well, *ugh.* He shuddered. *OK, shake it off.*

100

The shuttle lifted off the deck, rotating smoothly, heading out through the blue stasis field, passing over the Conquest's fantail. Lisa was still looking over her shoulder back at the flight deck.

"Stop it," hissed Jack. "Stop acting like a lovesick puppy..."

"But I really like him..."

"I think I got that," he replied, sarcasm dripping from his voice. "I think everyone on the flight deck got that..."

She shrugged innocently, "Don't care." She turned to him suddenly, "Ooh, I almost forgot! Did I tell you..?"

"What?"

"I don't care," she repeated smugly.

■ ■ ■

The landing bay of the Revenge was almost claustrophobic compared to the Conquest's, a mere closet, tightly packed, everything in its place. Tusker was busy securing the shuttle to the deck. Three shuttles shared space with cargo, parts and repair stalls.

Marine Sergeant Draza Mac dragged the duffel bags out of the shuttle's small cargo compartment. "Welcome aboard *the Raven,* Mr. Mercury, Ms. Stone..."

"Thank you, Mr. Mac. Are all of our temporary transfers aboard?"

"Aye, sir. All mission pertinent equipment and personnel aboard. The Skipper asked that we direct you straight to the bridge. I assume you remember the way?"

"Of course."

Draza Mac hefted the bags. "Good. I'll make sure your things get to your quarters." He paused, cocking his head, hearing the change in the tone of the ship's engines. "Sounds like the Skipper's got us under way. Once we clear this crap, it's less than an hour to the gate."

■ ■ ■

The bridge crew of the Conquest was watching the Revenge, *now the Raven,* pull out of formation, heading toward the gate to Rikovik's Reef. She was moving cautiously, out of the planetary debris, leaving the Conquest and Westwind behind, hidden in the clutter and metallic dust. Even in the zero

101

gravity, it clung to her hull, her movement leaving a trail of dust and ash like a wake behind her.

Captain Ryan stood up at his station and stretched, massaging his back with his hands as he watched the big screen. "Communications, I want double coverage on your station. I want full time monitoring on the Raven's emergency channel."

"Aye, sir."

"I want everybody fresh. Four hour shifts, no more. We're staying on yellow alert..." He looked over at his first officer. "You have the bridge, mister. I'll see you in four hours."

"Aye sir."

"I'll order up some food and drinks," said Ryan turning towards his ready room. "Good luck Mr. Mercury," he breathed without looking back.

CHAPTER EIGHT

RIKOVIK'S REEF: *DEN OF THEIVES*

"Rikovik's Reef in thirty minutes, Skipper."

"Understood." Commander Brian Carter reclined in his chair, feet on his desk in the Captain's ready room, "Your quarters OK, Jack?"

Jack extended his legs on the couch, leaning against the armrest, Fritz already sound asleep on the floor next to him. "Sure, they're fine."

"You didn't expect me to give up mine, did you?" Brian smirked crookedly.

"Nah," waved Jack, "it's your ship, man. I'm just a guest." He glanced over at the holo-chart hovering above the table. "So they had a set of beacons out of the Rikovik gate routing traffic around the danger in the system to a *third gate?"*

"Yep. We counted eight markers but I'm sure there were more beyond our sensor reach."

"Pretty smart idea."

"It is," gestured Brian. "But it shows planning and preparation. Whoever set them up knew what was going on here."

"Agreed." There was a silence and Steele found himself staring at the shimmering hologram.

Brian spoke first. "So, Mercury huh? *Quicksilver,"* he whispered dramatically. *"A highly toxic, amorphous liquid metal... some freaky symbolism there, Jack. Did you do that on purpose?"

Steele shrugged. "It's also in Greek mythology. Mercury was the Roman god of financial gain, commerce and communication. He also guided travelers, and more interestingly," he rubbed his hands together in an evil gesture, "escorted souls to the underworld."

Brian glanced, checking the time on his eGo-h. "Wasn't he the one with wings on his feet?"

Jack nodded, "That's the one. He needed them, he was a very *busy* god."

"Man, that's kinda deep," said Brian, cocking his head to one side. "But why did you have to call us the Raven? I've never really liked those birds, they always gave me the creeps."

Jack took a couple swallows of water. "Well, the common consensus associates them with death. But American Indian mythology paints them as a harbinger of magic, being able to travel between light and dark, life and death. Able to exist in either plane. The Raven's also supposed to be able to bring communications back and forth from the living to the dead, from the divine to the earthly."

Brian shook his head, "So traveling between light and dark, we really *are* the Raven then." He shivered outwardly, "You just gave me the chills."

"Suck it up buttercup, we need to look like serious badasses, here."

■ ▒ ■

"One minute to gate exit, Commander."

"On my way," confirmed Brian. "Looks like it's showtime, Jack."

Jack swung his feet off the sofa and took a second to adjust, taking a deep breath. He touched the surface of his eGo-h, "TESS, please find Lisa Stone and call her to the bridge."

"Certainly, Mr. Mercury," she replied in a sultry voice.

"And thank you for remembering to use my new name..." he ran his fingers through his hair.

"Of course," TESS replied, sweetly. "You only need to tell *me* once, I am not *capable* of forgetting."

Brian pulled the water bottle away from his mouth in a bid to prevent water coming out of his nose. He was unsuccessful. "Oh snap," he sputtered, wiping his face and pinching his nose. "Dammit, that hurt," he winced. "Did she just burn you?"

"It appears so."

"She's got *attitude!* How did that happen? Mine doesn't do that."

Jack rose from his seat, Fritz rising with him, stretching like a cat. "I don't know," muttered Jack, "just lucky I guess."

■ ▒ ■

Steele stood between Brian Carter in the Commander's seat and Raulya in the First Officer's seat, the entire crew dressed in civilian clothes of their own taste and choosing.

104

Fritz sitting by his side, Jack pointed Lisa to the second chair at tactical. "Do whatever Raulya tells you to do..." She moved without question, activating the screens at the station and tilting them to her liking.

Ahead of them, the splash of abstract color swirled in the center of the gate, undulating like liquid with a life of its own. "Entering gate corona," announced Ragnaar.

"All battle stations manned?" asked Jack.

"Aye, all manned, cells charged, systems dark."

Tendrils of color reached out and enveloped the ship as its bow neared the center, pushing though its surface. Punching through the other side, the colors spilled off the ship's hull like a whale breaching the ocean's surface, rivulets and droplets of light and color reaching outward like spray, only to fall back to the surface of the gate as if affected by gravity, recollected to an energy well.

"Five ships, Commander. *They have us locked and tracking! Weapons are live!*"

"Shields up, guns live..!"

"BELAY that order!" shouted Steele. "Stay the course, no deviations..."

Brian looked over his shoulder, "What are you doing, Jack?"

"You gotta walk in..."

"Like you own the joint," nodded Brian, finishing Steele's sentence.

"These are probably the security guards checking IDs at the door," explained Jack. He keyed his mic, "All hands, this is the bridge. I know we're all a little nervous, everybody just stay calm. Keep your eyes open and your systems dark."

"Incoming comm. I believe it's coming from the destroyer."

"On screen." Steele stood with his feet apart and his arms folded, his jacket's fresh leather squeaking. "This is all yours Bri."

"Gee thanks."

A single video square winked into existence on the big screen, a thin man with greyish skin and blue-black hair. "Who are you and what is your purpose here?"

"Who's asking? said Brian, rising from his seat and stepping past Jack. "I like to know who I'm talking to."

"Captain of the FreeRanger DD224. Now answer my question."

"Commander Brian Carter, skipper of the Raven. We're here to pick up a load of parts and equipment."

"Gunships closing in on either side, Jax," whispered Lisa.

Jack nodded once, almost imperceptibly to indicate he'd heard her.

"We don't have any record of you or your ship in this sector before..."

Brian folded his arms defensively, mirroring Jack standing behind him. "There's always a first time, isn't there... Do you greet all your first time visitors this way?" There was a hint of aggression in his voice mixed with aggravation.

"Who did you say you were seeing?" asked the FreeRanger Captain, stoically, unmoved.

"I didn't," countered Brian. "I didn't realize coming to this system for trade was restricted, I thought it was a free travel and free trade sector. Maybe we should take our business and money elsewhere."

The FreeRanger Captain's mouth curled at the corners, a hint of evil. "We just like to know who we're doing business with..." An inquiry and side conversation momentarily took the Captain's attention away from the screen. When he turned back he leaned forward, eyeing Jack. "And who are you?" he pointed.

"Jax Mercury," replied Jack. "I own this ship."

"Why aren't you sitting in an office somewhere, *mister owner?*"

"I like to keep an eye on my investments..."

"You don't trust your captain and your crew?"

Jack unfolded his arms, clasping his hands casually behind him. "I trust them just fine. It's the people we deal with I have to watch."

The destroyer's Captain roared with laughter, his head tilting back, revealing uneven, jagged teeth. "Who in hellion have you been trading with? Entertainment traffickers and Glacier dealers?"

"Oh, it's not the people we do business *with,* so much as it's the people we *meet along the way...* But I digress, I really couldn't discuss our business," said Steele as politely as possible. "If it got back to our clients or our vendors it might be bad for business. I'm sure you understand."

If the destroyer Captain noticed the intentional dig, he had no reaction. Turning away from the screen again, his side conversation lasting only a few seconds. He turned back, emotionless. "Enjoy your stay in Rikovik's Reef. Keep your nose clean." The comm's video square winked out.

Steele looked around the bridge, "OK, what the hell was that?"

"They were just about up our ass," commented Lisa.

"We were recording a low-yield scan," offered Raulya. "I believe the gunships were doing a cargo scan. They pulled away about the same time he signed off."

"What were they looking for?" asked Brian, returning to his command chair.

"Anything smuggled," explained Ragnaar, "that they could confiscate, or tax you on to let you pass."

"Hmm. A little grifting," grumbled Jack.

"Bribery is a survival staple of the pirate world," commented Ragnaar. "I'm sure the fact that the *owner* is on the ship, made them believe that it is a small operation not worth the effort. A larger outfit may have been worth more of a take."

Steele nodded, "Good point." He took a deep breath. "Stand down the crews. What's our time to Rikovik's planetoid?"

"We should make port in about two hours. Unless you want to jump."

"No, let's not give anything away, two hours is fine."

■ ■ ■

From space, Rikovik's Reef looked like a brown blob with spikes, dotted by lights and dirty neon... Upon closer inspection, it was much worse; a grimy brown asteroid, covered in cobbled black structures layered in red rust, covered in dilapidated lights and colored neon, probably scrounged from sign junkyards all over the star system. It looked like a decrepit ghost town, a place that hopes and dreams went to die. Die a long, agonizing death. "Such a happy and cheerful looking place," quipped Jack sarcastically. "Like the stuff of nightmares." He wasn't sure if the attempt at lighting and color made it look slightly more inviting or just more desperate. He was leaning toward desperate.

For Lisa, just the sight of the place made her stomach roll uncomfortably.

"The tower is requesting berthing preferences, skipper," announced Ragnaar.

"What are the options?" asked Jack.

"Internal or external, sir."

Jack and Brian exchanged glances. "Internal might be easier to load cargo if we're lucky enough to find what we need," said Jack.

Brian nodded. "Makes sense. Internal, Mr. Ragnaar."

After a brief exchange with the tower, a landing guide appeared on the big screen, displaying an approach pattern for the Raven, akin to stripes on a road, showing a traffic lane. Digital statistics and traffic information scrolled next to the approach overlay.

The grubby, desolate appearance of Rikovik's Reef was just that, an appearance. A false impression of her actual condition; which was a bustling urbanized planetoid... with a little frontier flavor. As they neared the cavernous opening the navigation aid was guiding them towards, they could see rows of windows in the rock face, whether they were offices or residences it was unclear. A train passed above them, the monorail following along the outside of the planetoid, disappearing into a tunnel, taking it inside the rock.

The Raven passed through the massive stasis field at the bottom half of the planetoid's waist, dwarfed by the open maw carved through the rock, before entering the interior spaceport of Rikovik's Reef.

"I think you'd be able to fit the Conquest in here," whispered Jack.

"Sure looks like it," agreed Brian. "My God, it goes all the way out through the other side."

"Probably to accommodate the ore freighters when they were mining," explained Ragnaar.

Ships of all types lined either side of the bay, the Raven was required to fit into a mooring space between two others. Alignment targets appeared on the screen as the traffic guide disappeared. At the helm, Quixetta maneuvered the ship gently into place, crabbing it sideways with maneuvering thrusters, maintaining her attitude. The alignment targets flashed green and he released the controls as docking clamps extended out to the Raven's hull. Two resounding *kachunks* reverberated throughout the hull, the floor moving slightly. "Clamps secure, we're in."

■ ■ ■

Jack, Lisa, Draza Mac, Brian, Ragnaar and Raulya stood at the open hatch to the gangway double-checking last minute details. "Everyone stays armed," ordered Jack. "And a full security detail here and on the ramp if we open for cargo."

Brian nodded. "I got it. Don't worry, I'm not taking any chances. We'll keep the warmers managing the core temps. Just in case."

Walking down the gangway to the dock, Jack, Lisa and Draza Mac set their TESS' to mark the location of the ship. Standing on the dock getting their bearings, the expanse of the interior spaceport only became more evident, ships moving through the interior past the Raven, past ships berthed on the opposite wall.

Offices above them carved into the rock of the planetoid, sealed with glass walls, stretched the length of the spaceport. Gantries reached across to the other side, moving cargo with cranes, material haulers moving back and forth along the docks.

"I feel so small," muttered Lisa.

"Welcome to Rikovik's Reef," greeted the man passing between them and the terminal doors. "Can I help you?"

"We're looking for parts..." offered Jack. The man was dark complected, the kind of color a man gets from years in the sun, his face lined and leathery.

The man scrunched his face in disbelief as he looked the Raven over, "She looks OK to me..."

"We're looking for parts for a client," explained Jack, "not for her," he motioned in the direction of the ship.

"There are several dealers here..."

"Who's the biggest?" asked Lisa.

"That would be *Deep Black*, young lady." The man looked her over, considering her curves in the leather and fabric bodysuit. "Not the best side of the city though..." He pointed at the 1911 charged particle blaster hanging on her hip, "You know how to use that thing?"

"We'll be fine," said Jack, cutting in. "How do we find this, *Deep Black?"*

The man pointed at the terminal doors, "Through these doors, up two levels to transport. You have several options; trains, cabbies, and slot trams. Unless you know the city well, I wouldn't recommend the trams. You need to go to the Peninsula Sector... if you go too far you end up on the Island. Stay out of the Island."

"What's the Island?" asked Lisa.

"Never you mind," he shot back. "You stay out of that area! The Island is not a place for a girl like you."

"What's *that* supposed to mean?" said Lisa defensively.

"People like you *disappear* on the Island," growled the man, walking away. Worn and faded, the word *Lawman* reached across the back of his jacket, a large, equally faded, number 42 in a circle underneath it.

■ ■ ■

It was almost immediate upon leaving the terminal and stepping out onto the transport level. Lisa made a face, swallowing hard, tasting the metal in

109

her mouth and at the back of her throat. "What the hell is that? It's disgusting."

"Scrubbed air," said Jack and Draza Mac almost simultaneously.

"Either ancient equipment or the filters need a serious flush," explained Draza Mac. "Some areas may be better than others, depends on the age and upkeep."

Jack motioned to one of the vehicles at the curb, the driver waving an acknowledgment. "Our ship's systems are far superior," commented Jack.

"It's also why ships have gardens," added Draza Mac, "they remove that taste."

The side of the cab slid open wide, cutting off any further conversation on the topic. The driver motioning them in. "No bags?"

"No bags," confirmed Jack, climbing in. "We need to go to Deep Black in the Peninsula."

"I can take you most of the way," said the driver, steering away from the terminal. The vehicle accelerated silently, floating on an anti-gravity cushion, heading for one of a series of tunnels in the far wall.

"What do you mean, most of the way?" asked Jack leaning forward.

"I do not go into the Peninsula that far. You can take a tram or walk the rest of the way, it won't be too far."

"Well if it won't be too far, why won't you take us all the way?" asked Lisa.

"It is not a safe area..."

"And you want us *to walk?*" she growled.

"I thought it was the *Island* that was the dangerous area," said Jack, cutting in.

"Oooh, yes. The Island is bad. *Very bad.* But the far end of the Peninsula is not much better." The driver swung the vehicle into another tunnel, weaving through slower traffic, rock walls passing by in a blur.

"What makes those areas so bad?" Jack was trying to pinpoint the type of dangers involved in traversing those areas.

"The criminals," shrugged the driver, oblivious to the benign banality of his reply.

"Specifically," said Steele through clenched teeth, trying to keep the snarl out of his voice.

"Oh I really can't say..."

"Can't say or *won't say?*" hissed Steele, his ire rising. From the back seat he wasn't able to see enough of the man's face to get a reading of deceit or avoidance.

"I've probably said too much already..." whispered the driver, barely audible.

Steele sat back in the seat, contemplating who might be listening in on the conversation. And when he saw Lisa lean forward he tapped her on the knee and shook his head no, sweeping his eyes around the inside of the vehicle. She nodded curtly and sat back in silence.

Some areas of the inside of the planetoid were well lit, looking upscale and well traveled, others looked like residential areas and yet others like manufacturing and commercial areas. All-in-all, it seemed to represent a well-rounded society. They passed a well-lit and colorfully decorated bazaar, with open stores and booths on either side of the street. Crowds of people were milling about, venturing into the shops and strolling through the eateries. It was a quick glimpse but Steele's artificial eye recorded the image of two men standing on a corner talking, the word *Lawman spanning* the back of their jackets. One had a number 23 in the circle below it, the other had a number 54. The fact that they had the exact same build and height struck him as slightly odd. He was still reviewing that image a short time later when the vehicle pulled to the curb in a darker, less friendly looking area.

"This is as far as I can go," the driver said cheerfully. "If you'll scan your ITC card," *Interstellar Trade Credits,* "with the reader on the back of my seat, we'll be all set."

"We couldn't pay you extra to take us all the way, could we?" asked Jack, holding his card up to the reader.

"No sir. Sorry." The driver looked back over his shoulder, a concerned look on his face, his brow furrowed. "Would you like a receipt sir?" He nodded slightly.

Jack caught the inference. "Yes, please."

"Digital or written?" The driver held up a stylus to indicate what Jack should choose.

■ ■ ■

Standing on the curb as the transport pulled away, Steele examined the clear rectangle of plastic film, then checked their surroundings quickly.

"TESS, scan this please," he laid the film over her screen. Lisa and Draza Mac watched the gloomy shadows uneasily. Scanning it from underneath, TESS bought up the scan on her holographic screen with a translation off to the side. *The girl is not safe. Keep her close. Never alone.*

"That's all of it, TESS?"

"That's all of it, Mr. Mercury," TESS replied, her face appearing. "Please be careful."

"Did you understand his directions?"

"Yes, Jax." She bought up a map of the area. "I have managed to tap into the Citymap System, he was being truthful in his directions."

"OK, let's go. Screen off TESS, but ears open. Use my earpiece for communication."

"Understood. External sensors active, earpiece linked. Connecting to my TESS counterparts."

■ ■ ■

It was odd walking through what in many places looked like a normal city in most respects, if it wasn't for the fact that it was all *inside* the planetoid. It equated in Steele's mind to an underground city. It might as well be. No sky, few open places, traveling through tunnels cut through its core. Stores, residences and businesses nothing more than rooms carved into the rock. It was a little claustrophobic. And dark.

It seemed the further they went, the darker it got, many of the lights broken or missing completely, with little if any traffic and fewer and fewer people. The fewer people they saw, the more Jack felt like they were being watched. "Just because you're paranoid..."

"Doesn't mean you're not being followed." whispered Lisa, finishing his sentence.

The area changed from a run-down retail area with decrepit stores, litter and vacant store fronts to commercial structures. Actual building fronts. And they hadn't seen a soul in at least five minutes. It felt like they were the only three people in the area. But Jack knew better than that, his senses reaching out, the little voice in the back of his mind screaming; *Danger! Danger!* at the top of its proverbial lungs.

"Wish I had my twilight vision with me," whispered Draza Mac.

"And a carbine... "

"Some armor..."

112

"A few grenades..."

Steele's earpiece chirped at the same time Lisa's and Draza Mac's did, each getting separate instructions from their TESS', the units working in unison. "I'm detecting two heartbeats ahead on the right, Jax. Sixty-feet."

Walking to the left of her brother, Lisa fell back a step to address a shadow detected on the left side of the street. Draza Mac spun around to watch the rear, walking backwards.

Steele slowed his pace, the little voice in his head still screaming. His hand resting on the grip of his hybrid 1911, he popped the holster's release. When the two men stepped out of a recessed business entrance just fifteen feet ahead, his firearm had already cleared the holster and he had dropped to a combat crouch. *"Stop!"* he commanded.

"Easy buddy. We don't want any trouble. Just give us the girl and we'll be on our way. No need for anyone to get hurt..."

"Step aside!" commanded Steele.

"Buddy, you are in the wrong neighborhood to be making demands like that... look around you. Just give us the girl and you can be on your way..."

Steele knew it was a distraction bid, so his eyes never left the two men standing nearly shoulder to shoulder, blocking the way. Weak details from distant lights highlighted their silhouettes. His sight picture was *Mr. Talker's* head. *"Step aside..."* Steele growled through clenched teeth, snapping off the safety. *"I won't say it again..."*

When the headlights of the vehicle parked in the blackness between the buildings across the street, suddenly bathed the trio from the Raven in harsh light, Draza Mac screamed, *"Ambush!"*

Time slowed down for Steele, as *Mr. Talker* lunged. He squeezed off the first shot, *Mr. Talker's* head disappearing from his shoulders in a crimson explosion, splashing the second man in gore. The vehicle charged out of its hiding spot to drive through and separate the group, triggering a hell storm of fire from Lisa. Shooting on the move, Steele cut the second man down with two fast shots to the body as he advanced. Massive gaping holes completely through his body that sucked his liquified organs out his back. He was dead before he hit the ground. The trio advanced over the prostrate and lifeless forms, Steele sweeping the street ahead, scanning for targets.

His free hand on Lisa's belt, Draza Mac trotted backwards, firing at the moving shadows advancing swiftly from behind, while Lisa's rounds blew through the windshield of the vehicle as she danced sideways to keep up with her brother's strides.

With golf ball sized holes in the windshield and hood area, the vehicle careened across the street and slammed into the building behind them, imbedding itself in the wall, temporarily cutting off the pursuers coming up from the rear. Seeing movement, Draza Mac added a couple holes in the vehicle's driver's door as he backed away, still tethered to Lisa by his grip on her gun belt.

"Truck! TRUCK!" screamed Draza Mac, the rear ramp of the vehicle dropping to the ground, two men jumping out with long guns who swung behind the vehicle for cover, firing as they maneuvered.

Hot magenta streaks of energy sizzled past, splashing on the building and ricocheted across the ground. Jack spun, planted his feet and the three of them pumped a rain of fire upon the truck and its occupants, the charged particle slugs punching holes through the vehicle like paper. A deafening, eyeball-searing fireball lifted the vehicle off the street, parts skittering across the ground, off buildings and the stone ceiling, the blast knocking them all flat on their backs. The heat took their breath away as it sucked in all the surrounding oxygen.

Laying on the ground panting, Steele struggled to get up, "We gotta go..." he wheezed.

"Can't breathe," gasped Lisa.

"Get up, get up..." Steele dragged himself to his feet, gun still in hand, pulling his sister up with his free hand. "Draza..?"

"I'm coming, boss..." The Marine forced himself onto his feet and immediately swung his pistol into action, scanning their surroundings. "Reload!" he called, seeing a respite long enough to do a tactical mag change. He captured the partial mag as he swiftly tapped the fresh one in place.

Sirens wailed somewhere, echoing through the tunnels and hollows of the planetoid. An automatic fire system somewhere on the ceiling started spraying fire-fighting foam on the burning wreckage.

Steele's headset chirped, "Lawmen are coming, Jax."

"I know TESS. How far to Deep Black..."

"Very close, at the end of this street. Six-hundred feet."

"Let's move..." Steele completed his own reload on the move, followed by Lisa whose slide was locked back on an empty chamber. Hustling into a stiff breeze generated by the air supply system trying to supply oxygen to the starved area, breathing became easier. Twice they had to conceal themselves in the shadows as emergency vehicles flashed past on the street. "Where were they a few minutes ago?" whispered Draza Mac.

"There's never a cop around when you need one," replied Jack sarcastically.

"A *cop?"*

"Slang for a policeman."

"Uh-huh," nodded the Marine. "You can explain that one to me later."

■ ■ ■

When the door to *Deep Black Supply* split down the middle, opening into the wall on either side, Jack wasn't sure what to expect. But this wasn't it. He stepped back a moment to look up at the sign, confirming they were in the right place. One half of the sign was lit, the other half flickered and hummed. The office looked like a warehouse had regurgitated; boxes, cartons, crates and equipment stacked everywhere, disorganized abstract columns reaching toward the stone ceiling.

The woman behind the counter had her back to the door, rummaging through the clutter on her desk, "Crap on a cracker," she muttered. 'Where in hellion did I put it?" Petite, no more than five feet tall, she had a shock of short platinum-blond hair that from the back made her thin five-foot frame resemble a Q-Tip. She looked up towards the open doors to the warehouse. *"Mouse!"* she shouted, "Did I leave my puff out there?"

"No ma'am!"

Walking into the lobby, if you could call it that, Lisa, Jack and Draza Mac exchanged curious glances before he rotated to watch the door behind them. Lisa folded her arms not wanting to touch anything. "Excuse me..."

"Just a minute," snapped the woman, who had resorted to throwing things on the floor in search of the object of her desire.

Jack spotted a thin stick protruding from her back pocket. "Could it be that thing sticking out of your back pocket?" he offered helpfully.

The woman paused momentarily patting her pants and finding the puff stick, straightening up slowly. "The question is," she said, turning around still irritated. "What were you doing staring at my a..." Her eyes scanned the trio, stopping on Jack. "Oh, *hello,"* she said smoothly, not missing a beat. Her short-cropped platinum-blond hair framed her pixie-like features, accentuated by one eye as blue as ice, the other as green as an emerald. She instantly broke into a coy smile. "Cheriska Skye," she announced, extending her hand. Each person took a turn to shake her hand but her eyes never left Jack. "And you are?"

"Jax Mercury. This is my assistant, Lisa Stone and my Chief Engineer, Draza Mac."

"Are you off that sharp little frigate that just came in?"

"The Raven, yes."

"Want to sell it?"

"Uh, no..."

"I had to ask," she shrugged, "I collect things..."

"I can see that," replied Jack, glancing around.

"Want to fix it?"

Jack shook his head, "No, nothing for the Raven."

"Then what can I do for you?" Cheriska asked, puffing on the stick. A smokeless menthol aroma drifted through the air.

"Hey boss?!"

"Not now, Mouse!" she shouted over her shoulder. "I'm busy..." she said sweetly, turning back.

"But Boss, I can't find that LG-542-Z you wanted!"

Cheriska pursed her lips before turning around, *"At the end of Aisle Five on the right! Eye level!"*

"I looked there!"

"I swear to you," she screamed, *"if I come back there and it's right where I told you, I'm going to kick your ass!"* She turned back. "Sorry, it's so hard to find good help nowadays."

"Found it!" shouted Mouse. Standing at nearly seven-feet, he decided there was a distinct difference between what *she* considered eye level and what *he* considered eye level. He hefted the sizable part over his shoulder and headed off to shipping.

Cheriska rolled her eyes. "Of course you did," she said to her guests. "It's surprising what they can accomplish when there's an ass-beating at stake." Her eyes sparkled. "So, what is it that you need?"

"We have a parts list..."

"Of course you do..." she said glancing over at the security monitor, waving them behind the counter. "I don't suppose you folks had anything to do with that little incident up the street in our fair neighborhood, did you?"

"Well..."

"Come, come," she waved. "Don't be slow; they'll be looking for you in a moment. Can't have them finding you. It will cost me," she urged, as the trio rounded the counter through the maze of boxes and columns.

"Cost you how?" asked Lisa.

"By ending your little shopping spree, of course," added Cheriska, ushering them through the open warehouse doors. Over her shoulder, she checked the security monitor on her desk. *"Too!"* shouted the woman, her voice larger than her size, "Escort these folks to the back of the warehouse!"

"OK!"

Cheriska pointed down a dimly lit aisle, stacked on both sides to the ceiling with crates, "Go that way, she'll meet you. *Stay quiet."* She turned back toward the office.

They walked down the aisle which seemed to reached into infinity. "TESS," whispered Jack, "any map of where we're at?"

His earpiece tweeted, "No sir. Just an open space on the map. This is the single largest room on the entire planetoid. Over twelve-hundred feet long and nine-hundred feet wide. It is interesting to note it also has its own bay doors to the outside."

"Space outside?"

"Yes, that is the *only* outside possible..."

Smart ass artificial intelligence...

When Cheriska silently appeared in front of them at the intersection of a cross aisle, it took the trio by surprise. Steele stopped short, Lisa bumping into him. "How did you do that?"

The woman cocked her head to one side, motioning them to follow. "Do what?" She turned away to lead.

"Get ahead of us..." Steele thumbed over his shoulder, "I thought you went back to the office."

"Cheriska went back to the office."

Steele was having a difficult time processing the third person reference. "Yes, *you* went back to the office..."

"Not me. *Cheriska."*

"But *you're* Cheriska." said Lisa.

"Well yes, but I am Too."

"Jack and Lisa glanced at each other quizzically. "You are too..?" said Jack, shaking his head.

"Yes."

"Too, what?" asked Lisa.

"Cheriska Too," replied the woman, matter of factly, leading on.

"Why am I not getting this?" mumbled Jack, running his fingers through his hair. "You're both named Cheriska?"

"Yes..."

"So she's Cheriska One and you're Cheriska Two?"

"Not two as in *numbers*, Too as in *also,*" she waved. I am Cheriska *also*. We are clones." She shrugged and waved again, "Actually, Cheriska is the original, I am the clone."

"That is *so cool*. So you're identical then..." commented Lisa, "interesting."

"Not identical," replied Too. "Cheriska has one blue eye and one green eye; I have one green eye and one blue eye..." She directed them to a back corner before reaching the end of the aisle. "Go all the way to the end and turn left. There will be a gap between the wall and the racks, squeeze past and go behind them. Stay there till one of us comes for you. And turn off your electronics, they can pick up the frequencies. *Stay quiet.* If they check the warehouse they rarely come back this far... but if they do, it could be bad for all of us."

"Where are you going?" whispered Lisa, suddenly aware of their precarious predicament.

"I need to go back up front."

"Why are they doing this?" whispered Lisa after Cheriska Too had walked out of sight. "Protecting us, I mean."

"For the money," replied Draza Mac, his voice hushed, walking behind Lisa and Jack. "I'm sure they have a rather diverse clientele... This is probably not the first time they've had to hide a client from the authorities."

"The question being," whispered Jack, "what it's going to cost us. I don't imagine this is out of the goodness of their hearts..."

CHAPTER NINE

RIKOVIK'S REEF: *DUALITIES*

"Skipper, there's a couple of Rikovik's Lawmen down here at the ramp. They want to come aboard..."

Sitting in the Raven's galley, halfway through his meal, Commander Brian Carter dropped his fork, activating his mic. "Absolutely not," he interrupted. "No one boards."

"They're being rather insistent..."

"I don't care, it's not negotiable," Brian cut in, rising from the table. "I'm on my way."

"Trouble?" Warrant Officer Dale Alaroot had pushed his plate aside and half rose from his seat.

"Maybe," replied Brian, "you're with me."

The boarding gangway attached to the starboard side of the Raven's hull was not far from the galley. Brian and Dale made it there in short time, two of the ship's Marines looking like scruffy freelance security personnel, were physically barring access to the ship, carbines slung across their bodies. To an average observer their positions were fairly casual. To someone knowledgeable, they were completely ready for a gunfight.

"Skipper's here, step aside boys," called Dale Alaroot.

Brian strode between them, stopping at the open hatch entry, standing squarely in front of the two Lawmen. "What can I do for you?" he asked politely.

"We need to see the Captain of your..."

"You got me," waved Brian, interrupting. "Commander Carter. *What can I do for you?*" he repeated, irritation creeping into his voice. It was then that he realized the two men were the exact same height, weight and build with the same facial features. He made no mention of it, despite his curiosity of their duality.

"We'd like to come aboard and speak with you about..."

"We can speak here."

The one with the number 42 on his jacket waved toward the ship's interior, "Perhaps we'd be more comfortable..."

"We can speak *here,*" said Brian adamantly, giving no ground.

"Fine." The Lawman sighed and glanced down at his e-Pad, "There's been an incident in the Peninsula Sector..."

"What kind of incident?" asked Brian, cutting in abruptly.

"We're not completely sure yet..."

"Then how does it concern us?"

"Because we believe it involves these people," said Lawman 42, handing the e-Pad to Brian. "Aren't these people, members of your crew? "

Brian glanced at the dark picture of Jack and Lisa who appeared to be sitting in a vehicle of some kind. "They might be..."

"They're being sought for questioning," said the Lawman, accepting the device back, "in connection with the incident in the Peninsula I mentioned."

"Which was..." prompted Brian with a wave, looking for more detail.

The Lawman looked mildly annoyed. "There was some property destruction, a few casualties..." He frowned, "Look, I'm not saying these... *casualties...* were star citizens. Far from it, but seeing as witnesses seem to be scarce, we would like the opportunity to interview your folks," he waved the e-Pad, "to find out what really happened."

"So you're not sure our people were even involved then...?"

"No we're not. But there are some strong indicators that they were there. I didn't catch their names..."

"Because I didn't give them," replied Brian, remaining stoic.

"Well, would you mind?" asked Lawman 42, his finger poised over his e-Pad.

Brian pursed his lips for a moment, trying to decide what to say to the inquiry, when a thought hit him. "John Smith, Mary Smith and Bob Smith..."

The Lawman's eyebrows arched. "Smith? That's kind of an odd name, isn't it?"

Brian shrugged, "Family name, what can I say?"

Lawman 42 looked down at his pad and back up again before deciding to make a note of it. "You'll give us a call if you hear from them, won't you?"

"Absolutely, of course," nodded Brian. He watched the Lawmen walk down the gangway, checking curiously over their shoulders as they headed back to the dock.

"You're not really going to call them, are you?" Dale whispered in his ear.

"Oh, *hell* no."

"You worried, Skipper?"

120

Brian shook his head, "No, if they can't find them, that's a good thing." He thumbed the screen on his eGo-h. "TESS, can you ping Jax Mercury?"

"Yes Commander, pinging." She was silent for a moment. "I am getting no response to my ping, it appears Jax Mercury's TESS is currently dark."

"Is his TESS shut down?"

"TESS units are never off in the conventional sense, Commander. We can, for the lack of a better term, hibernate. This allows the unit to be undetectable to nearly all electronic scanning systems."

Brian and Dale walked backed towards the galley, leaving the security team to resume their duties at the boarding hatch. "They're hiding then," said Brian to Dale. "Do you have a last known location, TESS?"

"Checking Commander." Her holo-screen opened with a map, her animated character to one side, an icon blinking on the far end of the planetoid. "It appears Commander, that they made it to a location marked as Deep Black. It is listed as a parts and supply warehouse..."

■ ■ ■

"I hear voices," whispered Lisa fearfully, barely audible.

In the darkness between the wall and the racks, Jack held his finger to his lips, listening intently. There was more than one male voice but only one female voice. Try as he might, he could not make out the actual discussion, just the fact that it was somewhat heated. Peeking between the crates and boxes did nothing to better his understanding of what was going on, his little voice shouting cautionary warnings in his ear.

When Mouse's hulk squeezed past the racks and silently appeared around the corner, Lisa almost screamed and Jack almost had a heart attack. *"Easy, easy,"* he urged, his voice hushed. "I'm Mouse, I work for Cheriska. We need to move you, the Law isn't taking the normal bribe, they want to search the whole warehouse, they're waiting for extra Lawmen."

Steele rose to his feet. "Where can we go? We're kinda trapped..."

Mouse pointed at the floor below his feet, "You're standing on the exit," the big man waved, "step back,". He pulled open the back of a false crate stacked on the nearest rack, revealing a hidden electronic command panel. Entering a code on the screen prompted movement of a panel of the floor. It swung up on hydraulic arms a tunnel shaft dropping away into the darkness below. Dim lighting flickered on, revealing a ladder reaching down into the darkness. "Go," he pointed. "I'll be last."

They descended through ten feet of the planetoid's solid rock to a level below, Mouse stopping a couple feet below the floor at another control panel mounted next to the ladder, to secure the escape hatch. Stepping off the ladder, stale, musty air clung to their faces, almost moist, its weight almost tangible.

"Sorry," apologized the big man. "We don't pull power unless we're actually down here for something." Calling up the controls on his e-Go, the lights flickered to life, the air system kicking on. "The air will get better in a few minutes... Cheriska said you have a shopping list?"

But Jack had already walked away, looking at all the dust-covered ships parked throughout the cavernous secret warehouse. "Sure, in a minute," he waved dismissively. Stopping and staring at two dust-laden Warthogs sitting side-by-side he reached up and wiped off the filth under the canopy release where the pilot's name would be, but it had been purposefully sanded off. The ship's name on the twin-tails still remained, the faded words *UFW YNOSA* still lettered on the tail.

"The Ynosa," he breathed, somewhat mystified to have found them.

"What is it?" whispered Lisa, sliding up beside him.

Jack cleared his throat. "The Freedom was the Ynosa before the pirates raided her... Before we had her..." he whispered back.

"How do you think they got here?"

"Captain Kidd must have needed the money and sold a couple of them off..."

"You don't want those dusty old relics," called Mouse, waiting patiently near the ladder. "We got those about four or five years ago and they were at least twenty-years obsolete back then..."

Lisa pointed further across the room, "What's that one? Isn't that like the one we lost?"

"Good eye, kiddo!" grinned Jack. "Hey Mouse, how much for that dark gray one over there?" pointed Steele.

"The Remora fighter?" he said, walking in that direction. "I don't know if you'd want her... she's an older model and she's stripped."

"What do you mean stripped?" asked Steele, heading towards the fighter with Lisa and Draza Mac in tow.

"No armaments. All her guns have been pulled off. She came in like that."

"She still run and got all her electronics?"

"As far as I know, yes. We can plug her in and you can take a look if you want..."

"I want." Jack walked underneath the fighter and started a precursory preflight inspection. "Doesn't look like she's ever been hit..." He was noticing small, flush, silver dots on her hull and wings – something he'd never seen before.

"She's been sitting for quite a while... she's probably dead." Mouse was dragging a heavy cable off a reel to the nose, popping open an access panel, plugging the cable into the fighter to power her up. He reached up and activated the pilot's access panel, the canopy motoring back slowly on its track. "I don't have a ladder but I can boost you up if you want to take a look..."

Steele accepted the lift and climbed over the side of the canopy into the cockpit, which despite the wear, was still clean and tidy. Cells charging, he began testing the systems. The dash, gauges, screens, sensors and air immediately came to life. Activating the flight systems, he watched the control surfaces match the flight stick motions along with the gimbaled maneuvering jets for space flight. *Two last tests...* He activated the anti-gravity system and the fighter quickly bounced off the floor.

"Hey!" shouted mouse, "What are you doing?"

"Easy Mouse," Jack waved over the side, I got to make sure everything works. You want to sell it, don't you?" He watched the big man nod slowly and shut down the anti-gravity the fighter settling back to the deck. *One last thing...* He crossed his fingers and hit the starter, hearing the engine spin up, releasing it immediately. *Nice.* Hitting the igniter button produced a throaty bump. "Looks like it's all good..." he called down. "What's this ARC system, Mouse? I've never heard of that..."

"I don't fly, I don't know."

"Well, we don't have any weapons to accidentally go boom so let's try it..."mumbled Jack, reaching for the switches. Activating the ARC system, a small independent screen swung into view, a message rolling across the readout. *Initiating ARC - Automatic Reflective Camouflage system.* A schematic of the spacecraft appeared, covered in markers. *STAND BY system checking emitters... System reading and calibrating... System active...* The whole process took less than thirty-seconds.

Shouts from the deck below him diverted his attention and he looked over the side, "What?"

"What do you mean *what?"* shouted Lisa. "You didn't notice your freaking ship was *invisible?!* All we can see is your damn head!*"

Steele did a double take, looking out over the wings and back behind himself towards the stern, seeing only the floor beneath him and the wall behind. If he looked hard, *really* hard, he could see the vague outline, a minor distortion."Whoa. *That's cool...*"

■ ■ ■

"Lawman 63 shoved the e-Pad in front of Cheriska for the umpteenth time, "Look at it again."

"I don't *have* to look at it again," she sneered, "I told you I haven't seen those people."

"One of our other Lawmen spoke to them on the docks, your business came up *specifically*. We know they were headed here... A transport driver dropped them off just outside the Peninsula on the outskirts of Town Central, straight up the street from here."

"Well they never made it here," Cheriska insisted. "That's quite a distance from Deep Black, and since it seems all the extra money I give you assholes doesn't buy the safety of my clients through this fucking area, maybe I should simply pay off the damn criminals. Oh that's right," she slammed her empty mug down on the table with a whack, "you're all one and the same, aren't you? Is that why you're mad?" She stood up, "Someone finally kill that ass you call a brother-in-law? Did he and his band of thugs try to nab the wrong person?!"

"That's enough!" shouted Lawman 63, slamming his fist down on the counter. "Consider Deep Black shut down until further notice!"

"Kiss my ass, you prick. Consider you and your goons cut off. Not another credit."

"We'll close down all your business, then," threatened the Lawman.

"You give that a try. In the meantime I'll be calling the Chief Constable, the Magistrate and the Primayor..."

Lawman 63 lunged across the counter at her and she jumped back meeting the frame of Mouse walking up behind her. "Problem..?" With one arm the big man slid Cheriska around behind him, eying the Lawman.

Sweeping his jacket, the Lawman rested his hand on the grip of his sidearm, "Back off you..."

Four Lawmen emerged from the warehouse brushing past Mouse and Cheriska, "Let's go..."

"You didn't find *anything?*" raged 63.

"No." The Lawman with the number 87 on his jacked paused at the end of the counter, studying 63 and his body language, glancing over his shoulder at the Deep Black employees. "Do we have a problem here?"

Lawman 63 straightened up, "No, nothing," he said slowly, staring evilly at Cheriska. He turned and followed the others out, not looking back.

■ ■ ■

The music was loud enough to dance to, but not so loud that you couldn't have a conversation. A layer of smoke hung near the ceiling and people milled about, some dancing. The clientele was mixed; some dressed for a night out, others like the rough neighborhood it was. An truly eclectic mismatch of patrons. A red-haired waitress with alabaster, nearly transparent skin came over to the table and laid an e-Pad down. "Here's a menu. Anything you want, Mouse said is on the house..."

Draza Mac leaned to the right, studying a half-nude dancer on the stage. "Uh, anything?"

The waitress smirked, "Food, drinks... or yeah, that too." She switched her eyes back to Steele. "Just tap whatever you'd like," she indicated the e-Pad, "and I'll bring it over."

"Thanks," nodded Jack. "So does Cheriska own this place too?"

The waitress bought her finger to her lips, her eyes shifting nervously around. She nodded once and hastily left the table.

"That was odd," offered Lisa.

"Hey, this whole rock is odd," commented Jack, studying the inside of the nightclub and the faces around them. "Like that maze of tunnels Mouse brought us through..." He paged through the menu and selected a handful of items.

"I was starting to get a bit nervous back there," admitted Draza Mac.

"You and me both," added Lisa. "How many businesses do you think Cheriska owns?" she wondered aloud.

"Judging by what I've seen so far," said Jack, running his fingers through his hair," I'm guessing a good part of the Peninsula."

Lisa's eyes were scanning the room. "Do you think those guys that jumped us were part of her, um, *enterprise?"*

"I don't think so. It would be counter productive. She stands to make a lot more from her legit business than smuggling girls..." He paused waiting for the waitress to finish depositing their food and drinks on the table, watching her walk away. "Though I'm sure moving women on the black market is probably lucrative in its own right, it can't possibly compare with her warehouse."

"You never know... They did seem to know we were coming," said Draza Mac, pointing out the elephant in the room.

"Yeah, that thought has been bothering me too," nodded Jack. "It seemed staged, not a crime of opportunity..."

■ ■ ■

"You OK Cheriska?"

She reached up and patted Mouse on the chest, "I'm fine. Good timing by the way, I think he really wanted to throttle me. So, how are our clients doing? Are they secure?"

"They're down on level three having dinner and drinks at the CherriPit. I comped them whatever they wanted..."

"Good deal. Let's hope their shopping list makes up for all the trouble..."

"Oh it *does,*" grinned Mouse, handing her his e-Pad, "it *does.*"

She scrolled through the items. "He wants twenty-five stasis emitter systems?"

Mouse nodded. "Full kits; emitters, reflectors, sensors and cabling. The SEk-2540 systems. New ones."

"I don't think we have that many, do we?"

Mouse pulled up a stool and swung a leg over. "Nope, we have seventeen. But we have enough rebuilts to cover the order. I told him they were factory warrantied rebuilt units and he OK'd it."

"Excellent," waved Cheriska. "But I wonder what he needs that many for? That's a *lot* of emitters..."

"He didn't say. Told me it was for a confidential client."

"If I didn't know better," she mused, inhaling on her puff stick, "I'd say he was building a ship. A big one..."

"Could be for a base too," offered Mouse, "you can run those units in series for bigger bays..."

"Did you tell her the best part?" asked Cheriska Too, strolling into the office from the warehouse.

"Scroll to the bottom of the order," prompted the big man, pointing at the e-Pad.

126

Cheriska scrolled to the stop. "By the Gods! You sold the *Remora?*"

"As-is, no guns. I had to throw in a full load of fuel, though..."

"Well done, Mouse! This definitely makes up for the rest of the day... How's his credit? Did you check?"

"No terms, he paid in full."

Cheriska stared at him, unblinking. *"Cash?"*

"An instant funds transfer..."

Her eyes narrowed for a moment, glancing at the order total. "He has some *mighty* deep pockets..." She inhaled on the puff stick, staring blankly. Suddenly something seemed amiss and it gave her an uneasiness she hadn't felt in a while.

■ ■ ■

"I'm telling you," whispered Lisa urgently, *"that's Nina!"*

Jack was trying to get a better glimpse between the passing patrons of the girl on stage in the red dress. "Nina's dead, Lisa..."

"Correction, Nina's *missing.* Her body was never recovered so her death is not *confirmed.* We do not know, for sure, what happened. "

"I suppose it's not impossible..." muttered Jack, trying to see through the increasing crush of people, "that we might have missed an escape pod... Dammit, it's too crowded, I can't see her now." He stood up, his CABL-enhanced artificial eye targeting the girl in the red dress, zooming in.

"I hate to rush things folks," said Mouse, appearing out of nowhere, "but we've got to go. *Now...* "

"What's going on, Mouse?" asked Lisa, trying to keep tabs on her brother at the same time. She snagged his sleeve, holding him from disappearing into the crowd.

"The Lawmen are giving us some problems... They're putting pressure on us trying to locate the three of you, we need to get you out and back to your ship."

Steele was torn, if that truly was Nina, and he was fairly certain it was, he owed it to her to get her back. "The girl in the red dress..." he pointed, glancing back at Mouse.

"You don't have time for fun and games," urged the big man, "Cheriska got word the Lawmen are going to raid this place..."

"Dammit," growled Jack, I don't want to have sex with her, I think she's one of our friends who went missing..."

"The *Syndicate* owns the girls, Mr. Mercury, you can't help her. Let it go. You'll only put her life in danger and get yourself killed..."

Reflections of flashing colored lights at odd angles danced across the walls and ceiling of the club, causing general panic, people screaming and pressing towards the exits. Jack shot a glance toward the stage and the girl in the red dress had disappeared.

"Dammit."

"We have to go *now!*" shouted Mouse.

Steele pulled his empty mag out of his belt pouch, handing it to Draza Mac, "Swap me." Draza pulled a loaded magazine from his belt and traded. Stuffing the loaded mag into his pouch, Jack grabbed Lisa's arm, "Can you fly the Ramora?"

She searched his face, she knew he was going after Nina. "I think so..."

"Think doesn't cut it, Lisa. Can you fly the Remora?"

"Yes."

"Then do it." Steele switched his gaze to Draza Mac, "You're her back seat..."

"Yes, sir."

The stampede of patrons was trying to force their way through the front doors to freedom, temporarily stalling entry of the Lawmen, but the raid was inevitable. The floor was littered with bottles, discarded food and broken glass.

"Use that side door, Mr. Mercury," pointed Mouse, "they'll be heading to the Island."

Lisa grabbed her brother's hand, "Maybe it's not worth it..."

"I have to try," said Jack. "Have the Raven launch, meet them in space, they can protect you." He looked over at Mouse, "You can deliver our parts via shuttle...?"

Seeing the Lawmen weaving their way in through the crowd, the big man pulled Lisa and Draza Mac toward the hidden back exit. "The shuttle's already packed. *Go now!*" he nodded towards the side door.

Steel bolted past the stage amid authoritative shouts from behind him. The corridor to the back door was narrow and he prayed the back entrance was unsecured, the only alternative hiding spots the restrooms he had just rocketed past. He hit the back door at a run, blowing it open so hard it slammed against the outside rock wall with a bang, the two Lawmen standing outside startled to see him suddenly appear. He didn't slow his pace, instead accelerating like a running back for open field, bulldozing the first

Lawman. The second managed a solid grab and Steele spun his body, viciously throwing an elbow, producing a juicy crunch, dropping the man in an unconscious heap.

He sprinted away, spotting an empty patrol vehicle at the end of the street, his senses suddenly picking up every shadow, every movement, every sound...

■ ■ ■

"It was nice of them to wash it off," commented Draza Mac, looking through the clean canopy from the back seat of the Remora as he fastened his belts.

Lisa climbed over the side of the cockpit with a boost from Mouse. "Uh huh," she grunted, dropping into the seat and scanning the controls. "Mac, call the Raven while I get us running. Get them moving." She belted herself in, taking a deep breath and closing her eyes for a moment, recalling her checklist in her head. She flipped on the main power and the flight control systems, testing the surfaces and gimbaled maneuvering jets. All the surfaces were free. *Locks, chocks, blocks...all clear...*

"We don't have suits or helmets," commented Draza Mac from the back seat, "what does that mean?"

"It means, we can't afford to screw up. So please shut the hell up and let me concentrate..." *Air system, communications, sensors, scanners, fuel pumps, jet systems, anti-grav...* The fighter bounced up off the deck. *Fuel levels are good, power cells are completely charged...* "Mac, we're head-in, I'm going to have to back us out the door. You're going to have to guide me out with your turret camera..."

"Got it. Stasis field on, door is open," he said, watching the monitor.

Hand on the throttle, Lisa paused. *What am I forgetting?* She scanned the dash and the systems. *HOLY CRAP! The canopy!* She pulled the lever, the long canopy motoring swiftly forward, latching down with a hiss, the green indicators coming on. "Good one Lisa," she muttered, "go into space with the canopy open. Brilliant..."

■ ■ ■

Commander Brian Carter was halfway to the bridge when TESS' holo-screen popped up, Draza Mac looking back at him. It was a short conversation, prompted by Brian who had to remind the Marine to keep a long story short. Now Brian was second-guessing himself, realizing he didn't fully know all the circumstances. Hopefully the missing details were minor. "TESS, forward the coordinates to the bridge..."

"Yes, Commander," she replied, almost seductively.

He swept the screen and it disappeared as he hustled toward the bridge at a trot, keying the mic on his earpiece, "Now hear this, all hands on deck, all hands on deck. Prepare to cast off *immediately...*" Lights strobed yellow, matching the gong, ending after several cycles.

"What's going on?" called Maria, catching up and pacing him.

"Hello, shit? Meet fan," replied Brian.

"Leave it to Jack..." she commented lightheartedly.

"I've learned to expect nothing less. Take the second seat?"

"Sure."

The hull vibrated, the deck moving beneath their feet as they neared the bridge. The bridge doors swished open, separating down the middle as they passed the sentry in the corridor. "Report," called Brian, sliding to a stop, dropping into the command seat.

"Umbilicals clear, gangway clear, docking clamps released, hull sealed. We're ready to get underway."

"Get us out of here, helm."

"Looks like we have an audience on the dock," announced Maria, pointing to the collection of flashing lights.

"Better luck next time, *Copper,*" sneered Brian. "Mr. Ragnaar, did you get the coordinates?"

"Aye sir, coordinates programmed in."

Brian called up tactical on his command screens. "Good. Follow the traffic lanes. Once we're clear, fly it like you *stole it.*"

Ragnaar glanced over at Quixetta at the helm and they shared a nod.

■ ■ ■

Lisa's headset chirped, "Remora, you're clear. The parts shuttle will be on its way as soon as I can get over to the other bay."

"She keyed her mic, Copy that. Thanks for all your help, Mouse." She watched the bay doors close as she rotated the fighter around, still coasting backwards. "Shields up," she announced, flipping them on, the field generators spinning up to a hum. The display showed all the shield emitters working at full capacity, something Jack could not test in the bay. She was glad to have the protection considering she was unarmed. She flipped the engine startup, listening to the spool-up, watching the readout, punching the igniter when the marker popped green. A throaty thump turned into a low growl, eliciting a sneaking grin and instant butterflies in her stomach. Hand on throttle, she was about to fly a fighter for the very first time.

"We've got company..."

Oh crap! Lisa snapped her head in a swivel, looking around, "Where?"

"Directly behind. Looks like a Law Enforcement bird of some kind... They're hailing... message is; return to the dock."

"Screw that. Hold on..." She slid the throttle forward, tentatively at first, then with a bit more authority, the engine coming to life, pressing them back into their seats.

"There's another one, bogey left!"

Lisa hazarded a glance, the second one cutting in at full throttle from around the tip of the planetoid. A threat indicator lit up, a warning horn squawking. "This asshole is *targeting* us!" She clenched her jaw, a sudden sweat breaking across her brow as the adrenalin hit, heart instantly pounding as she shoved the throttle to the far stop, thumbing the boost button. "Not today..." she winced, the G forces narrowing her vision. The cockpit gravity gyro was working to normalize the G forces but a flight suit was required for the best results. She let go of the boost button and eased the throttle back as her vision went gray, the G forces balancing out, allowing her to gulp some air. "You with me, Mac?" she panted, easing the throttle forward to the far stop again, the gradual increase easily compensated by the Remora's gyro.

"Still here... you almost had me there, though."

"Sorry about that. They still with us?"

"No," he replied, blinking hard, taking a deep breath. "They fell off the grid pretty quick when you hammered it." He tapped on his nav screen, "We're way off course..."

"I know." She rolled and pulled on the stick, putting the fighter in a wide arc, "No sense in pointing them to our rendezvous."

■ ■ ■

Maneuvering the Lawman's patrol vehicle down streets and through tunnels toward the Island, Jack Steele was wondering how he was going to find Nina in the red dress. It wasn't like there would be a sign with an arrow;

131

kidnapped girls here. He was beginning to doubt this particular line of decisions and the direction it was taking him. Of course that was the problem with decisions you had to make in short order, there was better than a 50/50 chance you were going to make the wrong one. And the farther you followed that path the farther astray you were going to end up. Unless of course you succeeded, in which case it was a genius plan.

And what the hell was he going to do if he actually found her? How in God's name was he going to get her off this rock? *Hmm, one thing at a time.*

He let the patrol cruiser coast to a stop, allowing cross traffic to clear an intersection, running his fingers through his hair. People standing on the corner looked curiously at the man in the battered Lawman's vehicle that was obviously not a Lawman. He ignored them and drove on, looking for signs of a red dress.

Out of the corner of his eye, the group of people walking down the street contained a splash of red and he slammed on the brakes, throwing open the scissor-wing door and jumping out. "Nina! *Nina!*" he shouted, rounding the nose of the vehicle and running toward the group.

"Back off, mister!" threatened one of the men, pulling a sizable blade.

"Easy, guys," said Jack, skidding to a stop, raising his hands, "thought she was someone I knew." The woman wearing a long red cape had fooled him. "No harm, no foul, just a mistake, guys." He turned and sprinted for the vehicle, slamming the door and driving off. *OK, OK, got a little over-excited there... running up screaming her name like a lovesick teenager probably wasn't the best tactic...*

Picking his way towards the Island, Steele checked two gentleman's clubs and a nightclub, hoping the Syndicate thugs protecting the girls would have stopped off at a local establishment to make up for the short night and money lost because of the raid on the CherriPit. Of course initially having to do a little fancy driving to lose the Lawmen, he managed to get himself temporarily lost. He might simply have overshot the area the girls were in. Reaching the end of the Peninsula, he decided it was at least worth driving through the Island to see if he could improve his luck.

Except there were no bridges to the detached Island. Only trains. *Crap.*

Abandoning the Lawman's vehicle in the darkest area he could find, he headed for the train station. Waking TESS, he checked the time. It had been two hours... with every minute that ticked by, his chances of finding her drifted further away. He shook it off, he had to try. Steele didn't want to delve too far into his own head why he needed to find her, but he felt responsible for her and decided to leave it at that.

Walking across the footbridge from the solid rock of the Peninsula to the station suspended between the main asteroid of Rikovik's Reef and the separate asteroid of the Island, was more than a little disconcerting. The trains that passed on either side of the main platform, rode through metal-bottomed glass tubes. Incorporated with an arched glass ceiling and glass panels in the platform floor, provided a view that was simply spectacular. It was a beautifully modern station... too bad it was so damn filthy and so poorly maintained.

Steele glanced up at the video monitor hanging on the support pillar above him, realizing his face was on something resembling the six-o'clock news. *Terrific.* At least the video clip was dark and blurry. He glanced around at the nearly empty platform, two people on the other side waiting for a train heading the opposite direction. He turned his back on them, waiting patiently for an Island-bound train.

■ ■ ■

Weaving in and out of tunnels through the rock of the Island, the train made stops all around the Island's perimeter. The Island was definitely the seedier side of the tracks and Jack had just walked a considerable amount of it, visiting more clubs and girlie bars than he could count. All to no avail. Wearily, four hours later, he dropped himself into a seat on a train heading back to the Peninsula. The serpentine train had no independent cars, winding its way smoothly, nearly silently through the tunnels like a metal snake.

He stretched himself out, closing his eyes in the nearly-empty train. He needed a shower, feeling dirty by exposure to the seamy underbelly of Rikovik's Reef. If he could make his way to Deep Black, he was sure he could arrange a shuttle pickup from the Revenge. He had run out of ideas and his luck was running on empty.

"Hey. *Hey you...*" Steele opened one eye, two men standing before him, unsteady on their feet from a combination of the train's movement and their alcohol content. "You're the guy on the news..."

"Nah, that ain't me," replied Jack with a wave, feigning intoxication. His right hand slowly crept toward the grip of his sidearm, pausing when his fingertips touched the holster on his thigh.

"Yeah man," chuckled the other drunk, "that's you alright..."

"Don't go back to the Main Rock," started the first, sitting down on a nearby seat. "Buddy, they're gonna catch you. Stay on the Island, the Law don't come out here."

"I gotta get off this rock," countered Jack. "I was looking for someone and I've come up empty..."

"You a bounty hunter, mister?"

Steele straightened up in his seat. "Nothing like that. I'm looking for a woman..."

"Lots of women on the Island."

Jack shook his head, "I'm looking for a specific woman. She was abducted..."

"Oh," nodded the man, "the Syndicate has her then."

"That's what I've been told. But I lost her when..."

"When you were running from the Law," interrupted the first man. "Yeah we saw some video on the news. You drive like *crazy!*"

Steele ran his fingers through his hair, "Yeah well, I got lucky..."

"You need to go to the Blue Moon, that's where they house most of their girls. You might find her there."

Steele frowned. "Is that a hotel?"

"Hotel, whorehouse, black market... It's four streets in, off the third station..."

"What about getting off this rock?"

"There are some transport pilots for hire on the far end, but they don't do long hauls."

"That's fine, I don't need to go far." Approaching the station, Steele could see flashing lights reflecting off the arched glass ceiling. *Dammit, cops.* They must have found the abandoned patrol cruiser.

"One more thing," said the first man. "If you piss off the Syndicate in any way, you'll never get a ride, no one will go against them. You'll have to steal something. Can you fly?"

"Yeah that's not a problem." Steele scanned the platform, it was empty.

"Good. Your best bet is to get off at the train stop past the docks. It's the yacht basin... Don't get caught though, the ships there belong to the Syndicate."

"Oh swell..."

■ ■ ■

Floating in the rubble of Rikovik's mined-out asteroid field, Lisa had shut down many of her systems, including shields, careful to set her drift to match the field. With the ARC system running, she would be nearly invisible to anything the Lawmen had while they waited for the Raven. "How are we doing, Mac?"

"We've got an inbound, good size."

"Not a Lawman?"

"No, way too big. She's really moving too. With our sensors on passive sweep I've got no details."

Lisa checked her systems. "Hope it's our ride. But we're staying put till we know for sure..."

"Works for me, Skipper. I'm in no hurry to get shot at."

As nervous as she was, that made Lisa crack a smile. She liked the way it sounded. *Skipper...*

"I've got another bogie," added Draza Mac. "Coming in on a similar vector that we took. It's small."

"Should be our parts shuttle. I hope."

"I've got a ping, Skipper... verifying... big one's the Raven."

"Sweet. Return the ping," Lisa instructed.

"Copy, ping returned. I'm seeing a comm to the Raven... confirming... got it, shuttle is from Deep Black."

"Good timing." Lisa activated her shields, deactivating the ARC system before relighting her engine, rotating the Remora in a direction for a clean exit from the rubble. She eased the throttle forward. "Remora to Raven, set me up for approach for docking procedure..."

■ ■ ■

Sitting in the Raven's command chair, Brian Carter shot a glance over at Maria sitting in the second seat. "Was that who I think it was?"

"That was Lisa," replied Maria. "She must be handling comms from the back seat."

"I thought Mac was in the back seat..."

"Then where the hell is Jack?" asked Maria, wide-eyed. "Lisa doesn't even have her wings yet."

"I don't know, I was trying to keep our comm short."

"There's only two seats in that thing..."

"I get it," snapped Brian. "First things first. Go down there and guide her in for a hookup." Maria slid out of her seat and hustled off the bridge without another word, giving Brian a little reprieve from Maria's concerns. "Helm, all stop. Instruct the shuttle to stand by until we've recovered the Remora."

■ ■ ■

The train eased away from the platform leaving the Lawmen behind. Steele took a quick glance around before sitting down, a group of people sitting several rows behind him, a streak of red near the outer window. Did his luck just change? "TESS," he whispered, "can you take a picture of someone behind us?"

His earpiece chirped, "Of course I can. Face my screen in that direction." He stretched, interlacing his fingers casually behind his head, leaning back in his seat. "Perfect. OK, I have it..."

"There she is..!" he breathed, examining the digital photo on TESS' screen. Six girls, three goons. And one of the goons looked like a neckless human wall with legs. Well, sort of human. Nina was sitting next to the window, half asleep, the girl next to her slumped on her shoulder, both of them disheveled and worn looking. A direct confrontation looked to be out of the question, she'd be in no condition to run. He was going to have to come up with a plan that minimized the risk of gun play...

His earpiece chirped, "Jax, if you're thinking of a recovery action, you should know the girls are wearing some type of control collar..."

"What does it do, TESS?" he whispered.

"I've searched my database and I don't find a match. Most commonly they issue a debilitating shock if the subject moves beyond the set boundary of the control unit.

"What are the other possibilities?" he whispered.

"Death. By lethal injection, by explosion, by electrocution... Considering that the women are valuable commodity, I would estimate the units are meant to temporarily incapacitate, nothing more. If I was to speculate, I would say the rather large man has the control unit."

Steele rubbed his eyes and exhaled heavily. "Yeah, that would have been my guess..."

CHAPTER TEN

RIKOVIK'S REEF: *WRONG SIDE OF THE TRACKS*

Steele had to be realistic; he wasn't going to get all three. One, maybe two, but not all three. And either the girls would take hits or he'd go down. He'd have to follow at a safe distance and see if an opportunity presented itself. He feigned inebriation, allowing the group a lead getting off the platform, following slowly behind. The Syndicate thugs were either tired, or lazy, or both. Not once had they looked behind them, plodding along, the girls shuffling between them. The girls were obviously worn out but he couldn't help but think they were either drunk or drugged. There was no animation or chatter from any one of them; girls or guards.

He sunk himself into the shadows as the group paused at a corner to let a vehicle pass through the intersection, the tail-end guard looking back for the very first time. Steele ran his thumb across the top of the holster release... the 1911 charged particle blaster would sound like a cannon on this narrow street. A suppressor would be really nice to have right about now... then he wondered if you could actually silence a charged particle blaster. He thought about the knife in his boot; he could fight with a knife but he had never managed to pass knife-throwing 101.

When the group turned the next corner, Steele hustled up to close the gap, peeking around the corner. They were gone. The street and sidewalk deserted except for a few parked vehicles. A spike of adrenalin hit him and he rushed, albeit cautiously, forward, drawing the 1911, keeping it close to his body. *What the hell, where did they...* His comm chirped, "Stop! Stop!" He stopped, flattening himself into an irregularity in the wall doing his best to be invisible as a set of doors less than ten feet ahead opened with force, banging against the rock wall. Two of the Syndicate goons strolled out into the darkness, their backs illuminated by the light inside the doorway until the doors automatically swung closed. It was the neckless walking wall and the tail guard, getting into the vehicle parked out front. Jack wasn't sure the wall was going to fit but he managed, the vehicle dipping on his side under his mass. The lights came on and they drove slowly away. Steele exhaled, looking up, listening to his heart pound. The neon blue, crescent moon hung above the doorway with no words. *The Blue Moon... how did I not see that?*

He stuck the 1911 into the back of his waistband and untied the holster from his thigh, folding it up against his body, covering it all with his jacket.

Steele walked through the door like he'd done it a hundred times, taking it all in as quickly as he could, angling for the front desk, surrounded with what appeared to be bulletproof glass, a teller's speaker above the payment tray.

The guy behind the glass looked like a permanent part of the chair he was sitting on. "What do *you* want?" he demanded gruffly, rubbing the scruff on his double chin.

"That beautiful girl in the red dress that just came in here..."

The desk man leaned toward the speaker, "Mister, do you have any fucking idea what time it is? *We're closed.* Those girls are going to bed; your dick can wait until later."

"But I'd like..."

"Beat it! Literally. Go home and take care of it yourself..."

"I'll pay you double," interrupted Steele.

That stopped the rant for a moment, his mind working. "Y'know," said the desk clerk, his attitude changing. "You look like a decent guy, all clean cut and whatnot... I'm going to do you a huge favor. I'm going to charge you triple. But to be nice, I'm going to throw in her little girlfriend. You'll like that. A little two-on-one? Yeah you look like the type, I can tell..." He tapped on the payment tray, "How you gonna pay for that?"

Steele dropped his ITC card in the tray.

"Real nice, not worried about the old lady finding out, eh?"

"Not married," lied Jack, accepting it back.

The desk clerk dropped a key card into the tray. "Room 410." He waved at Jack's ITC card, "I took a little something extra for myself. After they're done with you, you'll think I deserve it anyway. It'll save you the trip of coming down to tip me."

Jack smirked wryly, "I appreciate your thoughtfulness..."

The same type of threadbare carpet as in the lobby greeted Steele when he stepped off the elevator on the fourth floor, the musty, dimly lit corridor stretching out on either side, the directional placards missing from the wall. *So I guess they're not putting their profits into the décor...*

Finding room 410, he waved the key card in front of the reader, the door unlatching, sliding into the wall. The heady scent of incense rolled past him out into the corridor, stars twinkling outside the bay window on the other side of the room. *OK, now that's pretty cool...*

"I'm sorry mister," said the naked girl wearily, her back to him, "I didn't expect any more visitors tonight. I'll be right with you..."

Jack stepped into the muted light, letting the door close behind him, scanning the room for anything that might resemble a video camera. "Nina Redwolf," he said softly.

Standing in front of her wardrobe, pulling something sheer to put on, the woman froze. "How do you know my name...?" she whispered.

"Are there video cameras in this room?"

"Yes."

"Then don't overreact..." he breathed, "It's me, Jack."

She finished pulling what she was looking for, wrapping it around her and fluffing her hair before turning to him. She paused a moment, studying his shadowed features before moving to him with as much restraint she could muster, encircling him with her arms, burying her face in his chest, shaking. "Oh my God," she sobbed, "Oh my God. Oh my God... How did you find me?"

"By accident," he whispered in her ear. "We saw you in the CherriPit before the raid. I've been searching for you ever since." He squeezed her tight. "Hold it together, sweetie. Now I need you to remember something rather important; in this world I am Jax Mercury... can you remember that?" She nodded without pulling her face away from his chest. "Are there cameras in the bathroom?" She shook her head no. "The shower is running, who's in there?"

"My girl, Ruby."

"The second girl the clerk promised?"

"Yes."

"Can you trust her?"

"Yes."

"Good." He turned her toward the bathroom, its rectangle of light spilling out across the bedroom floor. "We're *all* going to take a shower together where we can talk and not be heard or recorded."

■ ■ ■

Jack leaned against the sink. "Any chance we'll get interrupted?" he asked, pulling off his boots.

139

"No," replied Nina, slipping into the shower, "unless we don't come out of here in an hour. All it takes is one of us walking around once in a while so they can see us."

"How long do we have?"

"I don't know what you paid him," replied Nina, "but he gave you all day."

When Steele slipped into the shower the girls were huddled under the dual shower heads, washing their hair, the steam filling the shower. Ruby was olive complected, all of five feet tall with waist length jet black hair, slanted oriental eyes and pointed ears that reminded him of every drawing of an elf he'd ever seen. Nina had shortened her auburn tresses to shoulder length and her skin had lost some of her natural golden color. But neither one could be ashamed in a bikini... *or* naked. *Wow!* panted the little voice in his head.

"Ruby, this is Jack, er, Jax. Jax this is Ruby," announced Nina.

Jack stuck out his hand, "Hi..."

Ruby put out her hand, "Hello... *Oh, look* someone else wants to say hello... *very nice,"* she smiled, crouching, reaching out.

Steele scooted back bumping into the shower glass, gently grabbing her by the shoulders, pulling her back to a standing position. "Eyes up here, sweetie" he motioned casually with a flick of his fingers, her eyes to his.

"But *he* wants to say hello," she motioned.

"Yeah well, he's got a mind of his own sometimes. OK, all the time," he waved. "But I'm a married man and we're not here for that..."

"It's cute," said Nina, "I've never seen you nervous before... and I've never seen you naked before. I like. And as much as I love women, I've got to say, I'd do you... And probably not hate it..."

Steele blinked hard, frowning, "Thanks... I think."

"I think we should do him," volunteered Ruby.

Steele held his hands out, "I can't, please don't..."

"She'll never know," coaxed Ruby, reaching out.

"But *I'll* know," said Jack, pained. "At another point in my life I would've jumped at the chance to be with two women as beautiful as you. In fact, you probably wouldn't have had to ask. After *hello,* discussion would have been rather unlikely. But now, well..."

"I think it's sweet," interrupted Ruby. "And I respect that. You're probably the first man I've ever met that isn't a total pig... She stretched her arms wide, "Group hug?"

140

Steele shook his head, "Lady, you're killing me..."

■ ■ ■

Brian took the mug of coffee handed him by the porter, scanning his screens. Blowing the steam away, he glanced up at the inset video on the big screen. The Deep Black shuttle rotated and pulled away, leaning over, lighting its engines and streaked away, arcing towards Rikovik's Reef.

"DB-One to the Raven, we thank you for your business! Come back and see us again..."

Brian rubbed his eyes. "Are we all buttoned up?"

"Aye, Skipper."

"Shields up, let the gun crews stand down..." Brian's TESS chimed, diverting his attention. "Carter, go..." he touched the glass face – prompting the holographic screen, Maria's face appearing. "Maria..." he acknowledged.

"Skipper, it looks like the parts delivery is complete. Jack got everything we were here for..."

"Do I detect a but coming?" he prompted.

"Yes. Several. Can you come down?"

"On my way. How did Lisa's recovery go?"

"Flawless," smiled Maria. "Flew it like she owned it."

"Excellent. Down in five." The screen disappeared as he rose to his feet. "Mr. Ragnaar, you have the bridge. Take us into the rubble field and let's minimize our signature."

"Will do, Skipper," replied the big man, moving to the command seat.

Passing gun crews in the corridor returning to normal duties, Brian's TESS chimed again. Well, ain't I the popular one today..." he touched the glass face – prompting the holographic screen, "Carter g... *Jack?*" Steele's face looked back at him on the screen. Brian kept walking. "Are... are you in the shower?"

"Yeah. Long story and not enough time to tell it. Tell Lisa I found her. We just need to find a way off this rock."

"Found who? Wait, we'll come get you..."

"No! We'll come to you. What are your coordinates?"

"TESS," said Brian. Her face instantly appeared on the holo-screen as a small inset, "Send Jax Mercury our coordinates."

"Stand by, Commander," she cooed. "Request complete, coordinates sent." Her head tilted to one side, "Will there be anything else?"

"That's all, thank you," replied Brian, her video square winking out.

"Got it," said Jack, "thanks, gotta go..."

"Wait," said Brian, *"who* did you find?"

"Nina Redwolf."

Brian's screen winked out, the connection gone. *"Nina?"*

■ ■ ■

Clean and dry, with the machinations of a plan, Jack, Nina and Ruby climbed into bed together for much-needed sleep. Aware that the video camera would be watching, they remained mostly undressed, cuddling, arms and legs intertwined. TESS was scheduled to wake them so they could execute their plan during Rikovik's peak business hours when the streets would be the most crowded with people.

"No wandering hands, OK?" mumbled Jack, getting comfortable.

Ruby draped her arm over his waist from behind, "I'm not making any promises. You point that thing at me and I might put it to good use..."

"Leave him alone," whispered Nina, "I've met his wife. If he doesn't split you in half with that thing, she's liable to do it with something else... And not in a good way."

It was quiet but there was something that had been plaguing Jack's mind since they spotted Nina in the CherriPit. "So what happened, Nina?" he asked softly, "In Velora Prime... how did we lose you?"

"When I came to, I was trapped in a damaged section of the Freedom, on level two. The comms were down, the section was filling with smoke and the pods were offline. I found an access hatch and was able to make my way down to level three where I finally found a live pod. I launched but I couldn't get the damn rescue beacon to broadcast. It looked like the ship was headed for the Velorian sun... was it?"

"Yes. We didn't want the Pirates to know what happened..."

"FreeRangers," she corrected him. "They call themselves FreeRangers."

"They can call themselves whatever the hell they want, they're still pirates. Was there anyone else? Alive I mean..."

"No, everyone I came across was dead. I checked. Anyway, I think I drifted for about three days before a freighter nearly ran over my pod. I was out of rations and nearly out of water. They picked me up and dropped me off here, sold me to the Syndicate."

Jack yawned, "Lisa will be so glad to see you, I'm glad we were able to find you."

"Me too," said Nina, yawning in response.

Seven hours went by quickly and Steele was enjoying a thorough examination of the inside of his eyelids when TESS' voice invaded his cloud of warmth and comfort. He opened his eyes, looking around without moving, getting his bearings. "Thanks TESS, I'm awake." When he rolled on his back and looked over at the girls, they were entwined, sleeping like curled kittens. Except they had switched sides, Nina sleeping between him and Ruby. *Thank you Nina... protecting me from Ruby the Rabbit.*

He rolled close to Nina putting his face in her ear. "Time to get up, Kiddo..."

"Stop poking me with that thing," she mumbled.

"Sorry," he replied sheepishly, "it's a morning thing..."

"If by *morning* you mean twenty-four hours a day, I totally understand..." She slid her arm out from under Ruby. "Doesn't that thing ever go down?"

"You're hot, so sue me..."

Nina brushed unruly bed-hair out of her face, "You really think so? I never thought you noticed..."

He chuckled, looking at her wild mop, "Well, maybe not right now so much..."

"Ass," she laughed, slapping him on the chest.

■ ■ ■

The girls surprised Steele, being dressed and ready to go in under ten minutes. Standing huddled at the door, the question would be, was the clerk paying attention to the videos or not? Strapped back to his leg where it belonged, Jack drew his sidearm and let it hang at his side, ready to pass his key card over the reader.

"Let me have your knife," whispered Nina.

"My knife?" He pulled his flat-gripped Ka-Bar from its sheath on his boot and handed it to her.

"I throw a ball like a girl," she admitted, "but I throw a knife like the Seminole Indian

that I am." She hefted the knife, feeling the heavy blade's balance in her hand. "This'll do. Go ahead, open the door..."

The corridor was empty except for the guard sitting in a chair down at the end, dozing with an e-Pad in his lap. "He'll have the controller and the collar key... I've got this..." whispered Nina. Checking the corridor toward the elevators, she pushed past, staying Jack and Ruby with her hand, walking quietly, holding the knife behind her back.

"What's she gonna do?" whispered Steele.

Ruby pressed forward to peek around Jack. "She's going to slit the bastard's throat."

The sound of the elevator starting, coming up from the lobby, made Nina cringe, hesitating as she saw the man in the chair, stir. She was still twenty-feet away when his eyes fluttered open, focusing on her.

His face immediately shifted to a grimace. "What are you doing out of your room, *bitch?*"

The knife felt natural in Nina's hand, like an old friend. She adjusted her grip, wound up and launched it like she was pitching a fastball, producing a wet *thwuck* as it buried itself up to the hilt in his neck, sticking into the back of the chair. He flailed uselessly as his life's blood spurted out in crimson streaks, his eyes wide, gurgling, unable to scream for help, clutching at the handle. Nina whipped around, "Check the elevators!" Watching the life pass from his eyes, she dug through the bodyguard's pockets, looking for the collar key and the floor's key pass. She had never killed before and was surprised at the lack of regret or remorse. In fact she really didn't feel much of anything. Except maybe contempt. Maybe that was the key, the contempt and hatred was shielding her from her other emotions. *No time to think about that now...*

Ruby darted out, retrieving the key pass from Nina, her stomach roiling as she gagged at the sight of the blood pool in the guard's lap. "Wait," called Nina, "hold still." She fitted the electronic key into Ruby's control collar and unlocked it, letting it fall to the floor. "Now do mine, do mine..." Ruby had some difficulty, fumbling to unlock the collar with her eyes closed in an attempt to avoid the bloody spectacle behind Nina.

When the elevator doors opened, the two patrons holding their room keys were confronted by the business end of a charged particle blaster. "Step out, gentlemen," waved Steele. The men entered the corridor, dozens of women running around in various stages of dress and undress. "This is your lucky day..."

"Really?" asked the first man.

144

"No. I'm afraid not," replied Steele, snatching their key cards at gunpoint. "And unfortunately for you there are no refunds." He guided them into Nina's old room and moved the girls' small duffel bags, the door closing and locking the two men inside.

Nina had to put her foot on the guard's chest to hold his body still and use both hands on the grip of the Ka-Bar while she wrenched it out from between his vertebrae, the blade scraping and crunching bone as it came free. She wiped it on his pants as clean as she could get it before sticking it into her belt. "His comm is getting a call, we've got to go!"

Jack passed her a duffel, "You're sure this is going to work?"

"Your guess is as good as mine. A breach is supposed to seal the room and evacuate the hotel..."

"Elevators and stairs. Go! *Go!*" he waved at the crowd of women in the corridor. "OK, here goes..." The sound reverberated in the narrow space as Jack fired two .45 caliber charged particle rounds through the closest open door, striking the outside window of the room, the heavy glass spidering. "Wow. *tough stuff...*" As he contemplated another shot, there was a strange crackling sound, the spider pattern widening, spreading. An ear-piercing whistle preceding his ears painfully popping as the room's door slammed shut like a guillotine, an evacuation alarm screaming in the corridor.

The elevators and stairwells quickly filled with screaming women, panicked patrons and pissed-off Syndicate employees all trying to reach the lobby and the safety of the street.

Jack, Nina and Ruby were making steady progress in the stairwell despite its congestion and the addition of people pouring in from the two floors above their own. The first shot sizzled over his head hitting the wall, cooking off the paint and leaving a sizable scorch mark. Jack spun as people around them panicked on the verge of stampeding but he could not see the shooter hiding in the crowd.

"How far are we?" he asked, leaving his firearm holstered.

"Second floor," replied Nina. "Follow me when we reach the first floor, we should be able to break from the crowd and go out through the kitchen..."

Another shot passed between Jack and Nina, hitting the girl in front of Nina between the shoulder blades, pitching her forward with a scream of agony, creating a domino of bodies, carrying Ruby with them. The fear and panic of the people behind them created a forward press and Jack and Nina went down as another shot passed over them. The pile of people on the landing was almost four deep and Steele fought to his feet, pulling Nina up and digging for Ruby. People scrambled and clawed their way over one another and it was getting increasingly difficult to remain civil and survive. Staying low and pushing with the rest of them like a rugby scrum. Jack could see the shooter over his shoulder on the landing above them, clutching a woman like a shield, shooting from behind her.

Steele drew and fired over the shooter's head, destroying the light fixture above him, making him duck. Reaching up and smashing the light above them with the muzzle of his gun, he sent the stairwell into darkness. He grabbed Nina and pushed forward, plowing people aside. "Ruby?"

"I've got her!" shouted Nina over the din.

Someone grabbed Jack by the shoulder, a strong man's hand and he sent him to the floor with an elbow. There was another pileup of screaming people at the bottom of the stairwell but Jack managed to stay on his feet, pulling Nina and Ruby along with him. "Are we on the first floor?"

"Yes, yes," pushed Nina, "go left here..."

"Dammit," spat Ruby, "I lost my duffel."

"Forget it," said Jack, hustling to keep up with the girls, "You can have anything you want *later...*" They followed the corridor through the deserted dining room of the restaurant toward the kitchen.

"You say that now," continued Ruby, jokingly, "but I know you're just going to turn me down..."

"Tell you what," said Jack, weaving between tables, "if my wife says it's OK with her, then it's OK with me..." *Like that would happen.*

The crimson shot flashed past Jack's ear with a static sizzle, the second sending Nina sprawling with a grunt, face first, Steele skidding to a stop on his knees, drawing his hybrid 1911 as he dropped. He fired two charged particle slugs behind him, the sound ringing off the walls, the rounds blasting through tables and chairs, much different than the energy weapons the Syndicate thugs were using. It served to get them to dive clear, allowing him a second to scoop up Nina and yank her to her feet, a smoking hole in the duffel bag slung across her back.

They plunged through the kitchen doors and towards the back, Steele dumping things behind them on the floor as they ran. He skidded to a stop at the walk-in refrigerator, yanking the door open.

"What the hell are you doing?" hissed Nina.

"Eggs."

"Egg – *Ohhh!*" She grabbed cartons handed her and began throwing them all over the floor.

"Screw that," said Jack, dumping entire cartons at once. He waved her to the exit, waiting behind the open, hefty refrigerator door.

The doors from the dining room swung wide, neon red lances coming from at least three shooters, the rounds crossing all over the kitchen. Protected, he waited. Aiming at a muzzle flash, his first shot producing an abrupt scream and another volley of exchange fire criss-crossing the room, minus one.

Steele blasted off another couple of rounds and peeled back to the exit, shooting as he retreated, realizing this was not a time to stay and fight. They needed to keep moving to avoid being cornered or flanked. The exit closed behind him and he backed away, shooting the control panel, the sound echoing in the narrow alleyway behind the Blue Moon Hotel. *Ooh, that can't be good...*

"Look at this, ruined half my damn clothes," grumbled Nina, examining the hole in her duffel.

"Better than a hole in you," he retorted, grabbing her by the hand and pulling. "Gotta go."

They did their best to blend in to the small crowds that walked the streets of the Island in its peak business hours, but there weren't too many women walking around loose. A transport slid to a stop alongside them and Jack's hand went immediately to the grip of his sidearm. "Hey," said the girl leaning out the window. "Room 410, right?"

"Who wants to know?" asked Jack.

"Room 405. Get in, *hurry!*" The door slid open, four more girls huddled in the back seat. As soon as Jack and the girls were in, the door closed and the driver took off. "So, where are we going?"

"We?" blinked Jack.

"You're the guy on the news aren't you? The one in the chase with the Lawmen?"

Steele's mouth screwed sideways in apprehension, "I might be."

"Then you need to get off this rock. The Syndicate has a bounty on your head... I heard five million. Preferably dead. So any idiot with a pulse pistol is going to be gunning for you. Including the Lawmen if you go back to the *big rock.*" She steered around slower traffic. "My guess is you're a pilot, am I right?"

"Yeah, you could say that..."

"Then anywhere you're going, we're going. Because we need to get off this rock as bad as you do. Do you have a ship - where are we going?"

"To the yacht basin..."

She glanced at him in the mirror, "The only ships in the yacht basin are Syndicate ships. And since you just made the biggest move against the Syndicate anyone's ever seen on this rock, I'm guessing you're not Syndicate..."

"No I'm not."

"So you're going to steal one?" She shook her head, "I can see you like to live dangerously, mister. You're either crazy or lucky..."

"A little of both," interrupted Nina, sarcastically.

"We'll never get into the basin by vehicle," said the driver, "we'll have to take the train and walk..."

■ ■ ■

The train wound its way lazily around the Island, ducking in and out of the rock, providing alternating views of tunnels and stars. Sitting in the window seat next to Jack, Nina kicked his foot, motioning toward a group of riders ahead of them with a discreet nod. They were huddled around a video screen mounted between the windows, throwing quick glances around the train.

"I've got a bad feeling about this," he whispered. "Can you see what they're watching?"

"Looks like a newscast..."

"Oh that's not good..."

"It's not," breathed Nina, "I think they've recognized you..."

One of the other girls from the Blue Moon leaned over Steele's shoulder from behind, "What's going on?"

"Nothing good... if anything happens, keep your head down. Tell the others." Jack's hand rested on the grip of his sidearm. He tried to appear casually disinterested, not making direct eye contact. "It'll be the big scruffy guy with the beard..."

"What about the skinny guy to his left?"

"He's a wannabe. The beard is the real deal, he hasn't taken his eyes off us and he hasn't blinked yet. The guy with the white hair on the other side is the wild card." Jack popped the released on his holster and pulled the hybrid 1911 clear, the muzzle pointing at the back of the empty seat in front of him. The charged particle rounds would pass through it without deviation.

"They both have their hands in their jacket pockets..."

148

"I see that." Steele flashed a wicked smile, "Do I know you, mister?"

The big man blinked, "What?"

Success, he'd broken the man's concentration. "I said, do I know you... You're staring at me like a long-lost brother or something."

"You... look familiar," announced the Beard.

"I have that kind of face," mused Jack. "Happens all the time. Forget it," he waved with his free hand. The Beard nodded and turned his back, the others redirecting their attention back to the video screen. The cop in him wasn't sure if they'd lost their nerve, like a shoplifter being engaged by a store clerk, or if this was a sly tactic. He was hoping they'd lost their nerve but the little voice at the back of his head was telling him they were simply rethinking their plan.

"This is our stop," whispered one of the girls from behind, "we must get off here."

"Use the exit behind us," he whispered back. "I'll follow you. Make it quick and don't stop, don't look back."

Steele slid out of his seat to let Nina pass behind him, his gun hand still hidden by the seat back in front of him. "Go, *go,*" he breathed. He dropped back into the seat, sitting on its edge as he quickly checked over his shoulder, almost all the girls were out on the platform. The Beard's men were watching casually, perhaps waiting for the right moment. He had a feeling they wanted to shoot him in the back. He wasn't going to give them that chance as he rose from his seat, his gun hand hidden behind his thigh, backing toward the rear door.

They all moved at once, shooting on the run, charging him. He fired once before diving between the seats on the other side of the aisle, their pulse lasers slashing past him on both sides, burning holes in the seats. To prevent catastrophic damage or explosive decompression, the pulse lasers didn't penetrate most cover. Unfortunately for the Beard and his men, Steele's charged particle blaster didn't suffer the same limitation. Crouching, he could see the top of white hair, a gun hand over the top of the seat back shooting blindly. Peering past the edge of the seat in front of him, Jack squeezed the trigger twice, the distinctive bark of the hybrid 1911 echoing in the train car, the rounds punching through White Hair's cover with ease, producing a scream and a flailing of arms as he toppled over, his pulse laser skittering across the floor.

"C'mon Jack! I can't hold the door much longer!" shouted Nina from the rear exit.

"Keep your head down," he shouted back, shooting over the top of the seat. Pulse lasers sizzled over his head.

"Give it up mister and we'll let the bitches go!"

"You can kiss my ass, fatman!" The train lurched and stopped, trying to resume its route, stalled by Nina at the door. Steele leapfrogged over the seat behind him, dropping to the floor, looking under the seats. *Feet and knees...* He squeezed off several rounds, the empty charged particle propellant casings tinkling across the train's floor. He heard the screams and jumped to a crouch, bolting into the aisle and heading for the rear door, crimson slashes flashing past him, one tugging at his jacket. With his free arm he collected Nina at the door as they rolled onto the platform in a tumble, the doors spasming. "Dammit," he said looking down, "this was brand new leather. Fuckers..." He quickly swung, leveling the 1911, snapping off two quick shots just before the doors closed, spidering an outer window on the train before it pulled away. "Deal with *that*, asshole."

"The girls went on ahead to see if they could pick a ship," said Nina, rising to her feet, offering Jack her hand. He took it and she pulled him to his feet.

"Do they know what to look for?" he asked, checking his magazine, swapping it for a full one.

■ ■ ■

It only took Nina and Jack about five minutes to reach the docks, a cavernous area five stories tall, with network of metal walkways that extended around the end of the Island in an arc, docking clamps on articulated arms holding ships of various sizes in place above and below them.

Pausing in a shadowed area, they scanned for the girls. "Where the hell are they?"

"You don't suppose they got caught, do you?" asked Nina.

Steele scrutinized the ships at hand. "I hope not." A jolt and rumble like rolling thunder shook the walkway beneath their feet, followed by sirens and flashing lights three levels below them. Nina shot him a concerned look. "Explosive decompression," he grinned, "train go boom."

Movement caught Nina's eyes, "Over there," she pointed. About halfway across, a group of girls was running up the stairs from a lower level. Reaching the same level Jack and Nina were on, they continued up the

150

winding staircase, taking two steps at a time. "Where are they going?" she wondered aloud. *"There,"* she pointed, answering her own question. The girls from 405 were leaning over the railing at the very top, waving the girls up, a ship berthed behind them.

"Let's go!"

Jack and Nina bolted out into the open, across the walkway toward the staircase. The girls from 405 were waving from above but Jack had neither the time nor the inclination to wave back. Thirty-feet from the stairs, he suddenly realized what they were waving about as two Syndicate men appeared from below, running up the stairs after the girls. Focused on the chase, they didn't give a sideways glance as they rounded the rail and up the next flight of stairs.

Stunned at his seeming invisibility, Steele lengthened his stride, pounding across the metal grating of the walkway, quickly pulling away from Nina. Closing on the two men ahead of him, he grabbed the rail as he neared, swinging the corner wildly and taking the stairs two at a time. Lunging hard he caught the closest man by the ankle, the thug lurching into the stairs face-first, splitting open his face on the edge of the stair in front of him, knocking him senseless. Steele scrambled over his body as the man's partner twisted in-flight, off balance, to confront him. Steele swung hard but the man was out of reach, leaning back to avoid the haymaker, still trying to maintain his footing. He backed hard against the rail, top-heavy and with a sweep Steele dislodged his footing and the man went backward with a scream, over the rail, falling onto a walkway rail two levels below with a bone-crushing thud.

Nina rounded from the landing below Jack, the Syndicate man behind him face down on the stairs, his face smashed and bloody, groggily fishing in his jacket for his pulse laser. She threw herself bodily on him, her knife grasped in both hands, her weight and momentum driving the lengthy blade between his shoulder blades to the hilt. Steele whirled at the scream but it was short-lived, Nina trying to wrench the blade free.

The sound of more footsteps ringing on the metal stairway from below seemed to be closing fast. "Forget it, kiddo," he said reaching back, grabbing her hand, "gotta go..."

The dash to the ship was a minor maze of walkways leading to different ships, some ramping up in odd directions, the girls cheer-leading from the ship's berthing dock. Somehow there were twice as many women as before and there were more coming from multiple directions.

"Where the hell are they all coming from?" asked Jack, tromping to a stop at the base of the boarding ramp. "And where the hell are we going to put them all?"

"Don't you worry about that," said the woman from 405, the driver of the transport, "I got this," she added patting his face. "You just get your ass in that cockpit and fly this thing. I'll work the dock controls." Winnipool was her name, she was the older sister, the matron, the mother-figure for most of the girls. She had been around longer than most and she knew more than she probably should have.

Without hesitation or further deliberation, Steele grabbed Nina's hand and dragged her up the short boarding ramp. "C'mon, I need you with me." The interior of the ship was a cross between a luxury yacht and a whorehouse, the warm, damp interior smelling musty."Oh, what the hell," he moaned, making his way to the cockpit, "it's a freaking party bus..."

"What's that smell?" asked Nina, wrinkling her nose.

"Booze, sweat and sex... if I had to guess," muttered Jack, plopping down into the pilot's seat, steering Nina to the copilot's seat. "A decade of it..." He started flipping switches, activating systems on a preflight checklist hanging on the flight yoke. Good thing the air system was one of the first things on the list... he dialed the anti gravity to ten percent, enough to make the ship buoyant but a stable neutral.

"Mister! *Mister!*" screamed a girl running through the ship's interior, appearing at the cockpit doorway, "they're shooting!"

Steele sprang to his feet, pointing at Nina *"Stay!* Don't touch *anything!"*

"I'm *not a dog,* you know!" she called after him as he disappeared.

Laser fire came and went in all directions. God only knows where the girls got the pulse lasers, but they were doing a fair job of protecting the last group of girls sprinting across the metal walkways toward the ship. *Where are all these girls coming from...?* Steele ran down the ramp passing Ruby who spun and went down as he passed her, screaming in pain. He doubled back, holstered his 1911 and scooped her up, carrying her into the ship, lying her on the floor, darting back out.

"Everybody inside! *Let's go!"* From the top of the ramp he was able to see the hiding spots of some of the Syndicate men, pumping rounds through their meager cover with his particle blaster. He quickly became the focus of return fire, the red hot slashes splashing on the ship's hull, scorching the surface, smelling like burnt electronics. He ran down the ramp, allowing the girls to board, the Syndicate focusing on him. He whirled at the scream behind him...

"Winnie!" screamed the girls still on the birthing dock.

"I got her!" he shouted, pointing at the ship, "get aboard!" They retreated from the rail, carrying the only survivor of the last group that attempted to make it across to the ship, her unconscious form hanging limply between two girls, three more firing as they retreated to the safety of the ship.

Jack dropped to a knee next to Winnipool, who was crumpled against the docking control pedestal. "C'mon, let's get you inside..."

"I'm not going anywhere..." she wheezed, looking down at the two gaping holes in her stomach and ribcage.

Steele tried not to look at her exposed ribs, his eyes tearing up, "You'll be OK, we have a good doctor, we'll get you all fixed..."

She put her fingertips on his lips, "So sweet of you to say, but I was a doctor... in a life before here. We both know..." she inhaled sharply, her eyes rolling up before coming back to lucidity again. "It's alright; I never expected to make it off this rock alive. But I'm fine with it..." She patted his face as before. "You go, get those girls to safety... a better life..."

Steele could hear the calls of the girls and the running of boots on the metal walkways. He was about to be overrun. He turned back and kissed her on the forehead, giving her a hug. Words failed him.

"Let the wings of the Lords guide you," she whispered. Go. *Go hard...*" She grabbed his arm as he rose, *"Go hard..."* her hand slipped away.

Torn, grieving for someone who he'd just met, he pushed the knot down in his stomach and mentally wrenched himself free, firing at the advancing thugs as he ran up the boarding ramp. He paused at the door looking over his shoulder, she smiled weakly and shot the first man to round the railing to the birthing dock.

■ ■ ■

Steele dropped into the pilot's seat and belted himself in. "Everybody sit or lie down!" He flipped the engine starters, listening to them spin up. "You might want to go sit with Ruby," he said to Nina without looking, "she's hit." It barely registered that Nina was up and out of the seat before he finished saying it, he was still thinking about Winnie's last words... *go hard*. His fingers poised over the engine igniters, he felt a little numb. A little numb and a lot angry. *This is for you Winnie...* The engines lit with a throaty

153

tandem *whump* and he could imagine whoever was controlling the yacht basin's traffic losing their mind over lit engines inside the Island.

Going hard, Winnie... When Steele shoved the throttle forward, three-hundred feet of flame instantly incinerated everything and everyone on the walkways. The metal stairways and walkways turned to molten slag, docking arms and supports melting, collapsing under their own weight. Weakened docking systems burdened with moored ships crashed through the levels below, crushing them on the Island's floor and cooking everything within about a thousand foot radius, leaving the Syndicate's Island in utter chaos.

Glancing at the sensor sweep, several light craft launched from Rikovik's Reef proper and Steele realized they were about to have some very unhappy company. He slid the throttle to the far stop and input the coordinates for a rendezvous with the Raven. "TESS, connect us with Brian Carter."

■ ■ ■

Brian's TESS lit up, her holo-screen popping into view above his wrist. "Incoming from Jax Mercury..." she cooed, smiling at him. Jack's face appeared, TESS' face becoming an animated thumbnail off to one side.

"I've got a little situation here, Bri..."

"Talk to me boss..."

"I've got fast movers at my back, and I'm flying an unarmed bus that can barely get out of its own way..."

Brian looked up from TESS' holo-screen, "Yellow alert!" The warning sounded, accompanied by flashing yellow lights throughout the ship. "Mr. Ragnaar, do we have his coordinates?"

"Aye, sir. Locked in."

"Best speed..." nodded Brian.

"Aye, flying it like we stole it..."

"What's your ETA Brian?" asked Jack.

"Fifteen minutes."

"I've got maybe five before they overtake me..."

■ ■ ■

The Lawmen were not particularly pleased with Steele's answers when they demanded that he return to Rikovik's Reef with the ship and its human

154

cargo belonging to the Syndicate. No, and he certainly didn't offer anything to assuage their already surly mood. In fact, he probably made it worse. Much worse. Admittedly, *kiss my ass,* was not a viable negotiation tactic. But in Jack's defense, negotiation is about give and take, coming to an agreeable middle ground where both sides make concessions and both sides enjoy some progress. But you had to have something to bargain with... with an empty vacuum of options, Steele probably let his attitude get the better of him.

Strapped into the copilot's seat, Nina closely monitored the sensors and shields, allowing Jack to concentrate on flying. "There's something big on the edge of our sweep..."

"Concentrate on the ones shooting at us please," he testily reminded her.

"Don't get your undies in a wad, I'm watching..." She adjusted the sensors, zooming in on the flight of pursuit craft which gave her a dimensional view, providing her with the details she needed. "They're bracketing left and right, you'll need to go up or down..."

Lances of intense green passed on either side, and Steele knew that was a warning shot. "Mmm, Boron guns. Lightweight stuff..."

"Can they hurt us?"

"Oh yeah. Our shields are light and we have no armor to speak of. Think you can route shield power aft when we need it?"

"Aft?"

"To the back, because it's about to get real dicey..." The ship bucked and the screen with the ships statistics showed an immediate drop in shield strength. "And that was just a love tap to remind us they mean business."

Nina busied herself with restoring shield strength to the stern of the ship. "Sweeping in on the left..."

Steele pulled left, hoping to cross them in front of each other. But it was like trying to outmaneuver a sports car with a school bus. A few shots went wide, green lances lighting up the darkness, but still more connected with the rear shields. Steele began weaving as unpredictably as he could, up, down, side to side but he realized the bus wasn't going to last long. The Lawmen would simply pick them apart at their leisure. "They're trying to take out the engines," he growled, manhandling the controls. "They're being careful not to damage the hull, they want their cargo back."

"Coming in on the left again..."

Steele broke low, not wanting to repeat his earlier maneuver, the green streaks passing over the top of the ship. He immediately changed directions, flashes of green passing over the port wing.

"The ones on the right are dropping back."

"Easier to match our maneuvers if they're not too close..." Steele wrenched the yoke over, barrel-rolling the bus as boron green streaks passed all around. The ship jolted once, then twice, the status screen lighting up with flashing yellow zones. "Shields can't take much more..." he winced. It jolted again, the screen flashing red as a warning buzzer sounded. *"Dammit...* shields are down!" He could feel his heart pounding in his ears, sweat stinging his eyes, helpless panic attempting to fight its way to the surface.

"I know, I know," said Nina fighting back tears of frustration, "I'm doing the best I can but she's not producing enough power to regenerate the..."

The next hit was jarring, sounding heavily metallic, like someone hit the hull with a sledgehammer, the ship lurching, warning buzzers and red lights flashing all across the status screen. The operating temperature for the Starboard engine shot up so quickly that the overheat alarm surprised Jack. In mid-reach for the emergency shutdown it let loose, grenading itself into confetti and spinning shrapnel, rolling the ship on its side from the torque of the remaining engine. "Son of a bitch," Steele eased the throttle back and wrestled with the controls.

"I lost one of them, where'd he go?" asked Nina.

"If we're lucky our engine took him out," replied, Jack, concentrating on control. "Dammit, we're losing fuel." He punched the fire control button for the right engine, hoping it might stop or at least reduce the fuel loss.

A Lawmen pursuit craft pulled up close on the starboard side, flying even with the bus' cockpit, the pilot tapping on his earpiece. "We have received clearance to destroy that ship if you do not return to Rikovik's Reef. Which I will happily do, considering you just killed my flight leader..."

■ ■ ■

The Raven's bow pierced the GOD portal, the filaments of color dancing, reaching across her hull like neon lightning as she pushed through into the black from her short jump.

"Forward gunners targeting..." announced Maria.

Commander Brian Carter leaned forward in his seat, peering at the big screen. "What *the hell* is he flying?"

The Raven's main tachyon particle drivers, opened fire, their heavy thumping felt in the floor, neon blue streaks passing through the Lawman's craft flying alongside the damaged yacht, cutting through it, instantly blowing it into pieces. The two remaining Lawmen split, one sweeping in on the tail of the yacht, the other breaking for Rikovik's Reef. Between the Raven's main guns and her mercury Gatling batteries, neither one made it very far. The Raven turning them into unrecognizable wreckage.

■ ■ ■

The Raven's sudden appearance was a welcome sight but the pucker factor when her main guns and mercury Gatling batteries lit off in his direction made Steele want to be almost anywhere else. One moment the Lawman was there on his right, then he was gone, replaced with a flash, a swelling spray of debris and spinning chunks of mangled wreckage fluttering outward.

He nosed the bus over hard to expose the Lawman sweeping in on his tail and the streaks of silver from the mercury Gatling batteries were so close their reflections flashed across the surfaces of the control screens.

"Damn, that's close!" shouted Nina, "Are they nuts?"

Steele saw the bogie disappear from the sensor grid. "Just that good," he croaked, swallowing hard. The Raven passed over the bus in a streak, chasing down the last Lawman.

His earpiece chirped, "Stay on course, Jax. We will circle back and meet you at the rendezvous, there's another bogie inbound..."

"Copy that," replied Jack. "Don't let them delay you; we need to get out of this system."

■ ■ ■

Slowly drifting in the rubble of Rikovik's mined-out asteroid field, Jack's chin was resting on his steepled fingertips, his elbows on the armrests of the bus' command chair. He was staring out into the darkness and flickering stars, his mind in neutral like the remaining engine. Though they had lost almost a third of the fuel the craft could carry, he dared not shut it off, not

157

knowing how much of the engine control systems were left intact. At least she'd stopped leaking fuel...

Nina reentered the cockpit with two bottles of water, handing one to Jack. "How are we doing?"

"Not great," he replied, popping the seal on the water. "I've run all the diagnostics she's got, but it's not telling me why our shields won't come above fifty percent." He took a long draw on the water. "We lost a third of our fuel load but we're running only one engine, so I have no idea what that's going to do to our range..."

"Navigation won't calculate that out?"

"She's pretty beat up, I'm not sure I can trust the navigation to get it right. It was off three minutes on our arrival to the rendezvous point. Stretch that out over a full system and we could be in big trouble..." He took another long swallow. "How are the girls doing?"

"Scared."

He nodded, "You?"

"Scared," replied Nina, picking casually at the label on the bottle.

He nodded again, he had some serious concerns too. "We'll be OK."

"Are you sure... or are you just saying that to make me feel better?"

"Maybe a little of both," he admitted. "How's Ruby?"

"Sleeping. She'll be OK. One of the girls used to be a nurse on Winnie's surgical team, she gave her a sedative from the emergency medical kit..."

"What about the girl that they carried on?"

Nina picked at the label on her water again. "She doesn't look good, she's real pale. And she hasn't come-to at all. At the very least I think she'll lose her left leg."

"Then maybe it's best she stays out."

Nina looked a little queasy, "Yeah, maybe."

CHAPTER ELEVEN

JENFAR SYSTEM, FREERANGER – DD217: *LITTLE WHITE LIES*

Commander T. B. Yafuscko propped himself up on one elbow to look at the flashing comm link in the darkness of his suite, blinking away the sleep from his brain. He reached over and tapped the screen, leaving the video off. "Report," he whispered.

"Sorry to disturb you Commander, we have recorded a FreeRanger general broadcast."

Tibby rubbed his eyes, "What's the topic Lieutenant?"

"There's been an incident in Rikovik's Reef and Command is looking for some support in the area."

"Details?"

"A few, but they're not terribly clear. Command suggests direct contact with Rikovik's for responding assets."

Tibby sat up and swung his feet off the side of the bed, staring into the darkness, "Any other responders so far?"

"No sir. Not at this time. There are a couple ships stationed in the system though."

"Hmm, well, we've got nothing else pending," said the Commander, thinking aloud, "send an acceptance reply. What's our ETA?"

"About fifty-two hours."

"Send us. Keep me apprised, Lieutenant." Tibby reached back over and tapped on the screen ending the comm. He could feel Grinah there in the darkness, stretching like a cat, her hand rubbing lazily on his back.

"Where are we going?" her voice said sleepily.

"Something going on in Rikovik's Reef... We're going to go and see if we can make some gold."

"Mmmm," she purred, half asleep, "I like gold... Come back to bed for a while."

■ ■ ■

This was not Commander T. B. Yafuscko's first encounter with Rikovik's Reef, he had been to the socially twisted and criminally overrun planetoid before, but he had never had the privilege of speaking with the Primayor. Not that Tibby considered it a privilege, no, but he was sure the Primayor considered it so, *pompous ass.* Tibby stared for a moment at the darkened screen in his office after the communication winked out, wishing he could have the last ten minutes of his life back. Remembering he was not alone, he swiveled his chair around, "So? Thoughts..?"

The three other officers present all began talking at once until he held his hand up, their chatter dying down. He pointed at Grinah, his most trusted confidant. "Ensign, your opinion?"

"Before or after we had to listen to him ramble on about how great and important he was..?" She waved her hand, "Sorry, had to be said. I think he's a shill for the Syndicate."

"There's no doubt in my mind," agreed the Commander. He pointed at his second in command, Dash Zarnev, "Lieutenant?"

The Lieutenant scratched his three-day stubble, "Hmmm, I think beyond the obfuscation and bullshit, there is gold to be had here. Do I trust him? No. Do I think there's a job here? Yes. But I think we ask for a good-faith retainer. That might tell us if they're willing to pay off on completion."

Tibby nodded. "Point taken, good idea. But what do you make of the other three ships they have in the region? Why do you think they want to hire outside guns to handle this?"

"As I hear it," explained Dash, "those guys are the gatekeepers. They're FreeRangers, but they're salaried by the Reef. I have a friend on a ship that runs supplies through that area, he says those boats never stray more than a quarter of a system from the rock, and never more than one at a time. Those would be the guys we'd be dealing with if this clown," he flipped a wave at the blank vid-screen, "decided not to pay off."

"Duly noted," Tibby stroked his own stubble, realizing he'd forgotten to shave. "More guns than we've got. Not something we'd want to tangle with."

"Three to one is bad odds."

"Still, I suppose we could involve the FreeRanger Council if things went into collections, they could impose some heavy sanctions..."

Dash made a face of distaste. "That takes time though. Meanwhile we're out the time and energy."

"Let's see what he says to a retainer, we'll make our decision then." The Commander pointed at the last contributor, "Doc, what do you think?"

The ship's surgeon was leaning against the holo-chart table, his arms folded across his chest. "Well, I'm convinced he's being one-hundred percent honest – about how important he thinks he is. But according to his eye movements and mannerisms, he's telling more than little white lies about everything else. There are some real whoppers in there. I'd go so far as to say some total fabrication woven in."

Tibby pursed his lips, "Yeah, that's about what I thought."

"I can go over the video playback of the conversation, Commander, I should be able to separate fact from fiction..."

"Sounds good Doc, get back to me with what you find. Should prove interesting. We'll give the good Primayor a follow-up call when we reach the Rikovik system." He pointed at Dash Zarnev, "Lieutenant, you've got the bridge, we need to get some breakfast..."

■ ■ ■

Jack Steele's TESS lit up, her holo-screen popping into view. "Incoming signal from Brian Carter."

"Connect, TESS."

Brian's face appeared, TESS' animated face sliding over to one side of the screen. "You OK over there?"

"Yes and no," replied Jack. "I lost an engine and dropped a third of my fuel load. She's pretty shot up... Navigation is glitchy and I'm not sure I can calculate my range accurately."

"Send me your Op Stats, we'll run it through our system."

Steele glanced at TESS' face and she acknowledged his need with a nod. "Sending."

"Nice timing, by the way," commented Steele, "they were about to finish us off."

Brian smirked, "Probably the shortest GOD jump ever made," he chuckled, "a whole four minutes." There was a pause in the conversation as Brian looked off screen to his right. "OK, Jack, our nav computer calculated out the best settings for your fuel situation. Set your power at seventy-three-and-a-half percent."

"How far will that get us?" asked Steele, adjusting his throttle setting.

"Through the gate and the transition. You'll run out of fuel halfway through the next system; Aegeron Pass..."

"Swell."

"We should be OK," waved Brian, "We're sending the Conquest and Westwind the coordinates, they'll meet us there."

"Don't they have two other systems to go through?" frowned Jack.

"Yeah, but at the snail's pace we'll be cruising, they'll probably beat us there. You sure you don't want them coming here to Rikovik's to get us?"

Steele chewed the inside of his lip. "They'll get jumped at the gate by our little pirate friends... not that they'd be much of a match but I don't want to risk it. Besides, I think this place can be useful if we don't blow our cover."

"Some cover," glowered Brian. "You really think they'd actually let you come back here?"

"Yeah, if they think there's money in it. I think our contact at Deep Black has a lot more pull than she lets on. And depending on her reach, which seems considerable, she may be very useful in more ways than one."

Brian shook his head, "I still don't see how you figure coming back here, waltzing in without them trying to shoot your ass..."

"Greed. Plain and simple. Greed overrides some pretty strong prejudices..."

Brian shrugged, "If you say so I guess. It's your neck." He pinched his lower lip and then waved, his mouth turning up a mischievous little crooked smile. "So OK, I gotta ask; you couldn't find something a little smaller or faster? Something you could have landed in our bay? Explain to me why you decided to steal the equivalent of a flying motorhome..."

Steele let out a slow breath, "We have a few extra passengers..."

"Come again?"

Steele pursed his lips pensively, "We, that is, Nina and I, are not alone... we have a few extra passengers..."

"Twenty-three," interrupted Nina. "Girls."

"Say what?!" exclaimed Brian, leaning closer to his screen.

Steele blinked curiously as TESS' holo-screen divided into two panels, then three, as Lisa and Maria almost simultaneously appeared *"Twenty - three girls?"* they said in unison. "Hiya Nina!" waved Lisa.

Nina waved back, "Hiya Lisa!"

"It's a long story," muttered Jack.

Brian glanced down at his wrist and pointed at a non-existent watch, "Ooh look, we have time."

Steele glanced out at the slowly passing stars. "Smartass," he grumbled.

■ ■ ■

162

"Jack... *Jack,* wake up!"

Steele's eyes popped open, bleary-eyed, "What's wrong?" He looked outside the cockpit, his mind taking a moment to register the shimmering silver transition tunnel, scanning around then back to her. Nina's hands were on the copilot's flight yoke, her eyes wide with a touch of panic. "How long was I asleep?"

"I don't know, five or six hours I guess. Focus Jack, the autopilot shut off and when I tried to put it back on like you showed me, nothing happened. So I've been keeping with the Raven manually. But now the navigation system went blank..."

"Where is she?"

Nina pointed over the dash at a wavering blue-white light, a spec in the distance. "Right there, the blue-white flame?"

"I see it. Let's give them a shout and get them to drop back a bit." Steele noticed his breath in the crisp air of the cockpit and suddenly realized the distinct chill in the air. "Why the hell is it so cold in here?"

"I don't know, I've been too busy steering..."

"Flying," he corrected.

"Whatever."

While still appearing functional, when the ship's comm system refused to broadcast, the first thing that entered Steele's mind was a cascading system failure. "Uh oh... comm's not broadcasting..."

"I can see my breath," said Nina, "I think it's getting colder..."

"TESS, contact Brian Carter." *Please connect, please connect, please connect...* Jack waited impatiently as the unit reached out, but he instinctively knew it was taking too long.

"I'm sorry, Mr. Mercury," apologized TESS, "I cannot reach Brian Carter. The transition tunnel is interfering with the range of my broadcast."

"Crap," he breathed. He grabbed the pilot's yoke, "I've got the bird, go check on the girls." Waiting until Nina was clear of the cockpit, Jack nudged the throttle up to nearly ninety percent to close the gap between the bus and the Raven, quickly initiating a diagnostic cycle on the ship's system with his free hand. Given her severely compromised condition, the ship refused to fly a straight course without constant attention. "TESS, cycle a continuous distress call, we need to get their attention."

"Broadcasting," replied TESS.

163

"Christ, it's freezing back there," huffed Nina, pushing past the curtains into the cockpit. "Everybody's huddled together in the salon. They took all the bedding, pillows and blankets out of the rooms and they're all scrunched together."

"How's Ruby?"

"Awake, in pain, about as comfortable as can be expected. I don't think the other girl is going to make it, though. She's as white as a ghost."

"The cold might actually help her."

Nina tilted her head to one side, "How so?"

Jack shrugged, his attention diverted, trying to get some of the systems to respond, "I just know that for some injuries, doctors will sometimes induce a coma and put a patient in a cold environment. I'm not sure how it works exactly, but I imagine it's like a suspended animation."

▨ ▩ ▨

Lisa Steele was sitting on the deck in the Raven's cargo bay, her back against the landing gear of a four man shuttle, half-watching some of the crew members exercise while she read an electronic version of the Remora's flight manual. She was tempted to sit in the fighter's cockpit while reading to review all the systems while she read. As a visual aid of course. Not that she considered taking it out on a joy ride. No, that wouldn't be safe in a jump tunnel transition. But she enjoyed the thought of an unsupervised flight anyway. Semi-lost in her daydream, the tone of the distress call broadcast by her TESS jolted her back to reality, spilling her coffee at her side and banging her head on the landing gear door. *"Son of a bitch,"* she hissed, crawling free of the nose and sprinting across the deck toward the exit.

▨ ▩ ▨

"TESS, put it on the big screen," commanded Brian Carter. "Helm, slow to one third, keep us above transition threshold protocols." The video was full of snow and the audio was distorted and loaded with static.

"Sir," said TESS, "It appears Mr. Mercury's comms are down. His signal is coming directly from his TESS unit and she does not have the power to generate a signal greater than the power fields of the transition tunnel. This is the best we will get at this distance."

"Will he receive what we send?"

"Yes, Commander. Since our signal is boosted by the ship he will receive a clean signal."

"Good." Brian plucked the holo-screen from TESS and moved it freely, setting it next to one of the monitors on his chair. Since it was well within its six-foot radius from the wrist unit, it floated motionless where it was placed despite the use of his hands on his command keyboards. "Jack, I know you can hear me," he spoke to the screen, "we have received your distress call and we've reduced speed to allow you to catch up. Your signal is too weak for video and audio. Ping my TESS every two minutes, she'll be able to tell when we have a solid signal..." The static and garble ended, with a single ping as a response. Brian sat back, pensive, deep in thought. "What's the status on the yacht?"

Raulya glanced over her shoulder, "It is moving up but her gain on our lead is slow..."

"We shouldn't have pulled so far ahead," Brian lamented.

"You were following protocol, Brian," reminded Maria from the first officer's seat. "We needed to be far enough ahead to exit the gate first and deal with any unknowns before an unprotected ship was exposed to a possible enemy engagement."

The bridge door swept open and Lisa tromped in at a trot past the Marines standing guard. "What's going on? I got a distress call from Jack but then nothing..."

"We don't know yet. He can hear us but not the other way around," replied Brian.

"But..."

Brian stayed her question with an open hand, an idea popping into his head. "Mr. Ragnaar, is there a speed differential between the Raven and the Remora in the transition? If so, what would it be?"

"There is," nodded the big man. "There is an equation of weight, physical size and overall mass that determines minimum speed for a ship in transition. A jump tunnel is created by the gates which are stable worm-hole generators. The tunnel is basically an electronic fabric tube, too slow or heavy and you tear a hole and fall through. But lighter ships can go slower without creating that stress."

"Can you calculate that speed for both the Remora and the yacht, please?"

"Aye, sir."

Brian turned to Lisa, "Suit up lady..."

"I'll go with her," said Maria, sliding out of her seat.

"No. You won't," said Brian, cutting her short with a wave. He looked at Lisa, "Take Draza Mac for your rear seat."

"But..." objected Maria.

"I need you here, Lieutenant. And she'll need someone to walk her back in for recovery." Maria sat back down without saying a word, looking like she'd bit into a lemon.

"Listen up, lady," said Brian, looking Lisa square in the eyes. "This is dangerous and you need to follow exactly what I'm telling you. Under no circumstances do you allow your bird to fall below the numbers Mr. Ragnaar gives you. And under no circumstances do you turn around to change direction. You must maintain forward speed and allow him to catch up to you. If he falls below his speed, don't be near him or you'll both drop out. Understand?"

"I understand. Where do you go if you drop out?"

"Null space."

"What's null space?"

Brian pursed his lips and shook his head, "Another system, uncharted space..." he shrugged, "nobody knows. But it's pretty certain we'll never see you again. Whether you live or not is anyone's guess."

"Swell," she sighed, "thanks for clearing that up."

■ ■ ■

Nina was scraping frost off of the inside of the cockpit glass with something that looked like a spatula she found in the ship's small galley. D-d-d-damm," she shivered, "how much f-f-fucking colder can it get?"

"More than a hundred degrees below zero," replied Jack through clenched teeth, his breath hanging in the air.

"I don't want to die like this..."

"We're not gonna' die, we're gonna' make it." Jack had TESS' screen sitting up on the dash, the only light in the cockpit, most of the other electronics dead or offline. "TESS are you broadcasting?" He pulled the cuffs of his jacket down over his hands.

"Yes, Mr. Mercury. We are not in sufficient range yet to communicate."

"Dammit," he breathed. Steele thought about his wife and son, his parents, friends, extended family, God and Voorlak. *Were they one in the same?* He wasn't sure it mattered at that particular point. "I sure hope you didn't bring me all the way out here just for this."

"D-d-did you say something?" chattered Nina.

Jack wasn't even aware he'd said it out loud. "No, nothing, just thinking out loud."

"Well if it's how to g-g-get us someplace warm, I'm all ears."

TESS' face appeared on her holo-screen, "I am getting a; *clear to broadcast,* message..."

"Then broadcast dammit, broadcast!"

Lisa's face appeared on the screen, her face framed in a helmet, the visor up. "How's it going big brother?"

"Lisa? Where are you?"

"Keep going straight, Jack. I'm ahead of you." She looked away for a moment. "We're sending you some adjusted performance numbers for the yacht..."

"Ship's computer is offline, I won't get it."

"It's coming through TESS," replied Lisa. "What's going on?"

"We're f-f-freezing our asses off!" shouted Nina. "That's what's going on!"

"Cascade failure," explained Jack. "System by system. The engine is still running, the oxygen system is still running, but nearly everything the computer controls has gone offline one at a time. We're cold and blind."

"Can you reboot or something?" asked Lisa.

"If I do and it affects the propulsion system, we're dead."

"Hmm. How's your fuel?"

"No idea. Last reading was about twenty percent before that system went dark."

"How long ago was that?"

Jack checked TESS. "TESS says it was an hour and thirty-seven minutes ago."

Lisa turned away from the screen to consult Draza Mac in the back seat who was running the calculations. She turned back to the screen, "You're going through your fuel faster than we had calculated..."

"How much longer do we have?"

"About an hour. You should make the gate, no problem..." she lied.

"Should?"

Lisa reached through her visor and rubbed her forehead. "Well we don't know exactly what fuel you have left and what you're burning or losing, so it's not concrete. But Mac figured in the difference from what was originally estimated earlier and what you actually had an hour and thirty-seven minutes ago. Is your power still at seventy-three-and-a-half percent?"

"No, I'm up at ninety percent trying to catch up."

"Alright," nodded Lisa, "let's get you an info feed... I'm linking my TESS with yours, she's going to feed you telemetry, navigation and scans so you can see. You may need to widen her screen so you can see it all. Let's get you back down to about seventy-five percent power and see if we can milk some more mileage out of that crate."

"Got it. Nice, thanks." Steele eased the throttle back, finally feeling a little ray of hope, praying the proverbial light at the end of the tunnel wasn't an oncoming train.

■ ■ ■

Fifteen minutes passed before Jack's battered ship finally slid alongside Lisa's unarmed Remora. She matched the speed of the yacht, slowly completing a circuit around it for damage assessment. With more than a third of the hull scorched, she was surprised it was still intact without a major hull failure of some kind. The extensive damage to the tail, stabilizers, their associated maneuvering jets and hull where the right engine used to be, revealed structural ribs and internal components.

"Well I think I've found the problem..."

"Really? Can we fix it?"

Lisa's mind drew a blank for a moment. "What? No! How would you fix... Never mind..." She realized he was pulling her leg when she heard him laughing. "Ass." She glanced over at the cockpit of the yacht, a dull glow inside. "I'm glad you still have your sense of humor..."

"And not much else..." he quipped.

While Draza Mac forwarded all communications and telemetry to the Raven, Lisa kept an eye on Jack via TESS' live video feed. He looked exhausted. She imagined the cold would compound that and his eyes looked heavy, so she did her best to keep him engaged. TESS's sensors were feeding Lisa atmospheric data from the yacht; oxygen supply was right where it should be but the temperature was down to twenty-two degrees and falling.

Draza Mac reached over his console and tapped on Lisa's seat back, " Raven has just entered Aegeron Pass," he said quietly.

Lisa gave him an abrupt wave to acknowledge she'd heard him. "So, Jack, I'm thinking steaks for dinner... what do you think?"

Jack nodded slowly, "Mmm, nice... medium well. Blackened on the outside to seal in the juices... a little pink on the inside. And some nice big steak fries..."

"I really want a nice tall cocktail," volunteered Lisa.

"Hot chocolate," countered Jack. "In a mug I can wrap my hands around..."

"I vote for the hot chocolate too," mumbled Nina, readjusting the blanket wrapped around her. "It would be great if I could drink it in a nice hot shower..."

It was subtle, but Lisa realized Jack's ship was falling back from her abreast position. Telemetry confirmed the yacht was slowing down. "Jack, have you adjusted your throttle setting?"

"No, I haven't touched it."

"You're dropping back, my speed is constant."

Steele adjusted the throttle, adding a little power to maintain his position. "I don't hear anything different, she sounds OK." He cocked his head to one side, listening intently, the growl of the engine droning on as before. "Maybe she's got a blocked injector or two."

"It's alright," said Lisa reassuringly, "the gate is coming up." She could see the gate's beacon on her scope, the gate itself not physically visible yet.

Draza Mac reached over his console again and tapped on Lisa's seat back, " Raven says Aegeron Pass is clear. They expect the Conquest and Westwind to be on time."

"Excellent..."

"What's excellent?" asked Jack.

"Ageron Pass is clear, we're good to go. Everything's running as plan..." She watched her brother spin in his seat. "What's going on?"

"I don't know, I just heard a boom."

"Hold on..." Lisa inched her throttle back, allowing the yacht to slide by as she eased past behind it, around to the other side. "Shit," she breathed.

"What? *What?*"

"You have a flameout. See if she'll restart."

She watched her brother on TESS' holo-screen, stab at the igniter switch. There was a sudden belch of flame from the engine as it relit, providing power for a moment, raising her hopes, before dashing them again as the engine went dark once more. After several tries the engine refused to relight even its igniter.

"He's out of fuel," said Draza Mac.

169

"How long can he coast at speed?"

"According to the computer calculations, he won't make the gate. They'll drop out of the transition tunnel at less than three minutes to the gate..."

"No. *No!* No that's not going to happen... we're so close. No I refuse to..."

"I don't think there's anything you can do about it, Skipper," offered Draza Mac. "It's not like we can refuel him."

■ ■ ■

The conference call over, Lieutenant Commander Brian carter and Lieutenant Maria Arroyo stared at TESS' blank holo-screen sitting on the desk in Brian's office. The Commander didn't want to go back out onto the bridge, he felt sick to his stomach. Death wasn't even certain in null space, not immediately anyway. The reality was no one knew. Or if they did they weren't talking about it. Was it like limbo? What happened next? Was it just a void, or were you dropped into an unknown system? If your ship was well supplied maybe you'd survive a while. Brian thought about his Catholic upbringing, maybe it was like Purgatory. He shook it off, he hadn't thought about that for years. It seemed so intangible when he was a kid. He wasn't sure it felt any more real now. What he was sure about, was that he was about to lose a friend he'd known for nearly a decade.

"There's got to be something we can do," sniffed Maria, fighting her emotions.

"I'm all ears if you have any ideas."

She shook her head without answering. "Oh my God, what are we going to tell Fritz?"

"Fritz? What are we going to tell *Alité?*"

■ ■ ■

Having nothing to lose, the systems reboot restored a couple of the yacht's systems, mainly climate control. The cabin was a balmy fifty degrees now. Without propulsion, uneven or otherwise, the ship needed no guidance, coasting along on its momentum. Steele sat with his arms folded and his feet up on the copilot's seat, Nina sitting in the salon with Ruby and the other girls. He stared out at the gate, so close yet so far. He glanced at what little readouts had been restored, the speed slowly ticking down as the ship lost momentum. Another minute and they would tear through the electronic fabric of the tunnel and disappear.

"The Lord is my shepherd; I shall not want. He maketh me to lie down in green pastures: he leadeth me beside still waters. He restoreth my soul: he leadeth me in the paths of righteousness for his name's sake. Yea though I walk through the valley of the shadow of death, I will fear no evil, because I am the baddest motherf..." *No hubris* he scolded himself. "I will fear no evil, for thou art with me, thy rod and thy staff they comfort me. Thou preparest a table before me in the presence of mine enemies: thou annointest my head with oil; my cup runneth over. Surely goodness and mercy shall follow me all the days of my life: and I will dwell in the house of the Lord forever."

He was surprised he wasn't angry. Or disappointed. He was accepting. Voorlak had told him he was special, that his destiny was to become something more than he was. Maybe this was the way it was supposed to be. Maybe this was the path to that destiny. He had no choice but to accept and trust what had been laid out before him. That is not to say he wasn't worried, concerned or fearful. But it was beyond his control. Steele regretted not being able to speak with his wife for a last time. He glanced at the speed and back up at the gate looming ahead... It was hard to believe it was so close...

He unmuted TESS' mic, the video having continued unabated. "OK Lisa, get clear and hit the gate. I don't want you in here, who knows what will happen... And don't forget to get that video to Alité for me..." He looked out of the right then left side of the cockpit, unable to see the Remora fighter anywhere. "Lisa?" He glanced at the speed sensors as they fell below their minimum speed, his heart skipping a beat, a spike of adrenalin shooting up his back quickening his pulse and his breathing, a sudden cold chill washing over his body as he saw stars through an opening in the tunnel wall.

"Hold onto something, Jack..."

"Lisa, where are you, what are you doing? It's time for you to get your bird out of here..!"

The sudden jolt nearly threw him from the pilot's seat, the slam resounding through the hull followed by a cacophony of squealing metal and screams of the girls in the salon. The sounds of protesting metal was replaced by a severe vibration threatening to tear the ship apart at the seams, the cabinets throughout the ship emptying themselves of their contents, a cascade of noise.

171

■ ■ ■

Even with her shields up, Lisa watched the nose of her Remora crumple as she shoved the yacht toward the gate, easing the throttle gradually higher.

"We're below speed protocols, Skipper..."

"I know, Mac. I know..."

"Sensors indicate an opening in the tunnel wall on our right..."

Lisa's heart was pounding and she couldn't tell if her hands were shaking or if it was from the vibration in the frame of the Remora from all the thrust she was applying. "Not something I wanted to hear..."

"Thought you'd want to know."

"I don't! How close are we to the gate?"

"Readings say sixty seconds."

"C'mon baby, you can do it..." she panted, near panic.

"Stars, I can see *stars* through the opening, it's *growing!"*

"Shut up, Mac!"

"Our trajectory is changing, it's pulling on us!"

"I swear to God, Mac..."

The tendrils of color from the gate reached out, dancing across the hull of the crippled yacht and the Remora.

"We're sliding!"

"Ain't gonna happen, that way," hissed Lisa through clenched teeth, "We're going through that *fucking gate!"* She nudged the throttle, imbedding the nose of her fighter further into the stern of the yacht, crushing one of her own sensor systems, half her dash going dark. The color swirl of the gate enveloped them and just as suddenly they slid violently to one side amongst a spread of stars, the two ships separating, debris and mangled metal floating between them. A surge of panic-induced electricity raced though her body, "What just happened?"

"Welcome to Ageron Pass, Skipper..."

172

CHAPTER TWELVE

FORT GEORGE G. MEADE, NSA HEADQUARTERS, MARYLAND :
SPY vs SPY

The sky was a crystal-clear turquoise blue, the morning mist having burned off, the sun shining brightly at the Fort George G. Meade Museum, a couple miles from the NSA Headquarters building.

Agent Doug Mooreland walked along the deserted concrete pathway from the nearly empty parking lot, flipping his collar up, a brisk breeze at his back. He was more than a little concerned, on edge, scanning the tree line, and the empty park. *Why were they meeting outside like this?* Nothing about it felt right. He approached the older man sitting on the park bench on the edge of the walkway facing an assortment of American tanks from various wars. "Deputy Director," he said, sitting down, his hands in the pockets of his overcoat.

"Douglas," acknowledged the man, staring at the tanks on the grass. "A bit different than Florida, eh?"

"About a forty degree difference..."

"Well don't worry, you won't have to endure it for long," he smiled. Out of the corner of his eye he could see Mooreland tense up. "Relax Douglas..."

"Why are we meeting out here?"

The Deputy Director crossed his legs at the knee, his gloved hands resting casually in his lap. "Because I rather enjoy these brisk mornings before the hotter months set in... So if you please, take your hand off the firearm I'm sure you have in your pocket before you accidentally do something we'll both regret." He turned to look Mooreland in the eye, seeing nothing but the agent staring stoically back at him. Unmoved. "Suit yourself, Douglas..."

"So why am I here?"

"Because you and your team have been getting rather sloppy of late, and it has to change."

"You want the equipment and I'm trying to get it for you..."

"You're calling too much attention to yourselves," interrupted the Deputy Director. "You're supposed to operate in the shadows not broad daylight with witnesses. Finesse not force."

"You've been putting a lot of pressure on us for results, we..."

"Have missed some prime opportunities," added the older man, hijacking his sentence. "Look, I don't want to take away your team, I think you are capable of handling this, but the Security Council thought you might be able to use a little incentive, a little boost. So we have a new member for your team..."

"My team is fine, I don't need anybody."

"Oh, but you do." The Deputy Director swept the cuff of his coat back to glance at his watch, "As of five minutes ago, your team is short a man."

"What are you talking about?"

"We decided to retire Pete Whitman."

"Pete?! Nooo not Pete, not Pete..."

"I can assure you, Douglas, it was quick and perfectly painless..."

"Death is never painless," hissed Mooreland, incensed.

"He never felt a thing..." said the older man, reassuringly. "Trust me. Besides, he was holding you back, he was a weak link. You cannot afford that on this mission. I decided to attribute that Chase Holt *catch and release* catastrophe to Peter. Had the Security Council suspected it was your doing... well, let's just say Peter would have had company." The Deputy Director shifted position on the bench, leaning closer, his elbow on the back of the bench. "Now, to your assignment; *find* and pick up the friends, the parents, the ex-wife, in-laws and anyone else you can think of. Bring them all in. In one piece. And for God sakes, you're *secret agents,* start acting like it." He rose from the bench and smoothed his coat, looking up at the sky, "Looks like it's going to be a beautiful day..."

■ ■ ■

Considering the late night he'd had with the Cape Coral shootings, Sheriff Frank Naywood was going casual today, a pair of black tactical pants and a black Sheriff's polo, his shield and rank embroidered on the shirt. He jammed the cruiser's key tag under the buckle of his duty belt and swung his leg out of the open cruiser door, not forgetting to reach for the travel mug of his wife's fresh, hot coffee. "Beautiful morning, eh Buck?" He glanced up at the pale blue sky, scattered clouds drifting past, the last remnants of morning dew drying off the parking lot pavement.

"Not for this guy," replied Buck Harper, walking up, thumbing over at the crime scene. A sedan, parked alone in a nearly empty mall parking lot at the far end of the row was shielded from prying eyes by temporary walls of blue plastic tarps. Curious motorists arriving at the mall drove slowly past, hoping to catch a glimpse of something they could gossip about while shopping.

"Let's try to keep the media out of this for a while. Where's the rest of our guys?"

Buck waved, "Still back in Bimini Basin interviewing neighbors, doing damage reports, collecting evidence..."

The Sheriff nodded, "OK, let's send some uniforms over to help them out and speed things up..."

"Did that boss." The detective glanced at his watch, "I'm hoping to have them clear by noon."

"Good deal." He eyed Buck, "When was the last time you slept?"

The detective shrugged wearily, "What day is it?"

Naywood nodded, he remembered those long days and nights as a lead detective. "Go home and get some sleep, Buck." He motioned to the crime scene, "CSI got here quick." He sipped from the travel mug, "Do we have an identity yet?"

"Drivers license and credit cards all say; Pete Whitman."

The two men walked across the asphalt, ducking under the yellow tape, past the uniformed officers. Detectives and crime scene technicians moved around the car, in and out of view. "The cup of coffee in the guy's cup holder is still warm."

The Sheriff looked into the car from the open driver's window, the victim's head leaning back against the bloodied headrest, his mouth slack, his eyes open, horribly askew, one looking up and left, the other looking right. Blood dripping from his nose had stained his shirt and tie. "How?"

"Two to the back of the head," replied Buck, making a finger pistol. "Small caliber, probably a .22 caliber. Scrambled his brains but good."

"Someone was in the back seat then, this was a hit."

"Looks like it."

Phil Cooper flipped his FBI identification at the officer standing outside the tarps before stepping through the opening, two cups of fresh coffee in his hand. He passed one to Buck Harper, "Here, you look like you need it." He motioned toward the doughnut shop across Colonial Boulevard, "Our cockeyed friend here, was in the coffee shop two hours ago with another guy. Their security tape shows both men in suits, coming in, getting coffee

175

and doughnuts and leaving. You can even see the nose of the car through the front door. It was this one," he tapped on the roof.

Buck glanced back into the car, "Doughnut's gone, half the coffee too."

"Last meal," retorted Cooper sarcastically.

"Pretty shitty last meal. Think he knew it was coming?"

Phil Cooper sipped his coffee. "I doubt it. It looks like business as usual, they picked up something to start their day before their meeting with a third party, here..."

Frank Naywood raised an eyebrow, suspicious. "What do you know about this? *Specifically?*"

"This is one of your actors from last night."

Frank's eyes widened, "What?! Are you *sure?* They offed one of their own guys?"

"Pretty sure," nodded Phil. "Look at his hands," he pointed, "well trimmed nails but rugged hands, those are not executive hands. His hair is tight, everything trimmed... look inside his suit, there won't be any tags. If they forgot to strip his watch, it'll be a very tactical timepiece, totally divergent from his conservative suit. No rings or jewelry and they'll have taken his cell phone. He'll have his driver's license, two credit cards and about a hundred dollars cash. If you run his cards, they will all have a zero balance and no history. When you dust the car, there won't be any fingerprints, probably not even his own." He took a moment to blow the steam off of his coffee, "I'm betting every door was unlocked..."

"They were," said Buck.

Phil took a sip, "Check the security tapes of that store there," he indicated the department store facing them. "If we're lucky, their security cameras will have picked up another car arriving and the Chinese fire drill after the fact, when they clean the car up. It'll go fast, they can sanitize a car in about sixty seconds. Did you find any disposable bleach wipes lying around?"

"The CSIs picked up a couple dry wipes off the ground..."

"Proves my point, I can guarantee you they weren't dry when used. So you won't get any DNA off of them, the bleach will see to that." He wagged his finger, "One more thing, run the plates and the VIN on the car, you probably won't find a thing, it'll be invisible..."

Naywood frowned, "But why would they off one of their own guys?"

"It's called *retirement,"* said Cooper. "Such a nice word; *retirement.* Sounds so innocent, so relaxing." He shrugged, "Evidently, someone was *not too thrilled* about his work... maybe sending a message to the team.

Maybe replacing the team leader... not sure." He sipped his coffee again, "I sure hope they're not retiring the entire team... or he won't be the last one you find..."

"Oh dear God," breathed Naywood.

■ ■ ■

The biggest problem with most of the island locations in the Cape Coral area, was that the mangroves made it nearly impossible to beach the Jet Skis. But Chase Holt had gotten lucky in the dark and stumbled upon a nice, smooth sand shoal that had built up in the center of the bay behind Pine Island. Dotted with small scraggly trees and tangles of mangroves on it, there was little shade as the sun came up. It had been a difficult night and Karen had slept fitfully at first, finally calming down a couple hours before dawn. Covering her face with a shirt for shade he let her sleep while he did what he could to patch the holes in the hulls of the Jet Skis. Aluminum AC duct repair tape should never be confused with the fabric duct tape. With an extremely aggressive adhesive, the heavy aluminum foil tape could even be applied underwater and was an effective emergency hull repair product, among other things. Keeping a roll in each of the storage compartments of the two PWCs, he had plenty to cover the multitude of 9mm holes. While neither unit was unscathed, Karen's boat had definitely taken more of a beating with holes at the water line. It was a wonder her's had not sunk.

With the upper cowling standing open on Karen's machine he was taping both the outside and inside of the holes he could reach, the foil tape adhering to itself in the center of the holes. The engine and transmission looked like it had been hit several times and although the block and casing had deformities there were no punctures. He wasn't sure if they were a result of low velocity ammunition for the silencers reducing their power, or if the rounds had dumped some of their inertia by hitting the water first. It truly didn't matter, except it busied his mind.

"How does it look?"

Chase straightened up suddenly, whacking his head on the underside of the open hull with an audible *thwunk*. "Son of a..." he groaned grabbing his skull, rolling on his side. He rubbed his head vigorously, looking up at Karen, "Hiya."

"Sorry," she sighed with sorrowful eyes.

"S'OK, I'll live," he winced, sitting up. *"Man,* that smarts."

177

Karen dropped limply on her knees to the sand next to the Jet Ski, "What do we do now?"

"We survive." he replied, reaching up and pulling the cowl down and latching it to the bottom half of the hull. "We'll need to find a place to hole-up."

"I can't believe she's gone," muttered Karen, her bottom lip quivering, her eyes full of tears.

Her mind had jumped the tracks and Chase needed her focused. He shuffled on his knees to her, taking her by the shoulders at arm's length. "Hey, look at me. I'm sad too, I loved Pam, but I need you here and now, I need your mind in the game, I need you thinking..."

"I don't know if I can, I don't know if I *want* to live..."

Chase fought back the burning in his eyes and the clutch in his throat. "I've lost Penny, I've lost Pam, and now you just want me to give up the person closest to my heart? Does that sound fair to you?"

Her eyes were wandering loosely but they locked with his, "You mean me?"

"I mean you. I loved you both, I always have. But I didn't love Pam like I loved you. Like I *love* you..." he corrected himself.

"Me? You love *me?*"

"Yes, *you*. I need you with me. I *need* you..." Chase *felt* as surprised at the epiphany as she *looked* at this emerging revelation. She threw her arms around his neck, kissing him hard, the two of them toppling over in the sand. They lay on their sides in that embrace for a while.

Chase's ears recognized the *thump, thump, thump,* of helicopter rotor blades. He lifted his head, "Uh oh, chopper." He raised himself up on one arm, searching in the direction of the sound, spotting the orange and white Coast Guard helicopter passing out over the water from the mainland.

"What do we do?"

"Hide." Chase jumped to his feet and began gathering their gear, stuffing it into the Jet Ski's storage compartments and slinging their backpacks onto the handle bars. He was praying the chopper would swing north and go up the coast, away from them. When it banked and swung south, his heart jumped as he wrestled the Jet Skis one at a time, into the water. "C'mon, c'mon..."

"Where are we going?" asked Karen, swinging her leg over the seat and thumbing the starter button, her PWC puttering to life.

"We're out in the middle here, we don't have time to make it anywhere else. We're just going around to the other side of the shoal where the mangroves are denser. Hopefully the overhang can hide us..."

■ ■ ■

Clinging onto branches of the overhanging mangroves, Karen, Chase and Allie had waited and watched through the leaves as the Coast Guard helicopter passed directly overhead, tensely waiting until it was well on its way toward Punta Rassa Point before venturing out from their concealment.

Around the southern tip of Pine Island, turning north, heading to North Captiva Island was a good thirty miles. Pine Island Sound, the bay between the islands could get choppy at times, like today. Traveling without life jackets, Chase had hoped out loud that they wouldn't run into any Coastguard, Police or Game Warden boats which would give them cause to be confronted. Being a relative novice on a Jet Ski, Karen was not encouraged by the lack of a life jacket, the choppy conditions of the bay, or the sketchy condition of her PWC. Twenty-five to thirty miles an hour, if her gauges could be trusted, was all she could manage under present conditions. She watched how Chase handled his machine and wished she had that much confidence in her abilities. Under different circumstances, *very different,* she'd probably be enjoying herself.

Reflecting back on events of the last ten days, Karen reminded herself she still needed to press Chase for answers. There had been no real opportunity for discussion or explanation. She was lost as to a reason why any of this could really be happening. It seemed like something out of an action movie and she was an unwilling participant. She just wanted to go home, she wanted her life back. She wanted Pam back. *Pam.* Her heart ached, her throat caught and she had to blink away the wetness around her eyes. Chase was not a criminal... at least she didn't get a sense of that. There had to be a reasonably sensible answer to all of this...

Karen suddenly realized Chase's PWC was gradually pulling away and she was having to add throttle to keep up. Except she couldn't. Her engine seemed to be working harder than it should, the hull wallowing. She was *sinking.*

"CHAAAAASE!!"

Allie woofed and strained to look back around Chase. He caught her cue and after failing to locate Karen in his mirrors, whipped his head around to see her waving wildly, her Jet Ski sitting low in the water, still under power, but just barely. "Hold on dog." He turned into the waves and waited until he was over the crest before goosing the throttle, *hard*. The PWC leapt out of the water, the German Shepherd clutching the seat with her nails as they pounded across the top of the chop like riding a horse at full gallop.

Chase cut the throttle early, his momentum sliding him past her, using the throttle to slingshot up next to her on the opposite side. "Pass me the bag!"

"What about me?" she asked, pulling the backpack off her handlebars.

"You can swim, the bag can't. *Give it to me!*" He reached out, trying to maintain control of his machine.

"Oh, nice," she snipped, reaching out to hand him the backpack with both hands. "Good to know where your priorities lie." Her engine puttered to a stop with a cough and Chase, still under power, idled away. "Hey, *wait!*"

Chase recognized the stress and fear in her voice, "Relax, I'm not going to leave you." He throttled the Jet Ski around in a circle, slowly passing her head-on, the machines bobbing opposite each other in the water. "Careful, don't tip us..." His small laptop backpack slung across his shoulders, he directed her to grab onto the straps as soon as she slid onto the seat. As Chase applied throttle to steady the PWC, Karen had to hold on tight to keep from sliding off the back, her face pressed against the heavy fabric of the flat backpack. They circled once around Karen's sinking machine, the nose barely protruding from the water's surface, bobbing in the waves. "Somehow, I don't think my insurance is going to cover that..."

■ ■ ■

North Captiva Island has no connection to the mainland. You can get there by boat, water taxi or the small airstrip on the island. Vehicles on the island are limited to scooters, dirt bikes and electric carts. With a small residential population, most people on Captiva are vacation visitors, attracted to the chilled, unconcerned, disconnected and laid back island life. If Chase and Karen could avoid more than passing contact, they should be able to stay long enough to make adequate plans. An unoccupied rental or an empty residence would be a perfect recipe for being anonymous, away from prying eyes and nosy people. But they had to get there first and Chase was losing confidence in his Jet Ski's ability to get them to the populated end of the island, obviously laboring, over capacity and somehow damaged. He angled toward Foster Bay and the narrowest part of the island, nursing the machine along, the engine sputtering and belching.

■ ■ ■

When Chase nosed the Jet Ski up on the sand and turned the key off, the engine sighed as it puttered down. "I think this one's done too..." he grumbled. Allie jumped down, happy to be off the machine on solid ground to stretch her legs.

"How far to food, water and..." Karen looked down at herself, "a shower?"

"Are you up for a walk?"

"I suppose, she groaned, "if that's what it takes."

"Then it's about a mile," said Chase, setting their backpacks on the sand.

"How far would it be if I didn't feel like walking?"

"Swimming would be about two miles... " He pulled Allie's tennis ball from a pouch on her harness and gave it a toss, "Did I mention the sharks..?"

■ ■ ■

After scuttling their crippled watercraft in the mangroves, Chase covered it with cut branches to camouflage it from the air and the water. Hopefully they'd be long gone from the island before anyone discovered it.

Karen had been thirsty for hours, It might have been nice if Chase had mentioned earlier that the backpacks had two-liter hydration systems in them. Even Allie's harness had a hydration bladder and a collapsible fabric bowl kept in one of her pouches to drink from. *Ingenious.* Karen suspected Chase didn't mention it to preserve their supplies as long as possible. The hike to relative civilization, such as it was, wasn't as bad as Karen had expected, following well-trodden paths through the mangroves. Chase hiked like he knew exactly where he was going – at least he made it seem like that. She was however, not too fond of the revelation that there were snakes to watch out for... poisonous no less. That lived in trees. *Yeah, great. Wonderful.*

At one point Chase broke from the path, using a hand held GPS to find a small, green, Tupperware-like container tucked into the crotch of two palm trees that had grown together. He removed a key and jotted notes in a small log book, leaving a hundred dollar bill inside it and resealing the container.

181

Geocache, was all he had said. He was a man in his element, he had a plan and he was executing it. Karen wondered if it should bother her that the whole survival, secret cloak-and-dagger thing seemed to be part of his comfort zone. Or that Allie seemed to suddenly be a different animal, almost instantly morphing into a work dog, all play aside. Karen supposed the thing that frightened her most was when she realized the key he retrieved from the Geocache belonged to a multimillion-dollar, Key West style stilt-house on the water, just beyond the mangroves... and that before he entered, he fitted a silencer to his pistol. He called it a *suppressor* but all she knew, was that it was the same thing the guys in black used on their guns during the raid.

■ ▧ ▨

"It has come to my attention," said Karen carefully, "whether by design or my naiveté, that I don't know you as well as I thought I did..." They sat across the table from each other in the kitchen, half naked, wrapped in bath towels, their clothes in the washing machine, churning away in the adjacent laundry room.

Chase fed a piece of cooked Spam to Allie off his fork, his plate nearly empty. She took it gingerly without even touching the tines. "Well," he sighed, "part of it is, that I'm not so sure how to tell you in a way where you don't think I'm totally batshit crazy..."

Her elbows on the table, Karen set her chin in her hands, supporting her head, "Try me. Truthfully, I can't see any scenario I wouldn't believe at this point."

"Ok, I'll start from here and work my way backwards... hopefully it'll be easier for you to follow that way..."

"One question first... what's with the silencer? You're not one of *them* are you?"

"No. I'm a security specialist, you know that. I've done some bodyguard work, it's just a tool of the trade. There's another one with the pistol in your backpack. They're totally legal..."

"My backpack?" her eyes widened. "I'm glad I didn't go digging around in there for anything!"

"No, no," he shook his head. "It's in a separate compartment. They're bugout bags, they have necessities in them. Food, water, clothes, a gun, ammunition, knife, a couple unused pre-paid cell phones, walkie-talkies, money... So you can be self sufficient for a while if you need to be. In addition, mine has a small collapsible shovel, yours has a collapsible tree saw, Allie's has her water, four days of food, her collapsible bowl and her tennis ball."

"That's why you were worried about losing the bag..."

"Yeah, and each backpack has ten grand in it..."

Karen sat up, "Dollars? In cash?"

Chase shrugged, If something bad happens, cash is your best friend, especially if you need to be invisible. Credit cards can be tracked, most cell phones can be tracked via their GPS whether you have it on or not... that's why we have the disposables."

Karen stared at the table, "My dad once told me people who expect conspiracies always seem to have a way of finding them. Or make them up... like a self-fulfilling thing."

"Just because you're paranoid," began Chase, "doesn't mean you're not being followed. Case in point, look at us."

"I guess. So what's with the secret key thing? How many people know about them?"

Chase sipped his coffee, " It's a private Geocache, only four of us. Me, the Realtor and two people who are not likely to be found. I've done some very delicate security work for the Realtor, she owes me. So there's almost always a key to a house out here for emergencies."

"In case you're being followed..."

Chase raised an eyebrow at her.

"Case in point, *us,"* she nodded, "I get it." She stared at the table, wondering what happened to her comfortable little world. "So what happened... what's going on? My entire life has changed to something I barely recognize in twenty-four hours..." She looked up at him, her eyes welling with tears.

Chase took a deep breath, "Here goes... Did you ever meet my friend, Dan Murphy, the Sheriff's Deputy?"

"Yes I think so."

"His wife was Caroline Murphy, the reporter that was killed right after that UFO news special aired on TV. Remember her?"

"Yes. That was so sad. I didn't know that was his wife, I never put the names together."

Chase fed another piece of Spam to Allie. "The crash that killed her wasn't an accident. It was intentional. OK, remember my friend Jack Steele?"

Karen chewed on her lower lip, "Didn't I meet him at your bar-b-que right after you got back from Afghanistan? Tall, mustache, had a German Shepherd too? He's a pilot or something, right?"

"That's the one," he nodded. "OK, remember on the UFO special, there was footage of two girls and a group of people running from a house across the beach and getting on the UFO?"

"I remember something like that... but didn't the government debunk that all as fake?"

Chase steepled his hands, "Stay with me here..."

"OK..." she leaned forward, listening intently.

"The two girls were Jack Steele's sister and her friend."

"Whaat?"

"And that was Jack's house."

Karen leaned back in her chair, "You're joking..."

"No joke. Jack has been missing for two years... but he wasn't lost... he just wasn't *here,*" he tapped on the table. "That video footage is as real as it gets. The ship was real, the people were real and they were sent by Jack to pick her up."

Karen's mind reeled, staring blankly at Chase, blinking. "Are you saying he's an alien?"

"No," he chuckled, "His plane disappeared over the Bermuda Triangle a couple of years ago, he's been off-planet ever since. Along with two Navy F-18 pilots. The FBI, CIA, NSA, CSS, have all been searching for him ever since."

Staring at the patterns of color on the marble tabletop until they began to move, Karen blinked again doing her best to digest it all. "So he was abducted then... by aliens..."

"By an alien ship," confirmed Chase. "Jack's parents were telling me that the incident wasn't intentional on the part of the aliens, some type of circumstantial *oops.*"

"Circumstantial..." her voice trailed off as she rubbed her face with the palms of her hands. "When I said there wasn't anything I wouldn't believe at this point... I wasn't expecting *that.*" She frowned momentarily, "Wait, you said his parents told you... how did *they* know what happened?"

"Jack came back a little over a year later to visit them and let them know he was alright. He had his own ship by then and he took them up to see it. Evidently he's married now and has a son..."

Karen waved her hand to cut him off, "This is getting deep, I need my wading boots..."

"Jack's mom said she's absolutely gorgeous and has purple eyes..."

"Oh, *come on..!*" she snapped.

"Hey I can't make this stuff up," laughed Chase, "my imagination's not that good. Anyway, Jack left something behind, some technology. Lisa, his sister, had it. It was some kind of a communication unit Jack's dad said was no bigger than a laptop. That's what all the alphabet agencies are wanting."

"I don't get it," said Karen, fluffing her damp hair. "All this fuss for what, a radio?"

Chase leaned forward his elbows on the table, his voice low like he was revealing state secrets. "A piece of alien communication hardware so advanced, a unit the size of a common laptop can transmit and receive real time audio and video signals from deep space. SETI's radio dishes are about one-hundred-fifty feet across, with literally tons of electronics running them and they can't even come close to doing what this little laptop does."

"So they want the laptop..."

"And anything else they think they can get their hands on..." Chase stared into his coffee for a moment before sipping. "The NSA is systematically and aggressively pursuing anyone and everyone who had any connection or contact with Steele. His family, his friends, I don't think *anyone* is safe. I haven't been able to reach Jack's parents in a while and that worries me. It's pretty obvious his sister was in danger... Dan's wife paid with her life for making it public, Dan has had to go into hiding, Penny and Pam are gone because they got in the way... It looks like they're willing to do whatever it takes to get the technology. I think they let me go so they could track me to other people. I'm guessing they're regretting that now."

"But *we* don't have anything... *do we?*"

"No we don't," he assured her. "But I really think at this point, fact and common sense are no longer in their vocabulary." He stood up moving to the counter, placing his plate and silverware in the sink. "Jack's dad did mention an FBI agent that he trusted, a friend of the family... supposed to know this whole story. But I can't for the life of me, remember the guy's name..."

■ ■ ■

The bullet-riddled Jet Ski sat on a cradle in the garage of the Sheriff's evidence yard, looking forlorn and out of place, surrounded by confiscated vehicles and crime scene equipment.

"Sheriff," acknowledged the girl without looking up, concentrating on dusting the machine for fingerprints. Her short-cropped red hair was a stark contrast to her white uniform polo, the Sheriff's Forensics Team embroidered on the left breast.

Frank Naywood rubbed his tired eyes, the bright lighting in the bay not doing his headache any favors. "Find anything?"

"A few partials, not much else. The saltwater pretty much washed away any chances of finding anything significant. It was submerged up to the bow."

Naywood pinched the bridge of his nose. "Any blood?"

"Not a chance."

"Have any aspirin?"

"Top left drawer," she pointed, "take what you need."

"Thanks. Where'd they find it?" he asked, staring at the machine as he fought with the bottle top. "Stupid child safety caps..." he grumbled.

If the tech heard his gripe, she made no indication of it. "It was headed to the Gulf, floating out of Pine Island Sound, through Blind Pass as the tide went out. A boater almost hit it before he realized what it was. Called the Coast Guard and they came and picked it up." She paused and looked up, "I heard there's a search on... Are we looking at a recovery or a rescue?"

Recovery meant bodies, rescue meant people. "Rescue... I hope." The Sheriff tilted his head back and tossed the aspirins back, swallowing dry. He winced as they went down with resistance. Capping the bottle, he tossed it into the open drawer. "Think you might get anything off that aluminum tape if you peel it?"

"On the glue side if we're lucky. The adhesive on this stuff is a beast, it usually destroys impressions but I have a new solvent I'm interested in trying, see if I can get some better results..."

Turning to leave, Frank Naywood's expression was pensive at best. "Let me know if you find anything..."

"Will do..."

He stopped just outside the overhead door, his back to the bay. The buildings cast long afternoon shadows across the evidence and impound yard. "Did you happen to find any spent rounds anywhere?"

"One. A partial..."

"A Black Talon?"

"Yeah, how did you know?" she asked, stopping her work and staring at his back.

"Same thing the M.E. found in our victim. Have you entered it into the report?"

"No, not yet..."

"Good. Don't. Leave it off..." he walked away without turning back, "bag it and send it to my office..."

CHAPTER THIRTEEN

UFW CONQUEST, AEGERON PASS SYSTEM: *BACK TO JACK*

The battered Remora fighter sat in a repair bay two levels below the Conquest's flight deck, its nose dismantled, skeletonized, supported on jacks, the mangled landing gear hanging loosely underneath, suspended off the floor. Jack stepped over and around the parts scattered about the floor, a maze of puzzle pieces. A mechanic standing on a short ladder was buried past his shoulders in the frame of the fighter, humming to himself.

Steele cleared his throat, not wanting to startle the crewman. "Will it fly again?"

"Oh sure," came the muffled reply from inside the fighter. "Not bragging but it's a good thing they gave it to me, I know this system..." The man began extricating himself from his position, "When I'm done it'll be as good as n... Admiral!" he straightened up and saluted.

"Toncaresh!" Jack stepped forward and instead of saluting, offered his hand to the engineer he'd known from the Freedom's early days. "How are you? I see you got your new stripe..."

"Thanks for that," smiled the mechanic, "Petty Officer means I have a little extra to send home..."

"I'll be honest with you Tonc," said Jack, "I need this bird fully functional, including her ARC system..."

"No worries Admiral, her Reflective Camouflage system will work like new."

Steele leaned casually on the frame of the Remora's nose, "What about teeth?"

Toncaresh smiled, "Guns are something we're not short of around here, we have some good choices. The only thing that won't fit is Mercury Gatlings. No room in her belly for the mercury tank or the cryo system. At least not without some major changes to her hull. The kind of enhancements which would affect her performance..."

"No," waved Jack, "don't do that. What *will* fit?"

"She's got plenty of power to run pretty much whatever you want, but space and fit is your issue. She's an older bird with some limitations. There's about four choices for wingtips and rear turret - depends on your flavor preference... But if you like projectile, I have a set of Gauss Coil guns for the nose. I have to allow for the ammo racks but I'm pretty sure if I stagger the setup when I mount them, I can tuck them in."

"I like that idea," agreed Jack. "Tell you what, you do as good a job as you say you can and I'll see what I can do about another stripe for your sleeve..."

■ ■ ■

Having a bite to eat at the Officer's Club, Jack was zoned out, not really thinking or seeing, his brain in neutral, staring at the wood grain on the wall as he ate his breakfast, his first real meal since the CherriPit back on Rikovik's Reef. When Lisa slid into the booth opposite him, it pulled him back into the living world.

"What's good? I'm starved." Lisa grabbed up the day's menu.

"Great omelet," he said mechanically, still partially lost.

"Mmm, not feeling omelet," she shook her head, "I'm feeling pancakes... something sweet." She looked up from the menu, "You OK? You with me?"

"I'm OK," he said slowly, yawning.

Lisa raised an eyebrow, a habit she'd gotten from her brother. "Have you slept yet?"

"No."

"What the hell? How are you still able to function *at all?* Go to bed."

"Had to clean up, debrief the senior staff, went down to look at the Remora..."

"Jesus, you're not even speaking in full sentences anymore." Lisa slid out of the booth and moved to his side, pulling him out by the arm. "Let's get you to your quarters."

"My omelet..."

"Forget your omelet, we'll get you another one later. Besides, you're liable to miss your mouth and stab yourself in the face with your damn fork." She shouldered underneath him and hefted him to his feet. She looked around, "A little help here?" Within seconds an off-duty bridge officer left his meal and appeared at Jack's other side. "He's exhausted," explained Lisa, "we just need to get him back to his quarters."

"No problem, ma'am," replied the Lieutenant.

189

"Y'know," said Jack, looking at Lisa, as they moved through the restaurant, "You're the first pilot I've ever seen who used her fighter like a push tractor... maybe we need to install a rubber bumper on it for you."

She smirked, "And you're the first person I've ever seen go after a woman and come back with a harem. So I guess we're even."

Steele's last words were still stuck in his tired mind as he motored mechanically up the corridor, supported under each arm, "Rudder baby buddy bumper... er, rubber baby bunny bunker... ah screw it, a bumpker for a baby bugger..."

The Lieutenant was doing his best to fight back a smile of his own. He was losing. Miserably.

■ ■ ■

Heart racing, Jack Steele watched as the wall of the transition tunnel separated, the gate within reach. Well below speed protocols, the ship slid sideways toward the opening, away from the gate. His breath hung in the frozen air as the ship passed through the massive tear, the ship's vibrations threatening to destroy itself, appearing in a sky of unfamiliar stars.

"Jack..? *Jack!*"

Steele sat bolt upright in the darkness, chilled, feeling a presence near him. "What's happening..?"

"You dream – bad I think."

"Lights!" called Jack. *"Lights!"* The illumination grew steadily, Fritz sitting on the bed next to him, watching over him. The vision and alternate reality still burned into his mind's eye, he failed to recognize his surroundings. "Where are we?"

"Quarters," annunciated Fritz, his head tilting to one side. "You sleep *long.*"

Jack swung his feet off the bed, staring at the floor, breathing deeply, working to clear his mind. "How long was I out?"

Fritz jumped to the floor and shook his head to settle his fur, "Long time..."

"TESS..."

The eGo-h lit up; the holo-screen popping into view, hovering above his arm, TESS' animated face appearing on the screen. "Good morning, sir. Are we back to *Jack Steele* and *Admiral?"*

"Yes, TESS. How long was I asleep?"

190

"You mean coma?" she smiled. "Just kidding. You were in a sleep state for nineteen hours, twenty-three minutes. Are you feeling fully rested now?"

"I think so, a little disoriented..."

"That does occur with extremely deep REM cycles like you were experiencing. You also need nourishment, your bio-levels suggest you are experiencing a near-hypoglycemic state. I suggest eating some fruit or drinking some juice as soon as possible."

Steele rose, slightly lightheaded and picked a piece of fruit out of a bowl as he passed the minibar on the way to the shower. It looked strangely like a cucumber but tasted much like a banana...

■ ■ ■

Lisa let herself into the Admiral's quarters, a small tray in one hand. "Jack... Jack?" She set the covered tray on the desk next to the computer and set down her e-Pad. Having heard his name, Jack stepped out into the bedroom from the shower. *"Holy crap!"* shouted Lisa, spinning away and shielding her eyes, "how about a freaking towel?"

Jack stood there, his hands on his hips, "What? I can't be naked in my own damn quarters?" He noticed the covered tray on the desk, "Ooh, is that an *omelet?"*

"Towel! *Towel!"*

"OK, OK," he waved, ducking into the bathroom. Jack reappeared wrapped in an oversized towel. "Better?"

Lisa peeked cautiously before relaxing. "Better." She handed him the tray as he dropped himself onto the sofa. "Yes, it's an omelet, sausage and some potatoes... *DUDE!" S*he slapped her hand over her eyes, "What the *hell..."*

"Sorry," Jack crossed his legs and pulled the towel around his knees. "So what's our status?"

"Captain Ryan has us back on course for Ossomon; the yacht was stripped of information and dumped overboard and the Remora is still undergoing repairs."

"What about the girls? How are they doing?"

"Fed, housed and all thawed out. Nina's girlfriend..."

"Ruby?"

"Yeah, Ruby's in recovery, she's doing fine. The other girl who was injured is in the ICU. She was in a pretty bad shape. The surgeon said it's up to her now."

"Did she lose her leg?"

Lisa's mouth tweaked crookedly, "The surgeon said it was too badly damaged..."

"Dammit..." winced Jack. He needed to push past it to fleet business but the thought of the young girl fighting for her life in the infirmary never left his mind. "Have we started the work on the stasis field emitters for the launch system?"

Lisa's mouth tweaked crookedly again, "Hmm, yeah about that..."

Jack raised an eyebrow, *"What..."* he said suspiciously.

Lisa bit her lip, "Um, well..."

"Spit it out."

"The factory new stasis emitters we got from Deep Black are as clean and perfect as the ones we got from Resurrection Station..."

"But..." prompted her brother.

"But the factory rebuilt units aren't. During the parts inspection, the Chief Engineer noticed an extra module installed on the emitters and broke one down to diagnose its purpose. He said it's got two functions; part of it is a short range tracking unit, with a system-wide reach. The other function is a remote control receiver wired right into the emitter package."

Jack paused, a forkful of omelet suspended above his plate. "Son of a bitch," he hissed. "I wonder if Deep Black knew... Can he tell if it the module was installed *at* the factory or after?"

Lisa, pursed her lips. "I wondered about that myself. He felt it was too perfect of an install to have been accomplished outside the factory."

Jack shoveled the last bit of food into his mouth, setting the tray aside. "Have the Chief and senior staff in my office. Ten minutes..."

■ ■ ■

After an hour-long meeting with his senior staff and Chief Engineers, Steele addressed the issue alone, with Task Force Vice Admiral, Vince Kelarez and Fleet Admiral, Warn Higdenberger, on a split screen in his ready room on the bridge of the Conquest. They listened intently as Steele explained the situation involving the sabotaged parts.

"My biggest concern is how pervasive the use of these compromised parts might be throughout our fleet..."

"I share your concern Mr. Steele," said Admiral Higdenberger. "Considering that those rebuilt parts originated from a UFW approved manufacturing facility, it is very dangerous indeed. We will take immediate steps to cancel that contract and close that facility..."

"If I can make a recommendation, Admiral..." interrupted Steele.

"By all means."

"Hold off on that. At least until we confirm or not, that any of the altered parts from this vendor are in fleet circulation. I'm not convinced the parts were intended for UFW Fleet consumption. And what we're seeing may not be actions condoned by the facility as a whole, rather by a few key people planted in the facility to produce randomly compromised parts. We acquired these stasis field emitters from a vendor that generally deals with the merchant and transportation trades..."

"What are you looking to accomplish, Mr. Steele?"

"Well, all parts from this manufacturer should be definitely checked, fleet wide... but my hunch is that the UFW fleet is not the target... These stasis emitters are used in ships and facilities all across space. Ports, warehouses, transporters, merchants... Circulate enough of these things and eventually you would have a secret key to the back door of every nook and cranny in the universe..."

Admiral Higdenberger's brow furrowed, head tilted to one side, *"Nook and cranny?"*

"Every corner and hiding spot..."

"Yes, I see. Go on."

Steele continued, "If we make overt moves too soon, we will most likely lose the perpetrators in the wind and forfeit a prime opportunity to know who's pulling the strings." Jack noticed the Admiral's curious head tilt again. *"Who might be running this little enterprise,"* he clarified. "If we can catch the infiltrators in the act we will have a chance to track their contacts up the food chain, if you get my meaning."

"I do..."

"Can we get a couple of our own people into the facility? It may be dangerous but it could pay off in a big way."

"I think we can..."

Steele rubbed his hands together, "Good. In the meantime, maybe we release a fleet-wide service bulletin looking for the emitters in question with their associated part number. We don't want to create any scuttlebutt or an information leak, so maybe we just say there is a general recall. Frequent failures or poor performance. To be replaced with stock units from the UFW Navy plant only..."

■ ▨ ▧

Sitting on a bench in the Conquest's sizable garden, Commander Dar Sloane sipped his coffee, watching Lisa's German Shorthaired Pointer, Gus, roll in the grass. "So I hear you might be getting a pair of flight wings..."

"Really..." said Lisa unemotionally, her back to him, staring at the birds flitting around in the trees. "You're not the first person to mention it, but I can't imagine why. Jack... er, the Admiral, was not terribly happy about what I did. I disobeyed a direct order. Two of them as a matter of fact. One from Commander Carter, and one from the Admiral himself... Not to mention that I single-handedly destroyed the Remora..."

"Pssh," waved Dar, "your brother doesn't give a crap about the Remora, that can be fixed, he knows that. What he cared about was your safety. And since you're safe, I think all will be forgotten." His face flexed in contemplation, "Or remembered – depending on how you look at it. What you did took *guts*. Lotsa guts... Not sure I would've tried it."

"You're so full of crap, Sloane," shot Lisa, "you wouldn't have even blinked. You're an adrenalin junky. In fact, you guys probably have a special technique..."

"Technique?" blurted Dar, nearly squirting coffee through his nose. "For using a fighter like a push tractor, to wrestle a disabled pleasure craft out of a collapsing jump tunnel? Yeah sure," he added with a touch of sarcasm, "we practice *that* all the time." The Commander shook his head, "No, Cookie, you invented that gem all by yourself. The damnedest thing is, it worked."

Smirking but unconvinced, Lisa watched Gus sniff at a stand of vibrant purple flowers. "I don't know..."

Dar leaned forward, his elbows on his knees, his hands cradling his coffee mug, "Look at the life pilots lead; we take risks, we do crazy things... it's what we get paid for. And we *love it*. Most of us would probably do it for nothing, for the privilege of playing with the coolest toys in the universe. It all boils down to doing a job most people would never dream of doing. And sometimes it involves making decisions on the fly, *pardon the pun*; decisions lesser men and women would never be able to make under normal conditions, much less under the physical and mental stresses *we* endure. Conditions they could not *begin* to comprehend."

Lisa chewed the inside of her cheek in reflection, "I guess. But I still don't get the sense that the Admiral is all too pleased..."

194

"Did he mention anything this morning?"

"No... not in so many words..."

"Not in so many words, or not in *any* words?" Dar shook his head and continued, "Y'know, orders are a funny thing..."

Lisa turned to face Dar and crossed her arms, "Funny ha-ha, or funny strange?"

Dar sported a mischievous grin, his naturally tanned face crinkling around the corners of his mouth, his slate-gray eyes dancing, "I've seen them both ways; funny odd *and* funny stupid. The thing is, it's up to *us* to make sense of them and carry them out. Sometimes we tread a thin line between following orders and doing something to get results. On occasion we need to cross that line to achieve the results they want. If we're successful, we're heroes, if we're not, it's our fault for not following their stupid orders." He sipped his coffee, "Because as the Gods know, orders from the brass are never wrong," he rolled his eyes in exaggerated sarcasm.

"Are Jack... my brot... the *Admiral's* orders ever wrong?" stumbled Lisa.

Dar Sloane shook his head, "Judging your brother's decisions are above my pay grade to question or find fault with."

"Nice dodge," she snickered.

Dar shrugged it off. Personally, he liked Admiral Steele. But giving any opinions at all could be a risky venture, especially to a member of his family... no matter how much he liked her.

"Now, Admiral Pottsdorn, *that* was a man who worked at perfecting stupid..." There was a pause, a moment where they just stared at each other. A moment that was both thrilling and uncomfortable at the same time. Up till now they had been kissing friends, pals, affectionate but not intimate. In his mind's eye he could see them going further with their relationship but was unsure how that might play out. Especially if it didn't work out. He wanted to avoid professional suicide. To break the silence and *that* train of thought, Dar flipped back to the conversation, "Um, back to Admiral Steele; I think you underestimate his appreciation of the circumstances. I don't see him as an obtuse man, do you?"

Lisa smiled wryly, *"Usually* not."

Dar caught her meaning and chuckled. "Then I don't think he's going to miss the significance of what you did. You made an on-the-spot judgment call. And a tough one. You have the guts, the brains and the nerves fighter pilots are known for." He leaned back against the bench, relaxing, "Don't let it go to your head, but it was *heroic*. I find it hard to believe your brother would see it differently."

Lisa blushed, "I don't see it that way," she shrugged, "I just did what I had to do..."

Dar countered with a crooked smile, "Cookie, that's exactly what a hero would say..."

■ ■ ■

Lisa and Dar Sloane walked around the noseless Remora, examining the work in progress, Lisa feeling more than a little panicked. "Where's the *rest* of it? Where's the *nose?* Oh my God, Jack is gonna *kill* me..."

"Easy ma'am" assured the mechanic, stepping away from his tool stand. "The Admiral has already signed off on all the work. It will be factory perfect when we get it all back together. We removed the entire nose sub-frame to rebuild her because it was damaged beyond straightening out. We'll install the nose turret carrier and and all the electronics on the sub-frame before reattaching it to the bird." The stocky gray man took her gently by the elbow and guided her around toward the rear of the fighter, pausing under the wingtip, pointing up, "As you can see we've already installed the new hardpoints on the wings. They can hold mission-specific rocket pods, missiles, special electronics or even gun pods..." Ducking under the wingtip, he guided Lisa to the rear of the fighter, pointing at the new articulated turret installed on the hull that extending beyond the flanking, twin engine nozzles. "That's the new stinger in your tail, a pair of Argon pulse lasers. I would have opted for Gatlings but there was no fitting them in the turret housing; too bulky."

"What will go in the nose?" asked Commander Sloane, following along on the tour.

"Mmm," nodded the mechanic approvingly, "Probably a nice pair of Particle Gauss Guns. We were thinking three, but that would seriously reduce magazine capacity. Since we're scratch building the nose turret housing, we can fit two comfortably with about two thousand rounds each." He looked over at Lisa, "It's not a true turret like the one in the back, it will track the target about ten degrees in any direction, the rest is going to be up to you..."

CHAPTER FOURTEEN

AEGERON PASS SYSTEM, FREERANGER – DD217: *THE SHADOW*

The gate in Aegeron Pass exploded with color as it deposited the FreeRanger destroyer, DD217, into the empty system, the sleek gray hull glinting from the system's sun.

Sitting in his command chair, Commander T. B. Yafusco casually sipped his coffee, his legs crossed at the knee. "All stations report." He really didn't expect to find anything; the yacht had too much of a head start. The lawmen at Rikovik's Reef claimed to have damaged the vessel, but he had his doubts as to what they would find. He made the Primayor agree to a non-refundable deposit before undertaking the mission assignment... something the politician was severely resistant to. Too bad, Tibby's crew wasn't in it for charity. Running a ship was a business and he had bills to pay.

"Picking up debris ahead, Skipper."

"On screen. Are we recording?"

"Aye sir. Recording."

The moment the image appeared his heart sank. The yacht was nothing more than an oversized party shuttle, its guts spread out around it, lifeless, dark, shot to pieces. He took a deep breath, letting it out slow, "Dammit," he hissed quietly. "Take us in, let's light her up... Getting any readings at all?"

"Not a thing, sir, no power of any kind."

"Of course not," sighed the Commander, "why should anything be easy..." He set his coffee mug on his console. "Just a little break, is that too much to ask?" He wasn't really looking for an answer, just complaining out loud. He leaned forward, as the floodlights set into the bow of the destroyer swept across the small hull ahead, making it shine in the surrounding darkness. "Hmm, the entry hatch is blown..."

"Think they were rescued sir?"

Tibby leaned back in his chair, picking up his mug. "I don't see any bodies floating around out there, so I'd have to say yes."

Ensign Grinah leaned over from the second officer's chair, "Think it's worth a walk through?"

Commander Yafusco thought for a moment, his mug paused midway to his mouth, "No... I seriously doubt there's anything of value left behind." He sipped before continuing, "Look at her, she's a mess. Something crushed the exhaust nozzles" he pointed. "How did it fly like that?" He shook his head. "I don't see how they made it through the tunnel like that."

"Could of happened here," suggested Grinah.

"I suppose," shrugged Tibby.

"The science officer turned in his seat, "I'm picking up Ion wakes at the reach of our sensors..."

"How many?"

"Difficult to tell at this distance, the wake is widely dispersed and quickly decaying..."

"Then guess, Lieutenant."

"Three to six."

In a moment of introspection, Commander Yafusco scratched his beard stubble, "Helm, new heading, follow that trail. Let's see if we can determine who's making it. Best speed. Communications, send an update to fleet dispatch, see if this might be one of our groups. If not, see if they have anyone they can spare to meet up with us..." He gestured at the yacht floating in front of them, "And transmit the data recording to the Primayor; tell him we've come to the end of our contract."

"We have the the mission deposit, what about our balance?"

"Tell him we're even. We were only able to complete half the mission, we're good with half the payment."

■ ■ ■

Deep in thought, Commander Yafusco was standing with his arms folded, his back to the chart table in his ready room, leaning on its edge, staring out of the observation window at the silently passing stars, a dusty red planet with streaks of green and blue in the distance, rotating slowly. A floating hologram of solar systems strung together by their connective gates stretched across the table, their golden glow the only light in the room. When the door to his office slid open behind him, it barely registered and he took no notice, maintaining his vigil of the passing celestial scenery.

Grinah slid silently up against him, her arm finding its way around his waist. "You OK Tibby?"

He was silent for a moment. "How long have we been out here Grinah?"

"You mean *this system?*"

"No. I mean, how long have we been in *space?* Personally I mean."

She looked up at his profile in the darkness, "I'm not sure, I've lost count... Five or six years I guess. You were out here first. We met when I was assigned to my first ship; the Harkener, remember?"

"I remember. Ten years..."

"You were out here five years before we met?"

He shook his head slowly, "No... I was out here four years already when we met. We met, *ten years ago.* I've been out here nearly fourteen years."

She pushed herself away a little, "I've been out here ten years already?" She shook her head, "Ten years..." she whispered. Suddenly the words seemed to hold no meaning. "No, that can't be right..."

"Ten years ago, today," added Tibby with a weak smile. He put his arm around her and drew her back in, "Happy anniversary, Grinah..."

"It all runs together," she breathed, "it just doesn't seem possible."

"What bothers me," he began, "is that I feel like I'm in the same place now that I was... that *we were,* ten years ago..."

Confused, she looked up at his profile again, "What do you mean? Where should we be?"

He played that back in his mind and realized it didn't come out of his mouth the same way that it sounded in his head. "No, us – we," he stumbled, "we're fine. I just hate after ten years we're still doing the same thing..." He held up his hand, "Wait, no - that's not what I meant it to sound like either..."

"I understand." She lay her hand on his chest, "You mean our circumstances, life. You thought things would be different by now..."

"Exactly," he sighed, relieved. "Do you know it's been seven years since I've set foot on soil?"

"So you're saying the ship's garden doesn't count?" she joked.

"No. No it doesn't..."

She smiled in the darkness, the soft light from the holographic table reflecting off her face. "Our vacation on Dineau... the waterfalls were amazing..."

"Remember the rental house on the lake?" He could still see it in his mind like it was yesterday.

She leaned into him, "It was sooo peaceful... We could go again..."

He rested his chin on the top of her head, his mind wandering. "Wouldn't it be great to own a little place like that? It would be a great place to raise kids..." He froze and stopped breathing the moment it came out of his

199

mouth. The silence was deafening and it seemed to last for eons. *Stupid thing to say. Idiot.* It was a topic they'd avoided for years.

"Children? With me?"

"Can't have them by myself..." he said cautiously.

"So, we'd get married then," she said slowly, still clutching him.

"If that's what you'd want," he ventured tentatively, unsure of the right answer.

She pushed herself slowly away, looking up at him, *"If?"*

"Yes. Yes of course," he smiled nervously, "we'd get married." She drew back to him and he took that to mean she was comfortable with the outcome of the conversation. They stood together, silently embraced, watching the stars pass the window.

Other than the FreeRanger articles of conduct forbidding it, he wondered why he'd never considered it before. It seemed a natural progression of their relationship. *Because he was afraid she'd say no, that's why.* And maybe the fact that he was up to his eyeballs in debt to pay off the ship. Yeah, that was in the fine print of accepting the command; providing enough income to the FreeRanger Council to cover the cost of the ship. And then some. Something called *interest.* He always wondered why they called it that, because he sure wasn't *interested* in paying it.

Yafusco's mind went back to their first meeting; the years since then, the friends come and gone, the adventures, the miles traveled together, the close calls... "Marry me. Be my wife." His heart skipped a beat, did he just say that *out loud?* Did his lips just form those words?

Grinah didn't look up, continuing her gaze at the passing star system. "Did you just say what I *think* you said?"

"I think so..." he mumbled.

"It wasn't really a question..." she teased.

"You want me to ask *again?"*

"She smiled to herself, "You didn't *ask* me the *first time."*

"Hmm, yeah, I wasn't even sure I *really* said it the first time."

"Consider it a dry run then," she patted his chest. "Try it again. A girl likes to be romanced you know."

"I don't have a ring or anything..."

"I don't care."

Despite his command presence and his rugged good looks, Commander T. B. Yafusco was not a man with a lot of romantic experience. The underpinnings of his character had begun at a parochial school level, through the military academy and into service. His exposure to members of the opposite sex and dating was limited at best, as was his skill in dealing with matters of the heart. He took Grinah's hand and took a deep breath, "On the anniversary of our first meeting..."

"Aren't you supposed to be kneeling or something?" she offered.

"Kneeling..? *Really?*"

She nodded silently.

"Do... *you* kneel too?"

"No, just you," she replied softly.

He dropped to one knee in front of the woman he'd known intimately for ten years and waited for her nod of approval. "Ensign Grinah..."

The ship-wide comm crackled, *"Attention; Skipper to the bridge, Skipper to the bridge please..."*

Grinah grabbed him by the shoulder with her free hand, "Oh no you don't! You're not going anywhere till we're done. A girl doesn't get one of these every day. Whatever it is, it can wait..."

Yafusco didn't even blink. "OK."

"Go ahead," she coaxed.

Still holding her hand he swallowed hard, suddenly realizing this was a little more difficult than he'd anticipated, "Ensign..." he paused for a moment, deciding her rank was uncalled for in this situation. *"Grinah,* from the first day I saw you, I knew there was something special about you. My only regret is that it took us two years for us to... well," he shrugged, "I'm not the best at this..."

"You're doing fine..." she cooed.

"My only regret is that it took us two years to connect. And for me to realize how truly amazing you were. Your presence in my life has been the best part of my existence. You are my confidant, my counselor, my love... and I thank the Gods every day for blessing me with your presence. I cannot imagine what life would have been without you and I cannot bear to think of what my future would be like without you. I would be forever incomplete without you... will you be my wife?"

Grinah dropped to her knees and put her arms around him, her lips in his ear, "That was absolutely wonderful. But you have it backwards, the Gods did not bless you, they answered *my* prayers - to find *you...* And I would love to spend the rest of my life proving that to you."

■ ■ ■

201

"Freighter coming up off the surface of the third planet, Commander..."

Commander Yafusco slid into his command chair, "Anybody we know?"

"He's a neutral. But he had some information for us. They picked up the group we're tracking from their position on the ground; three ships."

"Any details?"

"They were taking on cargo, their systems were passive, but they recorded two large, one small, no identity pings." The tactical officer pointed at Tibby's console, "readings are on screen; TAC 3."

Commander Yafusco flipped to his tactical readouts and paged to the third screen to see the scans and associated silhouettes. They were mostly featureless blobs but there was *some* shape – especially to the largest of the three. "That looks like a carrier..." he breathed, *"and escorts."*

"Didn't see any fighters, Commander."

Yafusco shook his head, "And you wouldn't, not at this resolution. But I'm betting they're there. That thing is a *monster..."*

"You need anything else from the freighter captain?"

In an exceptionally good mood, the Commander was still studying the digital recording of the ships and feeling rather generous, "No," he waved absentmindedly, "he's done us a service, let him be on his way..." Reviewing the replay, it suddenly occurred to him the next system was *Novellis.* There were two other gates out of Novellis besides the one they'd be entering through; Red432 and Ossomon. "By the Gods, *Ossomon..."*

"What about Ossomon?" Grinah slid into the first officer's seat, activating its vid screens.

Tibby rubbed the stubble on his jaw, "This group, they're heading directly for the Novellis gate... they're going for Ossomon."

Grinah lifted an eyebrow, "How can you be sure... maybe they're going to Red432."

"There's nothing in Red432. Or the next two systems... nothing worth the tour anyway. This group is on *patrol.* I'd bet gold they're UFW Navy..." He pointed to the Ensign at the comm station, "Comms! Call fleet dispatch, have them broadcast an all-call in Ossomon. They need to let everyone know there's a UFW patrol headed in."

"What if you're wrong?" whispered Grinah.

Yafusco leaned across the space between their seats,"Last I checked, we've got nothing in that system to fight a patrol group like that. If I'm wrong, a few people will be inconvenienced. If I'm right and we don't make the call, we could lose assets and people..."

"So what will they do?"

"Ground or clear anything pinging FreeRanger from the system. They can go to ground or evacuate, hide, go dark... The system's too big and too busy to search it completely..." He rubbed his stubble again, "At least they've never done it before..."

CHAPTER FIFTEEN

CAPE CORAL, FLORIDA: *DEEP WEB*

Under the cover of darkness, Chase Holt made the trek out to the beleaguered Jet Ski hidden in the mangroves, where it had remained undisturbed and undiscovered so far. Using his knife, he'd punctured the aluminum tape repairs and let the Jet Ski sink into the shallow water, burying it almost completely with sand and bending the live mangroves over it. It would eventually become a permanent part of the mangrove stand if it remained undiscovered. At least that was the plan.

The other part of the plan was getting off the island... quietly, without a lot of fuss. That required a boat or a plane. And since he had only a rudimentary knowledge of how to fly, acquiring a boat had become the new task at hand. Luckily there was a healthy selection around the island. He narrowed down the possibilities by size, availability, look and fuel consumption. Nothing too big, nothing too fast, nothing too flashy. He settled on a nice midsized sport cruiser docked behind a house with the keys hidden between the seats. The bonus was that it appeared the owners were one of the many part-time residents on the island and the house was dark.

"Where are you?" came Karen's whisper in his ear.

Chase adjusted the volume on the walkie-talkie's earpiece and brought the mic to his mouth, "I'm heading back to the house, I'll be back in about ten minutes... is everything OK?"

"It's fine. You've been gone quite awhile and I was getting worried."

"Everything's good..."

"Find the one you want?"

He took a moment to wave at a couple riding past on a golf cart with only one functioning headlight, its tires crunching softly on the crushed shell road as it passed. "Yep. Found a good one."

■ ■ ■

Chase plopped himself into a chair at the kitchen table in front of a plate of food, his German Shepherd, Allie, dancing around. "Any messages come through on the laptop?"

Karen shook her head, "It hasn't made a peep."

"Damn," he winced, disappointed. "C'mon Murphy, where the hell are you...?"

Karen held up a bright yellow sundress on a hanger, "What do you think? I found it in the closet..."

Chase looked up from his plate, "Wow... *bright.*"

She held up another, a Hawaiian print in blazing neon colors, "Is this one better?"

Chase's head recoiled like he'd been slapped, "Oh *God* no... We want to *blend in...* Nothing, um, *quieter?*"

"There's a white one..."

"OK, well, you need clothes... take the yellow and the white one I guess. Do they fit you?"

"Yeah," she smiled, "they fit pretty well." She laid the dresses on an empty counter and sat down at the table to eat. "So how does this thing work with the messaging?" she asked, pointing her fork at the laptop sitting on the kitchen's center island.

"Well," he started, sucking the fettuccine off his fork, "the internet isn't just the internet..." he made a contemplative face, considering his words. "I guess the best way to explain it is, it has layers. The internet you know and see every day is one of those layers... it's referred to as the Surface Web. The general term for the net you don't see, is Deep Web. That generic term covers; DarkNET, BlackNET, SIPRNet, CRONOS, NSANET, JWICS and a bunch of others. Those are all specific names for different networks. Secure networks. *Secret Networks...* Some are government stuff you seriously don't want to mess with. But they're accessible with the same internet connection the average person has at home. The difference is, these layers are invisible... unless you know how to reach them. They're the basement, sub basement, catacombs and dungeons..."

"If they're secret," interrupted Karen, "how do you know about them?"

Chase pointed at his plate of fettuccine, "Mmm, this is very good, by the way..." He twirled his fork to collect some of the noodles. "People are aware of the existence of the Deep Web like they are aware of a bad neighborhood. It's dark and intimidating and most people would rather not go there or even acknowledge that it exists. There's no real attraction; its sinister undertones and hidden, encrypted gateways are usually enough to deter the casual tourist."

Karen frowned as she fought with the fettuccine that kept sliding off her fork. "So what's the reason people go there?"

"DarkNET and BlackNET are for the most part anonymous, as long as you have the proper software to prevent tracing and invasion. The normal search engines on the Surface Web can't reach below to the other levels, so knowledgeable people, like me, use it for its privacy and greater freedom. You can find pretty much anything you want there; hackers, scammers, black market deals, weapons sales, drugs, gambling, information trading, spies, mercenaries, terrorists..."

"Good Lord... So how do you find someone?"

"Secure chat boards, prearranged meetings, codes. There's a bunch of different ways. I left a code on a board we use and I have to wait until he sees it and responds."

Karen sipped her soda, "What if he doesn't respond?"

Chase's face turned solemn, "It means he may be incapable of answering for some reason... or dead." He didn't like thinking it, much less saying it.

Karen stared uncomfortably at her plate, "If he's not... um, y'know, how long should it take?"

Chase shrugged, "Hours, days, weeks... it depends on his access. If he's hiding someplace remote, he may have no access." He pushed away from the table and stretched his arms above his head, "As soon as we're done we'll clean up and get some sleep, we're getting up before dawn. I want to clear this island before light breaks..."

■ ■ ■

Karen walked sleepily alongside Chase, their footfalls soft on the packed crushed seashell drive. "I'll have you know, I'm not exactly my best at five in the morning..."

Chase adjusted the straps on his backpack as they walked, hefting it to sit more comfortably. "It's OK, you can nap on the boat once we get under way."

"You say that like I actually have a choice," she mused. "So what's the plan?"

"Try not to get caught, try not to us get killed..."

"A simple plan with admirable goals..." she sassed.

"I'm glad you like it, I thought of it all by myself." Chase snapped his fingers to get Allie's attention as they neared the driveway of the house with the sport cruiser. She trotted silently to his side, abandoning her exploration. Mid-stride, Chase stopped dead in his tracks at the mouth of the palm tree-lined driveway, a golf cart with one broken headlight sitting in front of the house. "Son of a bitch," he breathed, unconsciously dropping into a crouch, "that's the one I passed last night on my way back. I was sure this house was empty... *Dammit.*" He scanned the area carefully.

"What do we do?" whispered Karen.

He looked up at the sky, changing subtly from star-studded black to deep blue. "We don't have a choice," he hissed, "we have to go for it." He grabbed her by her hand, "Low, fast and quiet, we don't stop for anything. Got it?"

"Got it."

Making a beeline to the back of the house where the boat was docked, they cut through the landscaping; weaving their way through palm trees and flower beds, motion activated landscape lights clicking on along the way, marking their progress. "Shit," growled Chase. He was doing his best to keep a good pace without dragging Karen to the ground but she was not used to running with a heavy pack. Running crouched, she lost her footing in the soft soil of a flowerbed and crashed to her knees with a grunt. Chase slid to a stop and doubled back, hoisting her to her feet with one hand under her arm. "C'mon, up you go... No stopping to rest."

There was a dog barking somewhere but there was no time to consider the direction or the cause.

As they crossed the patio, lights flickered on from the house to the seawall, lighting their way, the glow splashing across the dock and boat. "I guess these people don't believe in flashlights," panted Karen, struggling to keep up with Chase and Allie.

"None of these lights came on last night..." he replied. Leading the way, Allie cut the angle from the patio and slid on the dew covered dock, bouncing against the hull of the boat with a thud, scrambling to keep her footing. "Hup, Allie," commanded Chase as he slid to a stop at the first mooring line. "Get in, get in..." he pointed to Karen, "I've got the lines."

Karen moved past him, her running shoes squeaking on the wet surface, Allie jumping over the gunnel of the boat into the cockpit. Unable to climb over with her burden, Karen wrestled her pack off and dropped it into the boat before climbing over. Chase had the bow line free of the dock cleat and flung the loose end up on the bow as he pushed the boat away, hustling as best he could to the stern on the slippery dock.

"Lights!" shouted Karen in a hushed tone. "In the house next door! Hurry!"

The stern line free, he swung one leg over the side of the boat and pushed off on the dock with his other foot, the boat sliding silently away from the dock into the darkness. He shrugged off his pack and let it drop to the cockpit floor, digging between the seat cushions. The keys were *gone.*

"Lights are coming on in *this* house..." pointed Karen, whispering, "what do we do?"

A bolt of adrenalin shot up his back. "Sit! Sit!" he urged, looking around. He needed room, he'd never hot wired a boat before, but necessity was the mother of improvisation. He grabbed a mini flashlight out of his backpack and snapped a red lens over the front, "Keep an eye on the house..." he whispered.

Flashlight in mouth, Chase searched the seats and chart pockets again by a gentle red glow. Nothing. *Son of a bitch.* He dropped to his knees to feel under the dash for the back of the ignition switch, the tangle of wires running to a multitude of switches and instruments. It was in that position when the red wash of the flashlight reflected off the key fob dangling from the key plugged into the ignition. There was a wave of heat over his ears followed by an immediate cooling breeze when he realized, once again, his guardian angel had been watching out for him. He reached up and flipped on the bilge blowers, letting them run for a full minute before turning the key with his fingers crossed. The engine started up cleanly with a low burble, the exhaust bubbling up around the outdrive.

"The lights went out but there's a dog running around out there now," whispered Karen, peeking over the top of the gunnel from her seat on the floor.

"Doesn't matter," replied Chase, dropping the engine into reverse. He backed the boat away from the neighbor's dock and seawall where it had drifted. "Because we're off like a bad prom dress..." As the boat fell back into the darkness, he slid the boat into gear and spun the wheel, the boat sliding quietly around, idling away from the back of the island. The world around him nothing but ink and shadow, he flipped on the radar and adjusted the screen, pointing the boat toward the channel markers that would take them around the north side of the island and out into the Gulf of Mexico.

Karen sat down next to Chase at the helm, "Where to?"

■ ■ ■

Detective Buck Harper knocked on the open doorway to the Sheriff's office, "Boss, you got a minute?"

Sheriff Frank Naywood looked up from a stack of paperwork, "C'mon in Buck, I could use a break." He flexed his wrist and fingers, "Getting writer's cramp for God's sake."

Buck walked in and sat down, a manilla folder in his hands.

"Did you get some sleep?" asked Naywood.

"Yes, sir."

"Good. Watch'a got there?" asked the Sheriff pointing at Buck's paperwork.

"Well, you said to bring you anything that seemed out of sorts... anything that might relate to this whole thing in Bimini Basin..."

"Yeah..." Naywood extended his hand, waiting for the folder.

Buck handed it to him, continuing, "A boat was stolen from North Captiva sometime last night. The owners didn't notice till about 10am this morning. One of our marine units went out to take a report, we just got it back..."

The Sheriff glanced at his watch, "It's damn near six-o'clock... no wonder I'm hungry."

Buck shrugged, "I don't *ever* remember a boat theft out there, do you? I thought it might be our boy..."

The Sheriff shook his head, "I can't think of one. Well if it is our guy, he's got a ten or twelve hour lead on us... Did anyone see or hear anything?"

"Security lights and dogs barking at about five-thirty this morning. That's about it. If it is our boy, where d'you suppose he'd go?"

Naywood leaned back in his chair, rubbing his forehead, his eyes closed. "I don't know Buck. Conservatively at thirty miles an hour, if he went south, he could be in Key West or Cuba by now." He sat back forward staring at the report, trying to read between the lines, knowing the answer wouldn't be there. "No extradition with them either..." he mumbled. "If they went north, they could be beyond Crystal River. It all depends on the water conditions and his fuel consumption. File the report," he shrugged.

"Standard procedure, then."

"Pretty much."

209

"You don't think he would've cut across Okeechobee to the other coast, do you?"

Frank Naywood pursed his lips then shook his head, "Too slow. I'm guessing he went for speed and distance. Open water. I know I would..."

Buck's eyes narrowed, suddenly understanding the Sheriff's intentions, "You're letting him go..."

Naywood didn't acknowledge or deny the detective's assertion, and his expression remained poker-like, "Thanks for bringing that report to my attention, Buck..."

■ ■ ■

The River Inn & Marina was about four miles up the narrow, winding, Steinhatchee River from Deadman Bay inlet, and it was as far as Chase wanted to go by boat. He wasn't familiar with the panhandle and beyond where they were, marinas or safe harbors were a lot more scarce. Exhausted, he was glad to have made it before light failed and darkness fell. Even with the radar and GPS, the river would have made for tough navigation, lined with sandy shoals, docks, homes and scattered businesses. The boat securely moored at the dock, the marina quiet, music drifted from the restaurant and tiki bar at the far end of the marina.

Chase hefted his backpack over the side of the boat and set it on the dock. "Ok, let's get a room..."

"Why don't we just sleep on the boat?" asked Karen, handing him his laptop bag.

"Because I'm going to wipe down and dump the boat up river on a dead-end canal I saw on the chart. Hopefully it'll stay hidden for a while."

"Seems a shame, it's such a nice boat..."

"That's not ours," he reminded her.

"I know..." she shrugged, hefting her backpack onto the gunnel. She reached over the side to set it on the dock and its weight tipped her over bodily, bending her over the side of the boat, her feet coming off the cockpit floor. Chase caught her by the shoulders, her feet in the air, her head near his beltline.

"This is interesting..." he chuckled, grabbing her by her belt. Lifting her off the boat he set her on the dock across the bags like another piece of luggage.

"Well *that* was ladylike," she said, rising to her feet. She looked sheepishly around for a non-existent audience.

Chase pointed at Allie, still on the boat, "You stay. I'll be right back." She plopped her butt down, her head tilted to one side.

■ ■ ■

In her underwear and a t-shirt, with the television on low, Karen jumped up when the knock came on the room's door, Allie vaulting off the bed to accompany her. "Who is it..?"

"It's me," came a whisper, "let me in..."

"You have been gone two hours I was getting worri..." Karen opened the door and recoiled, Chase standing there, soaked to the skin, his hair matted to his head, "Ew! What is that *smell?"*

"And hello to you," he replied, entering the room, his muddy running shoes in his hand. He headed straight for the shower. "The river water's brackish and the mud in the mangroves is really nasty..."

"That's an understatement, " she attempted to wave the smell away. " Why were you in the water?"

"That dead end tributary is on the other side of the river. I took it to the end and ran her bow into the mud, tied her to the closest tree. Then I had to slog through the mud and swim back across the river..." He stepped into the shower, clothes on, shedding them in the safety of the tub. "There's nothing over there and the overhang is pretty dense... she'll be hard to find."

She stood in the bathroom doorway watching him shower. "I really don't think those are going to come clean. And I think your shoes are ruined."

"I passed the Inn's laundromat coming back, we'll have to give it a try."

She stripped her clothes, depositing them on the bathroom counter before climbing into the shower behind him. "Pass the soap, big boy..." She rubbed her naked body against his back.

He handed the soap back toward her, "I thought you'd already showered..."

"I did..." she purred, running her fingers across the muscles of his back.

■ ■ ■

Chase leaned back on the bed with his laptop on his legs. "Let's see if we can find a wireless signal..." he yawned.

Karen curled up next to him on the bed, "Where do we go from here?"

"We'll get some sleep, chill tomorrow and see if we can find a car tomorrow night..." Chase typed as he spoke. "Nice. Got a signal..."

"Find or steal?"

"I prefer to think of it as borrow..."

"You're just a one man crime spree aren't ya?"

"I remind you it is one man, one woman..."

"Yeah, thanks for that by the way..." she smacked his arm, "Until I met you I was a good girl who never got in trouble..."

He smirked crookedly, never taking his eyes off the screen, "So you're forgetting that little drunken fiasco at the prom?"

"I never said I was innocent, I just said I never got in trouble." She shrugged, "We never got caught..."

"Oooh," he laughed, "huge difference between good girl and never got caught."

"You're an ass," she laughed. It was something she hadn't done freely since Pam's death. It felt good to forget for a little while. Chase sat up quickly, typing, the keys clattering under his fingers. Karen leaned in, "What's going on?"

"Murphy's alive. Holy shit *he's alive!*" Chase pointed at the nickname on screen, "That's him right there..."

"Where is he?"

"I don't know yet, hold on..."

CHAPTER SIXTEEN

UFW CONQUEST, OSSOMON SYSTEM: *MOVE ALONG, NOTHING TO SEE HERE*

Lieutenant Commander Mike Warren settled into the deep leather seat of the Cyclone sitting in the launch rack, accepting his helmet from the rigger standing on the boarding ladder. The rigger assisted Mike with his flight harness, umbilical cord connections and safety checks. As his final task, he pulled the safety pin on the ejection seat and showed it to the pilot, getting a nod before dropping it into a gear pouch around his waist. He'd be reinserting it when the craft returned from its patrol.

Giving the rigger a thumbs up, Mike watched him disappear as he slid down the ladder to the deck. Pulling the lever that retracted the ladder into the Cyclone's fuselage, the light winked out on the console telling him it was complete. *Master power, air system, communications, fuel delivery system, electronics...* he progressed through his standard pre-launch checklist.

"Conquest Control to Black Leader..."

The Commander keyed his mic, "Black Leader, go ahead."

"Two minutes to launch."

Mike checked left and right exchanging a thumbs up with the other members of his flight as he pulled the canopy handle, the frame and perspex motoring forward on its track. "Good to go Control, we're saddled up and ready to ride..." Mike listened to the comm traffic as the flight tower checked in with White Flight, launching out from the other side of the Conquest's hull. Two flights of six to launch the moment they cleared the gate into Ossomon. As a precaution, two more flights of six were manned and ready to launch and probably another twelve were suited up on standby.

The Novellis System was such a major snoozefest, Mike wondered what they'd find in Ossomon. He knew the official story; that there had been considerable Pirate activity here but this felt like they were prepping for more than just a little resistance. In retrospect, that was OK with him, he hadn't pulled the trigger on anything since Velora Prime and he was jonesing for a serious hit of adrenalin. It wasn't that he wanted or longed to kill someone, it was more of a competition, a jousting match of sorts. It was only personal to the point of *his* machine against his opponent's, *his* nerves and talent in contrast to theirs. A challenge. It was irrelevant whether the enemy ship was destroyed or simply disabled... it was the winning that counted. A few drinks with Commander Dar Sloane and Mike was convinced he'd probably enjoy the thrill of canyon racing in Drifters.

He relaxed, leaning back against the headrest, staring straight ahead. The interlocking steel door in front of him was suddenly partially obscured by the translucent blue stasis field winking to life. Looking like an intense blue version of a television between stations, the electronic curtain moved and swirled and he pulled his helmet's sun visor down to preserve his night vision.

"This is Conquest Control; Black and White flights launching in; 5, 4, 3, 2..."

■ ■ ■

Captain Paul Smiley hovered over the situation table in the control tower, watching the movement, the positioning and make-ready of everything on the deck below them, the Conquest's experienced Mini-Boss watching the launch racks from his position at the tower's observation windows, "...3, 2, 1, *Launch!*" The tower's windows bowed as alarm klaxons screamed, red lights flashing throughout the flight deck, crates flying across the bay. *"Blowout! We have a blowout!"*

In the second or two it took Pappy to cross the gap between the table and the glass, the door on the rack where Black Three had launched was already closed, piled with debris the open maw had tried to suck out into space. "Cut the alarm. Did we lose anybody?"

"Not sure yet, Boss," replied his second in command. "We need to get a count. I'm working on it now."

"Any problems with the launch? Everybody out in one piece?"

"Black Flight is clear and operational," reported the crewman at the sensor station.

Jack Steele trotted down the steps from the main bridge, "What the hell's going on, Pappy?"

"Blowout, Admiral."

"Everybody OK?"

Pappy glanced at the Mini Boss and got a non-confirmation signal as he spoke on the comm to the deck crew. "We're still working on that, Jack."

Steele clenched his jaw, "Hmm. Was it one of the new units?"

"No, we haven't gotten to all of them yet..."

"Can we close off the ones that haven't been converted yet?"

Paul Smiley sucked air though his teeth in a sign of apprehension, "Man, Jack," he said quietly, "that would seriously hamper our launch abilities. We've only got about fifty percent of them installed."

"We need to step it up Paul..."

"I realize that Jack, but we can't sacrifice the launch readiness of this ship. We're a carrier; we live and die on our ability to field and recover fighters. Without them, were a big fat pigeon..."

"I get that, but..."

"No buts Jack, you know as well as I do, battleship escort or not, we'd be somebody's *lunch*. Look what you did to that Pirate carrier..." He waved, anticipating Steele's rebuttal, "Look, let me speak with the Captain Ryan, see if we can add some more men to the work crews. Maybe we can speed up the process."

"Please do," nodded Jack.

Paul pulled Jack to one side, "We still don't have enough of the field emitter sets though, do we?"

"We're golden," replied Steele. "The Chief was able to remove the modules. They're clean and ready to go... so we'll actually have some spares."

"Outstanding..." nodded Paul.

■ ■ ■

Admiral Steele and the Captain Ryan stood nearly shoulder to shoulder in the center of the Conquest's bridge, looking at the expanse of Ossomon, Black Flight and White Flight patrolling ahead, noted by markers on the big screen.

"Welcome to Ossomon, Admiral," commented Ryan. "Over there" he pointed to a blue and green planet on the right, "is Rega, capital of the system. She's a pretty large Class 014. Over on our left we have Ozira, a Class 09, not terribly habitable - fairly desolate really. Mostly desert. But there are several mining colonies there. There are also two stations in the system," he pointed at the markers on the screen, "one owned by Rega as a trade hub and another that is owned by a private franchise."

"Busy system..."

"Yes, sir," agreed the Captain, "it certainly is. And on a regular basis, we have to visit and chase out some undesirables."

"Pirates?"

Ryan pursed his lips for a moment, "Sometimes a little of everything. Minor skirmishes mostly. Peacekeeping."

"Does Rega have a military? Can't they handle it?"

"To some extent, yes. But in many respects they are like Veloria, a little light on population and technology. They are making strides in the right direction though. As a steady provider of agricultural goods, they have expanded their wealth and upgraded much of their equipment and technology. We just need to lend them a hand from time to time to make sure their growth remains unfettered." He glanced at Steele momentarily, "Something that should have been done with Veloria." He shook his head briefly, thinking about recent history. "It pains me greatly that Velora Prime was... overlooked. That we were not there when they needed us..."

"Your sentiments are appreciated, Mr. Ryan. Now they..." Steele caught himself, "*we,* must look to the future."

Anthony Ryan nodded solemnly, "Sometimes I forget, not only are you an Admiral, you are a King..."

"Mmm," nodded Steele, "I have to remind *myself* sometimes. Not something I am totally comfortable with yet."

"The Admiral or the King part?" mused the Captain.

"Take your pick..."

■ ■ ■

This was something new for Mike Warren, he had never seen this many civilian ships in a system at one time, his scope dotted with idents of all sizes. He keyed his mic on an open broadcast, "Unidentified freighter, one-five-seven-three-three-six, why aren't you broadcasting an ident? Identify yourself, please."

It took a moment before the response crackled in, a distinctly female voice, "Who the hellion is asking?"

"UFW Conquest, Black Flight Leader, Lieutenant Commander Warren. Now please activate your ident beacon..."

"Oh..." crackled the stunned reply. "Sorry, Commander... Our communications mast was damaged salvaging some mining equipment. Our ident beacon is not functioning; we're operating on a secondary array... We're with Omni Salvage and Transport."

"Where are you headed?"

"The only place with the parts and an interior bay where we can make the mast repairs; Rikovik's Reef..."

■ ■ ■

As Captain Ryan explained it, the Imperator of Rega was like the President of the planet. Immediately, with the Imperator's flamboyant mannerisms, wild hair and garish clothing, Steele got the impression he was meeting a circus barker. It was almost uncomfortable to watch.

"Greetings, Captain! Ooh, I see Admiral Pottsdorn is no longer with you... Whom do we have here?"

"Imperator, this is Admiral Steele..."

"Welcome, Admiral Steele!" exclaimed the man on screen, his arms spread wide. "Welcome to Ossomon and welcome to Rega! We hope you get a chance to stop at Rega Pinnacle Station, we're sure you will enjoy yourselves."

"Thank you, Imperator..."

"Oh, you are quite welcome, of course. Will you be staying with us long?"

And there it is... nervous concern. He wants me to say no, we're just passing through... "Maybe a couple of days, Imperator." Steele caught the Captain's shocked sideways glance out of the corner of his eye, but he was more interested in the Imperator's reaction. It was subtle but it was there. He did not want them there. Or maybe someone *else* didn't want them there. In either case he was worried. Truthfully, a UFW Task Force sitting in a system with *mixed company* might make a lot of people nervous. *Screw it, let them be nervous.*

"Well," smiled the Imperator, nervously rambling on, "you are of course welcome to stay as long as you want... If there anything you require, please do not hesitate to ask. Maybe we can get together..."

■ ■ ■

With the communication concluded, Steele and Ryan walked toward the holographic chart table near the rear of the bridge.

217

The Captain glanced in his mug, "Well that was... interesting..."

"That was *disturbing...*"

"Probably a better word..." nodded Ryan. "I've never seen that behavior from him before."

Leaning with his back against the chart table, his arms casually folded across his chest, Steele cocked his head to one side, "Mr. Ryan, that was probably the longest five minutes I've ever had the displeasure of enduring..."

The Captain sipped the remnants of his coffee, "He was nervous, *very* nervous. Almost frenetic. He's always been a bit... effervescent... "

The word struck him as funny and Steele laughed out loud. "The guy reminded me of a Muppet..."

"Muppet?"

Steele nodded, "A special type of puppet. They're famous back home."

Ryan raised one eyebrow, his expression dubious, *"Famous* puppets?"

Steele stroked his mustache in thought, "Yeah, I'm not sure I can explain it, but they're pretty funny."

"Hmm." The Captain looked unconvinced, motioning toward the screen with his empty mug, "So what do you want to do about our friend here?"

Steele was silent for a moment, formulating his thoughts. "Nothing." He turned around and pulled up the system map on the holo-chart; planets, moons, stations, sun and gates floating above the table. "What's your SOP in this system?"

Anthony Ryan set his mug on the console and called up the navigational history, the holographic image of their last visit displayed on the chart, colored lines snaking around the system, illustrating all ship movements and patrols. "This is pretty typical. The blue lines show the patrols we had out here, here and here," he pointed. "This blue line was our route through the system, and here is where one of our patrols engaged a pirate freighter smuggling contraband."

"First thing I'm noticing," began Steele, rotating the chart image around, examining it closely, "is there was a lot more ship traffic in this system on your last visit than we're seeing now..."

"Yes, sir. Considerably different..."

"What do you make of that?"

Captain Ryan pursed his lips in contemplation, "I honestly don't know, Admiral. I've been through this system about a dozen times, this is probably the quietest I've ever seen it."

"Could someone have tipped off the locals we were coming?"

"Anything's possible, sir. The transporter that Black Flight encountered was deadheading to Rikovik's Reef for repairs on a comm mast they claim they damaged while salvaging mining equipment. The closest mining operation would be the one back in the Gedhepp System..."

"The fifth planet... Or what was left of it," said Jack, correcting himself.

"Exactly. They came here to deposit their load and will likely head back to Gedhepp after their repairs."

"So we may not have been alone in that planetary debris field." Steele rubbed his chin contemplating their next move. He couldn't see anything happening at this juncture. It was a cat and mouse game; the task force was the cat and they had come late to the party. The mice had already scored their prize and successfully made away with it. Whether they had cleared the system or gone to ground to hide didn't matter, they had the time to wait the cat out. The Imperator, aka; *the Big Cheese* was nervous because a bunch of hidden mice could do a lot of damage if they got bored or resentful if their host wasn't graciously keeping them occupied. Whether he was a willing participant or simply tolerant of their presence was the question of the day. Steele suspected it was symbiotic relationship, a trade off of good and bad; their presence was bad, their money and trade products were good. It seemed clear the only result of remaining in the system would be to exacerbate the problem for the Imperator.

"Run the standard operations, Mr. Ryan. Let's head the task force to the nearest gate that puts us back on course for the Terran System. We've lost the element of surprise, we're not going to gain anything by hanging around or searching. We'll be back through here; maybe we'll have better luck next time."

"Aye, Admiral." The Captain left the chart table and headed for his command chair, holding up his empty mug, "Somebody bring me some coffee, please..?"

CHAPTER SEVENTEEN

FREERANGER – DD217, OSSOMON SYSTEM: *MOUSE CHASE CAT*

"Rega Pinnacle Control; FreeRanger DD217, you are number three in line for docking, the carousel is currently full. Please maintain your traffic pattern."

Commander T. B. Yafusco paced the middle of the bridge in-between the stations, "Rega Pinnacle Control, we need supplies and we need to make this quick, we're in the middle of a military mission."

"We sympathize with you 217, but we're a whole day behind in operations. I've bumped you up in priority three spots, I'm sorry we can't do any better than that, but..."

Commander Yafusco turned to his communications officer, making a slashing motion across his throat and she abruptly cut the comm connection. The square with Rega Pinnacle Station's traffic officer winked out, replaced by the view of a very busy space station and a line of ships snaking around the planet of Rega.

"Find us a comm to the Imperator." He strolled back to his command chair and unceremoniously dropped into it, barely containing his ire. There wasn't a single   FreeRanger ship in the waiting roster, they were all commercial ships. The Imperator was forgetting his place, neglecting the debt he owed to the FreeRanger Council. Military ships were supposed to come first. But then again that ridiculous buffoon had never served, he was a greedy politician, a charlatan.

"Comm up..."

"On Screen," barked Tibby, sliding out of his chair, standing in the center of the bridge, hands on his hips.

The Imperator of Rega sat behind his desk, hands folded calmly, looking fairly presidential despite his brightly colored clothes and wild hair. "Hello, Commander, how can I be of service to our FreeRanger friends?"

"Get me a spot on Pinnacle's docking carousel. Now."

"I'm sorry my dear boy, that is quite impossible, we..."

"BOY!?" erupted Yafusco, closing in on the big screen, *"You'd better check yourself, you pompous windbag!"*

"My apologies," waved the Imperator, attempting to placate the angry Commander. "We have a considerable backlog, as you can see. It is true they have placed you as number three in line, but we will have three docking spots opening nearly simultaneously. So you see, moving you up in the roster would do little to speed things up for you. We are doing our best, I can assure you."

"We are..."

"In a hurry, I understand completely," nodded the Imperator, interrupting. "If you would care to send your supplies list to the tower, we can help expedite things by organizing your order and having it ready to load when you get to the dock. That should save you quite a bit of time." He smiled, anticipating a positive response. Getting nothing but an icy stare, he waved an electronic stylus at the screen, "I heard you're on a mission. Might I inquire..."

"No you may not."

If nothing else, the Imperator was persistent. "It wouldn't have anything to do with the UFW group that passed though here, would it?" He watched Yafusco's expression change. "Might I say, Commander, you are a bit, um, *unprepared* to meet them?"

Yafusco didn't respond to the comment, remaining stone faced. "Tell me about the group, what kind of ships were they?"

"There were three ships; a carrier, a battleship and a frigate - not a type I'd ever seen before. And fighters, *lots* of fighters."

"What type of carrier?"

"An Oijin Class. And the battleship was a Chimera Class," he added with a knowing nod.

Yafusco paced, his head down, thinking. An Oijin Class was a heavy carrier, there wasn't anything bigger that he could think of. It was an older design; many of the newer types were smaller, lighter, faster... but with the fighter payload she carried, an Oijin could *own* a system. And with a Chimera Battleship, she didn't need to be fast. There weren't many around but the Chimera firepower was legendary. Could these be the ones from Velora Prime that came to the defense of the Freedom? It made sense. Commander Boxxe had said there were nearly a hundred fresh fighters coming into the fight; that certainly described the capabilities of an Oijin Carrier. What about the frigate? Could it be the same one Boxxe's DD158 was attacked by? Tibby had never heard of a Halceón until Boxxe mentioned it and the one in this UFW group remained unidentified by Rega Pinnacle Station. Coincidence? That was too many coincidences for Tibby's taste.

"What else do you remember?" probed the Commander.

The Imperator steepled his fingers, resting his chin there for a moment, "Well, the carrier and battleship have been through here several times before, but the little frigate is a new addition... Hmm... Oh yes, and the group has a new Admiral, I guess the old one retired or something."

Tibby stopped in his tracks, "New Admiral..? Name, name! What's his *name?"*

"Steele. Why, do you know him?"

"No. We've never met... but I've heard the name..."

■ ■ ■

Grinah strolled into the galley and slid into the booth next to Tibby, staring at his plate as he ate. "Slow down or you're going to make yourself sick."

He paused between fork-fulls, "I wanted to finish before they were done with our cargo..."

"Too late," she smiled, "the boys are securing the hull now. We'll be ready to go in just a few..."

"Commander Yafusco to the bridge, Commander to the bridge."

Grinah giggled lightly, glancing up at the comm speaker, "And there it is." She stayed Tibby's fork hand, "Slow down. *Eat* your meal, mister. Lieutenant Zarney is fully capable of clearing us from the station."

Tibby stared into her eyes for a moment before setting his fork on the plate and keying his mic, "Take us out, Dash. Best speed once we're clear."

"Aye, sir," came the response in his earpiece. "Also wanted to update you, the DD62 has arrived in system; she's been directed to follow our lead."

"Excellent, that's Kindre Thurmer's ship; she's a good skipper. Have them fall into formation, I'll be up after dinner."

"Aye, Skipper. Take your time."

Grinah tilted her head, "Who's Kindre Thurmer?"

Tibbe resumed eating at a more leisurely pace, "The DD62 is in system; they're joining up with us. I know Kindre from my Academy class, she's a good skipper. One of only a handful of women going through command class at the time."

"An old flame?"

"By the Gods, no." he laughed.

"So she's hideous then?"

Tibby had the distinct feeling she was toying with him. Like a cat toys with a mouse. "No, just way out of my league."

"You underestimate yourself," she said wryly, her eyes boring into his.

"No... you've never seen her..."

"So she's beautiful then?"

Yafusco could see where this was leading, and he had no exit strategy. "I really don't want to have this conversation, Grinah..."

"Is she more beautiful than me?"

Dammit. "No one is more beautiful than you..." It was the only logical answer he could think of.

Grinah leaned back against her seat, *"Good answer,"* she teased. "You do know I'm not the insecure type, don't you?" She touched his hand, "Stop sweating, dear, I'm just playing with you."

■ ▥ ▤

The conference comm in the Captain's ready room between the two destroyer commanders, lasted about fifteen minutes. Enough for a thorough situation report, with plenty of time left over for some friendly chatting and reminiscing. And more than enough time for Grinah to become uncomfortable. It was obvious Tibby approached Kindre Thurmer with a friendly professionalism, there was nothing that hinted at anything more. But there was something about that woman that told Grinah she would take more if she thought she could get it. She looked like a maneater, dangerously beautiful.

Grinah was still staring at the blank screen when Yafusco turned around, "You OK?"

She blinked away the image burned into her eyes of the striking platinum blond with the short hair. "Uh, I'm OK," she blinked, her eyes shifting to Tibby, "Alright, I might be a little insecure..."

He sat next to her, "She's not my type... *You're* my type."

"Pssch," snorted Grinah, "She's not my type either, I don't go that way. But by the Gods, *I'd make the exception.* Just so I could stare at her..."

"That's the problem," explained Tibby, "she's *too* attractive..."

"Sure, because *too attractive* is the new ugly," countered Grinah sarcastically.

Tibby burst into a belly laugh. "I don't know how to explain it," he said, taking her hand. "It's like she's *so* beautiful, it's distracting. She's *so* beautiful, looking at her makes my head hurt..."

"Stop saying *so beautiful,* you're going to give me a complex."

"OK. How about this, last one; she's so beautiful it scares me. *You're* so beautiful I fell in love with you."

Grinah laughed a short, unladylike snort, covering her mouth in embarrassment, "I can live with that one."

"Y'know, I could probably get you together with her," he teased, "I heard she likes women too..."

She shot him a sideways glance, "So you could watch? You'd like that wouldn't you..."

He shrugged, grinning, "Not *my* thing, just trying to keep my girl happy..."

"You are so full of it," she shot back playfully. "That's *every* man's thing..."

CHAPTER EIGHTEEN

UFW CONQUEST, RANGILEUR SYSTEM: *THE REAPER COMETH*

"Lt. Commander, Mike Warren, and Flight Cadet, Lisa Steele; report to the Admiral's office..."

Sitting in the crowded galley cafeteria, Lisa Steele glanced up from her breakfast and

the e-Pad she had been studying. She looked around, "Did they just call me?"

Commander Dar Sloane sat down across from her, setting his loaded tray on the table, "Yep, that's you, Cookie. What did you do?"

"Lt. Commander, Mike Warren, and Flight Cadet, Lisa Steele; report to the Admiral's office, on the double!"

Lt. Commander Mike Warren stood up on the other side of the room, slugging down his juice. "Let's go, Steele!" he shouted, leaving his tray on the table. Lisa jumped up and with one last inquisitive look at Sloane, began making her way toward the exit.

"Good luck, Cookie!" Dar called over his shoulder.

■ ■ ■

"What the hell's going on?" asked Lisa, hustling to keep up with Mike's longer strides as they trotted down the corridor.

"Your guess is as good as mine, Lisa, I haven't heard a thing. Are you in trouble?"

"Not that I can think of," she panted. "I have an e-Pad *and* an eGo-h, why didn't he just call me on one of those..." She slowed her stride when she thought of the Remora, *"Ooh..."*

Mike Warren slowed, grabbing her by the hand, "Keep up. What, *ooh?"*

"The Remora, I'm in trouble for the Remora."

"Doubt it," said Mike as they rounded a corner, "why would they need me? *Coming thru!"* he shouted, parting a group of crewman down the middle.

Lisa passed through the group behind him. "I don't know... Elevators?" she pointed.

"No time. Stairs," he huffed. They rounded another corner and he cut ahead of her, taking the stairs two at a time, his boots clanging on the metal steps. "Keep up, Kiddo."

"Doing my best, you're a lot faster than me..."

The run from the galley to the bridge was better than half of the Conquest's 1,987 foot length, through populated corridors and up six decks. Mike eased to a stop, pausing outside the bridge door, waiting for Lisa to catch up, making sure he was tucked and his gig line was straight before entering. "Tuck yourself," he prompted as she tromped to a stop.

"What?" she wheezed, pinching a stitch in her side.

"Straighten up," he whispered. "You can't go in like that."

"I just ran a half mile and you're worried about my shirt?"

"Fifth of a mile," he corrected her, taking her e-Pad so she could make her adjustments. "It wasn't the run, it was the stairs. Stairs are the killer." He pulled her belt buckle to the middle. "That's better. You ready?" He handed the e-Pad back to her.

"You mean... other than not being able to breathe?" she huffed. "Sure, I'm good... to go..."

The Marine sentry who had remained motionless and silent outside the door, activated the control and it split, disappearing into the walls with a metallic scrape. It was the first time since she'd been on the Conquest that Lisa was afraid to walk through the door onto the bridge. *What had it been, four months? Five months..?* Her internal dialogue abruptly ceased when Mike Warren paused inside the door, waiting to be noticed, saluting to the Captain when his attention shifted momentarily in their direction. She mimicked Mike's salute with almost perfect timing.

A quick salute and the Captain nodded in the direction of the Admiral's office, turning back to his bridge duties. Everything felt different and there was an impending sense of dread that rolled in her stomach, her heart hammering.

The door to the Admiral's office, the same door that she had passed through daily for months, suddenly seemed foreign. Mike stepped to the door without hesitation and it slid cleanly into the walls with a hiss. Stepping through into the office, he left enough room for Lisa at his side and saluted. She followed suit, feeling extremely uncomfortable.

226

She tried to read the Admiral - her brother, and for the first time she could recollect, found nothing there but a blank slate. It chilled her. He and Captain Paul Smiley rose from their respective leather chairs, returning their salutes. It looked like she and Mike had interrupted an important conference of some kind. She was more than happy to come back later.

"Do you know why you're here?" asked the Admiral.

"No, sir," replied Mike Warren, "but I expect you're going to tell us."

The Admiral smiled briefly, at least it looked like a smile to Lisa. "I'll let the Captain explain it to you," he said, sitting back down, crossing his legs casually at the knee. The smile disappeared as quickly as it came and Lisa felt weak in the knees. Her hands were trembling, having a difficult time holding onto her now sweat-slippery e-Pad. She pinched the leg seams of her pants to keep her hands still.

Paul Smiley glanced down at his own e-Pad, "This hearing is to determine if events recorded during the egress of Rikovik's Reef and the transition through to Aegeron Pass are properly recorded and accurate."

"Yes, sir," she replied quietly.

"I have not asked you a question as of yet, Cadet."

"Sorry, sir."

"Lisa Steele..." She twitched when he said her name like someone had just shouted in her face but the Captain took no notice and continued. "On or about interstellar date; 70522.523, did you or did you not, launch from the UFW Frigate, Revenge, in the ship's newly acquired Remora fighter during gate transit from Rikovik's Reef to Aegeron Pass, with the express mission of providing a communication link between the Revenge and a yacht, piloted by Admiral Steele?"

Lisa swallowed hard, "Yes, sir," she croaked, her mouth feeling pasty.

"And you were able to ascertain that the yacht was substantially damaged?"

"Yes, sir, it was."

"You were successful in communicating with both; Admiral Steele in the yacht and the bridge of the Revenge? Relay information?"

"Yes, sir."

"And you were issued clear, distinct orders by both; Lt. Commander, Brian Carter prior to launch and Admiral Steele, in flight, to vacate the vicinity of the yacht if it threatened to drop below safe transition protocols?"

"Yes, sir," she squeaked, her voice cracking. *Am I having a heart attack? I think I'm having a heart attack...*

227

"And, did you or did you not, disobey both of those *direct orders?*"

"Yes, sir," she replied, her voice quivering. *No, heart's still beating I can feel it in my ears. But I can't feel my hands... maybe it's a stroke... God, I'm having a stroke...*

"And in doing so, not only risked the safety of the UFW craft you were piloting, but your own life and the life of your crew member, Marine Sergeant, Draza Mac?"

"Yes, sir." She was clenching her jaw to keep from shaking. It wasn't helping. *Oh my God I'm going to prison...*

"And contrary to orders, common sense, better judgment and every known tactic or technique developed over eons of space flight, attempted to use a fighter craft like a lowly recovery tug? *Severely damaging* the craft entrusted to your care, nearly losing your bird, your life and the life of your crew member?"

"But..."

"Answer the question, Cadet." He tossed his e-Pad on the chair behind him.

She clenched, fighting her nerves. "Yes, *sir.*"

"And by sheer guts, fortitude, willpower and brute force, use every ounce of skill you'd developed, persevered to survive an event that has never been recorded before? And in the process, saved the Admiral and twenty-three other lives?"

Lisa took a deep breath, not only taking pride in the fact that she had not failed or abandoned her brother, but recognizing a different tone in the question. *"Yes, sir."*

"And *would you,* if presented with the same situation again, react in the same manner, risking your life, without hesitation or regret?"

"I regret nothing," she said, raising her eyes defiantly and looking at him squarely, her heart pounding.

"Then I cannot think of *anyone* who deserves these more than you do..." Captain Smiley extended his arm toward her, his opening palm revealing a pair of golden flight wings. Paul stepped forward, removed and pocketed the training emblem from her uniform tunic, replacing it with the polished pilot's wings.

The Admiral rose from his seat as the Captain stepped back from the speechless young woman. Mike Warren, standing silently, hadn't budged an inch since their entrance into the room.

"I think we have a problem mister Smiley..."

"What's that, Admiral?"

"This *pilot* seems to be out of uniform..." he stepped to his sister and pulled the cadet pips off her collar, taking a moment to replace them with a new set. Satisfied, he stepped back, "This *Ensign* is still dressed as a Cadet..."

Captain Smiley looked over the cow-eyed young woman, "That can't be right, can it?"

Steele shook his head, "No it's not. Please see to it that she visits the ship's tailor and is immediately fitted for the proper uniform of her rank.

Captain Smiley looked to Mike Warren, "Lt. Commander, will you see to it that Ms. Steele finds her way to the tailor for a new fitting?"

"Aye, sir. New uniform for the Ensign."

The Admiral rubbed his chin, "Something tells me we're forgetting something, Captain..."

"Ah yes." Paul grabbed his e-Pad off the chair behind him and paged to a new document. "From the office of UFW Fleet Command: In light of the actions of UFW Cadet, Lisa Steele, on or about interstellar date; 70522.523, in which she did willfully and without concern for her own safety, remain with a crippled, private space conveyance that had dropped below transfer gate protocols. At great risk to her and her crew, even as the transfer tube deteriorated, Ms. Steele used her UFW Remora spacecraft to push said private conveyance safely through the gate into Aegeron Pass. This heroic, selfless act of bravery, has duly been recorded and is being rewarded with the UFW Meritorious Halo Award, with *lightning bolt*..." Paul waved his hand, "Signed; UFW Fleet Command, Fleet Admiral, Warn Higdenberger."

Lisa recognized her brother in the Admiral now as he stepped forward with a warm smile, a small open box in his hand containing a campaign ribbon. "This is the Meritorious Halo ribbon, it goes under your wings on your uniform. An actual medal will come for you as well. The little silver lightning bolt on it, represents you surviving a tear during transition. There are only two people in the entire UFW fleet with this exact ribbon..."

"You..?" she asked, accepting the box.

Jack shook his head, "No, not me. You and Sergeant Draza Mac." He stepped back, shoulder to shoulder with Captain Smiley. "One last bit of business before we dismiss you..."

"Right," began Captain Smiley."Lisa, you will report to flight combat training day after tomorrow when our new class starts...." He nodded at Mike, "Mr. Warren here, will not only be one of the primary class instructors, but your private tutor. There is a lot to learn and we're going to push you pretty hard, both mentally and physically."

Lisa's pulse quickened, "I'm going to be a *fighter pilot...?*"

Paul smiled, "Lady, you're loaded with raw talent and a *huge* set of, um... *stones.* I'm expecting nothing but good things from you..."

■ ■ ■

Showered, refreshed and in a new uniform, sporting her new wings, rank and citation ribbon, Lisa Steele and Mike Warren walked the corridor toward the officer's lounge. She kept looking down at her new wings, the reality still sinking in. "I swear to God, I thought I was going to pee myself. Or pass out... In which case I would have peed myself anyway..."

Mike guffawed, "You did fine. You know why they did that, right?"

"No, not really... They wanted to mess with my head?"

"Heh," he snorted, "maybe a little. But mostly I think to impress upon you that being a bonehead is not going to have pleasant results. You screw something up you get reprimanded – and let's be honest, what you did was *insanely* stupid..."

"Hey..." she objected.

"Well it *was.* I'm not saying I or any other pilot wouldn't have tried it... Wait, I take that back," he said with a cancellation wave. "I probably would have *never* thought of something as ridiculous as crushing the nose of my fighter up the ass of another ship to push it..."

Lisa tossed her hair back in frustration, "Y'know if you're trying to make me feel better, you're failing miserably."

"What I'm getting at," explained Mike, "is you had a unique perspective; one of less experience, which benefited you. Working from a vantage point of less... *knowledge,* you did not know what you were doing had nearly a zero percent chance of succeeding. No one told you it couldn't be done, so it never entered your mind that you couldn't do it. So you just went and did it."

"Sooo, you *could* say I did something impossible then."

"That's what I'm saying," he said, punctuating with his hands. "It was against direct orders, so they had to reprimand you. But you succeeded, so they rewarded you. I'm pretty sure they just wanted you to understand that there are consequences to your decisions. Thank God it wasn't a posthumous award..."

"Pssch, yeah, that would suck."

"Fortunately for you, it all ended well... you have the Steele guardian angel on your shoulder... it must run in your family. We should drink to that angel and pray he's never asleep when you need him."

"Or her," mused Lisa, sighing. "Yeah, I could use a drink... a couple... or four."

"I hope you bought your ITC card, because tradition says drinks are on you tonight..."

■ ■ ■

"Li-sa! Li-sa! Li-sa!" chanted the people in the crowded Officer's Club.

"I didn't know I had this many friends!" Lisa shouted to Mike over the noise.

"Don't let it go to your head, you'd be surprised how fast *free drinks* spreads around the ship!" he shouted back.

"I have to pay for *everybody?* "

"Just one round," he nodded. "But *all night* for your friends," he grinned.

Lisa wove her way through the throng, running into Sergeant Draza Mac. "Hey Mac!" she hugged him then suddenly pulled away, "Wait, are you going to be in trouble for being in here? You're not..."

"An officer," he said, finishing her sentence. "It's alright, you can say it, it doesn't offend me." He pointed to his Meritorious Halo citation ribbon, "It's my night too..."

She took a drink handed to her by a passing waitress, "So do you have to buy drinks for everybody too?"

"I don't know, you might want to ask that guy over there," he shouted, pointing across the room to a far corner. Lisa turned to follow his finger, spotting her brother and Commander Dar Sloane standing together, waving at her over the heads of the crowd. "The answer is," continued the Sergeant, "the Admiral's got your back, your money's no good here." He grabbed her by the arm, "And if you ever need a back-seater, I'll fly with you... *Any time.* "

■ ■ ■

After more than a couple hours of noise, music and drinks Jack needed a break, dragging Lisa out of the Officer's Club by the hand, followed by Mike

Warren and Dar Sloane. "Wow," he opened his mouth and pulled on his earlobes, "my ears are ringing."

"Mine too," added Lisa as they strolled down the corridor.

"That bash is going to cost you a pretty penny, Jack," commented Mike in a moment of casual off-duty dialogue. "Er, sorry... Admiral..." he mumbled.

"Forget it, Mike. It's just us." He shot a sideways glance at Lisa, "It's worth every last dime," he smiled, "and then some."

"So where are we going, Jack?" asked Dar Sloane.

"You call me Admiral," teased Steele.

"Sorry, Admiral..."

"Kidding, Dar." He waved toward the elevators, "One last thing to show you, Lisa, then I'm headed off to bed. You all can go back to the party if you want."

"Not if I want to be able to get up in the morning," commented Mike. "Besides, I need my beauty sleep..."

Lisa and Dar exchanged glances and Dar wanted to say something but he dared not, especially in front of her brother. He decided to wait for a better opportunity.

The elevator ride down was silent except for the hum of the cab as it descended nine decks, the steel doors opening with a hiss on the hangar deck, directly below the flight deck. The smell of electronics, lubricants and metal were tangible enough to taste. "I'm getting to like that smell," said Lisa, "it makes my mouth water."

Jack slung his arm around her shoulder and gave her a little squeeze, "My little sister is becoming a *real* pilot, she's all grown up now..."

She pushed him off, laughing,"Quit it..."

Walking past several occupied repair stations, they came upon an empty stall and Jack came to an abrupt stop, looking around. "What the hell," he mumbled.

"What?" asked Mike.

"It was right here..." he pointed, "they must've moved it..." He waved his arms above his head in frustration, *"HEY!"* he shouted, "Where's..."

A head and shoulders popped up, suspended in mid air about seven feet off the deck, the mechanic looking down at the confused pilots, "Admiral! Wasn't expecting you tonight, just chasing down a few little things..." He reached forward, doing something with unseen arms and hands. An outline glittered, the shimmering shape of the Remora wavering as it gradually appeared like a mirage in the desert, finally becoming solid. The mechanic climbed down the boarding ladder of the flat-black fighter which had come to resemble a giant black wasp. He ducked under the nose and extended his hand as he approached, "Admiral." They shook briefly. "She looks great, doesn't she?"

"Astounding," was all Jack could manage, examining her new profile.

"She's not really a Remora anymore, she's way more advanced than that. Your engineer, Hoecken Noer... he's brilliant. Just amazing what that man can design."

"So what is she?" asked Lisa staring, mouth agape.

"Ma'am," said the mechanic with a sweep of his hand, "Meet *the Reaper...*"

"She looks *bad ass!*" breathed Mike. He reached up and put his hand on one of the nose guns, examining the turret. "These don't look familiar, what kind of guns are these?"

"Good question," gestured the mechanic. "We originally intended to install standard Particle Gauss Guns, but Hoecken Noer had a better idea... Cryo Gauss Guns..."

Jack raised an eyebrow, "Come again, Chief?"

"His new invention. Took a couple of standard guns and reverse engineered them, rebuilt them into these things right here in the machine shop."

"A Frankengun," mumbled Jack.

The Chief offered a puzzled look at the term but decided to ignore it, pulling a nine-inch steel spike out of his tool pouch, handing it to Jack. "That's your projectile. It's accelerated by Gauss coil magnets, barely touches the barrel, no friction. The tip is a super hard alloy, for penetration, as is the outer skin. The inside is another type of alloy, softer but very dense." He took it back and threw it on the floor with a clang and stopped its roll with the toe of his boot. "Totally inert. No explosive or propellant. On the other hand, a Gauss Particle is a super-hard steel ball, only does one thing." He bent over and picked up the spike again. "But this baby, will penetrate as-is and break up inside, or, when *frozen,* explode on impact like a frag grenade." He pointed at the turret, "The ammo rack is normally ambient temperature and dry. Want them frozen? Switch the system and it floods the rack compartment with refrigerant. Want them back again? Just switch the system back and the refrigerant drains back into the reservoir... of course it will take a while for the ammunition to warm back up..."

"*Very* interesting. How fast do they cycle and what's the round count?"

"Eight-hundred rounds per gun. They cycle considerably slower than the Particle Gauss, but the projectile mass is so much higher on the Cryo Gun, it will do a lot more damage."

Dar Sloane was running his hand across the hull, "What kind of paint is this? If feels almost... *soft.*"

"Non reflective, Commander," said the mechanic. "Light, Radar, magnetic, Lidar; it does a pretty good job of absorbing all of those. Not perfect mind you... but enough to give you an edge... "

"Something else Hecken Noer's been working on?" asked Jack.

"Yep. He wanted to test it on something so he thought this would be a good trial."

"It's OK by me... Anything else?"

"Some improvements on armor, brings it up to the level of some of our other birds, nothing hugely exotic. But I know he's got a few panels on it that are something he calls his *special blend.*" The mechanic shrugged and shook his head, "I don't ask."

Jack laughed, "Probably wise, Chief." He looked over the Reaper once more, walking around it before yawning wide. "OK people I'm done, I'm late for a date with my pillow."

"Yeah, me too," confirmed Mike, "I've got class prep to organize tomorrow."

The group said their goodnights and went their separate ways, the mechanic taking his cue and wandering off to finish his work, leaving Dar and Lisa standing alone under the right wingtip holding hands in an awkward silence. "So..."

"So..." replied Lisa.

"Big day, huh?" Dar knew what he really wanted to say. What he really wanted to ask. But it just didn't seem to dovetail into the here and now.

She nodded, looking down at her shoes, "Definitely one for the record books..."

"I bet you're tired."

She shrugged noncommittally, "Maybe a little. Not ready to go to sleep yet, though."

They started walking slowly toward the elevators. "Want to get a nightcap?"

Lisa tweaked her mouth sideways which usually meant it wasn't her first choice. "I think I'm done with the crowd for the night..."

"So, you want to be alone then?"

She smirked, "I didn't say that..."

Dar sighed, hoping he was getting a better handle on her line of thinking, "Well my quarters are on the pilots' deck..."

Lisa made the crooked mouth thing again, "The pilots' deck is like a frat house... I don't think I want to go there... Mine are on the command staff deck..." she said suggestively.

Dar pushed the button for the elevator. "Ooh, great, next door to your brother, just what I need."

She smiled as the door opened, "Same deck, different side of the ship..."

CHAPTER NINETEEN

BIRMINGHAM, ALABAMA: *MIDNIGHT AUTO*

Most of Birmingham was in the rear-view mirror when the old sedan began coughing up what felt like the equivalent of a lung. Chase knew from the beginning it would never last the entire trip, the sedan hadn't been quite right since they'd acquired it not more than a mile or two from the River Inn & Marina. Now he was hoping it would last just a few more miles.

Karen opened her eyes, stretching, "What's wrong?"

"Engine's almost done..."

"Poor thing," she mumbled. "Where are we? What time is it?"

"About one in the morning... We just passed through Birmingham." He hazarded a glance in the mirror as he moved to the outer lane. "Geez, she won't even hold fifty-five..."

Karen looked around, seeing nothing but a few scattered lights, "What's the plan?"

"I saw a billboard advertising a dealership ahead, I'm hoping she'll get us that far."

"You thinking of trading her in?" joked Karen.

"Funny girl," he shot back. "I'm hoping not to have to walk too far."

A gentle curve in the road and a break in the trees on the right side of the highway revealed a cluster of lights. "Is that it?" she pointed.

Chase had his foot buried in the accelerator pedal, half the cylinders firing in a lumpy, chug that was quickly dropping towards forty miles an hour. "I sure hope so..."

"I see the sign, that's it!"

"And no exit... oh well." Chase lifted his foot off the floored pedal and the engine immediately wheezed to a backfiring, belching idle as he steered it across the shoulder and onto the grass. The old engine groaned when it quit and he let it roll to a stop on its own, shutting off the lights. Chase made a finger gun and shot the dashboard, complete with sound effect.

Karen swung her door open, "What was that?"

"When your horse goes lame, you don't let it suffer, you put it out of its misery. I was putting it out of its misery," he shrugged, opening his door.

Hand sanitizer on a clean sock will work almost as well as alcohol or bleach wipes for removing fingerprints. It might not completely clean DNA but it would make it a great deal tougher finding any intact. His task complete, Chase stuffed the gear in his bag and hefted the backpack over one shoulder, heading for the tree line where Karen and Allie were waiting.

Moving through the trees, down the gentle embankment toward the lights of the dealership, Chase was running alarm systems through his head preparing himself for what he might encounter. As a security specialist, he had done his fair share of ethical security breaches for corporate and private clients. There were almost always weaknesses that could be taken advantage of; you just had to find them. Some were harder than others to find. The thing you couldn't plan for was the human element. Outside interference. A bystander, employee, security guard, cop, dogs... Dogs were a real pain in the ass, no pun intended. He even ran across a client in Miami that had a Bengal Tiger roaming the grounds of his estate. *That* was a tough one. But he usually had time to plan and make notes; going in cold was always the most difficult.

He crouched at the outer edge of the tree line overlooking the dealership, "You're going to stay here with Allie, I have to do this alone." He surveyed the lot, a low, heavy tubular rail surrounding the dealership with padlocked swing-arm gates. "Hmm, no tall fences, no barbed wire... I like it so far. We must be in a low crime area." He inserted the walkie-talkie earpiece in his ear and clipped the mic to his collar. "Let me know if you see anything," he whispered, moving out into the open. "And stay back in the shadows, not at the edge."

"OK," she whispered in his ear. "Um, what do I do if you get caught?"

"Find a way to Salt Lake City and call the number on your cell phone..."

"By myself..?"

"Ssshhh..." Chase crouched at the rear gate facing the access street running along the highway, checking up and down the empty road. Reaching back and pulling a pick-set out of the side of his backpack, he made short work of the padlock, leaving it in place but unlocked. He ducked under the gate and weaving between the rows of cars scanned the light poles for cameras. There was one on each corner pole looking in toward the building. Creeping between the cars being careful to stay obscured from the cameras he made his way to the furthest back corner. At the base of the pole was an electrical inspection plate. Removing it, he stuck the red-lensed flashlight in his mouth, holding it's rubber body between his teeth. Carefully separating the wires, he snipped the video coaxial cable and replaced the plate. Less than five minutes later the other video camera at the back of the lot was dark as well. "How are we doing?" he whispered.

"All quiet. Some light traffic on the street out front, no people."

"Good." Chase examined a used, white, sport truck on his way to the back door of the dealership building. *Nothing flashy, four door cab, four wheel drive, relatively new...* "I think I found us a new truck," he whispered, moving to the back door. Wearing blue Nitrile gloves he worked the picks on the lock of the service door. He figured at best he'd have two minutes to neutralize the alarm before it went off. At worst, a minute. He checked his watch before yanking the door open and slipping inside. It took him almost thirty seconds to locate the key panel in the front office near the receptionist desk, giving little more than a glance at the modern, well-appointed dealership or the new cars sitting in the darkened showroom.

Flashlight back in mouth, he unscrewed the front panel of the control panel, popping it open, "Oh what the hell," he mumbled past the flashlight, a spaghetti bowl of wires spilling out of the box.

"What's wrong?" Karen whispered in his ear.

"Sloppy wiring," he grumbled, fishing through the mess. He worked feverishly, separating the wires and contacts, jumpering several before the light on the front of the panel winked to green. He checked his watch, a minute and fifteen seconds had passed. He wiped the sweat off his face. "Everything OK out there?"

"Uh oh..."

"What?" he hissed.

"I have lights above me on the highway..."

"What kind of lights?" he asked, heading to the finance office.

"The blue and red kind... I think they're over by the old car."

"Don't panic, they're probably just checking it out to make sure someone isn't stranded..."

"Hurry *up* please..."

"Hang tight, I should be done in a few minutes..."

One sale missing paperwork might be suspicious, but two sales missing paperwork would more likely be careless. He snatched a completed file out of the finance officer's bin, looking at the salesman's name, "Sorry Bob," he breathed, "you got a little sloppy this week." He slid the file into his pack and hacking into the dealer's computer system, entered the associate's name on all the paperwork for the white pickup truck. Chase printed out a clear title, purchase, payment and transfer paperwork, assigning a license plate from the dealer's stash for new sales. He finished up, making sure he left no traces of his intrusion and headed off to find the security office. "How are you doing out there?"

"I think he left..."

Wiping the past eight hours of security video, Chase replaced them with video files from a week earlier, resetting the dates on the files and set the security cameras to restart

the next night. There would be a full set of videos for the day, before they realized the back lot cameras were inoperative. Satisfied with his work, he tucked everything into his backpack, slinging it over his shoulders.

"I'll be right out, be ready to go when I say so..."

"OK."

Chase checked his watch, opened the security panel and hit the reset before plucking off the jumpers, the alarm counting down from a minute and thirty seconds. He stuffed the wires back inside and closed the panel, screwing it shut. His eyes swept the area, making sure everything looked untouched before heading to the back door.

Halfway to the door he realized he'd forgotten the keys to the truck. *Son of a bitch!* He flung his backpack across the smooth floor and headed back to the front office as his bag slid toward the back door. As he rounded the service desk, the bright shaft of a spotlight reached through the showroom windows and swept slowly towards him. He dove to the floor and scooted across the polished tile on his belly to the sales manager's office, using the vehicles in the showroom for cover. Scooting through the doorway and around the desk, he could see the key cabinet above him but he couldn't stand up, the spotlight scanning the front of the dealership right through the glass offices. Peeking around the desk, he could see the nose of the police car sitting at the curb right in front of dealership's entrance. "Karen, use your cell phone, call 911! *Call 911!*"

"What? Why? What's going on?"

"I've got a cop out front, I'm trapped!"

"What do I say?"

"Say there's a man with a gun robbing the gas station up the street..."

"Which one?"

"Fuck! Pick one! Hurry!"

Chase took a calculated risk and rose to his knees to pop the cabinet open as the spotlight swept back in the other direction. He could see the key dangling on the hook above him, the truck description written on the tag. As he cautiously reached for it, red and blue flashes reflected off the walls and glass around him, refracting back and forth in dizzying directions. He froze, a sudden numbness in his hands, an icy chill racing up his back. The wail of the siren and squealing of tires almost made him piss himself.

With nerves jangling and muscles jittering from the adrenalin flood, he jumped up, snagged the keys and bolted for the rear door. One minute, twenty seconds. He scooped up the heavy backpack like it was a bag of feathers, spinning through the door, slamming it behind him. "Get the gate! Get the gate!" He fumbled with the picks to relock the back door fighting the trembles that threatened to spill the picks all over the ground. Somehow he lucked out and the latch dropped into place with a clunk.

Unlocking the truck's doors with the key fob, he slid to a stop and ripped the door open, chucking his pack into the back seat. Jumping behind the wheel he cranked up the engine and threw it into gear, tearing out through the open gate, flinging the passenger door open as he slammed on the brakes. "Come Allie!" The German Shepherd bolted from the tree line, diving through the open door and Karen jumped into the back, pack and laptop bag in tow.

"I'm in!"

Chase stomped the accelerator and the passenger doors slammed shut of their own weight as they raced down the access road in the opposite direction of Karen's 911 call, the truck's V-8 pumping out horsepower galore. "Give me your phone!" A hand appeared between the seats and he took the flip phone, wiping it on his pants and breaking it in two against the steering wheel, throwing the parts out the window.

Three miles were under the tires before he pulled off into an empty church parking lot. "I've got to put the plate on before we go any farther..." he stuttered, putting the truck in park and holding out his trembling hands. "Whew, you'd think I'd be used to these adrenalin dumps by now... amazing what it does." He looked back over his shoulder as he peeled off the blue gloves, Karen still laying across the seat on her stomach. "You're awful quiet, you alright?"

"Mmmhmm."

"You're stuck under your pack, aren't you..."

"Mmmhmm."

■ ■ ■

240

Jackson Mississippi behind them, Karen adjusted herself in the driver's seat, one hand on the wheel, holding the pickup steady just above seventy miles per hour, a hint of blue creeping into the night sky. "So we're taking I-20 all the way into Dallas?" She waved her hand, "I mean if we were going this way anyway, why didn't we take I-10 across from the get-go?"

His attention divided, Chase nodded staring at the laptop screen on his knees, a cell phone connection providing him with internet. "Yep, then I-35 up to Kansas City..." He glanced up for a moment, realizing she'd asked two questions. "I-10 is a popular smuggling corridor, lot's of police activity. We kinda want to avoid contact."

She nodded her understanding. "What are you doing..?" She tried to peek at the screen.

"Watch the road," he said without looking up. "I'm reactivating a corporation I set up a few years back. It's very secret, government-agency sounding and anyone running the plate is likely to want to avoid it. It's what I registered the truck to on the dealer's computer last night..."

"So this agency doesn't exist then..."

"Only on paper."

"Mmm, she acknowledged, half understanding. "So, Salt Lake City... too bad you can't fly, we could've swiped a plane, huh?"

"Well I know enough to get us off the ground. Landing, not so much," he shrugged. "That rather abrupt ending to the flight usually ruins the trip."

Karen toyed with her hair, twirling it around her finger absentmindedly, "I gotta ask, what the hell are we going to find in Salt Lake City?"

His work completed, Chase closed the laptop and unplugged the cell phone, packing them away in his laptop bag. "Southwest of there actually. Something called Dugway Proving Grounds..."

"And that is..?"

"Jack mentioned it once... in the same context as Area 51 and Groom Lake. Secret places that the government develops secret things... Places where the government develops science, weapons, more efficient and more violent ways of killing our enemies..."

"Oh *that's* nice..." Karen's voice dripped with sarcasm.

Chase ignored her caustic tone. "Citizens sleep safely at night because rough men stand ready to do violence on their behalf to those who would do us harm. There is a trust between those citizens and those men. And those rough men have issued our country a blank check for everything up to and including their lives. The thing that bothers me is that Washington has shown a propensity for abusing that checkbook. And instead of getting better, it's getting worse. I can speak from personal experience, it seems more and more, the current administration has come to view its own people as the enemy... including our returning vets."

She frowned, "Would the military really hurt Americans?"

Chase's frustration was reflected in half a shrug and a shake of his head. "Not the guys I know, but the military is a hierarchical chain of command and the guy in the White House is holding the top link of that chain. If he's abusing his power, the people down at the bottom are the ones who get shit on. In case you're wondering," he waved, "the citizens are the ones at the bottom and he'll use the military or Department of Homeland Security to do the shitting."

"I was never really clear on that, who *is* Homeland Security?"

Allie was sitting with her rump on the back seat, her front feet on the floor, her chin on the armrest between the front seats. She nudged Chase's elbow and he scratched her head. "DHS is pretty much everybody that's not military... they've all been lumped together under one umbrella - a domestic army. The administration has been working very hard to wear our traditional military down... constant deployments, budget cuts, reductions of support and recruiting... all the while strengthening DHS with more people, gear, weapons, authority..." He thought for a moment, "Look at what people put up with at the airports from the TSA; groping little children and grandmothers, crotch inspections, strip searches... what the hell is that crap? Then letting people who actually *look* like terrorists walk right through, because, heaven forbid, we wouldn't want to upset *those* people, it might be racist. It makes me sick."

He waited until Karen completed her pass on an eighteen-wheeler, the big truck's engine noise fading behind them. "Under the DHS umbrella, the government has militarized the IRS, the EPA, Social Security Administration, Federal Reserve Bank, Parks and Wildlife officers and even Property Code Enforcement teams... supplying them with weapons, and even SWAT teams. The IRS and Federal Reserve aren't even true government entities, they're basically private contractors. The EPA? Social Security? *Really?* What the hell do *they* need SWAT teams for? It's frightening."

"Karen reset the cruise control. "So what do you think will happen, then?"

"There is a growing group called Oath Keepers; people in law enforcement and the military that have sworn to disobey unlawful orders. Not sure what that will entail... Will they refuse with violence? Will they fight? I don't know. There will be plenty of men that will simply follow orders, do what they're told." He rubbed his face, "And the government won't play fair, they may use unconventional tools. Things they can deny or call an accident; like chemical, biological or weather."

"Did you say *weather?*"

"Yeah..." he waved dismissively, "but the real wild card is the *people.* With about eighty-million lawful firearm owners, they are the largest standing army on the planet... *If* they stick together. And judging by what's going on in some states, the *people* are just about fed up..." He looked down at his hands in contemplation, momentarily seeing the dried blood and powder-like Afghanistan dust covering his combat gloves, hearing the engine of the Humvee. He blinked it away. "Too many distractions..." he muttered.

"What?"

"Too many distractions," he repeated. "This administration operates like a shell game; every time something important comes up they distract from it with something else. And the media isn't doing its job either; they're complicit in all of this..."

Karen checked her mirrors and speed, "By the looks of it the house and senate aren't doing much either..."

"Yeah, don't get me started on that bunch, they're too busy stuffing their pockets to give a damn about the little people."

Karen took a deep breath and let it out slowly. "I'm liking this idea less and less. In a minute or two I'm going to start hating it." She shot him a sideways glance, "You want to explain to me why the hell we're going to this place? Isn't this the type of crap we're running from..?"

"I don't think we can run away from this anymore, Karen..."

"What are you saying, Chase? Exactly, I mean... is this some kind of combat mission for you..? I'm... I'm..." her voice quivered, "I want my old life back..."

243

CHAPTER TWENTY

UFW CONQUEST, TRANQUIL ECHO SYSTEM: *SCHOOL DAZE*

Lt. Commander Mike Warren paced in front of the class of twenty pilots, a large holo-screen behind him playing videos of their previous day's flights and maneuvers. "I think we made some good progress yesterday, and I want that to continue but we're going to study tactics and maneuvers in the classroom today." He pointed at the big screen, "We've seen some blatant mistakes that could get you in trouble so we're going to review video playback and see what you were thinking while you were doing it. Each pilot is going to give a verbal description during his video..."

There was a unified groan from the class.

Mike stopped pacing, his hands on his hips, a scowl, staring down the entire class. "Listen up boys and girls, when I want your opinion, I'll give it to you. Understand?" The group fell silent. "You are improving but some of you are sloppy and some of you are inexperienced... that will get you dead. A decent Pirate pilot, and we've seen some pretty good ones, would have owned half of you in a one-on-one confrontation. That's unacceptable. You should be able to handle two or three of them..." He folded his arms across his chest, his feet shoulder-width apart. "If there's someone here that can beat me in a one-on-one, I will sign off and dismiss you from the class..." He scanned the faces exchanging silent glances around them, a pilot in the back row finally standing up confidently.

"I can, Comman..."

"No you can't" waved the Lt. Commander dismissively, "sit down." He looked around, "Anyone else?" There were no other challengers, their confidence level wasn't such that they actually believed they could. He expected that near the end of the training if he asked the same question three-quarters of the class would stand up. Satisfied no one else was feeling bigger than their britches, he continued. "Good. Because you'd be wrong. It's OK to be confident," he indicated the pilot who had stood up, "but don't be overconfident. Don't let blind pride write a check your skills can't cash. Be realistic with yourself, know your strengths and weaknesses. Play on your strengths and practice to improve on your weaknesses. That's what this training is going to do, it's going to force you to focus on your weaknesses and improve."

He stepped away from the podium and held up his hand, "How many people here have had to eject or had ejection and recovery training?" He looked around the class, spotting Lisa Steele's hand in the air. "Anyone else?" He dropped his hand to his side, "Alright then, we have an exciting afternoon planned. After we review our flight videos, we will be practicing ejection and recovery survival..."

The pilot sitting next to Lisa had yellow eyes like a cat and short cropped blue-black hair. "You've had the ejection training?" he whispered, leaning in close.

Lisa shook her head curtly. "No, had to eject when we lost a wing over a planet," she whispered back out the side of her mouth.

"Were you scared?"

Lisa widened her eyes and nodded affirmatively without speaking, watching the first video start, the pilot narrating.

■ ■ ■

Considering she was the most junior pilot on the ship, Lisa had made a pretty decent showing. Nothing fancy, nothing spectacular, but she had hung with the instructor, taking his lead, doing what she was instructed without any preconceived notions or bad habits to have to break. She didn't want to end up in the dubious position of teacher's pet,   but she didn't want to be catching any flak for being at the bottom of the class either. Mike's teaching style wasn't overly complimentary, probably a good thing, but he had a way of conveying he was pleased without being overt. Equally, he had the ability to be critical without tearing down any progress that had been made and Lisa felt comfortable trusting everything he said, absorbing it like a sponge. Almost to the point of overflow. Thank God for the occasional break and a day off... if she wasn't flying she was studying, running or working out.

The days were blurring into each other and at times it was difficult to keep track of them. She showed up more than once for training on her off day, standing in an empty classroom. She couldn't remember working so hard for anything in her life. It was exhausting, nerve-racking, mind-numbing, but thrilling and exhilarating all at the same time.

"Lisa Steele..."

Waiting her turn in the ante-room to the ejector seat training module, Lisa looked up when the pilot with the dark hair and yellow eyes nudged her elbow. "You're up, they just called your name."

She blinked away her thoughts and rose, her helmet in her hand, "Thanks."

"Good luck," he smiled weakly, obviously nervous.

"No luck involved," she commented, pulling on her helmet. "Strap into the seat, hold on for dear life and try not to puke in your suit..." His face was pinched, almost dour, looking unconvinced. Lisa wasn't sure what he was worried about, Ensign Dado was one of the best pilots in the class; a fearless risk taker with fast reflexes and a fast mind, able to predict and mirror the instructors' maneuvers. Surely someone of his caliber shouldn't be bothered by a controlled ejection exercise with recovery birds waiting close by.

She shrugged it off, the heavy blast door to the training module sliding open with a hydraulic hiss. She stepped over the threshold and paused as directed at the hashed yellow line, the door closing behind her, the lock mechanism ominously winding heavy bolts that extended into the outer frame. The room, barely ten-feet by fourteen-feet, had one wall curved, from ceiling to floor, the room narrowest at the top. A door to her left opened slowly, a heavy robotic arm reaching into the room, clutching an ejection seat. Rotating precisely, the arm locked the seat down on the empty pedestal before releasing its grip and retracting, the door closing again. Then it hit her, she was ejecting into space. *On that.* She jumped when the bulky metal figure against the far wall moved.

"This is the outer wall of the ship," it commented with a metallic female voice, tapping on one of the room's exposed ribs. "Well the *inner wall* at least; there's two other layers and about two feet of armor."

Lisa stared at the figure, trying to see through the reflective glass visor.

"Step to the green box, Cadet," it said, pointing at a worn green square painted on the floor in front of the ejection chair.

"I'm an Ensign," Lisa corrected her, stepping forward.

"Good for you, sweetie," the figure replied flatly. "Inspection," it announced, checking Lisa's suit and helmet seals, moving her around. It paused for a moment, nearly visor to visor, staring back. "You can stop eying me, there's no one in here..." the visor flipped open and Lisa recoiled, her head hitting the padding inside her helmet. She was looking at a gaping hole filled with electronics, optical sensors and an array of lenses. It turned away to look at its own hand as it held it up in front of Lisa, wiggling padded, skeletonized metal fingers. "You didn't notice these?"

"No, sorry, I didn't."

"Oh."

It wasn't urgent but Lisa's nervousness probably prompted the feeling. "I don't suppose I could hit the head..."

"Oh sure, we have time," the robot responded flatly.

Lisa was relieved. "Really?"

"No." It pointed behind her, "Sit." The robot went about adjusting the seat's curvature and bolsters to fit Lisa's size and shape. "Comfy?"

"Comfy," replied Lisa, reaching for her belts.

"Don't help," corrected the robot, brushing her hand away. "Just sit and relax. I need to complete and confirm all steps in the process." Tasks executed, it stepped away to review its work; "Belts – secure. Restraint tension - within parameters. Umbilicals - secure and locked. Oxygen system - on and delivering. Climate control – active. Beacon – active. All systems functioning and stable..."

Lisa gripped the armrests, anticipating what would come next, her heart racing. Its visor closed again, the robot stepped back toward her and taking the pilot's arms by the wrists, crossed them over her body, "Grip your restraints, Cadet. You would normally eject with your hands on the launch loop between your knees. Your arms and hands should always be inside the armrests. A cockpit is narrow..." she made a cutting motion with her skeletonized fingers across her opposite metal arm as she stepped back to her original position near the outside bulkhead. "Stay in your seat and wait for recovery." The robot flipped a safety cover open and pushed the button it protected, a hatch in the ceiling above the chair blowing open, the atmosphere in the room exiting with an explosive roar. "Remember to breathe..." said the robot's metallic female voice in Lisa's headset. It flipped the cover on the remaining button...

Screaming.

Screaming seems to be one of the most natural responses for that first head-over drop on a roller coaster, the slingshot ride at the county fair, bungee jumps, skydiving, and, oddly enough, having the equivalent of a howitzer shell going off under your ass, blasting you and your seat out into the black void of space. The heavy frame of the hatch flashed past Lisa's eyes, a nanosecond later the darkness filled her view, the Conquest quickly shrinking below her. Being in a fighter in space, the vista surrounding the cockpit was awe inspiring. Being out there alone in a seat with an unobstructed view of nearly 360° was terrifying.

"Miss Lisa... *Miss Lisa...*"

"TESS?" gasped Lisa.

"Breathe, Lisa. You're holding your breath and your heart rate is at 142. Deep breaths."

Lisa forced herself to suck air in, she hadn't been aware that she was holding her breath. "Oh my God," she whispered, looking around. The ship had dropped below her, little more than a speck. Sensing a safe distance, the seat automatically fired deceleration thrusters to stop its momentum. The weightlessness immediately became apparent to Lisa, who had perceived gravity as the acceleration kept her backside planted firmly in the seat. It was a strange sensation but not altogether foreign as she recalled ejecting in the atmosphere over Veloria. The momentary weightlessness as her seat reached the pinnacle of its ride before plummeting back toward the surface of the planet was similar but short-lived.

"That's better," said TESS, "deep breaths... stay calm."

Lisa became a little braver, releasing the vice grip she had on her restraints, twisting from one side to another to look all around her. "I don't see anything around us..." She looked over the side below her, finding the speck that was the Conquest, and a flare halfway between her and the ship, moving upwards. "That must be Ensign Dado. I wonder if he's screaming... TESS, did I scream?"

"Like a banshee."

Lisa rolled her eyes, "Swell. I hope no one else heard it..." She tracked the flare as it rose, then suddenly going dark as it continued to shoot upwards. She lost it in the background of stars until the decelerators fired. "There he is..." she pointed, remembering there was no one there to share it with. Honestly, having TESS on her wrist made it easier, she didn't feel quite so alone. In retrospect, it would have been nice to have her along when she got stranded on Veloria.

The comm in her helmet crackled like an open mic somewhere, a voice suddenly breaking through the hiss. "Recovery Three to Ensign Steele, what's your status?"

"Awake and still breathing..."

There was a pause before the voice broke through the hiss again. "What is your *system* status?"

Duh... If Lisa could have facepalmed, she would have. Feeling a bit amateurish, she flipped open the panel on the armrest, reading her seat's power and system stats. "All in the green - top of the graphs."

"Copy that. We will be passing you to pick up Ensign Dado first, he seems to be having some system problems..." About a mile away, the recovery ship shot past on her left side, arcing in towards the area where she lost the spec that was Dado in the spread of stars.

■ ■ ■

The dinner rush was over but the ship's galley was still relatively busy, Nina Redwolf dropped into the seat across the table from Lisa with half of the volume of food on Lisa's tray. "Good *God,* woman..."

Lisa shrugged, "For some reason, that last exercise gave me a hellatious appetite."

"Ya think?" Nina poured dressing over her salad. "What exactly was the last exercise?"

"Ejection training. They put you in a seat and eject you out into space..."

Nina's fork stalled halfway to her mouth, "Say *what?*"

Lisa nodded, chewing, "Biggest rush I've ever had in my life... un*fucking* believable."

"Weren't you scared?"

"To death... but it was *soooo* cool!" She paused for a moment staring at her plate in thought, "I never got the attraction of roller coasters, I hated them," she said looking back up, "I understand it now. *What a ride...*"

Nina shook her head, finally getting to her salad. "It's like I don't even know you anymore. You're like this *warrior chick* or something..." She stared at her friend across the table, "It's kinda *hot,*" she smirked.

Lisa stopped mid chew, pointing her empty fork at Nina, "Behave yourself, you randy bitch."

"Greetings," said Ensign Dado, appearing at the end of the table, tray in hand. "Do you have room?"

"Sure," replied Lisa. She slid down to the next seat, dragging her tray along the table, giving him space.

He set his tray down and leaned across offering his hand to Nina, "Hi, I'm Torn Dado..." he shot Lisa a glance, "but she calls me *Tornado.* Not sure what that means, I guess I'm going to have to look that up."

Nina shook his hand, "Nina. Just Nina."

"OK, *Just* Nina," he joked, sitting down, a sparkle in his yellow-amber eyes, studying her satiny auburn hair and her fine features.

"So what happened to you out there, Tornado?" asked Lisa, sipping her drink.

"No idea. Something with the seat's air supply failed almost immediately on launch. I only had about five minutes of air. I remember seeing the rescue bird coming before blacking out, then nothing until we got about halfway back to the ship." He stirred his soup, "I didn't see you, when did they pick you up?"

"You were on Rescue Three. As soon as they got you aboard they headed straight back here," she tapped her plate with her fork. "Rescue One picked me up about ten minutes later..."

"Sorry they left you out there so long."

"No sweat, I was fine... After I stopped *screaming.*"

Ensign Dado almost spit his soup across the table, "I thought I was the only one screaming..." he said, choking it down, heat rising to his face. "Y'know, I heard they were going to play the launch recordings in our next class."

Lisa's eyes went wide, "Please tell me you're kidding..."

Dado shrugged, "It's what I heard. Something about reviewing how different people handle and deal with stress. It could just be a rumor."

"Oh God, I hope so..." She cut her meat and waved the knife casually in his direction while addressing Nina, "I don't know why he'd be screaming, he's probably the best pilot in the class. Flies like a bat outta hell... no fear, this one here."

Torn Dado's golden eyes shifted to Lisa, "Another reference I don't understand; *bat outta hell.* I suppose I'm going to need to look that one up too..?"

"Were you scared?" Nina asked, picking through her salad.

Dado tilted his head, thinking about it for a moment, "Yes. And no, I suppose. It's a surprise, not knowing what to expect. The acceleration is wicked and the vulnerability... I think the vulnerability is what hits you most. You have no protection at all, just this seat and nothing around you but space. It's humbling actually. For the training you can't hear the rescue birds until they want you to, you feel very alone. It's hard not to panic, I felt almost naked..."

"I *like* being naked," commented Nina, pushing a hot pepper to the edge of her plate with her fork.

For the second time, Ensign Dado choked on his soup, having to pinch his nose and cover his mouth with his napkin, coughing. *"Holy hellion..!* Have you two conspired to drown me in my soup?"

■ ■ ■

Admiral Steele looked up from the reports on his computer terminal when the door to his ready-room chimed, Fritz's ears perking up from his seat on the sofa. "Enter," called Jack.

The door slid open and Captain Paul Smiley entered, exchanging a casual salute. "Did you get a chance to review the reports?" Paul moved over to the mini fridge and pulled a bottle of water from the door, Fritz sliding up to his side to greet him and get a pat on the head.

Jack indicated the holo-screen hovering above his desk, "Yeah, checking it over now. Looks like a good class..."

Paul swallowed a sip from his bottle, his free hand rubbing the top of the Shepherd's head. "Mike's having some real success with this group..."

"Do I detect a *but* coming?"

"Nope, not a one. In fact I think after they've logged some flight time and live patrols, there are several I want to run through our advanced combat courses. Right now some are just short on seat time, like your sister. They need time to absorb what they've already learned and get truly comfortable in the cockpit."

"You think Lisa's good enough to go through ASTRA?" *Advanced Strike Training Academy.*

Paul pointed at the semi-transparent screen on Jack's desk, "Did you see her scores?"

"Yes..."

"Mike wasn't doing her any favors, Jack. For the most junior pilot on the ship with the least amount of stick time, she's passed half of her classmates... She really wants this. And we haven't had to break any bad habits with her, she never got the chance to develop any. Sometimes getting through their egos is half the battle, but she doesn't have one."

Jack leaned back in his chair pinching his lower lip in thought, impressed and proud of Lisa's dedication. "Wow..." was all he could think of to say.

Paul dropped into the sofa, crossing his legs, "Y'know," he said, his southern accent showing, "she snuck back into rotation and went through the ejection training a second time? For the *fun* of it?"

Jack's eyes widened, amazement in his voice, "No shit..." He shook his head, "Saying I was not fond of that part, would be an understatement."

Paul had an odd smirk, "I watched the video of her first launch, she was screaming like a scalded cat... most people do," he waved dismissively.

"I know I did," blurted Jack.

"Yeah, but on the second launch," continued Paul, "she was laughing her ass off..."

■ ■ ■

Nina was sitting on the couch in Lisa's quarters scratching Gus' tummy as he lay on his back, one leg bicycling vigorously in the air, making her giggle. "Aren't you done yet?"

"I haven't been out of uniform much lately," called Lisa from the bathroom. "I'd like to be a little girly for once... I figured the graduation party would be good timing."

"You like Dar enough to care, that's cute..."

"I'm not going for cute, I'm going for hot... We haven't spent any time together since I started training."

"Ooh, so you're going for the score..? Going to get some of that tonight?" teased Nina.

"I might," said Lisa striking a pose, framed by the bedroom archway in a pale yellow cocktail dress.

"Whoa," mumbled Nina, wide-eyed. "Meeeow, that's hot..! The little yellow fuck-me heels are a nice touch."

Lisa's mouth tweaked sideways in a smirk. "You're so classy, Nina," she sassed. "But thanks." She ducked back into her bedroom.

"I calls em as I sees em," chuckled Nina. "So, did you see they moved me and Ruby to a new room?"

"Quarters," corrected Lisa. "Where?"

"On this floor..."

"Deck."

"Whatever," sighed Nina. "I'm at the other end of the ship towards the back..."

"Stern."

"What?"

"Stern," repeated Lisa. "The stern is the back of the ship. Which side?"

"Left side..."

252

"Port side," called Lisa.

"Oh God, *who cares?"* moaned Nina.

"You live on a ship, Nina, you should at least know the basics... So who are you going to the party with? That girl from the bridge staff you and Ruby hang with... what's her name?"

Nina stood and smoothed her skintight slacks, "No, we're just cuddle buddies, nothing serious. Ruby's going to go with her, I'm going with Torn Dado..."

In a flash, Lisa reappeared in the archway, "You're going with *Tornado?* Wait a minute," she waved, "I thought you played for the all-girl team..."

Nina adjusted her blouse, purposefully popping an additional button open. "I like to keep my options open..."

"Since when?"

"Since I realized it doubles my chances of having a date. Besides, have you *seen* him? He's almost *beautiful."*

"I guess so."

Nina cocked her head sideways, "Guess so? You mean you hadn't noticed he was attractive? He's almost prettier than *me,* for God's sake."

"Uh-huh," grunted Lisa noncommittally. She strolled past, picked her clutch purse off the cocktail table and rubbed Gus' head, "Be a good boy for mommy, I'll bring you back something yummy." With a final pat, she headed for the door, waving at Nina, "Let's go, *Miss Trampy McTramperson."*

"You're just jealous," teased Nina as they passed into the corridor, "Torn is prettier than Dar..."

Unable to contain it, Lisa snorted a laugh of derision, "Oh please, there's no competition; Dar is a gorgeous *man,* Torn is a pretty *boy."*

"For now, he's *my* pretty boy. And from what I hear, he's a really good pilot..."

"He *is* a good pilot. Top of our class. I'd like to see him stay a good pilot..."

Nina shot Lisa a sharp glance, "What are you saying? Somehow I'll be bad for him?"

Lisa moved to one side as a group of uniformed crewmen passed, going in the opposite direction. "I'm saying," she hissed, controlling her volume, "he can't afford major distractions or someone fucking with his head. His life could depend on it. So if you're playing a game, don't."

"I'm not playing a game..."

Lisa stopped and faced Nina, her voice low, "Look, you went through some bad stuff... really bad. I can't imagine how hard it must've been to endure, but it's changed you. You have to know that. All I'm saying is don't let those inner demons cause you to do something that could risk someone's career or his life."

Nina was staring at the floor and when she looked back up her eyes were welled with tears. "I'm so confused..."

Lisa's heart ached for the pain she could only imagine was running around in Nina's head. "Then take your time to figure out how you feel. *Go slow.*"

"I love Ruby, but..." Nina's voice trailed off. "I wonder if there's more. Something I'm missing..."

"Like what?"

"I don't know... Stability? A man? True love? Everything seems so uncertain, so tentative... life is... "

Lisa put a hand on her shoulder, "That's all over. You're safe now."

"Am I? Am I *really?*"

"Yes, of course you are. Have you talked to Ruby about this? How does she feel?"

Nina shook her head. "No, not really."

"That might be a good place to start. I can also help you set up an appointment to see the ship's psychiatrist if you want. He can counsel you, alone or together with Ruby. I'm sure he can help." She took Nina by the hand and led her toward the elevators, "I don't want you to be *that* girl... the one everyone whispers about when you walk past."

"I think they do that already... about all of us from the Reef."

Lisa shook her head, "No, they don't. In fact most everyone knows what the circumstances and the conditions were like. Trust me when I say; nobody's judging." She tapped the elevator's call button. "You watch, someday we'll be going back there and Jack will lay waste to that place. Turn it to dust."

Nina shivered, "Don't say that word..."

Lisa raised an eyebrow, her head tilting to one side in curiosity, "What word?"

"Dust. I haven't had any Glacier Dust since the Reef. God help me, I miss it. Sometimes it was the only thing that could get you through the night."

"What is it, what does it do?" They stepped onto the open elevator and Lisa flicked the button for the deck with the Officer's Club.

"The worst thing I ever did at home was a little weed. This... *Glacier Dust,* I got it from one of the girls my second night on the Reef, I was scared to death... It took that all away. It took the fear away when you were scared, it made you happy when you were sad, it made ugly things pretty... you could see the music and hear the colors." She closed her eyes, "It made the Reef, as horrible as it was, almost pleasant." She opened her eyes, "And I wish I had some right now to take off this edge I feel."

"It's OK, you're just nervous. Relax, take a deep breath. You're just a girl going on a date with a boy. It happens every day all over the universe. No pressure. I'll be there if you need me..."

"Sure, Dar would be thrilled that you have to babysit me."

The doors opened and they stepped out, heading down the corridor. "He might not be thrilled, but he'd understand. He's pretty cool that way."

■ ■ ■

Dar Sloane made his way through the crowd, two drinks in hand, squeezing in next to Lisa, handing one off to her. "How's she doing?"

Lisa called his attention to Nina and Torn Dado holding hands and swaying to the music, talking closely. "She looks like she's doing alright. What did you say to him earlier?"

The Commander shrugged, "Not much. Told him to take it easy, follow her lead and not push. Told him it wasn't a request..."

Lisa patted the hand that had found its way around her waist, "Thank you, sweetie."

Dar smiled easily, "He was OK with it. Tell you the truth, I think he might be a little shy. So, how's her girlfriend dealing with it?"

"Ruby? She's over there with a girl who works on the bridge." Lisa discreetly pointed them out across the room.

"Hmm, *Zanzireen,*" nodded Dar, watching the two women who were glued together. "I've always wondered about her, I guess now we know." He rubbed his chin in thought, "So, um, how long do you want to stay?"

Lisa looked up over her shoulder, "You in a hurry to go somewhere, mister?"

Looking straight ahead, he pretended not to notice her mock scorn. "Meh, I don't know..." he countered, trying to sound lackadaisical, "someplace a little quieter. Maybe a little less crowded?"

"Like the corridor?"

He raised an eyebrow, looking down at her upturned face, "You're impossible."

"Not if you ask nice," she cooed.

"Y'know," he smirked evilly, feeling the material of her dress by stroking her hip seductively. "This is a real pretty dress... It would look nice in a heap on the floor at the foot of my bed..."

She turned around to face him, her eyes narrowing, "Has that line *ever* worked before?"

Dar's slate-gray eyes sparkled mischievously, "Nope. You'd be the first."

"What about my shoes?" she queried playfully.

"They're really hot, you could leave them on."

Lisa brought her glass to her lips and tilted her head back, draining her wine before setting it on the table at her elbow, "Alrighty then, *let's go.*"

Letting her lead him through the crowd toward the door, Dar looked back at the crowd, "What about Nina?"

"She's a big girl, she'll be fine. Time for momma to get her freak on..."

CHAPTER TWENTY ONE

UFW CONQUEST, WHISPERFIRE SYSTEM: *THE BOUNTY*

Standing at the head of the dimly-lit briefing room, a holo-chart of the system behind him, Lt. Commander Mike Warren clapped his hands, "OK we're done here, people. You all have your wing assignments so saddle up; we clear the gate in ten minutes." He waved them all toward the door, "And no excuses, bring my birds back in one piece!"

Her first real patrol, Lisa had to skip breakfast, the butterflies in her stomach refused to let her eat anything substantial. She managed a piece of fruit and some bread but that was the extent of what she could get her system to accept. Fully suited for flight, she rose to her feet, dumping her flight gloves out of her new helmet onto the deck at her feet. She bent down to retrieve them, a pair of flight boots stepping into her field of view.

"You the new girl?" asked a husky feminine voice.

Lisa straightened up, locking eyes with the Ketarian pilot standing in front of her. "Lieutenant Margareth," she acknowledged, trying not to look surprised. She extended her hand, "I'm Ensign Steele."

The Lieutenant JG ignored the extended hand, her bright green feline eyes regarding Lisa carefully, her small black nose twitching, one of her clipped ears rotating slowly. The Ketarian's mane of golden-orange with dark stripes, reminding Lisa of a tiger. "Follow me, *Princess,"* she scoffed, turning on her heel and heading for the door.

Left hanging without so much as a simple greeting, Lisa dropped her hand to her side and followed the Ketarian out through the doors and through the crowd of pilots. "Excuse me Lieutenant," called Lisa, catching up, walking parallel with her. "Is there a problem..?"

"No. No problem," the Lieutenant replied gruffly without slowing her stride.

Lisa caught her by the elbow, "Are you sure? Because it really seems like you have a problem with me. Or is that just my imagination?"

The Ketarian stopped and glanced down at the hand on her elbow, prompting Lisa to release it. "No. *Problem,"* she repeated deliberately.

Despite feeling the hair on the back of her neck creep into a standing position, Lisa felt the need to clear the air. "Look, if you're afraid to fly with me, I'm sure the Commander will assign..."

"I'm not *afraid* to fly with *anyone,*" she hissed, tapping Lisa's helmet with her index finger. "I don't like babysitting a *little Princess...*"

Lisa held the black helmet right-side-up, displaying the silver figure, "It's an *Angel,* Lieutenant. As in *Guardian Angel?*"

"You're the Admiral's sister," remarked the Ketarian flatly.

"Yeah, *so?*"

"So, *nepotism.* You're flying because of who you know not how you fly. Which means I need to babysit your ass and keep you out of trouble. Or *my* ass is *in* trouble."

Squared off, eye-to-eye, Lisa wasn't about to back down or be bullied out of something she'd worked so hard for. And while she didn't figure she was going to win a fistfight with a Ketarian, that fuzzy bitch wouldn't be walking away without at least a hitch in her giddyup. "I'm fully capable of taking care of myself, Lieutenant. *In or out* of a fighter. I don't need you or anyone else coddling me. And I find it amusing that you think *you're* good enough to do it, to begin with..."

With a couple of other pilots, Mike had been watching the exchange from the sidelines and decided to step in before it came to blows. *"Lieutenant JG!"* he shouted, stepping up. "Is there a problem here?"

"No problem, Commander," replied the Ketarian, stiffening.

Mike turned to Lisa, *"Ensign!* Is there a problem here?"

"No, sir," she replied calmly. "We were just discussing flight tactics."

"Fine. Stop jawboning like a couple of old biddies drinking Sunday tea and get your asses in those birds. ASAP." Without response, Lieutenant Margareth turned on her heel and strode off with haste. Mike caught Lisa by the wrist, giving her a quizzical look.

"I'm good," she nodded curtly, breaking free, hustling off for the flight line.

■ ■ ■

Lisa checked the chronometer on her Cyclone's HUD as the canopy motored into its locked position. Less than two minutes to the gate.

"Red Lead, radio check Red..."

"Red Two, check."

"Red Three, yeah."

Lisa keyed her mic, "Red Four, check." She adjusted the audio on her earpiece and increased the volume of her climate control, reviewing her systems, all in the green and in standby.

Lisa's earpiece crackled, "Just make sure you stay on my wing, Princess, I don't want to have to go looking for you..." The Ketarian's voice was instantly recognizable but Lisa didn't respond to her taunt or even venture a glance at the Cyclone in the next launch rack. Lisa wasn't about to give her the satisfaction. *Suck it, bitch.*

"Red Lead to Red Three, can the chatter."

Drawing in the cool oxygen to calm her nerves, Lisa closed her eyes for a moment, focusing on releasing the tension and relieving the jitters. The blue shimmer of the stasis field flickering to life glowed through her eyelids, making her stomach jump. *Stop it, you've done this dozens of times over the last few weeks, this is no different...* She opened her eyes just in time to see the launch doors split open wide, the flickers and tendrils of the gate iris washing back toward the stern as the ship passed through the gate into the system. The darkness and stars of Whisperfire visible through the crackling blue static of the stasis field, she listened to the tower countdown.

"Blue launching. Red, launching..." Before the words were complete, the catapult fired her Cyclone into the dark ink of space. Reaching forward and lifting the safety cover, she punched the engine igniter, rewarded with a satisfying thump and a kick in the seat. Scanning the sky over the canted gull wings of her fighter, she shoved the throttle forward, the engine roaring in response, pushing her into her seat, the Cyclone's gyro adjusting the gravity system to minimize the G forces. She swept in on the wing of Red Three as the flight arced away from the Conquest.

On their current heading, Red Flight would soon overtake the Revenge, currently flying point for the Task Force, its unique stealth abilities and array of specialized sensors their advanced eyes and ears.

The Whisperfire System had an interesting green hue washing through it, gentle waves with brighter ribbons streaming across the sky. To some extent it reminded Lisa of videos she'd seen of the Northern Lights on Earth. It was mesmerizing and she found it difficult to look away. When she caught the comet tail of Red Three on her left pulling away from her, she adjusted speed and course wondering if the Ketarian was purposely making random adjustments to make her life more difficult. They were cruising after all, everything should be fairly constant. *Should be - if you weren't flying wing for a bitchy, temperamental feline...*

Whisperfire's sun seemed weak, perhaps because it was filtered through the green haze stretching across the system, but it still prompted Lisa to lower her visor. There hadn't been much information in the database about the system, except, previously there had been mining operations on one of the system's planets which had been abandoned due to low productivity. Currently there were no known residents. As a matter of developing a habit with a positive bent, she had decided to check the database about any new system they were in before launching. It felt like a worthwhile effort, mostly for her own curiosity and edification, but you can never tell when some little scrap of seemingly useless random fact of information might prove useful.

Lisa eased the throttle back, adjusting for Lieutenant Margareth's antics. It was like trying to keep pace with a yo-yo. *Bitch.* She wondered how long it would be until the novelty of messing with the *new guy* wore off. Screw it, she was happy just to be flying... let crazy-kitty play her stupid game. Then another idea hit her, how wise is it to piss off the person supposed to be protecting your ass in a fight? *Hmm...*

■ ■ ■

Lieutenant Ragnaar adjusted the Revenge's sensor focus, a red target outline with adjacent notes forming on the big screen. "Picking up a structure in orbit around the fourth planet Commander."

Lt. Commander Brian Carter looked up from the maintenance screen he had been reviewing on the command chair's console. "On screen." From the red target square, a picture zoomed in as an inset on one side of the screen, a rusted, dilapidated mining station coming into focus. "Wow, she's seen better days... Any signs of life?"

"Some indication of low grade power usage..." Ragnaar sent the readings to the big screen, scrolling them next to the image of the station. "Everything you're seeing here is indicative of automated systems," he pointed. "Many of these older stations have no real *off switch*. Once they go live they run until they fail or they're damaged to the point of system collapse."

"How long will they run unattended?"

Ragnarr rotated his chair to face Brian, "I've seen stations over two hundred years old still running like the day they were put on line. As long as the solar collectors are intact, they have continuous power." He motioned toward the screen, "This station configuration looks to be a warehousing station for ore storage..."

Brian stood up and walked to the center of the bridge, staring at the image, "So why isn't this place listed on the charts?"

Ragnaar shrugged, "Probably because it's been inactive for a long time. It wouldn't be the first place I've seen that isn't recorded. There's a lot to keep track of out here and if it's not somehow interfering with ship traffic, it get's forgotten."

Brian pursed his lips, "Or maybe someone deletes it on purpose."

"Possible," countered Ragnaar. "More likely, the last survey ship through the system to take a scan, didn't see it because it was orbiting on the far side of the planet and they didn't bother to check. They may have assumed it shut down and dropped into the planet so they deleted it from the chart."

Brian folded his arms, "Can a station like this be put back into service?"

"Sometimes, depends on her condition. You wouldn't know that without paying it a visit. I wouldn't recommend that, some of them are death traps."

Brian raised an eyebrow, "How so?"

"This one," pointed Ragnaar, indicating the screen, "is a rust bucket. Docking and boarding could be a major problem. If she's not structurally sound she could damage the ship or trap you there once you disembark. Then there are the automated security systems... Some stay active."

Brian nodded, "Good point. Let's get a better look at her and get her back on the charts."

"Aye, sir."

"And let's inform the Conquest of our little course deviation..."

■ ■ ■

"One-hundred miles and closing, Commander."

Brian Carter diverted his attention back to the big screen, "Thank you Mr. Ragnaar, on screen. Let's do a circuit around her at about fifty miles... record of course."

"Of course."

Lieutenant Maria Arroyo, who hadn't been present for the first sighting of the station was seeing it with fresh eyes. "Shields up..." she called from the first officer's seat

"Aye, shields up."

Brian shot her a perturbed look,"What are you doing, Lieutenant?"

261

"Take us to yellow, Commander."

"What are you seeing, Arroyo?"

Maria pointed at the big screen, "Her positioning and navigation beacons are lit and there are signs of use here and here..." she drew with her finger on her task screen, making electronic notes on the wrap-around holo-screen for everyone to see. "Take us to yellow..."

Brian pursed his lips for a moment, thinking. "Go to yellow..." he agreed reluctantly. The klaxon sounded, yellow lights flashing throughout the ship. "What you missed earlier," he explained, "is that once these older stations were bought on line, they would run on their own indefinitely, until they broke down or were destroyed... sometimes for centuries."

"And in that time," she replied, what's to stop squatters from moving in and making it their own?"

"Security systems usually remain functional," answered Ragnaar without looking back.

"And for every security system is someone who can defeat it," Maria countered. "And what's to say the previous owners even cared enough to lock the door when they abandoned it?" She was watching her tactical sensor screen. "I'm reading passive sensor use... that wouldn't be something they left functioning..."

Brian wasn't taking his eyes off the big screen, "Any information on this structure? How big is it?"

Maria began reading off the statistics. "The ID says it's a *MineSpec VS200*. It has two external docking gantries for freighters on opposite sides of the station. An internal bay big enough to hold a fleet of work shuttles and consumable goods or cargo. Storage for up to a quarter-million tons of ore, and accommodations for up to two-hundred people. It says minimum crew requirement for mining operations is seventy-five."

"Orbiting, Commander. Video recording in multiple spectrums."

"Thank you Mr. Ragnaar. Looks pretty much as you'd expect it to..."

Maria stiffened, "Power spike!"

"Movement!" called Ragnaar, zooming in on the image. "There!" he pointed.

"Defense turrets... *Dammit!*" Brian slapped the red button on his console, the red alert klaxon screaming through the ship, red lights flashing. "*All hands to battle stations!* Helm, *break!* Get us out of here!"

At the helm, Quixetta leaned the Revenge over, making best use of her main engines' directional thrust, pulling her through an evasive arc away from the station, her engines vibrating throughout the ship.

"Those are *not* on the standard specs!" shouted Maria, flipping back to her tactical screens.

"Son of a bitch," hissed Brian. "Think they're automated?"

"You wish," countered Maria, an adrenalin hit thickening her Spanish accent. "We have company... *Fighters!*" she pointed at the screen, long-tailed points of light appearing from the back of the station.

"How many?"

"Three... Four... Six... No, *seven!*"

"Craaaap!"

"And a bonus... *a heavy gunship!*"

Brian shot Maria an unbelieving glance. "Helm, head for the task force..."

Maria shook her head, paging back and forth on her screens, searching for information on the ships in pursuit, "I've got nothing on these things, they're not in the damn database..."

"Fuck me," muttered Brian under his breath.

"That gunship is about half our size with twice as many guns..."

■ ■ ■

The Conquest's alarm klaxon sounded, red lights flashing in the tower and elsewhere about the ship, the call to battle stations echoing through the address speakers.

Commander Paul Smiley turned away from the comm on the holo-screen in the flight tower, tapping the flight controller on the shoulder with authority, "Launch White and Black Flights, *immediately!* Activate, Green and Yellow and at least one rescue bird..."

"Aye, White and Black." As the assistant Controller called up the additional pilots to the flight line, the Controller keyed his mic, "White and Black Flights, confirm launch ready..."

"Black Flight, ready."

"White Flight, ready."

He scanned the deck below, confirming personnel and equipment were clear and ready, his fingers dancing across the glass floor plan of the flight bay, arming the launch racks and activating the stasis fields in front of the doors for the two flights of Lancias, blue strobes calling the pilots attention to the active stasis fields. The Strobes turned solid green when the doors reached their locked open position. "Launch in three, two..."

■ ■ ■

"Seven-to-one are bad odds, Admiral..."

Jack Steele, Captain Ryan, and Commander Paul Smiley occupied insets on the Revenge's holo-screen . "Nobody's debating that Mr. Carter," admitted the Admiral. "You did the right thing. Can you stay ahead of them?"

"So far, so good..." Brian glanced off at Ragnaar who nodded a quick confirmation.

"Good, have you taken any damage?"

Brian's attention went back to the comm on the big scree, "No sir, they haven't fired... *Yet.* But we can tell their weapons are hot and shields up."

"Red and Blue Flight's are vectored to intercept," added Paul, cutting in. "White and Black have been launched for cover. You've got sixteen birds out there with you..."

"Don't outrun them, just drag them to us," instructed the Captain. "The Westwind has swung wide, pass between us."

Brian rubbed his forehead, "Will do. Listen, we can't find any matching information on these ships, we don't even know who they are. Have you come up with anything?"

Jack shook his head, "We looked at your data feed, nothing in our database either. We'll worry about who they are at a later juncture."

■ ■ ■

Lisa's comm crackled in her helmet, "Red Leader, go hot people. Arm all weapons systems, guns ready." She reached forward and lifted the safety covers, flipping the toggles, arming her systems, the Cyclone's targeting screen winking on, immediately searching for targets. The weapons stores menu opened and the status gauges for her guns lit up, showing their ammunition count and charge level, the generators whining momentarily as they woke up. It was all a bit unnerving... and exciting at the same time. Her fingers tingled and she found herself breathing heavily, her hands sweating in her gloves. *Shit was about to get real.*

"Red leader to Red Flight, we're swinging wide right, Blue is going left, Black and White will go above and below; the Revenge will pass through us. We're going to flank these jokers and cut off their exit... Like it or not, they're going through a meat grinder. Break in three, two, one."

Lisa was expecting a comment from the Ketarian but got nothing. *Good.* She gritted her teeth as she rolled her fighter and pulled, craning her neck to keep an eye on her wing leader through the sweep, maintaining her distance and relative speed.

"Stay with me Princess..."

Lisa bit the inside of her cheek. *Dammit!* Red Flight rolled back in the opposite direction, arcing back to parallel Blue Flight, White and Black appearing on her scope, high and low, a little further back but closing quickly to parallel the flanking flights. In position, the flights slowed, the trap ready to spring.

Lisa watched the Revenge streak past, its dark shape a mere blur momentarily blotting out everything beyond it, driven across the field of stars by her engines' blue halos.

"All ships, ident beacons on..."

■ ■ ■

Standing between the stations in the center of the Conquest's bridge, Steele stood facing the holo-screen, Fritz sitting at his side. "This is Admiral Steele, UFW Task Force Lancer... please identify yourself." The group of unidentified ships sat motionless, facing the task force, the Revenge falling back into formation between the Conquest and the Westwind.

Eager to catch their prey, affected by tunnel vision and a singular mindset, the unidentified ships were a little late in breaking off their pursuit. Too late to avoid the surprise party thrown in their honor. All this fuss and they had completely forgotten to bring a gift for the host when they ran out the door with haste... Of course, in all fairness, that's when they thought the surprise party was theirs and the Revenge was the gift.

Studying the ships on the holo-screen - zoomed in, Steele felt a familiarity and he was running through his memory to figure out why. His eyes narrowed, *"Greirggådariopshé senvou mé, I uso té strument Ö té cŏnstruktures, as markez Ö té antiqos arkuitekos..."*

The bridge was silent when Captain Ryan leaned over to him, "What in the hellion did you just say?"

"It's Gogol," whispered Jack, "I said: *Greg sent me, I wear the tools of the builders, marks of the ancient architects...* The ships look Gogol to me."

"You speak *Gogol?*"

"Just the one sentence," admitted Steele. "I'm taking a stab in the dark here..."

A tactical officer turned in his seat, "Captain, the ships are powering down weapons and shields..."

"All of them?"

"Yes sir. All of them."

An inset comm-frame winked into existence on the holo-screen, the Gogol Commander looking back at them with a sallow, greenish hue to his thin, smooth skin, veins visible beneath the surface. When he blinked, translucent eyelids swept across his large glassy eyes. "We apologize for the intrusion, Admiral Jack Steele of Earth. I am Captain Céaraviŋŋeågŏlshun, and this is my squadron. We are bounty hunters..." He noticed Fritz at the Admiral's elbow, his eyes widening. "Is that the animal who speaks?"

Jack reached out reflexively and patted Fritz on the head, "It is. His name is Fritz."

"He is as handsome as I have heard..."

Steele held up one hand to politely interrupt, "Thank you Captain... may we call you Ceravin? It is easier for us..."

"Of course, Admiral."

"Thank you. Now, about what brought us to this moment, and just as important, why you seem to know so much about *me?*"

"Ģreirggådariopshé, the Gogol you call Greg; has informed the Imperial Gogol Senate of your fairness, light, and honor. When you let him act as a liaison for Veloria instead of killing him, they expressed a great deal of respect for your thoughtful treatment of him. I understand he is thoroughly enjoying studying with the person called Professor Walt Edgars."

"I am glad of that..." Jack couldn't help but crack a knowing little smile. As an Archeologist, anthropologist and historian, the Professor could not resist the temptation to compare the similarities between the Ancients, the Builders and the Masons. The best way to do that was to become a Mason. And in his twenty-odd years on Earth, he made his way through all the fascinating levels, astounded by the parallels. However, when Jack paired Greg with the Professor he had no idea the Professor was a Brother, it simply never occurred to him. Until he received his royal ring from Alité, the Masonic engravings perfectly representing his achievements. In retrospect,

266

Jack couldn't have paired Greg up with anyone better suited to teach him about the truths he sought. "I'm hoping Greg's involvement will help us better understand each other; our society and yours..."

"As well as some ancient history perhaps..." added Ceravin.

"I look forward to that," nodded Steele. "In the meantime, what happened here..?"

"Well, we are bounty hunters..."

"So you said," replied Steele.

"And you..." Ceravin waggled his finger at the screen, "you Admiral, were running with your ident beacons off."

"Yes we were. But I don't see how that brings you to pursuing and attacking a ship..."

"To be fair Admiral," interrupted the Gogol Captain, holding up his hand, "we never fired... In driving off an unwanted visitor from our home, we realized..."

"Home? Did you purchase or lease that facility?"

"No Admiral," countered Ceravin. "That base has stood empty, unused and unmaintained for over fifty years. According to interstellar law, after that period it is open for claim. We have been in that facility for a little over a universal year. In that period there have been no occupancy or ownership disputes. By law it is legally ours..."

Steele glanced over at the Captain Ryan, getting a curt confirmational nod. "I see. I'm sorry I interrupted, you were saying..."

The Gogol tapped his bottom lip with his index finger in thought, "Oh yes, while we were in pursuit of your frigate, we realized we had a bounty order for one quite similar. According to our data, it is called the Raven... It is reported the Captain was a *Commander Carter* and the owner of the ship, a man named *Jax Mercury...*" His eyes narrowed, eying the Admiral, a wicked little smirk creeping across his reptilian features. "The bounty was placed by a business consortium on Rikovik's Reef... You wouldn't know anything about that, would you?"

Under the watchful eye of the Gogol Captain, Steele remained stoic. "I'm sorry Ceravin, I'm afraid the UFW would probably be the last to learn of a bounty order. It's not exactly our line of work..."

"Interesting thing, Admiral, the data packet included some images..." he touched his chin in contemplation. "They weren't the best mind you, but you seem bear a considerable resemblance to the man called Jax Mercury..." With a sweep of his hand he waved it off a bit too nonchalantly, "But of course, that would be ridiculous. What would you, an Admiral, be doing in a degenerate dung-heap like Rikovik's Reef... it's absurd." His eyes shifted slyly.

Dammit, he knows. Steele tried to remain detached, rubbing the top of Fritz's head, who had pushed against his hand for attention. The distraction helped. "You are quite right, Captain... It is absurd. And my advice to you would be; to choose more carefully the contracts you accept. There are a lot of unscrupulous characters out there and my understanding is that Rikovik's Reef is lousy with them. This encounter could have ended very badly for you and your squadron..."

"Wise words, indeed," agreed the Gogol Captain, nodding. "Bounty hunting is inherently dangerous, and we quite often take the work at face value, having to work with clients of all sorts, good *and* bad. But we will endeavor to choose more wisely in the future."

"Might I suggest you dispose of that contract," pointed Jack. "I seriously doubt that it's wise to pursue it to its conclusion, it sounds dubious at best..."

"I am sure you are correct, Admiral," he replied slowly, unconvinced. "I don't see it as something we can fulfill..." Scanning Steele's expression, he was both disappointed and impressed that there was nothing there that he could read.

"Good," nodded Jack emphatically. "I'm glad we see eye-to-eye on that." He brought his hands together, his fingers steepled, "I thank you for your cooperation, Ceravin, but we really have to continue our patrol..."

"Of course, Admiral. May I beg of you one indulgence before we go?" He did not wait for an answer, indicating Fritz, "Could we hear him speak..?"

Jack looked down at Fritz, "He really only speaks when he has something to say... what do you think dog?"

Fritz stood and moved forward toward the screen, his tail swaying, looking up at the Gogol Captain, "Two dogs walk into a bar..."

■ ■ ■

Suffering from the energy void left by the receding tide of adrenalin, Lisa Steele felt drained, sitting in the cockpit of her Cyclone as it gently settled to the deck with a bump. She hauled back on the canopy release lever and it broke seal with a hiss, a wash of flight deck air with its warm metal, oil and tangy electronic smell filling her nose. It smelled like home. She rested her head back against the headrest and dug a power bar out of one of her suit's utility pockets. She knew she was going to have rubber legs without a little boost.

A deck-hand slapped the fuselage of her fighter, "Ladder! Ladder!"

Stuffing the last half of the bar in her mouth, crunching on the sweet, toasted cardboard, Lisa flipped the release and the ladder unfolded from the belly, allowing him to climb up. Leaning in, he helped her disconnect and unbelt, taking her helmet, reaching over and setting it on the wing. "You doing alright there, Ensign?"

"Sure, yeah, I'm fine..."

"Jittery?"

"Yeah, a little. How'd you know?"

"Happens to everybody. Here," he handed her a small 8oz. bottle of dark red liquid pulled from his waist pouch. "Suck this stuff down and you'll be fine in a couple of minutes."

Lisa examined the liquid and how it clung to the insides of the bottle. "What the hell is it? It's kinda gross looking, like blood..."

"It's a juice. No idea what all the ingredients are but it's salty-sweet. Most everybody calls it Jungle Juice. Gives you energy and takes away the wobblies."

"OK..." she replied suspiciously, popping the cap. A tentative sip revealed it was definitely unique. As odd as it sounded in her head, it reminded her of a combination of tomato juice and cherry juice. It wasn't great but it wasn't objectionable either. She finished it before standing up and attempting to climb out of the cockpit, the deck-hand having moved on to the next Cyclone. Stepping to the deck and retrieving her helmet, she ducked under the fuselage and headed toward the locker room, Mike approaching with a wave.

"How was your first patrol..?" he queried, knowing full well what had transpired.

"It was..."

Lieutenant Margareth strode up from behind, punching Lisa in the arm as she passed, "Good, Princess..."

Lisa lunged with a swing that whiffed through empty air and Mike bodily intercepted her, *"Whoa there..."* the Ketarian pilot walked on, unawares. Or maybe unconcerned.

"I've had it with her..."

"Easy Lisa," he urged, voice lowered. "I think you just got the Lieutenant Margareth stamp of approval..."

"I'll stamp *her*..." She looked back at Mike, confused. "What?"

"If she was unhappy about your performance, you can be sure she would have let you know in no uncertain terms. She's not shy about that. Considering she had nothing negative to say, I'd say you passed her standards..."

Lisa looked unconvinced, "So next time I fly with her I won't have to hear her ration of shit...?"

Mike took a step back, waving a non-committal, "Oh, now I didn't say that. She has something to say about almost everyone she flies with..." They started walking across the deck toward the locker room.

"You?"

"Yeah," he shrugged. "I think the only person she *hasn't* said anything to, is probably Pappy."

"Smart. Jack?"

Mike smirked, "I don't think he's ever flown with her, but wouldn't *that* be a show to watch?"

CHAPTER TWENTY TWO

TAMPA, FLORIDA: *REPLACEMENT & REGRET*

After a winding drive through the grimy old commercial park, the taxi pulled to a stop in the middle of the street, the area nearly deserted. A humid Florida breeze blew dust and paper across the adjacent parking lot past a derelict truck sitting on flattened tires.

The cabbie looked over his shoulder at the woman in the back seat, "Lady are you sure this is the right place? I don't see anything here... leastways no place *you'd* want to go."

Mercedes Huang scanned the rusty building, her keen eye for detail catching the rim of a transmitter dish nearly hidden behind the building's roofline. *Cameras... there should be, ahh, there's one.* "Pull up to the door," she pointed, "there."

The cabbie shook his head and let the car roll up the drive and through the useless gate hanging limply off its hinges, stopping in front of the corrugated building's steel front door. He popped the trunk release and got out to help her with her luggage. "I hope you know what you're doing young lady," he winced, hefting out a long, flat, black bag.

She hefted the bag by its sling, swinging it effortlessly over her shoulder, the contents producing a metallic rattle. "I'll be fine, thanks." She handed him a fifty, "Keep it," she smiled, pulling the handle up on her roller bag.

He set her laptop bag on top, wrapping the sling around the roller bag's handle. "Look, the company won't send any cabs here after dark, it's not safe. Which means you've got about half an hour..." he handed her a card. "But you call my cell and I'll come get you. I ain't afraid of this area... I pack," he tapped his ribs. "But I'm only on for about another two hours..."

Mercedes smiled warmly, "You get along, now," she shooed him with her free hand, "I'll be fine, I promise." She tucked the card away, "Thanks." Four inches taller than him in her *sensible heels* he looked up and nodded, climbing back into the cab, waving as he idled away, back out the way he'd come.

Satisfied she was unobserved; she dug a key-card out of her pocket and passed it over the push-button keypad, the face popping open with a chirp, revealing a digital screen hidden underneath. Checking her surroundings first, she stooped and stared at the screen placing her right thumb in the corner of the screen. The thumbprint reader initiated a retinal scan and a pale green halo swept over her face, the door next to her unlocked with a distinctive *clack.*

She pulled the door wide, grabbing the handle of her roller, the keypad face swinging shut on its own. Stepping in, the door behind her swung closed, locking her in a cubicle, her eyes fighting to adjust to the sudden darkness. A momentary green halo above her flickered for an instant before the metal wall in front of her slid aside, disappearing, allowing her entry to the building.

The last of the day's light angled through the greenhouse style skylights, a grid of golden light splashed across the warehouse floor and the scattered workstations. At first glance the organized chaos resembled a maze, but as she approached there was a clear path. The building opened widely to her right, a fleet of four black SUVs parked inside the adjoined bay.

"Pete's replacement is here...!" called a disembodied voice.

"Aw man..." groaned another, "they sent us a bitch..."

"Bros before hos, man..."

Her eyes still adjusting to the muted light, Mercedes could see men moving through the shadows, between the lights, having the impression they were converging on her. Doug Mooreland got to her first, stopping in front of her with his hands on his hips.

"You Mooreland?" she asked.

"Yeah..."

Agent Huang reached down and pulled a manilla envelope out of a pocket in her laptop case, handing it to him, "Agent Mercedes Huang..."

Doug looked her up and down as he took the folder and flipped it open, taking in her straight smooth hair, caramel skin, chiseled features, fine suit and stature before paging through the sheets. "Hmph," he snorted, "Air Force intelligence analyst? No combat?"

"Holy shit, she's blackanese..."

"And she's *hot..!*"

Doug shot an evil glance around him, *"Shut up."* He looked back at Mercedes, "So what's an intelligence analyst do..?"

"Try to figure out why you clowns can't find your asses with both hands, and yeah, I've seen combat..."

"Really? What kind would that be..? Because we don't count sitting on your ass in a *zone* as comba..."

She unslung her weapons bag and dropped it unceremoniously to the floor, pointing her finger in his face, "Flying past Mach 1 and trying to take pictures while they're shooting SAMs and anti-aircraft at you is not as easy as you think."

"Bitch, please..."

"Fuck you, Mooreland," she spat. "You got a problem with it? Speak to the Deputy Director because he's the one who picked me. And if you're even remotely curious about my background or experience, I'd suggest you read the *entire* folder. You do remember how to read, don't you Doug?" She glanced around, "Or are you the same as all the rest of these mouth-breathing Neanderthals?"

"Ouch," mumbled a voice in the group.

"Yeah... uncalled for..."

"Screw the lot of you." she shot back, widening her stance. "I'm not going to tolerate your bullshit. Any of it... if you have any more disparaging comments about my race, my color, my mother, whatever... let's get it over with now!" She glanced sternly around at the shadowed faces. "Anybody? Nobody? Good. You can call me Mercedes, Agent Huang or Mercy. I'll accept nothing less..."

"Mercy?"

"Mercy," she said through gritted teeth, "cuz that's what you'll be begging for when I'm kicking your *fucking ass..."*

"Geez, what a fucking..."

"Your mouth better be forming the word, bitch," she snapped, scanning the faces that were becoming clearer, her eyes adjusting, "because if you say the *C* word, you'll be wearing your nads for a hat."

"Alright, that's *enough!"* waved Doug. "You guys get back to work. Huang, my office. Now." He turned on his heel and headed for the other side of the vehicle bay.

■ ■ ■

Doug sat with his feet up on his desk, reading the file in the manilla folder, trying to ignore the woman sitting in his office and how attractive she was. There was a lot of the usual information; Mother: Black, Father: Chinese, Born: New York, New York... schools, hobbies, grew up an only child, yada yada yada. Which all changed drastically the day after 9/11.

"Your parents..?

"Both killed," Mercedes replied flatly.

"I'm sorry..."

"Thanks, I'm over it now."

He paged through her spotless service records. "Why the Air Force?"

"I wanted to fly. I wanted to bomb them all into dust. I figured I could get more of them that way than with a gun."

"So how did you end up as an intelligence analyst?"

"I didn't like flying." Huang swept her hair back and sat back in the chair a little, crossing her legs at the knee. "I went with my strengths. I have an eye for detail, figured I could do the most in target assessment and after-action damage assessment. Worked on the ground, in the field and in the E-3 Sentry..."

"The AWACS?"

"That's the one."

Doug cocked one eyebrow, "So you never flew Mach 1 in a photo mission then..."

"No, I told you what you wanted to hear..."

Doug dropped his feet off the desk and leaned forward, his elbows on the desk, "You *lied...*"

"Yes, I did," she nodded nonchalantly. "Get over it. When I walked in here," she waved, "the testosterone count was off the charts. It didn't matter what my experience was; I could have been the fucking *door gunner on the space shuttle...* You were going to find fault with it. So I threw you a bone."

"So you have *no* combat experience then..."

Mercedes pointed at the folder, "Keep reading, Mooreland."

After two more pages he looked up, a little wide-eyed, "As an analyst, what the hell were you doing in the field?"

"We had to wear multiple hats. I volunteered as a forward observer. We'd consult, record, film, direct air support... sometimes we'd get *too forward,* and sometimes we had to do more than *observe."*

Mooreland tapped on the page, "This Marine commendation says, you actively assisted this Marine unit to repel an insurgent counter-attack on your position...?"

"Yeah. What's the date on that one?"

"That one? You mean there's *more?"*

274

"Sure," she replied casually, "I have several. But the office was pressed for time and couldn't get me all the copies for your file before my flight. I can have them send you the others if you'd like."

She knew that she had skewered him, he could see it in her eyes, and now he knew it too. Did she know that he knew? Of that, Doug couldn't be sure. But he should have known better than to second guess a personal pick by the Deputy Director. Was she there for his position? Could he trust her? He didn't know that either. The guys would watch his back, but he was going to have to watch her. Closely. "Welcome to *The Barn*, Huang..."

■ ■ ■

By the time the guys wandered into the operations area, morning sunlight poured through the greenhouse skylights. Mercedes Huang was already showered and dressed, sitting Indian-style on the situation table, coffee mug in hand, studying the materials posted all over the white board. In her lap she poured through the documents scattered across the table, carefully placing them back in their respective piles before moving on to the next.

"Hey, Doug! She took Restonovich and Brodermeyer off the white board!"

"So what," she shrugged. "They're dead, they have no other connections to our guy and they were peripheral at best. They were only linked to Steele through Maria Arroyo. And if I remember right, she's with Steele, right?"

"Right..." Doug Mooreland approached from around the table looking at the changes to the board, coffee mug in hand. "You moved the sister and her girlfriend up under Steele. Why? She entered the picture later, down here..." he pointed at the time line toward the bottom.

"Because you're looking at this as a time line, I'm looking at this as a relationship tree. We need to determine who is loose, who is in play, what their relationship is and who we can leverage. Like this guy," she pointed, "Stephen Miles."

"He's a CIA *Director...*"

"Yes, I can see that, Doug. Fuck, it's right on his tag, I'm not blind. But at this point no one is above reproach. Maybe they've repatriated him and they're hiding him... They won't share that with us without some leverage..."

"Steele is currently out of the picture..."

"How can we be sure of that?" she countered. "He could be..."

"Wait," grinned Mooreland, holding his hand out, "Hold on, you *have* seen the videos, right?" He turned to his right, "Lou, run the DVD..."

"Yeah I've seen..." she looked at the flat-screen next to the white board, her eyes narrowing, "No I haven't seen *that* part..."

"Some of this is our video, some is footage we confiscated and some came from files we found hidden on the Deep Web. We also have the news broadcast that TV bitch aired on here as well."

"I thought this was something we did to confuse the public and discredit..." she shot Doug a glance, "It's not manufactured..?"

Doug Moorland was enjoying this part, blowing her mind. A little payback for her ruse last night. He shook his head with a Cheshire Cat grin, "No. This is the real deal, lady..."

"Whoa!" she jumped, her head pulling back as a quick lance of light came from the darkened doorway of Steele's beach house towards the camera, destroying a black SUV in the intersection below, debris flying up past the camera's lens.

"Yeah got that from the lady filming it from her balcony. That was *our unit* he blew up, by the way..."

"What the hell was he using? An RPG?"

Doug shook his head, "Laser, particle weapon, rail gun, we have no idea." He pointed back at the screen, Here, watch *this* part... don't blink or you'll miss it..."

She watched the hand-held shaky video zooming in slowly from a vantage point down the beach. "It's hard to tell, is that a Coast Guard chopper..?"

"Yep. MH60T Sea Hawk..."

"It's a real UFO..." she breathed, enlightenment creeping in. "Oh!" she pointed, "they're shooting at the people in the sand, that can't be a good idea...*" Mercedes recoiled as the ship returned fire, the helicopter disappearing in a fireball, reduced to flaming confetti floating through the air. *"Shit..!* What it God's name..."

"Exactly," he nodded. "I missed that part, I was still inside the house..."

Her brow furrowed, not taking her eyes off the screen, watching all the different angles and clips as the video continued. "You were *there?"*

"Me," he thumbed in Lou's direction, "Lou, Pete..." he cleared his throat as the name stuck, "and a couple guys we lost there. That weapon you saw blow up our vehicle cut two of our guys in half. Our body armor doesn't do anything against their stuff."

"Jesus... OK, so I don't get it, what are we in this for? Payback? The ship?"

Standing next to her, Doug pointed at the screen, "Here, check out the departure of this thing. The footage is from the F-16s that came out of Homestead." He touched her shoulder, "Keep in mind they're at full afterburner doing Mach 2..."

The F-16s closing in from above, recorded the engines of the UFO glowing blue, pulling away slowly at first, then accelerating hard, disappearing in a matter of a couple of seconds in a blue flash, a comet tail chasing it out of sight.

"My God..."

"Yeah. They estimated it somewhere between Mach 5 and Mach 7." He leaned back against the table, sipping his coffee. "We realize, barring mechanical failure grounding that thing, it's unlikely we'll ever be able to capture it. But there is a piece of portable communications equipment..."

She turned and glared at him, "Say *what?*" Communications equipment seemed a bit of a letdown.

"Communications equipment," he continued, "the size of a laptop, powerful enough to reach deep space, faster and more efficiently than anything we have." He turned and backed away from the table with a wave of his hand, "Just think, no more transmitter dish arrays, no more giant banks of computers to control communications... we might not even *need* satellites. The U.S. could monopolize all communications on the planet. No one could communicate without us knowing about it."

Mercedes slid herself off the table, "How many of these units are out there, do we know?"

"We're not clear on that yet. The sister had one, we know that for sure. SETI saw the incoming signals and got all excited, thought they were receiving messages from ET. When they realized the communication was going both ways, then they panicked. They thought ET was here, phoning home. Our guy inside dropped a dime and alerted DARPA..."

"Who handed it to us..." she finished his sentence. "So what were the communications about?"

"We don't know. DARPA, CSS and our own cryptography are all stumped. The sister took the unit with her when she bugged out. We believe the parents may have one and there are a couple more people including Chase Holt," he pointed at the white board, "this guy here."

"Sooo... are these people *aliens?*"

Doug shrugged, "You guess is as good as mine. Maybe, maybe not."

"Why haven't we picked these, er, *people* up yet?"

Doug thumbed at the white board, "The sister was the only one with a signal. Between Holt's background in electronics and security and his tight ties to everyone in the family among other key people, he seemed to be the lynch-pin and possible direct link to Steele himself."

"So that's why you picked him up," she added, paging through Chase Holt's file. "Hmm, too bad Pete Whitman fumbled the ball." She closed the folder, "What about the parents?"

"Our ace in the hole," replied Doug, ignoring the comment about Pete. "We're sitting on them. Steele came back for his sister, we're sure he'll come back for his parents. If we leave them alone, he'll know where to find them and we'll know where to find him."

She tapped on the photo of Stephen Miles, "Let's not forget this guy. It all started with him..."

"Fair enough," agreed Doug. "Then we should add this guy to the list," he said, tapping on the photo of Phil Cooper. "FBI agent, good friends with Steele's father. Something's always told me he knows more than he's letting on."

"Hold on," interrupted Lou Geller, stepping in, "we're crossing a line here targeting members of other agencies... this could go upside down real quick."

"Think of it this way, Lou," began Mercedes, "what do you think would happen if we got our hands on one of these things and called Steele to bargain something bigger for his parents? Like a ship?"

"Ya mean *ransom?*" said Lou sarcastically.

"No, like *negotiation,*" countered Doug. He was beginning to like the way Huang was thinking.

"Potato - potahto," mumbled Lou.

Mercedes stepped up to the board and studied the photos. "I think we need to go back to basics. Some of these people are in the wind and we should go back and rewire their pads in case they return for any reason. That's step one. Step two, we tag anyone mobile so we can keep track of them. And step three, starting at the bottom," she pointed, "the peripheral folks. We start picking these people up."

"And what do we do with them?" asked Lou.

Mercedes shrugged, "Hold them, question them."

"For how long?"

"As long as it takes. If we let them go we run the risk of them informing others. We'd have to hold them until the investigation is resolved and the equipment is acquired. This is of national importance, our country's security and safety is at risk." Mercedes Huang was staring intently at the board. "Mooreland, what is that symbol?" she pointed, waving her finger at three photos.

"Steele, Holt and Murphy are Masons. That's how they know each other, they're in the same lodge..."

"Then we need wires in that lodge, see what they know."

"Um," Doug rubbed his chin, "that's not as easy as you might think..."

Mercedes rolled her eyes, "Oh for God's sake, you're spies, get creative. Figure it out. Hell if you can't figure it out, *I'll* do it."

"You won't get in," commented Lou, "women aren't allowed in the lodge... Besides, being an enormous fraternity, with a very influential enrollment..."

"Like the CIA or the FBI?" she interrupted sarcastically.

"Like Presidents, heads of state, judges, lawyers, heads of industry, and other stuff we shouldn't really mess with... from all over the planet."

Not totally convinced, Mercedes scrunched her lips together. "Hmm. Maybe we'll have to think more on that, then."

"Yeah, think it over real hard, lady," admonished Lou Geller. "They're not just Masons, they're *Knights Templars...*"

She looked at him with a blank stare.

"Hoo boy, she has no idea who they are. Doug, you want to take this?"

Doug Mooreland rubbed his forehead. "I'm not going to do a full history here, some of this you're going have to study up on for yourself... That being said; the Freemasons are arguably one of the oldest secret orders on the planet. The *Order of the Knights Templar* dates back to the early 1100's and is an integral part of Freemason history. You could say that Masonry was borne from the ideals, principals and code of ethics, of the Knights Templars. The Templars invented the earliest forms of banking and checking, developed massive wealth, had their own navy, had their own army, and their first headquarters was the Temple Mount in Jerusalem... The Crusaders called it the Temple of Solomon. They protected pilgrims traveling to and from the holy land of Jerusalem from Islamic raids, ensuring their safety. Developing over about two centuries, their financial network and massive influence extended across the Middle East and all of Europe. At one point they owned the entire island of Cyprus."

He took a sip of his nearly cold coffee, producing a look of disdain. "At the beginning of the 13th century, King Philip IV of France had racked up a great deal of debt owed for their services. To avoid paying it he hatched a scheme to discredit the Templars, allowing the crown to seize their money and assets. After some planning, he made his move on Friday, October 13th, 1307, arresting and incarcerating as many as he could find."

He shot Mercedes a glance, "That's how the 13th got its bad rap. Anyway, King Philip pressured Pope Clement to work with him to declare the Templars heretics so all their properties and assets could be seized internationally, which the Pope finally did a month later."

Mercedes Huang was listening carefully, her hands tucked in her pockets, leaning against the table. "Weren't these the Knights with the red cross on their uniforms that fought in the Crusade against the Muslims?"

"Yep. The red cross that the Templars wore on their robes was a symbol of martyrdom, and religious piety. They were essentially warrior monks. I've seen several references to them being called the *soldiers of Christ* or the *warriors of Christ*. What most people don't realize is that the Templars fought the Crusades as a response to more than a hundred years of attacks by the Muslims. It wasn't initiated by the church; it was an effort to stop the attrition brought on by the Muslim aggressions. Because the Templars had the experience and resources, they were called upon to do battle, along with other religious orders like the *Knights Hospitaller* and the *Knights of St. John*. Their uncompromising principles, along with their reputation for courage, excellent training, and heavy armament, made the Templars the most feared combat force in medieval times..."

"OK," waved Mercedes, "this is all fascinating enough, but how does that relate to the here and now?"

Doug handed his coffee mug off to another agent quietly listening, "Would you mind?" The agent gave a silent shrug and headed for the coffee pot sitting on the warmer. "Alright," continued Doug, "Friday the 13th, the King and the Pope conspired to wipe out as thoroughly as they could, the Templars and all their holdings, yes?"

"OK..."

"So," he said, accepting a refilled coffee mug, "the Templars were famous for something else; their use of pigeons for communications and their secret codes. As soon as the arrests began, messages were sent out by courier pigeons. And hundreds if not thousands of the Templars simply disappeared. Some went to other orders, some blended back into normal life, a large number regrouped under the name, *Knights of Christ.* They had an *exit plan.* The King confiscated all the properties and some of their monetary assets... but much of the wealth disappeared with them..." He waved his hand, "Poof. Gone. They ended up in Spain, Portugal, Mexico, America, England, Ireland and scattered throughout Europe. The ones captured were imprisoned, tortured, killed, some burned alive at the stake..."

"Jesus," she breathed.

"Yeah," nodded Doug, "but the rest survived, lived on, and continued the legacy of some of the most influential people on the planet... In 1492, a hundred-eighty-five years later, Columbus sailed to America. You noticed I didn't say discovered, because he didn't really, the Templars had already been here. In fact they provided him with charts and information on the winds and currents. If you've ever seen drawings of his ships, the sails carried the cross of the Knights Templars..."

"Columbus was a *Templar?*"

"Yep. A member of the *Knights of Christ.*"

"Wow... But I still don't get how that applies..."

Doug slapped his forehead, "Don't you get it? They may be civilians, and they certainly don't carry swords and armor anymore, but the dedication is the same now as it was back then. The oath they swear, the secret ways they communicate, their influence and power... If you go stomping into a lodge and ask questions, start hauling them in for questioning... it will be a replay of Friday the 13th all over again. I think we've already seen that with Dan Murphy and Chase Holt. Unfortunately, 20/20 hindsight; we weren't initially aware of the connection."

"What do we do then?"

"Careful observation, tapping, listening... they'll resurface."

"How can you be so sure?"

Doug cracked a crooked little smirk, "Because they still have family..." He waved his finger in the air, "As a final side note; one of the Knights Templar burned at the stake, Jacques de Molay, called out from the fire that a great calamity would befall those who had condemned the Templars to death... Pope Clement *mysteriously* died a month later and King Philip died in a hunting *accident* before the end of the year."

"Fuck, that's creepy."

Doug shook his head, "Gotta respect someone with that kind of mojo," he sipped his coffee. "So I don't intend to underestimate this organization or their members."

CHAPTER TWENTY THREE

SALT LAKE CITY, UTAH: *DOUGWAY - THE RABBIT HOLE*

After exiting I-15 toward Salt Lake, State Road 6 was a bit of a shock, a two lane road winding west through the desert and between the mountains. Eureka popped up out of nowhere, a little mining town with two gas stations. One of those places you'd miss if you blinked too long. After the necessary pit stop they continued on, facing the brutal glare of the afternoon sun.

Utah State Route 36, ran west before it swung north and they almost missed the turnoff because it looked smaller and more worn than the road they had just been on. The narrow two lane road ran through desolate desert with little traffic, save a tumbleweed crossing every now and again. The setting sun on their left was a reprieve from directly facing the intense, unrelenting ball of fire now dropping though a cloudless sky towards the distant peaks. Only an occasional sod farm broke up the flat, lifeless stretches of nothing, their giant green circles the only color in a brown and gray world. It reminded him of another place... a place far away, where war never seemed to end.

Chase Holt lifted his foot off the accelerator, letting the truck slow down on its own, staring out at the desert on the right of the road. He angled gently and the truck rumbled across the rough scrub on the unpaved shoulder paralleling a short barbed wire fence in serious disrepair. Karen was watching him but trying to see what he was looking at out the window at the same time. "What are you looking at?" she squinted, scanning the terrain.

"Bunkers.... I think." Looking around suspiciously, he climbed out of the cab and into the truck's bed for a better view, standing on his toes. "Yep, bunkers. Rows and rows of them..."

She stuck her head out the window, "How the hell did you even see that?"

"Practice. Certain things in the desert look natural, some don't. These don't, though I suspect they're more worried about them being seen from the air than the ground."

"Whose are they?"

"No idea. Army probably. They look abandoned though. I don't see any vehicles or security..." He jumped down to the ground and climbed back into the cab, putting the truck back in gear and angling back onto the empty road.

"What are they used for?"

Chase checked his rear view mirror, "Trucks, tanks, fuel, weapons, ordnance... anything they want to protect from bombs or missiles." He pointed to the right, "There's the road going in. I don't see a gate or anything... interesting."

■ ■ ■

Passing the Tooele Army Depot on the outskirts of town as the sun slid behind the mountain ridges, Chase wondered if what they'd previously seen was truly deserted, or more likely remotely monitored. The second question would be what is the response time for an encroachment? That was probably going to run around in his mind for a while.

Thankfully, Tooele was a decent sized town with enough amenities to provide them with a decent, clean motel room and the first real dinner they'd had in days. It was a bit of normalcy that seemed to be rare in the maelstrom of crazy that had become their lives.

Coming back to the room from the restaurant, Chase stalled Karen with a wave, swiping his windbreaker aside, silently drawing his Glock. "Door's open," he whispered, holding it at low ready. He looked up and back down the corridor, checking his surroundings.

"I watched you pull it closed," she whispered back.

He nodded, pushing the door open with his foot, greeted by Allie, wagging her tail. "Hi girl," he breathed, "did we have a visitor?" The German Shepherd danced around, glad to see her human, kicking something black under the desk. Quickly scanning the room, Chase holstered his Glock and stooped down to pick up the MagnaCard.

Karen closed and locked the door behind them, "What is it?"

"An electronic master key card. This thing'll open any door in any hotel. I'm guessing they didn't count on Ellie being here. She must have scared them off..."

"Are we talking hotel staff?"

"No, they'd use one of their own cards. This card plugs into a decoder device the size of a cell phone. It probably popped off the cable while he was trying to get out. This is spy stuff..."

"Not a burglar, huh?"

Chase tossed it on the nightstand, "Nah, too high tech for this neck of the woods..." He wedged a chair under the door handle. "This is a military town. We're not military and we're not from around here. Maybe it was a security sweep." He turned out the lights and peeked out the window at the truck. Everything appeared normal.

"Are you trying to make me feel better, or is that really what you think?"

He scanned the cars in the lot, all of them empty. "Uh-huh..."

"Nice ambiguous answer," she remarked sarcastically, plopping onto the bed.

"It's the only one you're getting," replied Chase, pulling the curtains shut. "You can go ahead and give Allie her food..."

■ ■ ■

A few hundred feet from Utah State Route 36, Chase pulled the pickup off the road onto the rough scrub along Utah State Route 199, the desert running right to the edge of the pavement. The morning sun peeked over the ridge behind them, scattered clouds creating a colorful play of light. They were trading one desolate two-lane road for another, with one difference; this one pointed them toward the mountains. "There's the start of the barbed wire fence..." Chase put the truck in park.

"Are you sure this is right?" asked Karen, swiveling around and scanning in all directions. "There's nothing here..." She pointed up the road, "I take that back, there's a tumbleweed crossing the road."

"It's exactly where Dan's instructions said... he said to wait here." Allie stuck her head between the seats and nudged Chase's arm.

"What are we waiting for..?"

Chase glanced over his shoulder when he caught the flash of blue and red light out of the corner of his eye, his stomach taking a rolling leap before balling up into a knot. *"Ooh crap..."*

Karen's eyes flicked out her window to the mirror on the door, "Oh God, what do we do?"

Chase swallowed hard. "Nothing, stay calm... Don't say anything unless he asks you a question. We're tourists..." He watched the Sheriff exit the cruiser and adjust his gear before reaching through the open window and pulling his cowboy hat off the dash, placing it on his head and adjusting it with a tug on the front of the brim. Chase caught that he was wearing cowboy boots and wondered if that was standard uniform out here.

"Mornin' folks," he said leaning close, eying Allie. "Does he bite?"

"She," corrected Chase. "And no," he lied. "Did we do something wrong, officer?" The Shepherd watched the officer over her human's shoulder with interest.

"Not that I know of..." replied the Sheriff, lifting the brim of his hat with his index finger, looking in around the cab of the truck. "Mind if I see your license and registration?"

"Sure," nodded Chase, fishing things out of his wallet and center console. Along with what was requested, he included his concealed weapons permit and instructor ID.

The Sheriff glanced at it briefly, handing it all back except the driver's license, "Don't need those. Where's your gear?"

"Back seat in our backpacks," replied Chase without moving.

The officer straightened up with a curt nod, "Let's leave them back there for now, shall we?" With a polite smile he headed back for his cruiser.

"Was it me or was that a bit odd?" whispered Karen.

Staring in the rear view mirror, Chase was watching the officer in his cruiser, the door standing open, "Yeah, little bit." A Jeep without top or doors drove past in the opposite direction, giving the scene only a casual glance.

"Here comes our boy..."

The officer strode up to the truck and leaned, handing Chase his license back, a piece of paper wrapped around it. "Y'all have a nice day," he smiled, tipping his hat before heading back to his cruiser.

Chase checked his mirror and shot Karen a quick glance, "What the hell..?" Unwrapping the paper he realized it was a note; *Brother: follow me but not too close. Turn right when I go Code 3, follow it to the end.* He looked up as the cruiser pulled back onto the pavement, passing them, heading west on 199 without so much as a glance in their direction from the officer.

"I don't get it," said Karen picking up the note as Chase put the truck in gear and pulled back onto the road.

"Dashcam video..."

"Like on the cop shows..."

"Yep. Most cops have dashcam video and mics on their uniforms. He probably couldn't say anything, he wanted it to look like a routine traffic stop."

"What's this, *Code 3?*" she pointed at the note.

"Lights and siren."

Karen sighed, "You'd think there would be an easier way to do all this..."

■ ■ ■

Ten miles later after winding through climbing narrow canyons and passes cut through the foot of the mountains, the Sheriff's cruiser pulled off into the dirt, his lights coming on, his siren wailing as he spun his cruiser in a semi circle using a controlled slide. He appeared out of a swirling cloud of dust, racing past them on the road in the opposite direction, his engine roaring.

Karen's head whipped around as she watched him scream past, "Holy shit he's flying... do you think he got a call and had to leave..?"

Chase steered the truck off the pavement in the same place the cruiser went off the road, a rutted sand and dirt trail angling up and away into an unseen canyon. "Nope, that's what Code 3 looks like. It's part of the show," he pointed, "see there's our road..."

"That's *not* a road," she argued. "That doesn't even qualify as a driveway. It looks like a wagon trail..."

The canyon walls rose up on either side blocking out the early morning sun, the narrow track winding its way left and right, up and down. "This is kinda creepy... are you sure we won't get stuck in here?"

Chase's mouth cocked crookedly, not so sure himself, "Four wheel drive, I hope not." He caught a glimpse of the trail around a bend, climbing up the side of the mountain. "Oh hell no... this thing ain't going up that..."

Opening up into a small, cozy valley, a motor home, tents and dirt bikes populated the area, hidden under a sizable camouflage net, the trail reaching up beyond the camp. A young woman with long black hair braided past her waist, and golden skin waved them to a spot to park. An animal that looked like a mix of coyote and wolf appeared from one of the tents sidling up beside her.

"I have my dog," called Chase, "Is your... is he animal friendly?"

"Yes," replied the woman, approaching, "she's wonderful with other animals." The woman extended her hand as Chase slid out of the truck, Allie climbing over the seat, eager to get out. "Hello, you must be Chase. I am; *Two Dogs Fucking.*" She shook his hand.

"Excuse me?"

"She grinned at her own humor. "Bad Indian joke..." she mused.

"You're Indian, then," he replied, still off balance.

"You couldn't tell?" she smiled, her white teeth a contrast to her golden skin, a wide, colorful, beaded choker around her neck. "Shoshone..."

Karen made it around the front of the truck, extending her hand, "Karen..."

"Dancing Rain."

"Oh, that's beautiful..."

"Thanks, just call me Rain," she said with a casual wave. "Dan and Jesse took a couple of the dirt bikes to the top before dawn, they should be back for breakfast soon, you folks hungry?"

■ ■ ■

Dan Murphy, tanned and bearded, pushed away from the table under the shade of the camouflage net, his plate empty. "That was good, sweetie... it really hit the spot," he remarked, rubbing his stomach. Rain kissed the top of his head as she moved past, picking up empty plates and silverware. Dan stroked his beard, "Man, that's quite an adventure you've had, I'm glad you made it... Again, I'm really sorry to hear about Pam. I only remember meeting her the once but she seemed like a sweet girl."

"Thanks," nodded Karen.

Chase leaned forward, his elbows on the table, hands clasped. "So Dan, why are we here? What's going on?"

Dan leaned back, his hands laced behind his head in a long stretch. "Brother Chase..." he paused and eyed Karen.

Chase didn't so much as shift his eyes, "Karen, honey, would you mind helping Rain? Give us a few minutes?"

"Nothing doing," she snapped. "I'm in this up to my eyeballs just like you. My life is on the line just like yours. I have a right to know what the hell is going on..."

"OK," nodded Dan, leaning back in, "fair enough." He accepted an open laptop handed him by Rain, setting it on the table. He shot Chase a glance, "She is bound by *your* oath, she is *your* responsibility, understand?"

"Understood," agreed Chase.

287

"Good." Dan brought the laptop out of sleep mode, "Ever heard of Project Zenith?"

"No..."

"How about Project Ascension?"

"No..."

Dan spun the laptop around so they could see the screen. "Alright, we have a lot of ground to cover... But before I show you that, you should know where you stand."

"That might be good," snipped Karen.

Dan ignored her attitude, understanding her angst. "The Brotherhood's Commandery has three divisions; the Watchers, the Guardians, and the Crusaders. We are the Watchers. Teams like ours all across the country gather information from people inside and outside the government loyal to the Order. The Guardians are tasked with protecting the people, the defenseless citizens. And the Crusaders are tasked with restoring order, restoring government..."

Karen's eyes were wide, "Are we talking about a revolution?"

"Hopefully it won't come to that," replied Dan, shaking his head. "But the possibility *is* there. Thomas Jefferson said; *The tree of liberty must be refreshed from time to time with the blood of patriots and tyrants.*"

"That sure sounds like a revolution to me..."

Dan's eyes narrowed, "The people of this country need to awaken from the reality TV induced, self indulgent coma they've allowed themselves to be lulled into. People sit across the table from one another, transfixed by their technology, oblivious to everything around them, ignoring the truly meaningful warm blooded social interaction the human race craves. They've become zombies, replacing quality with quantity, so tied to their gadgets they are controlled by them. Yet they are so woefully uninformed it is staggering in scope. And the media has stopped doing their real job, which is being a government watchdog. They are complicit in the deceit and corruption."

"Nothing new," commented Chase, "it's been like that for years..."

"Has it?" Dan touched Rain's hand as she walked past, "Do we have any iced tea?" She nodded and headed into the RV, Dan turning back to the table. "Why do you think we went to digital TV instead of analog? To drive people to cable and satellite. Sure the signal quality is better but that's not the point. The point is that the government can more easily control cable and satellite. And while we all pay through the nose for our cell services, the government hands out free phones with free calling and free data to the low information voters. Like samples from a drug dealer to a crack whore."

Rain placed glasses of iced tea on the table for each of them, "They want a nation of addicts..."

"And now they have it," added Dan. "What do you suppose would happen if it all just suddenly... *stopped?* No TV. No radio. No internet. No cell service...*"

Chase touched the beads of moisture forming on the sides of the glass, "Anarchy..."

"Control the information, control the people," said Dan. "Kiss it all goodbye. Your rights are gone. You'll get what they decide you should have... martial law, complete and total government control..."

Chase watched the beads of moisture race down the glass, "But how? And why?"

"Enter the how..." Dan tapped the laptop keyboard, starting the video. "Project Zenith." He took a sip of his iced tea. "You're watching a video we took early this morning, about 4:30, of Dugway which you can see from the top," he thumbed over his shoulder at the peak of the ridge line. "That bright green flash and beam you're about to see..."

"Whoa!" Chase and Karen both snapped rigid.

"Yeah, they're testing that laser on debris in orbit. Remember that Russian reconnaissance satellite that came down in February...?"

"Yeah..."

Dan pointed at the screen, "Bang. Dead satellite. It was an old Russian spy rig our folks figured would be mistaken by the Ruskies as an age-failure thing. They didn't set to totally destroy it, just disable it with a narrower beam. All the evidence would burn up on reentry. It worked. The Russians might have suspicions, but if they did they didn't say anything. Because there was no proof. The unit fires from one of the hangars down there. The hangar roof opens and closes for operations. This one's a prototype, but there's a facility in Nevada called the National Security Device Facility, south of Area 51 in Groom Lake, that's building operational units for Navy ships and for the X-37B Spaceplane."

"Alright... if that's the how, what's the why?"

"Global communications control. *Everything,"* waved Dan expansively. "The US would be the only country left with operational satellites, communications, GPS, etc. If they have any of those things mounted in our satellites they could kill ground radar and other important targets. Then we're talking global domination. Anywhere, anytime, no nukes... unless they're ours."

The video complete, Chase sat back in his chair. "That's *insane...*"

"Yes it is..."

"It would take them days, maybe weeks to kill everything up there. The Russians wouldn't just sit around..."

"Reports we've seen say once all the units are deployed," offered Rain from the RV's doorway, "Project Zenith would have them relatively blind and deaf in two hours or less. In twenty-four hours, the only satellites in orbit still functional would belong to the USA. And if they time the attack to some serious solar activity it might be long enough to cripple anything with offensive capabilities before they shake off the confusion."

Chase waved his hands, "That's a big fucking *if*... No, I'm sorry this is all just too insane. We're talking World War III, here... Wait, then why all the military cutbacks on manpower and benefits?"

"They're going to convert to a conscript military," shrugged Dan. "Fight a war, thin out the population a bit, no benefits to worry about... One of the reasons they don't care about the illegals coming over the border; they get those votes with the promise of free stuff and with a military draft they get free manpower."

Karen had been silent, the prospect of it all so overwhelming. But there was something that seemed to be missing. "So how does all this tie in to us? I mean, why were we being stalked and shot at?"

"Ah," nodded Dan. "Good question. As hard as all this has been to fathom, it all ties together. It seems our friend, Brother Jack, left a little device with his sister; an alien communications unit of some kind. What I read was that it was about the size of a laptop and the signal could reach and receive from deep space, in real time. So they want it *bad*. It makes all communications technology we have, look like a stone tablet and chisel by comparison. The group hunting you, hunting all of us, is the NSA. And they think Chase knows something about the unit, or maybe has one..."

Chase nearly spit out a swallow of iced tea, *"Me? What the hell gave them that idea?"*

"Probably your close relationship with the family."

"Fuck me," he muttered.

Dan took a swallow of his iced tea. "Here's another piece of the whole puzzle, a pretty important piece as far as I'm concerned; all the calls for repealing the Second Amendment, gun registrations, bans etc... are because they know they can't pull this off if the people are armed..." He stirred his iced tea. "It's also why the administration has been purging military leaders that won't walk lockstep with their ideology. They want military leaders that will follow orders; whether it be firing on American citizens or going along with a plan for world domination."

"A hundred-forty-five dismissals by last count. Good people..." Tense, Chase's jaw muscles were working. "If the people would just wake their asses up!"

"I think that is actually happening," offered Rain. "Did you see what's been happening in Nevada?"

Chase frowned... "No..."

"They've been on the road, Rain," said Dan over his shoulder. He leaned forward, his elbows on the table. "The government is testing the waters, seeing how far they can push, how much they can get away with. Something they've been incrementally doing for years using the EPA, IRS and the Bureau of Land Management. The BLM has forced ranchers in this valley of Nevada off their lands and out of business. There's only one family left and the BLM has been in conflict with these people for over a decade. Suddenly it's urgent; they're claiming eminent domain, safety of an endangered species, he owes grazing fees or something..."

"For his own land?"

"Yeah, only the BLM claims it's not his land, it's theirs. Problem is not only are they running roughshod over him they're stepping all over the state's rights... If it's actually government land, it belongs to Nevada, not Washington. And the state has no argument with the rancher..."

"So what happened?"

"The BLM shows up with two hundred armed officers, helicopters, snipers and range hands to start confiscating this guy's cattle and take the land. They were threatening people, getting rough like schoolyard bullies, telling people they would arrest or shoot anyone who interferes..."

Karen was transfixed. "Jesus," she breathed.

"But this time there was push back. This rancher, a tough old bird, asked for help. It went viral. In a couple of days there were almost two thousand citizens there to protest and protect him and his ranch, from all over the country. A fairly sizable portion of those people were armed."

"The Three Percenters," nodded Chase.

"Yep. And about half of those were our Guardians," added Dan. "No shit dyed-in-the-wool patriots, willing to do whatever was needed. The end result

291

was the BLM returned most of the confiscated animals and pulled out. They knew they were seriously out manned and outgunned."

"Nice..."

Dan smirked, "Here's the kicker; the BLM wanted the entire valley for a solar farm deal one of Nevada's very own senators cooked up with a Chinese conglomerate. Selling out Americans to line his own filthy, greedy pockets."

Chase rolled his eyes, "Holy shit... not just Americans but his very own constituents. Can't get much lower than that."

"Snake's belly in a wagon rut," chirped Rain.

"Sadly," added Dan cutting back in, "I think it's a short-term win. The BLM will wait it out and when there's less coverage, less attention, they'll sweep back in. Probably at night... scoop up the entire family. Then they'll have free reign to do whatever they want to."

"That's not going to be pretty..."

"No it's not. One way or the other those folks are going to disappear; a dark cell or a bodybag... At this point I don't think the government's going to be picky."

"That may be the second shot heard round the world..."

Dan sipped his iced tea, "I'd like to say I hope it will end all *peaches and cream* but I think that's ignoring the white elephant in the room. I hate to say it, I really do, but I think there's a good chance things could get really ugly... for all of us."

Chase stared at his glass in silence for a long moment. "So what's Project Ascension?" he asked slowly.

"The X-37B Spaceplane. The first one set a record at four-hundred-sixty-nine consecutive days in orbit. A *secret* mission for the military... directly tied to Project Zenith. Everyone thinks there's just one of these but there's a second one in orbit that's been up there over five-hundred days. Same mission."

Chase sat back unconsciously biting his lower lip, "Intelligence gathering on all the satellites in space..."

"Exactly. And just FYI, those two are not the only X-37s they have. While the latest one has been orbiting up there, three more have been completed. There's about ten now."

Chase rubbed his face, "One is research, two or three is transport or testing... ten is weaponizing."

■ ■ ■

The small established observation area near the peak of the ridge overlooked Dugway and the cloudless sky full of stars promised a night for clear photos and video. Chase adjusted the camouflaged poncho with the foil lining around him. "Do these things really work?"

"So far so good. Can't wear the damn things during the day, too fucking hot. But then trying to pick us up with thermal during the day surrounded by hot rocks in the sun is fruitless. As long as we stay hidden we're golden. At night though, as soon as everything cools off..."

"Yeah we used thermal all the time in Afghanistan. It has its limitations though. Range mainly... So what are we looking for?"

"UFOs, helicopters, convoys that disappear into the ground, lasers... whatever."

Chase was staring through the telephoto lens on the digital camera, "Y'know, I can see a service road just inside the fence line... not much of a fence either..."

"Don't need one, it's mined."

Chase pulled away from the camera looking over at Dan in the darkness, barely visible, "You're shitting me."

"Nope. Warning sign's say unexploded ordnance but that's to cover their asses. They have it mined."

Chase shook his head, "I don't know if I totally believe that or not... I don't want to believe it. But if it's true it's a sad comment on what's happening in the United States," he sighed. "Sometimes I don't recognize this country anymore."

It was silent for a while, nothing but the desert breeze and an occasional cricket.

"So um, you and Karen... you a thing?"

"Yeah. It was a fate thing. But it's good. You and Rain?"

"Yeah, she's terrific. She's a lawyer... or was. Worked in a big firm in Salt Lake, did pro-bono work on the side for the tribes in the area – give back to the community and all that. She took a client suing the government over a death that occurred at the military depot on Route 73..."

"We passed two; one on the right side of Route 36 then later one on the left... The one on the left looked like the biggest."

"The one on the right. It stretches between routes 36 and 73."

"It looked abandoned..."

"That's what they want you to think, but not hardly. Anyway, some teenage Indian kids were out there exploring and base security stopped them and held them. Killed one *accidentally* while they were in custody."

"Oh God..."

"Turns out, Rain's firm does a lot of government work and they ordered her to drop the case. It was on her own time and her own dime so she refused. They fired her; she sued her own law firm and won."

"Nice. What about the lawsuit for the kid?"

"She had to abandon it, she started getting death threats. Then of course there were the black SUVs following her. She hid out on one of the local reservations. With a little digging, the Order found that her firm secretly represented the DOE."

"Department of Energy," groaned Chase, "previously known as the Atomic Energy Commission... terrific. So these guys then," he thumbed over his shoulder at the base below.

"Yep."

"Purveyors of the finest, most thorough, most horrific destructive devices known to man. They're going to figure out yet, how to make the human race extinct..." he sighed.

"Here's the kicker," added Dan, waggling his finger. "With a *little more* digging, we found that the base in question, which everyone thought was an annex of the larger Army depot closer to town, is actually a CIA weapons, ammunition and equipment depot. Code named, *Midwest Depot.*"

Chase rolled his eyes. "Let's go home, Dan..."

"Florida? I'm not going back," countered Dan, "there's nothing for me there..."

"Fine," interrupted Chase, "screw it, I'll go back."

Dan Murphy started to laugh, "Man, you can't go home. You can *never* go home... *Ever.* If they caught up with you, you'd never see the light of day again. You'd probably end up in a shallow unmarked grave."

"Yeah, I know, it just sounded good. For a minute." Frankly, this situation didn't seem to have a very bright future either.

■ ■ ■

The night had passed quickly and it was active enough to keep them both busy. Under the shade of the camouflage net, reviewing the night's photos and video footage on the laptop at breakfast, Dan busied himself with uploading everything they had gotten onto a server hidden somewhere on the Deep Web. "This is some good stuff... Uh-oh, what's this? Hmm, interesting, we're being directed to Groom Lake..."

Mechanically eating his scrambled eggs, Chase Holt was staring blankly at the back of Dan's laptop. He raised his eyebrows, "Area 51?"

"Yep. I don't know about you but I'm bushed. We'll get some rest first and leave this evening; we should be there before morning."

Chase's mind was still playing back the night's events. "There's got to be a huge base underneath... over fifty deuce-and-a-halfs and MRAPS went into that hangar. I'd love a chance to see what's down there. Where did the helicopters go? I was concentrating on the ground vehicles."

Dan shook his head, "You mean after they buzzed us? I thought they'd seen us for sure. Two landed between the hangars on the other side and the other two flew off."

"Any idea what those other lights in the sky were?"

"You mean the..."

"Yeah, those."

Dan looked up over the screen of the laptop. "Nope."

CHAPTER TWENTY FOUR

FREERANGER – DD217, WHISPERFIRE SYSTEM: *MEE-OW*

Sitting at a dead stop a quarter of the way through the system, Commander T. B. Yafusco and Lieutenant Dash Zarnev were comparing notes on the holo-chart in the ship's ready room, examining the Whisperfire System.

Tibby Yafusco dropped himself into the lounger and kicked his feet up. "I don't know Dash, I think we've lost them. Sensors aren't picking up a damn thing. That ass at Rega Station screwed us bad; put us too far behind. Somewhere between Rega and here, they altered course.

Dash Zarnev rubbed the back of his neck in exasperation. "I swear to the Gods, Tibbs," he waved at the chart, "I was studying this route and this system twenty-four hours ago, and *that station...*" he pointed, *"wasn't* on the map."

Tibby wasn't so much listening as he was brooding. "I think that pompous ass lied to us... I'm betting they paid him to stall us. It makes sense," he mused, bringing his steepled fingertips to his lips in contemplation. "Why else would he have held us off station for so long...? We should go back to Rega and have a little old-fashioned talk with him..." He was staring at the wall deaf and blind except for the daydream in his mind's eye.

"TIBBY!"

Disrupting his plot, Yafusco shot Dash a scowl, *"WHAT?!"* he barked back, throwing his hands wide.

"Forget the fucking Imperator, will you please?" He stuck his arm into the hologram, his index finger touching the marker of the unnamed mining station orbiting the fourth planet. "This station wasn't on the map twenty-four hours ago..."

"Aaah," Tibby waved it off like he was physically casting the idea aside, "you probably just missed it..."

Indignant, Dash Zarnev straightened up and turned his back to the table, leaning back against it, his head cocked to one side, staring at his commanding officer, "When have I *ever* missed something like that?"

Yafusco nodded acknowledgment, "OK, never. But that doesn't mean anything... It could be a glitch in the chart system or a simple update."

"Or someone entered it into the system."

"Yeah, *maybe,*" shrugged Tibby. *"*But that could be *anybody.* Any ship traveling through a system can submit a navigational or structural position report."

"Or *maybe,* that UFW task force did it."

"At this point I think that's a big maybe..."

"C'mon, Tibby, it's a pretty big coincidence that we're following this group and this station suddenly appears."

"Yeah but it could be just that, a coincidence. I'm not sure I want to risk going any further. We're getting a little stipend from the FreeRanger Council to investigate but we can't count on that if there's nothing to report. Expenses and supplies will be coming out of our bottom line."

The door from the bridge slid open with a hiss, Grinah stepping in and standing in the doorway, "Sorry to bother you, but Kindre Thurmer and her first officer are shuttling over from the DD62..." She placed her hands on her hips with a snarky little smile creeping across her lips, "I guess she figured it was time for a little reunion..?"

Tibby pointed accusingly at his wife to be, "Don't start with me, woman..."

Grinah's snarky little smile remained, "As long as she doesn't start anything with you..."

▪ ▪ ▪

Commander Kindre Thurmer was at least a head taller than Grinah but that was not something Grinah was concerned about. The woman walked like a jungle cat looking for something to kill. And eat. It was simply unnerving to watch her walk into a room. Of course you wouldn't know it by looking at the men; drooling and panting like horny little puppies wanting to hump her leg. It was almost sickening to watch. Tibby was right, she was almost so beautiful it was distracting... disturbing. She was perfect. All the more reason for Grinah to dislike her, which she did almost instantly. It was an impulse. Like the impulse to tear at her face and scratch her eyes out... *Whoah! What the hellion was that?* Grinah shook off the feeling.

"Kindre Thurmer," she said, extending her hand, "and this is my first officer, Lieutenant Heunter LeStarn."

297

"Grinah." She politely shook the hands of the enchantress and her officer, who looked too much like a boy-toy. "Commander Yafusco thought it might be best dining here in the ready room; a little more privacy."

Kindre made herself at home on the leather settee, her first officer inspecting the holo-chart. "And where is Mr. Tibby this evening?"

For some reason that irked Grinah. "He and our first officer, Mr. Zarnev, will be with us in a moment. Can I get you a drink?"

"Why yes my dear, how nice," she waved regally, adjusting the hem of her skirt; an odd uniform choice for a ship's Commander. "So what is your position here, *Ensign...?*"

With her back to the Commander, Grinah caught the antipathy, wickedly reversing the proportions of Kleer and mixer in the glass. She turned and walked the drink over to the woman on the settee, "Bridge officer and *wife,*" she replied casually. The change of expression was brief and slight but Grinah caught that too. The first sip was a visible shock and *s*he rather enjoyed seeing the instant change in complexion as Kindre Thurmer forced it down, eyes watering. "Oh, *I'm sorry,*" Grinah said innocently. "Did I make that too strong?" She shook her head accepting the glass back, "I'm so used to mixing them for Tibby. He loves them that way, you know... Let me try again."

"No need," coughed Kindre, "I can... wait... for dinner..."

"Nonsense, can't have our guests going thirsty..." She remixed the drink in palatable proportions, walking it back over to the more humble Kindre who accepted it with a measure of caution. "Can I get you something Mr. LeStarn?"

Eyes wide, he shook his head and waved it off, "No thanks, I'm fine..."

■ ■ ■

Dinner was completely informal, conversation light and casual; overall friendly and uneventful, Kindre behaving herself under Grinah's watchful gaze. Wine glass in hand, the Commander was still sitting on the leather settee, watching the holo-chart animations. "I'm not sure just giving up our pursuit is a good idea Tibby."

"You just don't want to lose the Council's mission stipend..." waved Yafusco.

"No, of course not. Do you?"

"There's a point of diminishing return here somewhere, Kindra, and I think we're at it. Or near it. If we don't have something to report soon, they're going to pull the plug. And we'll end up deadheading back on our own dime. In case you hadn't noticed, this is not FreeRanger territory and we're alone out here..."

"I understand what you're saying..."

Yafusco shook his head, "If our ships had GOD drives, I'd feel a lot better about a hasty exit if we had to make one. But..."

"But we could get jumped by fighters if we're not careful. I get it."

Tibby sipped his nearly straight Kleer, producing a wince, its sharp heat burning on the way down. "There's at least six other routes between Rega Station and here. They could be anywhere. Two years ago, I would've been able to tell you where they probably went. Their patrols were predictable..."

Kindre uncrossed her legs and stood up, smoothing her skirt, moving over to the holo-table. "They've definitely changed tactics and patrol patterns, I've noticed that."

"According to the Imperator's description, this may be the same task force from the fight in Velora Prime..."

"I heard that was a mess for us..."

Tibby's face tightened, "You heard right. We missed it by half a day but we saw some of the ships coming out of the area. They were in bad shape."

"We never got close, we were doing escorts on the Fringe."

"Probably a good thing. There weren't many survivors."

Kindre sipped her wine. "What was the name of that ship...? The one with the bounty on it...?"

"Freedom," replied Heunter LeStarn. "And nobody seems to be able to confirm what happened to it..."

Kindre nodded, "I heard there are a few claims on her demise but the Council is refusing to pay out the bounty because there's no confirmation..."

Tibby smirked and shook his head at the same time, "I had a feeling that was going to come back and bite them in the ass somehow." He sipped his Kleer, his mind wandering back to his conversation with the Imperator of Rega Station. "Something the Imperator said keeps bothering me..."

"What's that?"

"The task force had a new Admiral. *Jack Steele...* Ever heard the name before?"

"Can't say that I have. Have you?"

Tibby's eyes narrowed. "Yeah. In Zender's Trek from a Maultier ore transport crew we rescued. They barely made it out of Velora Prime. Got shot up in the process. Their ship was owned by McSuddeth Mining..."

"Who is a subsidiary of VirTech Mining," interrupted Grinah. They lost a ship a couple months earlier in Haruna Tier... to the *Freedom.* VirTech's communications with the Freedom listed the captain as Jack Steele."

"A cruiser with fighters," added Tibby. "They're the ones who took out our cruiser later that day. The Skipper overextended our GOD jump and we went in depleted. We were a sitting duck."

"I remember reading that report," said Kindre. "I didn't realize... You've got a bit of history tied up in this."

Yafusco stared at his glass, "A little bit. But what the hell is he doing on an Oijin class carrier. As an Admiral? Did he lose the Freedom?"

Kindre Thurmer leaned against the holo-table with her hip, "It's an obvious reward for the victory in Velora Prime, if you ask me. And I think we should keep going... you'll never forgive yourself if you don't."

"Maybe..."

"You know as well as I do, it'll eat you up if you just let it go now." She pointed at the chart, "Look, if you had to guess... your *best guess,* where did they go?"

Tibby motioned over at Dash Zarnev. "The Lieutenant noticed an anomaly on the system chart that wasn't there on earlier review... It could be nothing..."

"But if it's *not,"* urged Kindre, "if it *is* them, then they're heading that way," she pointed at the gate to Elyse Core.

"Doesn't make sense though," said Tibby, shaking his head. "There's nothing in Elyse Core. The Terran System beyond that is populated but they aren't spacers yet, and you have to go two more systems from either one of those to find..."

"You said yourself they've been unpredictable," interrupted Grinah, "isn't this unpredictable?"

Yafusco stared at the chart and scratched his head, "So now we're trying to predict unpredictability...?"

"You have a better idea? Because sitting here isn't doing anything for us." She pointed her finger at him, "You know I'm right."

He slipped his arm around Grinah's waist and pulled her close, kissing her forehead. "Yes, dear," he smiled. "Dash, make for Elyse Core as soon as the Commander gets back to the DD62."

"Aye, sir."

"Kindre, it was good to see you again... you're welcome to tag along, but I understand if you decide to turn back..."

Commander Kindre Thurmer shook his hand and gave him a quick hug, keeping in mind Grinah was watching closely. "The 62 will be right beside the 217. We're in it for the adventure."

"And the mission stipend..." teased Yafusco.

Kindre smiled, "The stipend doesn't hurt." She turned to Grinah and shook her hand. "Good to meet you. Take care of each other... Let's go Mr. LeStarn."

"Yes Ma'am..."

■ ■ ■

Lieutenant Dash Zarnev poured himself a cup of coffee, to accompany his late night snack.

"You still awake?"

Dash glanced up, "Skipper," he acknowledged. "Can't sleep."

"You have Kindre on the brain...?"

The Lieutenant nodded uncomfortably, "Yeah, how did you know?"

Yafusco grinned, "I've seen it before. In the academy we used to call it Thurmer fever."

"I don't think I've ever seen a woman that beautiful... can't seem to get her out of my head."

"Shake it off, Mr. Zarnev. She'll chew you up and spit you out. And you won't even enjoy it..."

Dash cocked a curious eyebrow, "Is that the voice of experience?"

Tibby poured himself a cup of coffee, "Not personally. But I've seen the aftermath. The wreckage isn't pretty."

Dash laughed, "Guess I don't need that."

"No. No you don't."

"So where are we headed?"

Tibby blew the steam off the coffee in his mug, "I've been thinking about your station..."

"The one around the fourth planet?"

"Yes. We're going to do a close pass on our way to Elyse Core, see if it's occupied."

"You want to ask if they've seen anything..." pointed Dash.

301

"It had occurred to me..."

CHAPTER TWENTY FIVE

UFW CONQUEST, ELYSE CORE SYSTEM: *THE HOME STRETCH*

Admiral Jack Steele pulled the canopy release as his Lancia coasted across the deck, angling towards a rearmament stall. The canopy seal popped like a cold beer, lifting up with hydraulic arms, the warm smells of the flight deck mixing with the cold wash of the fighter's air system. He slid his visor up as he systematically went through his shutdown procedures, miniature holo-screens automatically folding in and tucking away. The Lancia settled to the deck softly and the twin engines whined down as he began to unbuckle himself.

"Getting in some flight hours I see..." said the Crew Chief as he climbed the boarding ladder, his head appearing over the left side of the cockpit. "How was your flight Admiral?" He busied himself with removing the pilot's connections and harness, re-pinning the safety on the ejection seat.

"Good, Chief. Thanks for asking." Free of his connections and belts, Steele handed his helmet to the Chief before standing in the cockpit to climb over the side.

Dropping to the deck below, the Chief waved at the tower with his free hand, returning the Admiral's helmet as he stepped off the ladder. "Hold on sir..." he pulled his e-Pad out of his cargo pocket, the screen instantly waking up. "Tower wants you to see this," he said, paging to the report. "Near perfect gunnery score, ninety-nine percent..." he smiled, "looks like you ain't too rusty just yet."

Jack reviewed his gunnery stats with a smirk, "Good to know..." He tapped on the screen, "Though I gotta work on my time a bit..." He handed it back to the Chief's waiting hand.

"Better than Miss Kitty," he whispered nodding in the direction of the Ketarian Lieutenant climbing down from her Lancia in the next stall.

"How'd she do?" asked Jack leaning in to get a look at Nera Margareth's score.

The Chief tilted the screen for him to see, "Ninety-four percent..."

"That's nothing to sneeze at, Chief..." The man shot him a questioning look and Jack realized it didn't translate well. "That's nothing to be ashamed of..."

The Chief nodded his understanding, paging through a few more reports. "Thought you'd like to see this one too... Miss Lisa did really well for a young'un. Ninety percent."

Jack edged in to see the screen, "What was she flying?"

"Says here, the Reaper, that new two-seater for the Revenge... No one in the back seat though, she was alone." He tapped on the screen, "They had her flying *flight lead.* Green Flight." He slid the e-Pad back into his pocket, "That's impressive that they put her in as a flight leader..."

Steele wedged his helmet under his arm as he tugged on his gloves while they walked. "Agreed. Personally I would have waited a bit, but Captain Smiley and Commander Warren know what they're doing..." He wondered who was in her flight and how they did overall. He headed for debriefing.

■ ■ ■

Still in flight gear, Steele grabbed an empty seat next to Nera Margareth. "Lieutenant..."

"Admiral," she acknowledged, her eyes reflecting surprise. "Didn't expect you to be here..."

"Why not? It's flight debriefing, isn't it?"

"Well yes, but..."

"Have they read any of the scores yet?"

Nera looked at him with glass-like green eyes. "No, the Commander hasn't started the meeting yet."

Steele smiled at her warmly, disarming her visible discomfort. "So how did you like being our flight leader?"

She looked him up and down, "Can I be honest, sir? Off the record?"

"Sure. Off the record."

"I don't like flying with you. Sir. You make me nervous."

"Why is that? Do you think maybe I'm rusty? Can't cover your wing?"

Nera's ear twitched nervously. "No, sir. I felt like you were watching everything I was doing. Looking over my shoulder."

Steele chuckled, "As your wingman that was kinda my job."

"Maybe," she admitted. "But I felt like you were grading everything I was doing."

304

"That's not *my* job," he nodded toward the podium, "that's *their* job." He turned in his seat and casually crossed his legs at the knee, leaning closer. "I get the feeling you don't trust too many people on your wing..."

Nera shot a quick glance in Lisa's direction two rows over, "Why, what have you heard?"

Steele schluffed it off, "Nothing. Just my personal observations. Like your constant speed and attitude adjustments; either you were testing my competence or you're a nervous pilot. I sense a high level of confidence in you, so I have to figure it's the first option."

"Are you thinking of filing a report?"

"I hardly think that's necessary, do you?" She remained unresponsive, watching his eyes. "You're a good pilot, I saw your score and..."

"What did I get?" she interrupted.

"Ninety-four percent..."

"What did *you* get?"

"Ninety-nine."

Nera's eyes narrowed, "I was sure I did better than you..."

"Look, Lieutenant," he began in a hushed tone, "this is *not* a competition. It's a way of staying sharp and gauging who's in need of skill improvement. From what I saw tonight, there isn't anyone I *wouldn't* trust on my wing. Whether you're a flight leader or just a wing leader, you have enough to worry about without having to fly for your wingman too. Let your wingman do his job." He looked around, "Is there anyone here that you wouldn't fly with? Someone whose scores you don't think were good enough?"

Nera looked around, pausing briefly on Lisa and a couple of the newer pilots.

Steele took the non-answer as mistrust. "Let me ask you a question, what do you think the lowest score was?"

Her eyes shifted around the room, eying the newer pilots again, "Seventy Percent..."

"And what would you say is an acceptable score? One that would allow you to concentrate on your job and let your wingman fly with trust?"

"Ninety percent," she shot back without hesitation.

"Honestly? You can't do better than that?"

She sighed, closing her eyes for a moment. "OK, eight-five percent. That's as low as I can go."

"I can live with that," grinned Steele. "I've got a wager for you; for each pilot with a score under seventy-five percent, I'll buy you a steak dinner.

And, you won't have to fly with anyone with a score lower than eight-five percent... "

"*Deal...*"

"Waaait... there's a catch."

Nera rolled her eyes and folded her arms, "Of course there is." *I'll have to fly with your sister no matter what...*

"Since eight-five percent is acceptable, and you won't have to fly with anyone below that, no more screwing around. Do your job, let your wingman do his job."

She eyed him suspiciously, "What's in it for you?"

"Peace and harmony. Everybody's happy."

"Deal..."

■ ■ ■

Nera waited outside the briefing room, her flight helmet dangling from her hand, watching the pilots file out in clusters, chatting amongst themselves. When the Admiral appeared, his sister at his side, she intercepted them. "Admiral, Ensign," she acknowledged. "Admiral, I feel like I owe *you* a steak dinner, nobody was under eighty-five percent." She tapped Lisa on the shoulder in an uncomfortable attempt at camaraderie, "Congratulations," she added awkwardly, "ninety percent... that's... a really good score."

"Thanks," replied Lisa, a little taken aback. "Of course not as good as Torn Dado, our class star. *Ninety-four percent...*"

"Why don't you come to dinner with us, Lieutenant?"

"Thank you Admiral, but..." as inclined as Nera Margareth was to decline, she couldn't for the life of her, think of a good reason not to. "Sure, thanks. Steak?"

"Whatever you want, Lieutenant. It's on me." She shot him a questioning glance. "I'm buying," he clarified.

■ ■ ■

Watching the big screen intently from the back of the bridge, Steele was leaning against the holo-chart table, his arms folded, watching the Captain and the Conquest's bridge crew work like a well-oiled machine. He was happy to have been right not to replace him. Free from the madness of

Admiral Pottsdorn, Anthony Ryan had quickly reverted back to the command officer he needed to be.

On the big screen the splash of hypnotic, abstract color swirled in the center of the gate, undulating like a living, breathing, liquid kaleidoscope. Tendrils of color reached out their dancing fingers toward the approaching Conquest.

"Entering gate corona, Captain."

"Maintain course and speed. Where's the Revenge?"

"She's through, sir. Commander Carter's reporting all clear."

Lisa leaned close to her brother, "I don't get it, you've seen this dozens of time, why are we up here?"

"Hold on..." He leaned around the corner to his left looking down the steps to the flight tower. "Pappy, you seeing this?"

"Yes, Admiral..."

Jack leaned back, whispering to his sister, "Don't you think it's beautiful?"

"Well yeah, but they all start to look the same after a while. Don't you think?"

"Don't be so jaded... they're *all* a little different. Some are more beautiful than others..." he never took his eyes off the screen. "Each one seems to be more beautiful than the last. This one seems to be the most beautiful of all."

She raised one eyebrow, "You feeling alright? Because you're sounding a little weird."

The Conquest pushed through the iris of the gate leaving the silver lining, entering a star-filled sky with a purplish-blue planet prominent as the wash of colors slid off her hull, dropping behind. Two inset comm squares appeared off to one side on the big screen, the Captain of the Westwind in one, Brian's face in the other.

Brian saluted, "Welcome to the Terran System everyone. People from around these parts call it the *Solar System. Damn* it's good to be home!"

Lisa discreetly elbowed her brother in the ribs. *"Nice.* Could've *told* me! Dick..." she whispered.

Steele smiled an evil little grin. "Go pack. We're moving over to the Revenge. We're going to be over there for our duration here in the system. Gus, Fritz and our gear can go over in a shuttle. Who do you want as a rear seat for the Reaper?"

"Sergeant Draza Mac. He's already on the Revenge."

"Good deal, we'll call Maria for a pickup when we're ready... You and I will fly the Reaper over."

Lisa indicated the big screen, "What planet is that?"

"Neptune." He pointed off to the right, "Pluto's out over that way somewhere. We have to go all the way across, Earth is on the other side of the Solar System right now."

■ ■ ■

Jack's impromptu meeting in the Admiral's ready room was attended by; Paul Smiley, Mike Warren, Derrik Brighton and Captain Ryan. "OK guys," began Steele, I know I'm not the only one here that might have unfinished business or loose ends that need to be taken care of..."

"Yeah, I skipped it last time," volunteered Mike, "but I'd really like to see my folks if I could. Let them know I'm... well, *not dead*. They're about twenty miles outside Fort Dodge, Iowa..."

"There's only my Mum," offered Derrik. "She knew I was leaving with Uncle but he only told her we were traveling abroad... She's in Vauxhall London, Borough of Lambeth."

Steele raised an eyebrow, "That's a mouthfull..." He turned to Pappy, "Paul..?"

"I'm good, Jack. There's nobody, really... Mom and dad are gone, just a few cousins and we were never close. Jill's the only one of any importance and I'm sure she's moved on..."

"Wife?"

"No, no," waved Pappy, "best girl. We were sort of engaged..."

"How can you be *sort of* engaged?" asked Steele. "You're either engaged or you're not. Kinda like being *sort of* pregnant..."

"Nothing official," waved Paul, chuckling. "No ring, just a promise... If I went back to see her I'm sure it would only disrupt the life she has now..."

"Are you positive?"

"I'm positive," nodded Paul. "You know Myomerr's my girl. I wouldn't want to do anything to jeopardize that... She's the future, everything else is just the past."

"Alright. Then I guess you won't mind coordinating the visits for whoever needs to go?"

"Done," agreed Pappy.

"Brian and Maria might be in the mix somewhere as well; I'll discuss it with them when I get over to the Revenge. I would suggest any shuttle going down get an armed escort. Or simply let them go down in fighters..."

308

"Don't sweat it. I'll handle it. I'm more concerned by your visit; yours have a history of being a bit more complicated..."

Sitting behind his desk, Steele put his feet up, casually leaning back. "I'm going to check on mom and dad real quick and then see if I can scare up a meeting with one of the Florida senators I've had some contact with."

"I know Admiral Higdenberger and the Madame Directorate wanted you to approach Earth about being a UFW Alliance member, but do you really think they're ready?"

"Only one way to find out, Pappy," shrugged Jack.

"Do you have a plan?" asked Mike. "You can't just walk up to the White House and knock on the front door..."

"I'm working on it..."

"Oh, we've heard that before," groaned Pappy. "I didn't like it then either..."

■ ■ ■

Lisa Steele adjusted the airflow to the rear cockpit as she reviewed the Reaper's sensors and turret controls. "I thought this was *my* bird, why do I have to sit in the back?"

"It's your bird unless *I'm* flying it," retorted Jack.

"Funny, I don't remember seeing that provisional clause in my contract..."

Completing his preflight, Jack flipped the anti-gravity on and the Reaper bounced a few inches off the flight deck. "Exactly the reason I don't do contracts..." he snickered, "I can make it up as I go along."

"You're an ass..."

"I thought that was the very definition of a big brother..." He got the nod from the lineman on the deck and slid the two-seat fighter sideways out of its revetment. Not configured or designed for the launch racks, he would launch manually over the Conquest's fantail.

"It's sometimes difficult to tell whether you're my brother the ass, or my commanding officer the ass, " she quipped.

"OK then, I'll do my best to clarify. Commanding officer; check six, tell me if we're clear and if the shuttle has launched or not..." He watched her check over her shoulder in his canopy mirror. "Brother; you're doing it wrong, use the turret camera."

"Mmmm," she growled. "Six is clear, shuttle is out the door."

"Tower to Reaper; traffic pattern is clear, you are free to launch. Happy Trails, Admiral."

"Thank you tower." Steele rotated the fighter on its own axis until it faced the stern, the static blue haze of the stasis field wavering and shimmering. He returned the lineman's sharp salute and accepted the launch wave, nudging the throttle. In a few mere seconds they passed through the wash of blue into the inky blackness of Earth's Solar System, the stars of the Milky Way a spectacular backdrop. "Gear up, AG off," he announced. "Vector to Red Flight's patrol?"

Lisa pulled up the screen for long-range sensors. "We're not going straight to the Revenge?"

"Nope," he replied, adjusting his oxygen. "I want to play with her a bit, see what she feels like." Punching the igniters, both engines lit simultaneously with a deep thump.

"OK, gotcha. Sending navigation coordinates to your screen."

"Thank you..." he grinned sardonically, easing the throttles forward. "Visors..." He pulled the Reaper into an arcing turn, the Sun passing across the sky. "Damn, that's bright," he breathed, still squinting with the gold visor down. "Ready kiddo?"

"It's dark, *sort of,*" she squinted, "we're wearing sunglasses and we're in a badass ship... hit it."

"Hold on, going full-on Mach-stupid..."

"I haven't gone ffunnhhhhhh..." Lisa's body was squeezed mid sentence as her brother hammered the throttles the full length of their travel, the ships artificial gravity gyro fighting to equalize the cockpit gravity.

Steele's vision narrowed, his field of view going momentarily gray before the gravity system began to stabilize and the pure oxygen automatically pumped into his suit brought him back. "Still with me?" he panted.

"Barely," she wheezed, gulping oxygen. "I haven't had the opportunity to push her that hard... *holy crap...*"

Jack eyed his scope, "Coming up on the Revenge..."

■ ■ ■

"Somebody's in a hurry," noted Ragnaar, watching the incoming marker on the sensor screen.

"Ours I hope," commented Brian without looking up.

"Aye, sir..."

"Lieutenant Arroyo's shuttle in and secured?"

"Yes sir."

"Then that's probably Admiral Steele, you can clear him for approach..."

Ragnaar was double checking the Reaper's incoming telemetry, "I don't think he plans on stopping, Commander..."

"Why not?" Brian looked up as he brought his coffee mug to his lips, the Reaper flashing past the bridge in stone-throwing distance at full throttle, a thousand foot long trail of *fire breathing dragon* propelling it through the darkness, the full burn lighting up the inside of the bridge like daylight. Proximity alarms were sounding throughout the ship and Brian suddenly realized he was wearing his coffee. Very fresh, very hot coffee. "Jesus H. Chr... Son of a fucking bi... *Dammit!*" He pulled at his shirt and pants trying to hold the steaming cloth off his body, his empty cup rolling on the floor. "Admiral or not, I swear I'm gonna kill him..."

Maria pounded down the corridor toward the bridge, passing the Marine sentry on duty and through the blast doors, sliding to a stop at the bridge's upper ring, Brian Carter dancing around in a coffee stained uniform. "What the hell was that? Are we hit?"

"Steele..." growled Brian.

Maria angrily placed her hands on her hips, "What did he do *this* time?"

"Crazy bastard," was all Brian managed to say through clenched teeth as he staggered past her off the bridge to change his uniform.

■ ■ ■

Throughout Jack's rigorous test flight of the Reaper, he maintained a watchful eye on her engine temperatures, forcing cones and thrust nozzles. The new metal treatment protocol that Chief Engineer Hecken Noer had been testing on her was successfully proving out his theories on heat dissipation. Temperatures edged into the yellow, but just barely. And any reduction in throttle allowed them to cool down swiftly. Although the treatment he'd devised was a time-consuming process, it was a substantial improvement on performance. If applied across the board to the Conquest's stable of fighters, she would have the fastest fighters in the fleet. Whether it improved fuel economy or not was another question to be answered. It reasoned out that way, but it would bear out with time.

Steele lined the Reaper up with the stern of the Revenge, matching her speed, automatically triggering the docking computer. A small HUD screen in his cockpit mechanically unfolded and lit up. Carefully following the guides on the dedicated docking HUD, he eased the Reaper underneath the Revenge and held it steady when prompted; a pair of docking clamps reaching down from the belly of the frigate, locking onto the fighter and drawing it up. The throttles, now controlled by the docking computer, zeroed themselves and Jack released the fighter's controls. Fitting into the impression in the hull of the Revenge, the Reaper became part of the bigger ship.

Halfway through shutdown, the engines silent, the only remaining sound being the air system, Steele shut down his electronics and sensors. "Do me a favor, send our test data over to Engineering for Hecken Noer..."

"Sure." Lisa pulled up the data file from the Reaper's computer, her gloved fingers pipping on her keyboard, sending it to the Conquest. "Sent."

A sliver of light appeared from above, widening as the frigate's hull plating opened, a face peering down through the top of the canopy. *"Seal is good Admiral. You can release your canopy... We'll get you out of there."*

■ ■ ■

"I have a bone to pick with you..."

Steele knew it before Brian said it, and not just because of his irritated look. "I know, I heard... Sorry about that."

Brian's eyes shifted around, lowering his voice, "I almost burned my... junk off. That's not funny..."

Jack did his best British accent, "Your fun things and wiggly bit? Heavens no..."

Brian frowned, "You were so close you set off our proximity collision alarms..."

"I was a good two miles away..."

"Twelve hundred feet," countered Brian.

"And you've flown an arm's length from the hull chasing a bogie, what's your point?"

"That's in a fight, that's different..."

"That reminds me," interrupted Jack, "pack an overnight and head on over to the Conquest..."

"For what?"

"Pappy's got you scheduled for a flight. You need to put in some stick time."

Lisa strolled past, heading to her quarters, her gear bag slung over her shoulder. "You'll love the ejection training. Fun ride."

Brian shot Jack a quizzical look, "What's this then?"

"Don't worry about it, Bri. I think he just wants to get you some stick time to keep your quals up to date. Gotta shake the rust off once in a while." He patted Brian on the shoulder, "Don't worry, you'll be back before we get home. I'll take care of things around here till you get back."

"That's what I'm afraid of..."

CHAPTER TWENTY SIX

GREEN BANK, WEST VIRGINIA, NATIONAL RADIO
OBSERVATORY: *ICU*

Dr. Michelle Fabry, at a petite five-foot-two with blond hair and blue eyes, was not your typical astrophysicist. While she was a research fellow at the largest fully steerable radio telescope on the planet, she was not quite a fashionista, but she preferred her heels to flats, she never wore her hair in a bun, and a pocket protector would never have the audacity to sneak into her wardrobe.

Morning had been a nonstop attack of meetings and it was good to be off her feet for a few minutes. With her feet propped up on an open drawer of her desk, she sedately ate her deli sandwich, occasionally sipping her diet soda while reading the news on the laptop perched on her desk. They were starting to call Chicago, Chiraq because of all the violence and murder there. The Chief of Police was blaming it on the weather... again. First it was too cold, now it was too hot... whatever.

"Mitch..! *Mitch..! MICHELLLLE..!"*

Prompted by the urgency, she dropped her half-eaten sandwich on the deli paper and bounced to her feet, running out of her second floor office overlooking the control room below. She leaned on the walkway's railing, "We do have an intercom you know..."

"Mitch, *get down here...!"*

"I'm eating lunch can't it wait..?"

"Now, Mitch, *NOW!"* Sitting at the control console, David was beside himself with excitement, the others in the room as visibly agitated as he was. He was holding the headset tight over his ears, "Hurry Mitch, I'm losing it, *HURRY!"*

With quick dainty little steps, her high heels clicking on the concrete, she ran to the stairs. "I'm coming, I'm coming..." She was forced to slow for the stairs to prevent pitching herself down to the bottom and breaking her neck. "Pipe it, David, put it through the speakers..." Her heels clacked across the floor towards the console.

David Weller slid the headphones off his head and tossed them on the console in disappointment, "Never mind," he mumbled, "its gone. I lost it."

"Please tell me you were recording..."

"Well yeah, but..."

"Play it back then," she waved. "What was it? What did you hear?"

"A conversation."

She paused mid-reach for a set of headphones at a neighboring station, her eyes narrowing, "Are you sure?"

"Positive."

"I... whe... what's our target?" She lifted the headset off the console and held one earpiece to her ear.

"We're mapping Harding-Konos 452..." he replied, punching the playback key.

Michelle Fabry covered her other ear with the palm of her hand and closed her eyes, listening to the quiet hiss and rhythmic sound of the cosmos. "All I hear is the pulsar from 452..." Her eyes popped wide open and then her face relaxed, tossing the headset onto the console. "That's English," she pointed at the console. "I don't know how, but you caught a military flight or something..." David shook his head and rewound the digital recording back again. "What do you mean, *no?*" she asked.

He picked up the headset and held it out for her, "There are more voices. Listen until it all fades back to the pulsar." He shook the headset in her direction, *"Listen..."*

She slid the headset over both her ears and David set the recording back in motion. Knowing what to expect, Michelle listened intently watching the faces of the others around her, listening on their own headsets. There was a second voice, and a third. She felt unsteady on her feet, lightheaded, she reached for a chair, sitting down. Then there was a fourth voice. The first was definitely English, American-English. Although it was too laced with static to catch more than word fractures. The others didn't sound like anything she'd ever heard before, but they were definitely in a conversation, the banter going back and forth. As if it was moving, it dropped off into the quiet sounds of the cosmos again and she sat there staring at the smiling faces staring back at her.

Michelle's brain was still processing it all when she jumped to her feet still tethered to the console by the headset which shot off her head when she lurched forward. "Give me those coordinates!" she pointed, moving to the center station looking up at the flat screen readout. "Find it! *Find it!"*

315

She started looking around vigorously, "Glasses, where did I put my glasses?" David tapped his forehead and she reached up realizing they were sitting up near her hairline. Pulling the gold rims to her nose she began reading the spatial coordinates on the big screen. *"RETASK!* Come to..."

"You can't do that, Mitch! We're in the middle of a map..."

"Save it, where it's at," she said frantically. "We'll come back to it and start with an overlap..."

"Mitch, you know that never works. We'll have to start all over again..."

"This is me not caring," she snapped, pushing him out of the way, he and his chair rolling clear of the station. She dropped to one knee and began entering the new coordinates for the dish, pulling it off station. The one-hundred meter dish began to swing away from Harding-Konos 452. "Samantha, are you listening?"

"Yes ma'am."

"Record at the first sign of a signal..."

"Yes ma'am."

"David, do something useful and call NASA. I know they don't, but see if they have anything up there and tell them what we're listening to. See if they have any answers." She looked to her right, past Samantha, "Sean, call Hat Creek Observatory and see if SETI has ears on this. If not, send them the coordinates. The more confirmation we get on this the better..."

Samantha suddenly perked up, sitting rigid in her chair, "I've got something..."

"Record," ordered Michelle, pulling on her headset. She was watching the numbers change on the screen as they marked the swing of the dish, still heading to its intended mark. When it finally slowed to a stop the target was no longer in the center. "It's moving," she breathed.

"What?" David rolled up alongside her. He had the phone handset tucked under the earpiece of his headset, cradling it on his shoulder, chatting simultaneously with someone over at NASA as he typed on the keyboard around Michelle. "Yes, that's right, it's moving. Yes, I'm setting the dish to track the target. Hold on a moment..."

"What do they want?"

"They want to know the distance of the contact..."

"I've got it here," shouted Samantha. She turned slowly to look at them, her eyes wide. "It's IN *our Solar System...*"

Sean waved his hand from the other side of the room, phone receiver still clutched to his ear, "Hat Creek just said the same thing! They say it's near Neptune!"

■ ■ ■

Moments after David's phone call with NASA, the NSA was aware of the developing situation. During the last half of Sean's phone call to SETI, the NSA was listening in. And less than an hour after they'd first discovered the signal, a black helicopter from NIOC, *Navy Information Operations Center,* at the neighboring Sugar Grove Research Facility, made a low pass near Green Bank. Following a low circuitous approach so as not to interfere with reception of the Green Bank dish, it landed out in the field near the control building. The NIOC over at Sugar Grove was home of the NSA's ECHELON program and the black helicopter was *not* a welcome sight. Neither was the group of men in black who were climbing out of it. When the nervous secretary in the front office attempted to call the Pocahontas County Sheriff about the wayward helicopter, she discovered the phone lines were inoperable. And in the heart of the *United States Radio Quiet Zone,* cell phone service simply doesn't exist. Even their internet was down. They were cut off. Isolated.

Michelle Fabry caught the panicked secretary by the shoulders as she ran into the control room, pointing and stuttering. "Deep breath, Katie, deep breath... what is it?"

"Helicopter... guns... black... coming... front door..." she gasped.

"Is the front door locked?"

Katie nodded vigorously, her strawberry blond locks bouncing. "Door... glass... they break..."

"I know, they can break the glass. Stay calm." Michelle glanced around at her team, "Back up the signals, thumb drives, satellites, whatever you have... hide them."

"We have triple redundancy," offered David.

"I know, do it anyway. *Hurry* people!" She hustled toward the front office expecting an urgent tap on the door glass any second. "Katie, how many of them were there?"

The secretary kept up alongside Michelle, "Six. I think..."

Michelle pointed toward the front office as she headed for the front door, "Call the Sheriff."

"The lines are dead..."

"Try again," she instructed curtly. But halfway between the office and the entrance she could see there was no one at the door, which gave her pause. She turned back to Katie who was attempting to get a dial tone. "Are you sure they were coming here? Because I don't see anybody..."

The secretary held up the phone's receiver and shook her head, setting it back onto the cradle, "Still dead..." She blinked, staring past Dr. Fabry out through the glass door at the empty field, "The helicopter," she pointed, *"it's gone..."*

Michelle turned back toward the door, "It was right out there?"

"At the top of the hill," added Katie, appearing at her side. "Right there," she pointed.

They walked closer to the door to get a better look and Michelle studied the wild grass between the hill and the entrance. "Are you sure you saw..."

"I swear," promised Katie, her hand resting on the door's push bar. "I saw them climb out..."

The face that suddenly appeared, spied at them through mirrored goggles, the face and head obscured by a black tactical balaclava. Michelle's heart jumped and she started, jumping back with a scream, staggering on her high heels and landing on her butt, Katie dropping to the floor beside her, unconscious with fright. Her heart pounding in her ears, Dr. Fabry could barely hear the man outside the door.

Dressed completely in black tactical assault gear, he tapped on the door glass with the muzzle of the M4 carbine that hung casually across his chest. "Ma'am, open the door..." He waited momentarily, staring at her, another man arriving at his side dressed in a black business suit. *"Ma'am,* open the door. I don't want to have to break the glass..."

The man in the business suit stepped up to the door holding his government credentials against the glass. "We're not here to hurt anyone, Dr. Fabry. Just open the door please."

Michelle Fabry rose to her feet, a bit unsteadily, her heart still pounding, brushing herself off, divided between opening the door and helping Katie.

"Open the door and we will help her, Dr. Fabry. I apologize; we didn't mean to frighten you..."

Michelle reached over and rolled the deadbolt open, backing away and dropping to her knees at Katie's head. "Nice going whoever you are. Get your jollies from scaring women...?" she commented gruffly.

318

The man in the suit walked past her, motioning towards the women, two agents in tactical gear entering behind him, locking the door behind them. One agent took a knee next to unconscious secretary; the other pulled Michelle to her feet by her elbow.

"Walk with me, Dr. Fabry. Let's have a little chat."

■ ■ ■

Sitting behind her desk, Dr. Michelle Fabry felt like a cornered animal, the man in the suit pacing back and forth between her desk and the door.

"I hope you understand Dr. Fabry, this is not personal, this is national security..."

The words didn't chill her as much as the perceived intent. "No I don't. It seems to me that we're all on the same side here. We're looking for the scientific truth..."

"Well yes and no," he countered. "Our truth is a tad different from your truth. My job is to keep your truth from scaring the hell out of the American public."

"I don't think the American public is as fearful as you think."

The man in the suit stopped pacing, folded his arms and stared her down. "Alright then, let's look at this from another angle; your contact never happened. Period. It's our gig now, capiche?"

"And just *who* are you?" Michelle asked angrily.

"Nobody. We were never here, we don't exist. And I would suggest to you, today never happened..."

There was screaming in the control room below and it launched Michelle to her feet, the man in the black suit swinging the office door wide as he lunged for the railing. When Michelle got to the rail she was terrified of what she was about to see, her hands shaking.

"Mitch, *Mitch..!* They've erased *everything!*" She stared down at David who was beside himself with grief, pacing around the man in the black tactical gear sitting at the console working at the keyboard. The rest of her team sat quietly to one side, frightened and sullen.

"*Let it go,* David," she called down, turning on her heel and walking back into her office. She gritted her teeth. "So what now?"

"As soon as we're done, we're out. You and your crew are free to go."

"Just like that," she quipped sarcastically.

319

"Just like that. It will be up to *you* to keep your people on the program; *today never happened.* Because you really don't want us to come back..." He leaned on the desk with both hands, his eyes cast down. "I don't like it when I have to come back." He looked up into her eyes with a steely glare, "*You* won't like it if I have to come back."

A chill ran up the back of her neck and she had to fight off the instinct to back away, "What about our calls to NASA and SETI?" she breathed cautiously.

The man in the suit didn't even blink, "That's not your concern. And you will never mention it again..."

■ ▦ ■

In jeans and tennis shoes, attire that was seriously more casual than her norm, Dr. Michelle Fabry was back the next morning along with most of her team. They sat around quietly drinking their coffee.

Samantha looked around, "Where's Katie?"

Michelle pursed her lips, "I don't think she's coming back to work, Sam. Ever."

"Can't say I blame her," mumbled David. "I can't believe those assholes erased everything. Even the coordinates for Harding-Konos 452..."

"Over a week's worth of mapping," interrupted Samantha.

"Uh, guys..." Sean was holding a Styrofoam cup of cold, day-old coffee in one hand, and a small chain between the fingers of his other hand. A waterproof thumb drive dangled from the chain, dripping stale coffee.

Michelle's eyes widened, "Is that what I think it is?" she whispered.

He nodded silently, motioning to where he left the cup in plain sight on the console overnight. "Should I..." he motioned to the computer, indicating a restoration of data.

"No, no," waved Dennis. "Not until we sweep all the software..."

"And everything else," added Michelle.

■ ▦ ■

Just north of Alamo, Nevada, along State Road 93, was the only motel in probably a fifty mile radius with real walls, indoor plumbing and electricity. The small aging cottages, while a tad musty, were surprisingly clean. Thankfully. Chase and Karen occupied one cottage, Dan and Rain occupied another and Jesse stayed in the motor home parked between the buildings with the pickup trucks and motorcycles.

The sun had set, the cloudless sky a deep purple, the moon and stars were already visible over the desert.

A small flashlight in his mouth, Dan methodically checked the tie-downs holding the three dirt bikes in the bed of Jesse's pickup truck, re-wrapping the tarp tightly around them with Chase's help.

The task completed, Chase leaned back against the side of the pickup and stared up at the stars. "So what's Jesse's deal?" he whispered. "Who is he?"

His elbow on the side of the truck bed, foot on the rear bumper, Dan looked up at the same sky and stars, wondering if they were both seeing the same thing. The more time he spent out in the desert, the more fascinated with the stars he became. It had almost become an obsession. He wondered if Steele was really out there somewhere. "He's an Indian kid... A friend of the one that was killed – the one in Rain's wrongful death lawsuit. She met him when she was doing depositions for the case..."

"Was he there the day that kid was killed?"

"No, and she didn't see him again until she went to hide on the reservation when the black SUVs were stalking her. He's a loner but a decent kid. No family, he bounced around in the tribe, seemed to be well liked. Everybody took care of him. The tribal council gave him a little cabin and he did odd jobs. When he hid her out he never asked her for anything in return... I suspect there's a little crush going there, although he's never acted on it."

"So he feels tied to her..." nodded Chase.

"Yeah... which is good I guess. He's the best trail guide we could've ever hoped for. He knows this desert like the back of his hand." He thumbed toward the tarp, "Bought him a new dirt bike - you should've seen the pile of shit he was riding... held together with baling wire, tape, hopes and wishes..."

Chase chuckled, "Sounds like my first car... An old T-Bird I inherited from my grandmother when she passed."

"What year?"

"A sixty-six..."

"The ones with the sequential taillights, a very stylish car."

"Complex though. It had a lot of little problems... nickel and dime stuff, drove me crazy." They watched the stars in silence for a while, a white streak crossing the sky directly over them, heading west. "What the hell was *that?!*" asked Chase spinning around to watch it disappear.

"Whatever it is, it's headed for Area 51..."

"It didn't make a sound," interrupted Chase, astounded. "We should have been able to hear *something...!"*

Dan smirked, "Spooky, ain't it? Welcome to Area 51..."

■ ■ ■

Dan, Chase and Jesse sat around the table in the motor home, a detailed fabric map spread across the table, laptops and a hand-held GPS unit sitting around them. "Right here," pointed Jesse. "is where the GPS signal will cut out. From there on, you need to use the map and your eyes." He pointed to another spot on the map, about halfway to the end of the GPS signal, "I'll ride with you to here, and drop the fuel. There will be enough to fill both your tanks and get you back even if you're almost empty. I don't expect you to use that much, but you never know... We'll also leave a couple gallons of water and some food."

"We'll mark the fuel stop on the GPS," explained Dan. "Once we're clear of the dead zone we'll be able to pick it up on the way back with no problem."

"Why the dead zone?" asked Chase.

"Jamming," said Jesse. "No cell, radio, GPS, walkie-talkie..." He waved, "Doesn't affect their frequency of course." He pointed to a place along Route 375, known as the Extraterrestrial Highway, "We'll pull off here and drive in about a mile or so and unload the bikes. From the refuel spot I'll head back to the truck. I will be back in twenty-four hours to see if you're back yet. After that I will come back every twelve hours. After four days... I, um, will have to assume you're dead or they picked you up..."

"Terrific," mumbled Chase.

"We'll be fine," assured Dan.

"How far are we actually going?" asked Chase.

Jesse tapped on the map, "Here. You'll get decent video and photos from this area..."

Chase blinked, comparing the map to the images from the online satellite map on the screen of the laptop. "You can't be serious... that's *on the base."*

"Not really, it's actually considered the gunnery range. You're up in the mountains. They won't be able to get to you in their four-by-fours..."

"They don't need to, kid," argued Chase. "They have *helicopters...*" He rubbed his face in frustration, "Helicopters with door gunners trump pretty much anything on the ground."

"That's why you're going it at night without lights."

Chases' eyes widened, "Out there? Are you nuts?"

Dan patted him on the shoulder, "Don't worry, we have night vision."

Chase nodded, "Oh good, because that was the thing I was most worried about." He shot Dan a sharp glance, "That was sarcasm in case you're wondering..." He stood up and walked to the front of the motor home and stared out through the windshield into the darkness, his hands in his pockets. "You know, they have night vision too... and thermal and a few other things to see in the dark..."

Jesse folded up the fabric map, "Because the path you are taking is a more difficult way to go, it is much less patrolled and has fewer monitoring stations. They have seen dirt bike riders out there and usually watch without interfering. This route has been used before; it does offer us the best chance for success. Especially since no one has done it in the dark."

"That's not exactly reassuring," remarked Chase. "So what are we supposed to be looking for here? More stuff like at Dugway?"

"A little different. We've had reports of increased activity of UFO-like craft and since I've seen one up close they've put me on rotation here..."

"So since you've seen a UFO you're an expert?" asked Chase sarcastically. "That's like saying since you've seen a car you're a mechanic..."

"Look I get what you're saying," interrupted Dan. "But I was in shooting distance. And apparently that's closer than anyone else has been. They want me to look."

"Mmm," grunted Chase. "I can't say I'm not curious... or even intrigued. But dammit, this is espionage. At least at Dugway we were on public land..."

"There is no *intent* here," corrected Dan, "to..."

"Pshh," waved Chase, "you're entering a high security, military research base. They're not going to ask your *intent*. They're going to shoot your ass first and ask questions later. That's assuming we don't run across a mine first, if there are any. In which case you'll get a new nickname; *stumpy*, or *shorty* or something."

"You don't have to go... Jesse can go with me instead..."

Chase sighed with exasperation, "No... I'll go. *Somebody's* gotta keep you from getting killed..."

323

CHAPTER TWENTY SEVEN

UFW FRIGATE REVENGE: *TERRAN SOLAR SYSTEM*

With Brian heading to the Conquest to fulfill his in-service training and keep his flight credentials current, Jack Steele did not hesitate to make the Captain's ready room his own, commanding the Task Force from there. It was much smaller than he'd become accustomed to on the Conquest, but it would suffice. Though in a direct comparison, the appointments were definitely more modern than in the one-hundred year old carrier.

Sitting in the Captain's chair on the bridge, Lieutenant Maria Arroyo was acting commander of the Revenge during Brian's absence, and she was enjoying the proverbial view from the top.

Jack reached over and keyed the comm button on the console mounted into the desk, "Lieutenant, might I see you in the ready room, please?"

"Aye, sir." As Maria swung herself out of the most coveted seat on the bridge, she waved Raulya from her spot in tactical to take the command chair.

Lisa was switching between hijacked Earth television signals on the holo-screen in the ready room when Maria entered from the bridge, the door sliding into the wall with a hiss, closing automatically behind her. "What's up, Jack?"

Steele didn't react to her casual demeanor as there were no other crew members present. "Have you been watching any of the news broadcasts from home?"

"Yes..." Maria pointed at the sofa, "May I?"

Jack waved casually, "Sure."

She sat down next to Fritz who was lounging comfortably, giving his head and ears a stroke. "I started watching when we first pulled them in Elyse Core. The signal was pretty sloppy and they were a few months old when we pulled them, but it was still interesting..."

"Right," he interrupted, "and when we gated into the system we jumped ahead to current broadcasts, so we've missed everything in-between. But considering that many of the topics are unresolved and continue, I'm not liking what I'm seeing. What the hell is going on?"

She motioned toward the current broadcast on the screen, "You know about as much as I do..."

"No," said Jack shaking his head, "Your *professional* opinion. As a CIA agent. What do you think is going on?"

Maria made a face like she'd tasted something offensive, "I think there's a meltdown coming. How big or how wide I can't tell. Even with what I've been able to find on the internet, I..."

Jack did a double-take, "Internet? How did you get the internet?"

"We hijacked a signal and tapped in on a satellite service. A little more complicated but similar to what we did with the broadcast stuff. There's a lot more news content than the media is carrying."

"Like what?" asked Lisa, cutting in.

"Well, assuming twenty-five percent of it is conspiracy theory thinking and another twenty-five percent of it is intentional misinformation, the answer should be in the remaining content. The truth is; that the *real truth* is where the first and second twenty-five percent collide and overlap. The rest is white noise. Diversion."

Lisa's face scrunched in contemplation. "Sooo..."

Maria shrugged, "So when the *push-back* on critical conspiracy theories is equal to or greater than; the effort, volume, frequency and duration of those theories, it validates the theories."

Jack leaned forward, his elbows on the desk, his hands clasped. "You're saying the conspiracy theorists are right?"

"Yes, I'd say so. There has to be a lot of truth to what they're saying if the push back is this tough. The disturbing part is the media seems to be complicit in disseminating the disinformation..."

"So what's the *Net* got that's not on the news?"

"Widespread upheaval. Citizens rebelling against their governments. A meltdown in Greece, revolutions in Venezuela, Egypt, and the Ukraine. A civil war in Syria, anti-Christian terrorism in Somalia, Kenya and Nigeria... slaughter and kidnappings... North Korea testing nukes, Russia flexing its muscles and bullying the Ukraine and Iran is threatening nuclear annihilation of Israel and the U.S." She shrugged noncommittally. "And, the Middle East is well, the *Middle East;* mayhem and misery as always..."

"Jesus," breathed Steele. "What about home?"

Maria looked pensive, apprehensive... "I can't say that it's much better. There's a war going on in Mexico and the southern border is a mess. Whatever the administration is doing, it seems to have destroyed all respect in the global sense. The United States has lost footing as the World leader and it seems Americans are fed up in general. By all accounts there's been a considerable amount of civil protest nation-wide for a wide variety of things. I'd have to say the fuse is lit."

Jack stood up and began to pace, suddenly restless, his hands clasped behind his back, a hot flush washing over him.

"We have to get mom and dad *out,*" cautioned Lisa.

"I know, I know... I just can't believe we're coming back to such a damn mess... I don't like it. There are so many ways this could go bad..." He stopped pacing, "Maria, do you have anyone you need to see? Not that I want more of our people on the ground but there's no telling how long we'll be gone this time."

She shook her head, "Nope. I go down there, it would only be to murder a couple of people. I can do without the stress."

Steele snorted a short-lived chuckle. "What about Brian?"

"No idea, he hasn't mentioned anything. You'll have to ask him yourself." She glanced over at Lisa then back at Jack, "With everything going on, are you still thinking of approaching the U.S. About UFW membership?"

His heart and body felt suddenly heavy with dread. He stopped pacing and leaned against his desk, "It's part of our mission. I have to at least try."

The comm crackled, *"Captain to the bridge. Captain to the bridge, please."*

Steele stared at Maria who sat comfortably on the sofa, anticipating the conversation would continue. He pointed at the ceiling indicating the page, "I think that's for you..."

She bounced to her feet, "Oh my God! I totally forgot..." she dashed out the door onto the bridge, barely clearing the door as it slid into the wall.

The comm crackled again, *"Admiral Steele to the bridge, please."*

He glanced at Lisa, "Me too, huh? OK, let's go see what's going on..."

■ ■ ■

Raulya turned in her seat, "Commander, we've been monitoring a radio signal from the surface of the planet. It was originally positioned in a scanning pattern past the Task Force but has been readjusted in our direction..."

"Show me..." ordered Maria.

Lieutenant Raulya provided red markers on a zoomed image of the planet on the main holo-screen from her control panel. "The signal originates from this area on the northern continent..." An outline appeared around the shape of North America.

"Hmmm," growled Maria, that's either Green Bank Observatory or the Sugar Grove Research Facility..."

"There were originally two more, here and here..." added Raulya, red markers appearing on the image of the continent.

"Alright," pointed Maria. "That one on the bottom is NASA in Houston. I'm guessing the one in the west is SETI at Hat Creek."

"So there's only one signal now?" interjected Steele.

"Right," said Raulya, removing the extraneous markers, her fingers pipping across her keyboard.

Maria shook her head, "Has to be Sugar Grove..." She turned to Jack, "Naval Intelligence... and your friends at the NSA."

"Oh craaap..." he breathed.

"They're about to lose their declination," pointed Maria, they've got about another ten minutes before they lose us. The dish can only turn and angle so far."

"Then what?"

She shrugged, "Maybe they activate another one somewhere. Or not. Knowing them, they want to control the signals and the exposure..."

"How do you think they picked us up?"

"Luck," commented Raulya, relinquishing the command seat to Maria. "They were scanning another system; we must have crossed their field of view."

Steele ran his fingers through his hair, "Once they lose us for the day we should alter course."

A quick flicker of information appeared and vanished on the screen. "What was *that?!*" demanded Raulya, lunging across Maria at the keyboard, her fingers pipping on the keys.

Sitting in the command chair, Maria raised her hands, "What the..."

"A comm signal..." Raulya paged through to the communications screen, scrolling through the logs. "From the Task Force to the planet..." Highlighting the most recent entry, it showed a one-second comm burst. A second comm signal, identical to the first appeared on the log above it, bumping it down. "There's another one... Someone sent another comm to the planet."

"From where? And where's it going?" asked Steele leaning in over Maria's other shoulder.

"I'm getting a little claustrophobic, here," complained Maria.

"Sshh," corrected Jack. *"So..?"* he insisted, glancing at Raulya's profile.

Still leaning across Maria, Raulya pulled the comm record and opened the details on the left command screen. "Looks like..."

"Can't you do this at another station?" pleaded Maria.

"Sshh," scolded Raulya. "The signal is coming from the Conquest..."

"From the bridge?"

Raulya shook her head, "No Admiral, it appears to be a portable comm unit. And I cannot pinpoint such a short signal... Also too short to tell where it went. I don't see any replies. Yet."

"Can you pull up the message itself?"

Raulya opened the commuication, the signal decoder automatically spitting out a series of cryptic hieroglyphics on the screen. Her head tilted one way then the other, her feline ears rotating. "That's odd... I don't understand Admiral..."

"Ciphers," breathed Maria. "Intelligence agency cipher code..."

Steele straightened up, looking sideways at her, "We have a *spy?"*

■ ■ ■

Steele wasn't so much pacing the ready room, as he was walking laps around the holo-chart table, Fritz strolling along behind him. His eyes cast to the floor, Jack's mind was racing in high gear. Sitting on the sofa with Gus, Lisa played silly games with his ears while Maria sat on the edge of the desk patiently watching him do his laps.

"If you weren't here on the bridge at the time, I would have assumed it was you," he commented as he passed Maria.

"Hey," she objected, pointing her finger at him, "not cool."

"I suppose you could have set up an automatic transmission and hidden the unit somewhere on the Conquest. The radio signal from the surface could have triggered it..."

"This is *not* funny, Jack, you can't be serious."

"Not trying to be funny..." he mumbled, still walking.

"I haven't been over there in weeks except for shuttle runs. And I never get a chance to even get off the shuttle..."

Lisa was evaluating her brother's face and his demeanor, "I think he's messing with you, Maria..."

"You're *impossible,*" sassed Maria, folding her arms across her chest in defiance.

Jack smirked, "Since *I am,* it is not possible for me to be *impossible.*"

"Are you having a stroke or something?" She shot a glance over at Lisa, "What is *wrong* with him?"

"The list is sooo long," quipped Lisa. She watched her brother rounding the far end of the table, partially obscured by the hologram hovering above the table. "Are you thinking it's one of our people?"

Steele had been running the possibilities through his mind. "I'm not sure. I don't want it to be..."

"Are you thinking NSA?"

Steele stopped dead in his tracks, Fritz head-butting his legs. *"Fuck.* I am now..."

"It makes sense," commented Maria. "Right timing after the contact by Sugar Grove."

Steele chewed on his lower lip, "But who?"

"It was right after Brian went over there..." offered Lisa.

Jack's stomach knotted. "I've known Brian for over ten years, I can't believe it would be him."

"People get recruited as a matter of convenience. Right time, right place. It doesn't necessarily mean they're an agent. It could have been to keep tabs on our CIA operation..."

Steele raised an eyebrow, giving Maria *the look.* "Like an informant. Is that even a thing? Our own agencies spying on one another?"

"Sure. Happens all the time."

Lisa shook her head, "Spying on your own spies... that's just nuts. Nobody trusts anybody any more."

"Does seem kind of a redundant waste of resources," added Jack.

"I'm not saying he *was,* I'm just saying it's not impossible..."

Steele started his laps again, "I'm going to have to say no on Brian. I just can't see it."

"What about Mike Warren or Pappy?"

Steele paused and peered at Maria through the holo-chart, "They're fighter pilots..." he said dismissively.

"But they're Navy," countered Maria. "Military Intelligence, especially the Navy, is tightly linked with the NSA."

Steele shook his head, "Nah. Carrier duty is too restrictive. It would serve no purpose there. Now if they were fleet NCIS agents, *Naval Criminal Investigative Service*, that would make more sense. They do a considerable amount of intelligence and advance prep work before a fleet heads into port."

"Well the only two others are the Professor and Derrik Brighton..."

Jack came to a stop again. "And the Professor is back on Veloria."

Maria shook her head, "Derrik and I cohabited for nearly a year, I would have noticed *something*... Honestly? The man was an open book."

Jack leaned against the holo-table, "We're missing something somewhere... what are we missing?"

Maria turned to Lisa, "Your friend... what's her name..?" She struggled with her memory, shaking her hand and pointing at Lisa, "Nina Redwolf!"

Jack and Lisa shared a glance before they simultaneously burst out laughing. "Sorry," waved Jack, still chuckling. "That is just so absurd..."

Annoyed, Maria raised an eyebrow as she tossed her hair, "Glad you think it's funny, Jack. Those you suspect the least are the most likely candidates..."

Lisa waved it off, "Nina's an electronics neophyte. She's lucky if she can figure out how to make a flashlight work..."

"Actually," interrupted Jack, pinching his lower lip. "That's not true. Now that I think of it, she handled the shields and anything else I directed her to do on the yacht pretty well. She even flew it a bit." His eyes widened, "I think we need to put her in the *maybe* section..."

The door chimed before swishing open, Raulya stepping into the open frame. "Sorry to interrupt Admiral, just thought you'd like to know, the system was finally able to decode your cipher..."

"What did it come up with?"

"Kingfisher One."

Jack scratched his forehead. "That's it? Nothing else?"

"That's it, Admiral."

"Thank you, Lieutenant." He watched her go, the door hissing closed. "Wow, that was a lot of computer power used for two damn words..."

"I think I know what else you're missing, Jack," volunteered Lisa, scooting forward on the sofa. "There are at least two-hundred people on the Conquest that would pass as human back on Earth..."

He pondered that for a moment. "Maybe more, except for language..."

"Except for language," she agreed. "But how hard would it have been to learn a second language? People do it all the time. The Professor's an alien;

didn't you tell me the Professor speaks like six or seven different languages?"

"Something like that," nodded Steele. "If that's the case, we have over two-hundred suspects."

It was silent for a few moments before Maria rose and moved over to the holo-chart, staring at the 3D image of the system. She stuck her hand in and grabbed the earth, bringing it closer, enlarging it with a motion of her hand. "We're going to have to let him commit himself... *or herself,*" she added, concentrating on the spinning globe. "Our advantage is that he or she is exposed and doesn't know it."

Steele's eyes widened with a sudden realization that sent a shot of adrenalin through him. "Oh shit..."

Lisa stood up, joining her brother and Maria at the table. "What..?" she asked cautiously.

Wide-eyed, he turned slowly, staring at the holo-planet, his mind unraveling a frightening scenario. "What if the communication isn't for the CIA or the NSA or any other alphabet agency?"

"You mean what if it's for the KGB or..."

"No," he interrupted. "What if it's a FreeRanger signal..?"

"Oh my God," whispered Lisa.

"Yeah," he breathed. "What if everything we're seeing going on is a repeat of Veloria? An effort to destabilize the entire planet?"

Maria glanced up at the news broadcast, "I'd say it's working..."

Lisa turned away and covered her mouth, "Oh my God, this is *horrible...*"

Maria reached out, "Easy now, no one is saying this is the real truth. It's just a possibility..."

"Think about it," continued Jack, "Maybe what we're seeing is FreeRanger influence. Maybe FreeRanger infiltrators in government. The design would be to cause widespread destabilization. Set the people against their governments, cause critical governmental and infrastructure failure. If they can cause a collapse the rest would be easy. They could step in and run the planet. Veloria had a much smaller population but it's a freaking blueprint of what's going on here... you've got to see that."

"I do," nodded Maria. "But it's just as likely being torn down from the inside via incompetence and greed. Believe me; I've seen my fair share of that first hand. And it's a meat grinder for hopes, wishes and good intentions." She turned and passively watched the Earth news feed on the ready room's holo-screen with unseeing eyes. "People enter service in the government without realizing it's a pact with the devil. It devours them and spits them out as wasted, soulless, husks of humanity."

"Why couldn't it be both?" observed Lisa.

Jack and Maria shared a silent look, both nodding slowly. "She could be right," said Jack.

Maria shook her head in disgust, "I wouldn't put it past the incompetent and greedy to collude with the evil and criminal. Infiltrators or not."

"It would explain a lot."

Maria walked over to the sofa and dropped herself down on the vacant cushion. "And probably the most dangerous of the options. So, what are we going to do?"

"I'm not sure yet. But whatever it is, whatever we decide, it can't leave this room..."

"What about the bridge crew?"

"Inform them they are not to speak with *anyone* about what transpired. Remind them they are a small group and any leak will be thoroughly investigated."

Maria rose and smoothed her uniform. "Alright, back to work then?"

"For now," replied Steele, running his fingers through his hair. "In the meantime, if you think of any good ideas, don't hesitate to let me know..." He leaned back against the holo-chart table. "I think Lisa and I are going to review the Conquest's personnel files and see if we can identify any of the crew that could pass as human, and then see if any of them have ever been to, or come from Earth..."

Maria's eyes went wide with surprise, "That's nearly three thousand people!"

"A little over that, actually..."

CHAPTER TWENTY EIGHT

OFFICE OF THE DIRECTOR OF NATIONAL SECURITY, UNITED STATES

When *he* entered the room all chatter and banter ended. Immediately. "Door," he commanded, pointing at the door at the far end of the room. He pulled the leather chair out at the head of the long conference table, glancing at the faces lining each side, tossing a manilla folder down on its glossy surface. He sat carefully, neatly, smoothing his slacks, adjusting his suit jacket and straightening his tie. Only then did he address the people waiting around the table for him; division heads, agency liaisons and military brass. He opened the manilla folder and laid a pen on the top document, "What's the status at Sugar Grove?" The inside cover had a paper-clipped photo taken by the radio telescope of the ships in space. It was dark and blurred but definitely recognizable as something intelligently designed.

A Rear Admiral with salt and pepper hair opened his own manilla folder, reading from the file; "Sugar Grove Radio Telescope contact was lost with the targets at 18:47 hours yesterday with planetary rotation. Back on line at 07:30 this morning, Sugar Grove is searching for the targets along the projected trajectory... All information is being fed live to NORAD and USSPACECOM at Cheyenne Mountain."

The Director glanced at his watch, "It's 09:15 hours; they have been unsuccessful in locating the targets?"

"So far, yes sir. I fully expect the targets will be located and identified..."

"Are we going to have any issues with Green Bank or SETI?"

A man in a dark suit sitting next to the Admiral cut in. "Our inside man at SETI will alert us if anything there changes. I don't foresee any problems with the civilians. The security team that visited Green Bank introduced themselves to the good doctor and her people. I think they fully understand that it is in their best interest to forget the event and never discuss it..."

"What kind of assurances do we have from..."

"Dr. Michelle Fabry..." offered the man in the dark suit.

"Right. What kind of assurances do we have to make sure this stays... *permanent?*"

"They have no evidence left. Their data was lost... an unfortunate digital mishap."

"I take it we acquired a copy of that data before its loss?"

"Yes sir."

The Director nodded his approval. "I see. Anything else?"

"Our team left behind a few monitoring devices..."

The Director nodded again, interrupting, "It has occurred to me that we might reacquire the target faster with more eyes on the sky. Any chance we can use Green Bank to scan additional sectors?"

"We already have Houston and Kennedy Space Centers employed in that task. I do not think using Green Bank and their staff is worth the security risk..."

"Then send them home and use staff from Sugar Grove."

"We do not have the additional staff," interrupted the Admiral. "Budget cuts have reduced the Grove's capacity."

"Hmm." His brow knitting, the Director picked up his pen, making notes on the first sheet in his file, turning it over to reveal the next. "Have a team revisit Green Bank. I'm sure your people can persuade the doctor and her staff to work quietly with us on this. Give her whatever assurances you think will be effective. But get it done." He made some cryptic notes and turned another page. "Where are we on projects Zenith and Ascension?"

Across the table from the Admiral, an Air Force Brigadier General flipped open his folder, "Zenith is undergoing continued testing at Dugway. Successfully I might add..."

"And Ascension?" interrupted the Director.

"X-37B number Three has been in orbit for five-hundred-twenty-seven days and counting..."

"Is it armed with Zenith?"

"No sir," replied the General, "that is Project Equinox. We have two X-37Bs in the fleet that are Equinox capable, but the software is still being debugged and updated..."

"How fast can you get them up?"

The General raised his eyebrows in surprise, "Sir? In orbit? Equinox isn't ready to be field tested yet... A month maybe. And that would be pushing its timetable..."

The Director held up his index finger, "In case you haven't noticed, General, we have some extenuating circumstances on the horizon. Equinox and Zenith may be our most capable defense in dealing with this possible threat." He scribbled some cryptic notes on the facing page before flipping it aside for the next page. "As of now, those units are operational and cleared for immediate use. Get them up."

"Yes sir."

"And bring all the Zenith systems on line. How many are available shipboard?"

"None," replied the Admiral. "The first Zenith capable frigate is still being built in Norfolk. It is slated to be completed in Spring of next year..."

"My understanding was that we had three cruisers planned for the upgrade, what is the status on them?"

"The shipboard Zenith system is not ready for installment or deployment. It was expected by the time Zenith was ready later this year, it would be installed in the new frigate under construction. At the same time, one of the cruisers would be pulled into Norfolk for the upgrade. All three cruisers are expected to be complete mid-summer next year; each ship taking sixty to ninety days to upgrade."

The Director laid his pen down on his files and rubbed his forehead, "That is not helpful for our current situation..."

A man in a blue suit at the far end of the table raised his hand, "Why are you automatically assuming these... things, are hostile or have hostile intent?"

"And you're assuming they're not?" The Director looked up from his notes, his eyes narrowing, "We're not in grade school, put your hand down. And who are you...?"

"Liaison to the House Armed Services Committee..." said the man with a mere sliver of confidence remaining.

A smirk passed over the Director's face. Briefly. It was more a sign of contempt than amusement. "I suggest you remain silent while the adults are talking..."

"I just meant..."

With a silencing motion of his hand, the Director's eyes shifted to the faces around the table. "Bureaucrats," he sighed in disgust. He locked the man with the blue suit in a steely gaze, "Get out."

"Sir, I have clearance to be here, I am an official Liaison to the..."

Slamming his hand down on the table brought the man in the blue suit to startled silence. "You," growled the Director, "are interrupting *my meeting*. A National Security Meeting. Would you like to find out, first hand, how long you could be in a cell before someone notices you're missing..?"

■ ■ ■

Dr. Michelle Fabry was both surprised and pleased to see Katie walk through Green Bank's front door about an hour after everyone else got there, her normally bouncy strawberry blond locks pulled back into a ponytail. She looked stressed but softened after some coffee, a doughnut and a little warm praise from her fellow employees. By her own admission she hadn't planned on returning, ever. But she decided she loved both her job and the people she worked with, and recent events had not changed that.

What had changed, overall, was the fact that the folks at Green Bank suspected they were being watched, although to what extent they were uncertain. With groups of school children touring the facility, they used the background noise of their voices for quiet conversations.

Katie trotted into the control room, her eyes wide... "They're *baaAack!*"

Standing next to David, looking over his shoulder, Michelle Fabry looked up from the data screen, "Who's back?"

Hands on her hips, Katie's head tilted at an angle, "Who do you think?" she replied a little sarcastically. "The assholes are back..."

"Oh, *maaan...*" Michelle headed across the control room floor, following Katie towards the lobby door, "What the hell do they want now..."

Two men in black suits waited patiently in the lobby amidst the children, indifferent to their presence. "Dr. Fabry..."

"What do you want?" she crossed her arms defiantly, her gaze sweeping the room. "Where's the rest of your storm troopers? Scaring little children today?"

The two agents ignored her obvious stab of sarcasm. "We'd like to speak with you in your office..."

■ ■ ■

"Mitch? *Mitch..!*"

"*I'm fine,* Dennis," called Michelle Fabry, waving over the railing. She entered her office and closed the door behind her, moving to her desk, passing the two men in black sitting on the sofa against the windows. "So what do you guys want now?" She turned to them, pointing an accusatory finger, "You know, you assho...," she bit her tongue. "You and your *people,* and I swear to God I'm using that term loosely, deleted two weeks' worth of work? We were mapping Harding-Konos 452 when you..." she recognized the blank looks. "Yeah, no idea how much work you destroyed or how important it was. Typical," she waved dismissively.

Doctor, we apologize for the inconvenience. *We really do...*"

Michelle's face flushed red, "Inconvenience? *Inconvenience..?!* You destroyed over *four-hundred* man-hours of research!" she interrupted, talking over him.

"We are dealing with," he continued, "a matter of national security and we need your assistance..."

"Now you want my help...?!" she laughed out loud. "Are you freaking kidding me? You people are really unbelievable..." she shook her head in disbelief. "And what if I say no? What then?"

"It's not really a *request* per Se..."

Dr. Fabry's eyebrows lifted in astonishment, *"Excuse me?"*

"We have been directed to seek your cooperation in this matter of national security. You and your staff will be treated with the utmost respect, as two of our *monitors* tasked with tracking your progress, share your findings *live* via a direct link with NORAD and USSPACECOM at Cheyenne Mountain. Your facility may remain open to the public as it is today. You and your staff will be fully acknowledged for any discoveries or findings and rewarded for your full cooperation at this crucial time in our nation's history..."

Michelle's eyes narrowed, "That's if I say yes. What if I say *no."*

"The outcome will be much less favorable for you and your staff."

It was a flat, open-ended, frightening response, void of emotion and it chilled her to the bone. Whether driven by morbid curiosity or blind courage she felt compelled to ask what he meant by that statement. "Really," she said flatly, "you want to elaborate on that?"

"If you insist... The facility will be closed. To the public. To you and your staff. The government will seize control of the facility..." he added, adjusting his tie for emphasis. "A team of our own will be deployed to run the facility," he lied, "until which time the situation comes to a conclusion."

"Oh, you can kiss my ass," she shot back. "No one touches my equipment but my team..." She waved her hand, "And yeah, I just heard that in my head, but you *know* what I mean..."

"Then it appears your decision is an easy one, doctor..."

■ ■ ■

Chase Holt let the dirt bike roll to a stop, his feet dragging in the sand on either side, a cloud of dust and grit passing him, carried by the heated desert breeze. The sun had dropped below the far ridge line and the purple of the cloudless sky deepened, flecks of stars appearing all around them. He hooked the heel of his boot and dropped the kickstand, swinging his leg over the back of the bike. Jesse was already off his bike, pulling the two fuel cans and water from his saddle racks. "You might want to top off your tanks before you go, there will still be plenty left in these to get you back to our rendezvous."

Chase pulled his helmet off and scanned all around him, "I thought this was supposed to be Cutler Reservoir. I don't see any water..."

Jesse opened his visor, "Dude, it's a desert. Did you see those deep depressions on either side of the trail when we came up out of the wash?"

"Yeah..."

"When it rains, that wash turns into a raging flood zone and the reservoir fills. There's also a pump that adds water to it from the wash." He pointed north, "There's a set of solar panels out there about a hundred yards that charge the pump batteries. If the reservoir is full, it'll hold for about a month or so."

"My tank took about a gallon," commented Dan as he recapped the gas can.

Jesse took it from him, tucking it up under the pumping station's water pipe, "That'll give you another gallon and a half to refill with on the way back, you should be good to go."

Chase topped off his bike's tank and handed the other can back to Jesse. "What do we do with the cans after they're empty?"

"Don't worry about it, just leave, em."

The three riders huddled around the GPS unit with the fabric map laid out on one of the dirt bike's seats. "South on Road 41," began Jesse, "West on Basin Road. If you get to a gate on 41 that says anything about area 61 Bombing Range, you passed Basin Road..."

Dan entered the fuel into the GPS. "OK, fuel's logged in. I think we're going to have to slow our roll since we're going dark with night vision."

Chase nodded, "Open visor means we need a dust buster..." he pulled the military Shemagh he wore in Afghanistan out of his backpack, handing another to Dan that he'd requisitioned from Karen's pack. "Here, I'll show you how to wrap it."

■ ■ ■

Darkness fell fast, a deep, dark black with only a sliver of a moon and a sky full of stars. Chase had a minor flashback to a war torn desert a half a planet away, making the hair stand up on the back of his neck. He found himself eying the edges of the road looking for signs of planted IEDs, *improvised explosive devices*. He had to force himself to shake it off, keep his eyes moving. Riding side-by-side on the gravel road, puttering along between ten and twenty miles an hour, allowed them to see details and hazards in the road, see the terrain and minimize the dust off the road. If you could call it a road. Dan motioned to a vehicle trail that intersected, breaking off to the west. Dan checked the GPS and nodded, they were going in the right direction. So far, so good. Heading west on Basin Road, they caught a glimpse of a headlight glow that appeared to be heading east back toward the main highway. It disappeared as suddenly as it had appeared leaving Chase to second-guess if they'd actually seen it. He wondered if Jesse had made it back to the truck yet. The road, such as it was, swung northwest. They crossed several dry washes that would be treacherous to cross in a rainstorm, a flash flood filling them to capacity in a matter of minutes.

They slid to a stop at a crossroad that looked measurably more traveled and well maintained. "Do we turn left here?" asked Chase looking up and down the road.

Dan shook his head inside his helmet, "No, straight across and up into the mountains... now it gets rough."

Chase adjusted his Shemagh, shaking out the dust. "OK," he breathed, "let's go..." he held out his hand, "Wait!" He shut off his bike. "Turn it off," he waved, pulling off his helmet, listening intently. "Look!" He pointed north over the top of the mountains, two large aircraft heading toward Area 51 trailed by several smaller aircraft. They quickly dropped out of view. He wiggled his helmet back on, "Let's go."

■ ■ ■

The GPS no longer receiving, it was sheer luck they'd found the opening in the fence. *Nellis Bombing and Gunnery Range – Restricted. No Trespassing.* The heavily weathered sign looked ancient. It was a simple barbed wire ranch fence, nothing special, and several of the rotted fence posts were broken off at the base, the rusty barbed wire laying half-buried in the sand. Looking at the sign, Dan shrugged, "I like the *photography is prohibited* part at the bottom..." He kicked the dirt bike in gear and motored through the gap in the fence, "We'll only take video then."

His mind buzzing, Chase felt pins and needles all over his body, his eyes searching for even the faintest of visual clues. Unaccustomed to being unarmed, he felt seriously vulnerable without a firearm. The Ka-Bar knife webbed to his backpack, while useful, was not much of a consolation.

They wound their way up between the ridges and peaks. When Dan finally angled off the trail he pointed at a stand of twin Joshua trees at the top of the ridge line just above them. "We're here..."

"You're going by a tree?" lamented Chase. "Those things are all over the place."

"No, this is it. It matches the photo Jesse showed me. See the crooked branches?"

Chase Holt was just glad to be off the bike, his ass was sore. "Whatever dude, they all look like they have crooked branches to me."

Hiding the dirt bikes between boulders, they covered them with a small camo net before climbing up to the ridge line. Standing at the top near the Joshua trees, Area 51 lay spread out below them on the valley floor. Chase suddenly felt visible and dropped to a crouch. *"Wow..."*

Dan grinned. "It sure is something. Worth it, huh?"

"I'll let you know tomorrow," breathed Chase, looking through binoculars. "Let's get our gear set up."

■ ■ ■

Considering it was midnight, the base in the valley below was a hub of activity. Two flights of fighters sat on concrete aprons at the north end of the base; four F-16s and four new F-35s.

"Ugh," grumbled Chase.

Dan peered through his viewfinder, "What?"

"F-35s."

He glanced over at Chase. "Isn't that the new stealth fighter that can take off vertically?"

"Don't. Don't be that guy..."

"Which guy?"

"The one who believes all the crap about that brick. It can't turn, it can't climb, and it can't run. It's a decade overdue and about a half a trillion dollars over budget. The F-16 is over thirty years old and is still a better plane."

"I thought the F-35 was supposed to be the answer for air superiority..."

"Pssh," hissed Chase. "The F-35 weighs 10,000 pounds more, costs literally ten times more per plane, is slower, can't turn with other modern fighters, and it was recently revealed, isn't all that stealthy."

"Jesus."

"Yeah, the Aussies and Brits have been smart enough to back out of the orders they placed." Chase went back to the viewfinder. "The idea was to build a fighter that could do it all. Turns out that's not possible... so they built a fighter that can't do anything. Except take off vertically. Because, well, that's really important in a dogfight."

Dan shook his head, "Sorry, didn't mean to touch a nerve..."

Chase sighed, "No, sorry, it's on me. I'm just sick of the military pandering to whomever is handing out the biggest kickbacks. It's always the guys dodging the bullets that have to deal with the garbage equipment they commit to."

"I feel ya brother," admitted Dan. "Police Departments are guilty of the same crap... Like buying ballistic vests from the cheapest bidder. Seriously? Fuck that, I bought and paid for my own."

"Left hangar," announced Chase, "The big one, what the hell are they rolling out onto the apron?"

"I see it. That's an X-37B Spaceplane... Hmmm, except it looks a little different. That one's shaped a little fatter... must be a new variant or something."

"There's another one in the hangar behind it..." Chase pulled away from the viewfinder shooting Dan a glance. "It looks like they're going to mount it on top of that first 747..."

"That doesn't look like a standard 747 though, look at the engines, they're *huge...*"

Chase adjusted the focus on the lens, "I know they used to transport the shuttles on a 747, maybe that's what they're doing..."

Dan pulled away from the eyepiece of his camera, "Is it possible they've come up with a 747 that can fly high enough to launch the X-37B off its back?"

Chase pulled away and stared back at him, "I don't know. That would require a completely different kind of engine..."

"Ramjets? Because they have been experimenting with them out here..."

Chase rubbed his face, "Well above my pool of knowledge, that's for sure." He held his hand out, his voice suddenly hushed, *"Helicopter..."*

"Where?"

Chase watched for movement and pointed it out, appearing as a dark silhouette above the base, heading on a circuitous route to patrol the periphery of the area. "He's blacked out." Sliding slowly, quietly, backwards off the ridge, he pulled the camouflaged foil blanket over his head. "Cover up and stay quiet," he whispered.

"How come we don't hear anything?"

"It's classified equipment. Special rotor blades and engine mufflers. The SEAL teams use them too. Look, they'll have FLIR and listening equipment, so stay covered, stay quiet and keep still..."

■ ▩ ▩

Absent the traditional thump, thump, thump that you could physically feel as well as hear, the whooshing of the rotor blades faded after passing almost directly overhead, it's shadowy form disappearing in the darkness unseen by the two hiding in the desert below it.

"I think they're gone," whispered Dan.

"Not yet, stay put." Chase lifted the corner of his cover high enough to be able to see out from under it with his camera lens, watching the camera's articulated digital screen. The sensitive night setting picked up a moving shadow in the distance blocking out the stars, continuing its patrol without deviation. He watched the form continue to shrink. "I think we're clear," he whispered, sliding out from underneath the blanket. "I guess these things really work..." He looked over at Dan's form that was still hidden underneath his camo blanket, "Dan?"

"I don't think I'm alone under here..." came a faint whisper.

"Oh crap," growled Chase, digging into his backpack. "What side is it on?"

"Left side..."

Locking the folding shovel into an open and extended position, Chase cautiously moved over to Dan's position and stepped on the left edge of the blanket with the toe of his boot, gingerly at first then with his full weight. "I'm holding the left edge of the blanket. On the count of three, roll out to your right. Fast. *One... two... three...*" Dan appeared at about the same time Chase heard a very distinctive rattle before his overhand swing landed the shovel on the left half of the blanket with a resounding *whump*. Several more whacks and the blanket stopped moving and making noise.

Having rolled down the ridge a good fifteen feet, the veteran Sheriff"s deputy knelt in the sand and shook himself violently, *Yeaaach!* Dammit, I *hate* snakes..."

"He seemed to like *you...* "

"Bite me..."

"You would have *loved* the Camel Spiders we had in Afghanistan..." offered Chase as he crawled back to the edge of the ridge.

"Fuck you, I hate spiders too..."

Chase scanned the base below with the camera, "Oh, these were not ordinary spiders..." he paused, "Damn, they have one mounted already, looks like they're rolling out the second one."

Dan was watching though his own camera, zooming in. "Same wider body X-37B as the first one."

They watched as a tow tractor moved the first 747 with its piggyback payload out of the way to make room for the second. Dan pointed at the fighters, "Looks like one flight is getting ready to leave."

"The F-35s."

Within minutes the fighters were on the move, taxiing down the field for takeoff, the loaded 747 starting it's engines. Using their adjustable thrust nozzle and mid-body vertical thrust turbofan, the F-35s executed a short runway takeoff in pairs. Climbing to a thousand feet, they circled the valley, while the 747 they were to escort, taxied to the end of the runway.

The streak of light that crossed the sky looked to be thousands of feet up but just before it disappeared over the horizon it arced back, and came screaming silently back.

"Are you watching this?"

Chase squinted through the viewfinder trying to track it. "Yeah... what the hell is it? Same thing we saw the other night?"

Dan glanced down at the base, "Uh oh. Whatever it is they don't like it..." he pointed. Red lights flashed on the hangars and a voice could be heard on a PA system though it wasn't clear from across the valley. Figures scrambled around the F-16s and another hangar at the end of the strip opened. Suddenly the base went dark, the only lights remaining on, the blue globes along the runways and taxiways.

A dark spot appeared on the valley floor nearest the observers on the ridge and Chase focused on it. "Fuck, where the hell did that come from?"

"What is it?"

"A Patriot missile battery just appeared from out of the ground..."

"F-16s are taking off..."

Chase swung the lens, catching the first pair coming up off the runway from the opposite end as the 747 which was still sitting on the runway. The fighters thundered into the sky, lighting their afterburners. "See, now *that's* how you're *supposed* to take off! Where'd our little UFO go?"

"I lost it... too much going on..."

The F-16s swung in unison, flying a diamond formation, passing right over their heads, forcing both men to cover their ears, the massive thrust vibrating their bodies and the ground underneath them.

Chase Holt was struggling with his better judgment to leave, compelled to stay and witness the unfolding events. The 747 began its takeoff run, the sound of its engines heard across the valley floor, the F-35s still patrolling the area in wide circles to the west, the F-16s out of sight somewhere.

A tart, electric smell in the air puzzled Chase, his mouth watering, his skin buzzing like pins and needles all over his body. He glanced at Dan, "What the hell is..."

Daylight came instantly from above them, the blue-white light washing over them erasing all shadow and features. Chase cursed his drop in situational awareness. *Dammit, he'd allowed the helicopter to sneak up on them. This was bad...* Chase gnashed his teeth, his stomach knotting in protest. He rolled to his side to look up, freezing in disbelief, his mind trying to convince him his eyes were lying. That the fifty-foot oblong disk hovering motionlessly and silently above them could be something other than what it was... or wasn't. And it wasn't a helicopter. At this juncture he almost wished it was. "Oh fuck," he breathed.

A toxic swamp of panic, elation and adrenalin, surged through his body. He opened his mouth but could not speak, he reached out his hand but could not move, he tried to look away but his mind refused...

It was impossible to tell if the light went out first or if the disk shot away first. Maybe it was simultaneous, the blast of air creating a small sandstorm on the ridge. Covering his face, Chase felt numb, drained. The F-16s were not far behind, storming across the sky in pursuit, playing tag with the UFO they could not catch.

Feeling slowly returning to his shaking hands, Chase began slowly stowing his camera equipment into his backpack with clumsy fingers, trying to blink away the white-out. "Time... to... go," he said shakily. Dan was laying on his back mumbling, staring at the sky. "Dude," urged Chase, "we really gotta get out of here."

"We need to keep filming," mumbled Dan.

"Fuck no," objected Chase, lucidity returning. "Pack it up, we're done. I don't know who that was... I'm still processing that. But *someone* knows we're here. And with that little light show, I'm guessing so does everyone else."

Begrudgingly, Dan began packing his gear, shaking the dead snake and its guts out of the camo blanket. "Just when it was getting interesting..."

"Not interesting," corrected Chase. *"Terrifying."* Making his way back down the ridge from the Joshua trees to the dirt bikes a flicker of light off to his left caught his attention... *headlights.* "Hurry the hell up, Murphy, we have incoming!"

Dan was still stuffing things in his backpack on the way down the slope, half on his butt, half on his feet. "How far?"

"Neighboring ridge. Doesn't look like a four-by-four..."

"Dirt bikes or ATVs, can't get anything bigger up here."

Chase swung his leg over the seat of his motorcycle, "I'm torn between coasting them down quietly, or going all *bat outta hell...*" He hurriedly tucked his Shemagh into his jacket before easing his helmet over his night vision.

Dan slid to a stop and mounted his bike in one motion, quickly fitting his helmet over his night vision, "Those guys are moving, I vote for bat outta hell..."

Chase squeezed the starter button, "Bat outta hell it is."

▦ ▦ ▦

What's more dangerous than off-roading in the dark? Off-roading in the dark at breakneck speeds with your lights off, using night vision and wearing no protective gear save boots and a helmet. Try as they might, they could not run side-by-side; someone had to lead and someone had to follow. Following was not a place you wanted to be; gravel, rocks, sand... riding through an all-obscuring sandstorm. Close calls were abundant as they descended the winding trails from the mountain ridge to the floor of the desert; passing giant rocks, boulders, Joshua trees, an occasional cactus, bramble scrub... all at a pace that was far from sane.

The lights behind them came and went, a flash here a glimpse there. They didn't seem to be losing or gaining ground. "Don't get us lost up here, Murphy!" shouted Chase. A cactus appeared out of the swirl of dust ahead of him passing his peripheral in a blur, eliciting a burning pain across his left leg as the needles slashed through his pants into his calf above his boot. He grit his teeth, blocking the pain out of his mind as he maneuvered his sliding bike through a bend in the trail.

Running down the stretch of trail toward the damaged fence, Dan slammed on the brakes, almost laying down the dirt bike, a gray pickup truck with wide desert tires straddling the downed fencing. "Oh, shit!"

Chase skidded up next to him trying to avoid a pileup, "It's empty, don't stop!" He twisted his body around as Dan kicked his bike back into gear, accelerating through the gap between the truck and the fencepost. Chase caught movement on the ridge to the left, two heavily armed men making their way back down in his direction. They were already halfway back to their vehicle when he swung his bike around and headed for the gap. Sparks off the gravel told him all he wanted to know about their intentions. Dan was already out of sight when Chase paused next to the truck, semi-protected from their gunfire by its body. Pulling the Ka-Bar from its sheath he stabbed the sidewall of the vehicle's back tire, having to twist and wiggle it to get it back out, ripping a sizable hole, the air whooshing out with a whistling sound. Returning the knife, he accelerated away hard, the front wheel of the dirt bike momentarily leaving the ground. In his right peripheral vision he saw an explosion of splinters, the trunk of a Joshua tree catching a rifle round. Laying low over the handlebars he weaved until he made the next bend, accelerating hard again.

Dan was waiting for him at the bottom where the Basin Road crossed the intersection to the trail they were on; Chase slid to a stop on his left.

Dan dumped the sand out of his Shemagh, "I thought I lost you, what happened back there?"

"They're in a shooting mood, so I flattened one of their tires to slow them down but there'll be others. You got GPS back yet?"

"Yeah. *They shot at you?*"

"Yeah, so let's get the hell outta here. Head for our gas stop."

Dan pointed past Chase to his left, *"Headlights."*

"Shit! Those trucks are no joke, they can go almost anywhere we can..." Chase kicked his bike into gear, *"Move it! Move it!"*

Basin Road was far from smooth but it was the best that they were going to get. It wasn't the best place in the world to run flat-out but they really didn't have much of a choice. The DOE trucks were nearly Baha capable and had a serious horsepower advantage. Chase and Dan's only advantage was that they were small objects in a big desert.

■ ■ ■

The DOE Security truck roared down the gravel road, bouncing and vibrating, rattling, launching airborne across a dip, "This is Unit T4, we're on GP Road closing on Basin Road from the north. Unit T7 what's your location?"

"T7 is at the head of Basin Wash Trail. Our unit is down, I repeat, T7 is down with a tire... They made it past us."

The two agents in T4 had a few choice words, the passenger keying the mic, "Copy that, T7. T4 is now primary unit... T6, location?"

"T6 is heading north on Road 41 from Reservoir Branch Road..."

"T4 copies. Step it up T6, they're coming your way on Basin, maybe you can cut them off."

"T6, roger that. Do we have air?"

"Negative T6, go-fasts are dealing with a visitor. Rotaries are grounded." The agent in the passenger seat was pointing at the lights along his side of the road where Basin Wash Trail crossed over to Basin Road. "Nate, stop, stop STOP..!"

The driver jammed on the brakes, the truck sliding on the gravel road, jittering on the uneven surface, the oversized all-terrain tires growling. The driver expertly steered into the slide, a cloud of dust and sand carried through the air as the truck finally lurched to a stop next to the two agents on dirt bikes.

"You guys have a Jerry can?" The closest of the two agents swung his leg off his bike, stepping to the open window of the truck. "Can we grab some gas? We're almost empty."

The security agent sitting in the passenger seat thumbed over his shoulder at the bed of the truck, "Sure, grab one out of the rack, we gotta go!"

"They're crazy bitches... running dark," said the rider, dragging the heavy five gallon gas can over the side of the truck. "Must have night vision..."

"Sounds like outside talent," commented the driver of the truck, turning the wheel toward Basin Road on his left. "Catch up when you can..."

"Two minutes!' shouted the rider as he turned away, closing his visor. The gravel thrown up by the truck's tires pinged off his helmet and back plate of his off-road armor as it sped off, roaring down Basin Road in a cloud of dust.

"Well *that* was rude," joked his partner, climbing off his own dirt bike.

■ ■ ■

There was no conversation riding at the speeds they were going, it was even difficult to maintain control, the gravel rolling like marbles under the tires of their dirt bikes. Hand signals had to convey what they needed to say. With the headlights ahead on Road 41 it was clear that they were going to have to leave the road or be cut off.

Chase Holt waved off at a nearly right angle and they slowed enough to leave the road, catching air over the soft lip of soil along the edge of the gravel surface. Cutting a more severe angle away from the road, they would have to slow down to cope with rolls, dips, soft spots and sudden changes in the rugged terrain.

The spot on Chase's calf where the cactus had slashed through his pant leg was burning like it was on fire, and as much as he wanted to glance down at it, he knew that would be the exact time something solid would appear in front of him. It was intense heart-pounding work that required one-hundred percent concentration to read the desert around them, interpreting the shadows and shapes in the night vision, things whipping past, anticipating the difference between a jump and a drop. Managing to follow the GPS, Dan pulled slightly ahead, angling toward their fuel stop. They needed to cross Road 41...

■ ■ ■

The gray DOE Security trucks T4 and T6 slid to a stop alongside each other, door to door, facing in opposite directions, three-quarters of the way to Road 41, a cloud of dust drifting between them, their headlights glowing through it like fog.

"Nate..."

"John," nodded Nate. "You see anything?"

The driver of the other truck shook his head, "Not a thing."

"They must've left the road somewhere along here..." Nate thumbed behind them along Basin Road.

"That's a lot of desert. This would be a lot easier with air cover."

"Tell me about it. Let's head down 41 to 51, see if they're heading to the highway. We should be able to run them down. We'll call the bikes and head them across the middle, see if they can pick up a trail..."

"Want *us* to cut across?"

Nate shook his head, "It's hard enough in the daytime, besides you're liable to break something trying to cross the Central Wash. Leave it to the bikes..."

"OK, we'll follow you..."

■ ■ ■

When Dan slowed, easing to a stop, Chase pulled up alongside him. "Why are you stopping?"

Dan nodded up 41, "Headlights. There's two of them."

"If we cross now they'll see our dust trail. Let's drop into the wash and wait it out. Hopefully they won't be able to see us down there..."

"You sure?"

Chase nodded, "Yeah, cuz I gotta check my leg too. It's burning like a bitch..."

"Did you get hit?"

"Cactus," winced Chase.

They idled carefully down between the gully ridges, and stopped at the bottom on the flat riverbed-like wash. Turning their bikes off to prevent detection, Chase unsaddled and sat on the ground. "My pants are wet..."

"Did you piss yourself or are you bleeding?"

"Funny man..." Touching it tentatively, he smelled his fingertips, "Damn, it's gas..."

Dan dug a small first aid kit out of his backpack, "No wonder it burns, we need to clean it."

Looking a little like raw hamburger, Dan first rinsed it with water from his hydration bladder then sterilized it with a small squirt bottle of alcohol.

Chase sucked wind, *"Holy mother of... sonofafuckingmotherbitch..."*

Dan couldn't help but snort a chuckle.

"Glad you find that amusing, Murphy."

349

"Sorry. Most convoluted swearing I've ever heard." He finished wrapping and taping the wound. "Now let's see if we can find that gas leak..."

Tightening a loose fuel line fitting on Chase's bike with the blade of a knife, they were ready to go. "Damn, I hear dirt bikes..."

Dan started his bike, "Me too, let's get the hell out of here."

■ ■ ■

They heard the DOE Security team bikes but never saw them. Cutting across 41 they paralleled it, finally jumping up on Cutler Road and heading toward the reservoir and their fuel stop. Chase's bike began chugging along as it ran out of gas and he nursed it along until it eventually quit, coasting silently up to the reservoir pumping station.

Emptying both fuel cans into their tanks, Chase required the lion's share to fill his motorcycle, Dan's bike having had about a third of a tank left. They topped off their hydration bladders and prepared to leave, when they heard the DOE dirt bikes again.

Dan swung his leg over his bike, "Damn, these guys are persistent..." He squeezed the starter button and his motorcycle puttered to life, "Let's go, buddy..."

"Shit. She's not starting..." Chase jumped off and began to push it toward the ridge between the reservoirs and the wash below. "Go, *go,* I'll catch up once I get her started..."

Dan pointed back behind them, "They're coming up the road!"

"Go! Go!" Chase's legs were pumping like a linebacker trying to punch through the line as he ran alongside the bike, pushing the button, the starter turning the engine over, trying to get the fuel to the carburetor and prime the engine. Dan disappeared over the edge and down into the wash, leaving him alone, rolling his stalled bike along the ridge between the dry basins. He was just out of the spread of headlights that were closing on him from behind. Once they turned into the pumping station he'd be visible.

The edge was so near and the damn sand was so soft...

Suddenly seeing his own shadow in front of him, he ignored their shouts, determined to make the edge of the wash. The pop-pop-pop of the DOE Security team's 9mm pistols sounded weak in the wide open desert. The front tire crested the edge of the wash's ridge when he felt the hammer blow hit him almost dead center of his back, pitching him forward as his bike dropped over the edge. He fell across the bike like a surfer flat on a

350

surfboard paddling towards a wave. Through pain and stars floating through his vision, he struggled to get himself upright on the bike and maintain control. Flying down the steep wall of the wash between the gully ridges he managed to get the bike in first gear and pop the clutch, the stubborn engine roaring to life, almost redlining. Kicking it into second gear he navigated to the bottom, turning northeast, searching for Dan. Each breath produced stabbing pain and he could feel moisture running down his back. Finding Dan ahead waiting for him in the shadows was a relief and a blessing.

Seeing Chase had caught up, Dan turned away to take the lead again, almost missing the fact that Chase was waving at him, rather weakly. "I don't think we should stop at the rendezvous," commented Dan, "we should ride back into town in the dark if we can..."

Chase eased to a stop next to Dan, killing his engine and rolled off into the sand, the bike dropping over on its side. Turtled on his back in the soft sand he tried to shrug off his backpack, *"I'm hit,"* he wheezed...

Turning off his engine, Dan vaulted off his bike, dropping to one knee alongside his fallen friend, unbuckling the backpack that was holding him immobile, sliding his hand along Chase's spine and the padded side of the pack. He could feel a hard pronounced deformity which peaked his interest and he opened the bag to check the contents. "It's water..."

With the weight removed Chase was able to breathe again. "It's not blood?"

"Nope. You got hit alright, but your gear took it. It went through your camera and into the spade of your trenching shovel. It was hard enough to rupture your hydration bladder. The shovel acted like a trauma plate and the water in the bladder dissipated the energy."

"I thought for sure..."

"You might have a broken rib or two... you'll definitely be black and blue. Can you ride? We really need to get out of here. As determined as they were, I'm surprised they didn't follow..."

The sky flashed as a lance of green neon shot up into the sky, the source invisible over the ridge of the wash, but obviously coming from Area 51. At over ten miles away there was still an audible crackle and the tart smell of ionized air. It was sufficient to make both men jump and set them to motion. "Time to go," they said in unison, their voices overlapping.

Inexplicably, the game had changed. This did not fit in with the rest of the night's narrative; although neither did the UFO. Or why it had chosen to park itself over them, no matter how temporarily.

351

Chase winced as he re-shouldered his pack and righted his dirt bike, looking back at the empty sky, not sure what he was looking for or what to expect, if anything. "What do you think is going on back there?"

Dan swung his leg over his bike and squeezed the starter button, the bike sputtering to life. "No idea. More testing maybe? I didn't even know they had one here, I thought all the testing was done at Dugway. We need to add this to our report..."

"Chase started his bike, "Maybe they were trying to hit that UFO..."

Dan kicked his bike in gear, "I don't know, that thing didn't look anything like the ship that came down on Fort Myers Beach..."

A crisp, vibrant, neon magenta line flashed from the stars, producing a sharp thunder crack, following the same path down as the green line fired up from the Zenith weapon on the base. The horizon, as seen from the bottom of the wash, flashed yellow-white, the sound of a rolling explosion crossing the desert, vibrating the sandy soil beneath their feet. Something up there didn't like being fired upon and fired back. Exchanging startled stares, neither one of the two riders wanted to wait around for whatever would happen next...

CHAPTER TWENTY NINE

UFW FRIGATE REVENGE, EARTH ORBIT: *WHAT THE HELL?*

Fritz stretched, dropping himself off his human's bed in the muted light. "Room is a lot smaller here..."

"I know," nodded Jack, sliding a sheer form-fitting t-shirt over his head, "it's a much smaller ship. You understand that, right buddy?"

Fritz nodded his head with a snort. "Yes. Just no room to run here."

"Don't worry," replied Jack, slipping a protective combat vest over his head "We'll go back to the Conquest soon. You like the Conquest, right?"

"Is okay," replied the Shepherd, looking up at Jack mischievously, his head cocked to one side. "I would rather run on the beach..."

"Uh huh," nodded Jack, zipping up his flight suit. "I knew this was going somewhere... I don't know if we're going to get to do that this time, buddy..."

"Gus wants to run on the beach too."

Steele raised a dubious eyebrow, "Did he tell you that?"

"Yes..."

"Hmm." Steele checked himself in the mirror as he slid into a leather flight jacket, hiding his shoulder holster and hybrid 1911. A dark gray flight suit, black boots and dark brown leather jacket... "Meh, looks civilian enough I suppose. If you're half blind and running for your life..."

Sounding like a bass drum strike, the floor rocked, staggering Jack . Red alert klaxons blared throughout the ship, lighting flashing red.

"All hands to battle stations! All hands to battle stations! Gun crews report in..!"

"What the hell..?" Steele activated his TESS, "Lisa, on the bridge..."

■ ■ ■

Jack sprinted down the corridor paced by Fritz, slowing to pass the Marine sentry and through the opening bridge doors, tromping to a stop between the command chairs. *Sitrep, "* he commanded. "What the hell was that?"

Brian spoke without looking back, "Someone on the surface took a shot at us..."

"And *hit* us..." added Maria.

"Damage?"

"No sir. Our shields were up as a precaution in this floating junkyard of satellite orbits," he waved at the screen littered with markers and declination trails. "It might've hurt us if we didn't..."

Steele was aware of Lisa's presence behind him but did not acknowledge her there, concentrating on the situation at hand. "What the hell did they hit us with?"

"An energy weapon..."

Raulya looked over her shoulder from tactical, "We're still being targeted, the weapon is recharging for another shot..."

"Take it out," commanded Steele.

Brian swiveled around, *"Admiral,"* he said slowly, "It's in the *U.S."*

"What's your point, Commander? They're being *hostile.* Take. It. *Out."*

"Sir," called Raulya over her shoulder, "I'm reading a similar power buildup in another area. I believe there may be another weapon..."

Steele pointed at the big screen, "Can you bring it up on screen?"

"Aye, sir." Raulya's fingers danced over her glass keyboard, the big screen zooming in to the North American continent, markers appearing on screen in the west, the icons showing a circular power gauge around the target. "First target is approximately ninety percent, the second at about thirty percent..."

Steele could see Brian's hesitation to fire upon the hostile weapon batteries, his indecision jeopardizing the ship. "They're both out in the desert, Commander..." prompted Jack, hoping it would move him to action. Watching the levels on the on-screen icons, the first target neared one-hundred percent. "Tactical, target the weapon only. *Take it out..."*

"Yes, Admiral."

Zwump, Zwump. The floor vibrated, the forward turret firing one volley. "On target, Admiral. Direct hit, weapon destroyed."

"Any collateral damage?"

Raulya zoomed in as close as she could get, a flaming crater showing where it was obvious a building had stood, several nearby structures appeared damaged, and images of men and equipment moved quickly about. Steele recognized Area 51 but said nothing to Brian who stared silently at the screen.

Steele eyed the icon of the second weapon nearing seventy five percent. "Lieutenant, if they shut it down, mark its location but leave it intact. If it passes ninety-five percent, take it out."

Raulya nodded, "Aye sir."

Steele pursed his lips, "Mr. Carter, ready room. Now." He turned on his heel and headed for the Captain's Ready Room, staying Lisa with a discreet wave of his hand.

■ ■ ■

Jack Steele sat on the corner of the Captain's desk facing the door, Brian walked in looking troubled. Jack waited until the door closed before he pointed in the direction of the bridge, "You want to tell me what the hell happened to you out there?" Brian Carter shrugged, shaking his head as he stared silently at the floor. "I can't read your mind, man. Tell me what's going on in your head." Steele ran his fingers through his hair. "Do you need a break? Should I put someone else in command..?"

"No, no..." waved Brian weakly.

"Then what?" gestured Jack, his palms facing upward in question. "Was it just because it happened to be the United States?"

"I don't want to kill Americans..."

Zwump, Zwump. The floor vibrated beneath their feet.

Jack nodded, "OK, I get that. So you're saying if it was someone else it would have been alright?"

Brian took a deep breath, "I really don't want to kill *humans..."*

Steele pointed to the bridge, "In case you hadn't noticed, they, *we...* are pretty much all *humans.* The only ones I have a question about are the Gogol's..." he mumbled, thinking about that for a second. "Not really sure what *they* are..." he waved away the thought. "What I think you really mean is; you don't want to kill *Earthlings..."* Brian looked up, seemingly satisfied with that assessment. "OK look; I see someone shooting at people, I don't take the time to find out who he is, what Godforsaken armpit he's from, what demon he worships, the color of his skin, or what kind of fucked-up childhood he had... I take the bastard *out.* Period."

"I get it..."

"They threw the first punch. We offered no threat, we weren't bothering anyone..."

"I get it," insisted Brian.

355

"Are you sure? Because that can't happen again..."

"I'm sure."

"Fine then get back out there and let's get back to work..." Steele stood up, "We good?"

Brian nodded, looking relieved, "We're good."

Jack caught Brian by the shoulder before he turned for the bridge, "You sure you don't want to go see your mom and dad?"

Brian's mouth skewed crookedly, "Just to say hello to say goodbye again? I don't think I could do that to them. I gotta think it's better this way. They have their lives, I have mine, they don't have to worry anymore..."

Jack patted his shoulder, "Alright, it's your call. But if you change your mind..."

"Thanks."

■ ▦ ▩

Having delayed their launch several hours to determine if there would be any new developments or threats put Jack and Lisa behind their preferred schedule but it seemed a reasonable precaution.

Steele glanced up through the Reaper's canopy, the last sliver of interior light coming from the belly of the Revenge disappearing as the armored hull closed above them. Inside the cockpit, the air system pumped cool, clean air into the silence and he adjusted his flight gloves.

"I still think I should get to fly," mumbled Lisa from the back seat. "It's supposed to be *my* bird..."

"Hush." He ran through his checklist as the crane arms extended, easing the Reaper out of the nestled belly slot in the hull of the Revenge, the silence retreating to the sound of electronics waking up, the sudden growl of the engine warmers and the hum of power units. "Position of the rest of the Task Force?"

"Dark side of the moon," replied Lisa, going through her own checklist. She glanced up as the crane's claws released with a metallic *kachunk,* their magnetic surfaces reversing polarity, pushing the Reaper away from the Revenge. She watched the arms retract, "We're clear."

"R1 to Revenge, we're away..." He tapped the igniter, lighting the twin engines with a twin thump and swung the nose of the fighter to the right, adding throttle as he rolled, arcing down towards the planet.

"Copy R1, happy trails."

"Plotting you a course down..." announced Lisa. "Did Fritz mention to you he wanted to go to the beach?"

"Did he try to run that guilt trip on you too?" chuckled Jack.

"Yeah, and he tried to tell me Gus told him he wanted to go too..."

A plotted trajectory appeared on Jack's navigation screen, "Well I gotta hand it to him, he's thorough." He reached forward and flipped on the shield system, the generator spinning up with a whine. "Do me a favor and monitor a Fleet screen, keep an eye on things?"

"Got it." Her TESS covered by her flight suit and flight jacket, was set to voice recognition. "TESS, holo screen please..."

A holographic screen appeared above her wrist, TESS's face appearing, "Hello Lisa, what can I help you with?"

Lisa grabbed the frame of the screen and moved it to hover independently above her main screen, only blocking her view of the back of her brother's helmet, adjusting its size by the corners of the frame. "TESS, tie me in to Conquest Control and the Fleet Information. I need plotting, movements and communication..."

"Does that include Conquest's Flight Operations and patrol movements?"

"Yes, TESS."

"Connecting and assembling information," confirmed TESS, her interactive animation minimizing up to the right corner of the hologram. "Lisa, there is too much information for a single screen. You will have several tabs at the top, just select the one you need to examine, they are all live feeds..."

■ ■ ■

Lisa tabbed through her Fleet Information screens. "You want to tell me why we're coming down over the Arctic?"

"No eyes... unless you want to count polar bears and penguins. We'll level off over Hudson Bay and move south over Ontario. A lot more of nothing there too..."

"Seems like a real roundabout way... just saying."

Jack adjusted his sensor screen, "They saw us coming... which in itself is troubling, but they fired on us. And I don't know what they're using or how they got it, but they shot at us with something that seemed considerably more advanced than I would expect. Without so much as an attempt to find out who or what we are..."

"I guess a; *Hello, who are you?* woulda been nice."

Steele shook his head inside his helmet,"Makes me wonder if duck hunters would be so eager to shoot at ducks if they knew the ducks were carrying grenades..." He held the throttle at zero, letting the Reaper drop through the atmosphere, adjusting attitude or power as needed for stability.

Checking her Fleet activity screens, Lisa paged to a global plot, "Looks like we've got two of our birds dropping in over the North Atlantic... one fighter, one shuttle."

"That would be Commander Brighton, his mom lives in; Vauxhall London, Borough of Lambeth..." he added with a British accent.

She raised an eyebrow, "Uuhh, OK... And we've got two more dropping in behind us, both fighters."

"That should be Mike Warren, his folks live on a farm in Iowa..."

Lisa reached forward and adjusted her airflow, "Why is Commander Brighton using a shuttle?"

Steele adjusted the Reaper's attitude, the sparkling blue water of Hudson Bay rushing up at them. "London is like New York, it's big, busy, crowded and really doesn't sleep. If he took two fighters it meant one would be sitting empty on the ground. If it got discovered it could go all sorts of wrong. A shuttle with a three man security team can move and come back for extraction if needed."

"Chicago's big, busy and crowded..."

"Well," waved Jack theatrically, "the Reaper has the magical cloak of invisibility..."

"You think the Automatic Reflective Camouflage system will be enough?"

"Yes," he declared with a booming voice, holding up his hand. "We have the wondrous, mighty ARC to conceal us from our enemies..."

Lisa rolled her eyes, *"Oh, brother..."*

At ten-thousand feet, Jack pulled the throttle back into the negative which fired the breaking jets. Pulling the stick back, the Reaper arced gracefully to level flight at four-thousand feet. Gently dropping the nose he let her sink to a thousand. The sparkling blue water of the massive Hudson Bay soon gave way to the gray glacial bedrock and thousands of lakes in northern Ontario. The closer they got to the top of Lake Superior the greener it became, turning into endless lush rolling green forests only broken by long, winding rivers.

Jack rolled them upside down, looking up through the canopy which was actually down, *"Man,* there's a lot of nothing down there." He rolled the Reaper upright again, "Seems like such a waste of space, doesn't it?"

■ ■ ■

"You'd better back it down, Jack..."

Jack eyed his telemetry screen, as he walked the throttle toward the zero mark, "What month do you think it is, Lisa? May? June..?"

"Has to be June or later... otherwise we would have seen snow and ice."

"Hmph," Jack acknowledged. "There was some just off the bay, some ice on the Hudson but not much. Not sure if it ever melts completely up there."

"In any case," said Lisa, tabbing through the Fleet screens, "It ain't Christmas like you promised mom and dad. They're going to be pissed."

Dropping under Mach 1, Jack reached over and switched off the shields, trading them for the ARC system. "ARC is on and active," he noted, looking out over the right wing. The Reaper faded to an outline, the shining water of Lake Michigan visible through it.

Lisa looked left and right, "I always feel like I'm flying a video game when that's on."

"It's hard to appreciate how effective it is in space... but here, the effect is quite amazing." He throttled back as the skyline of Chicago grew ahead of them, bringing the speed down to something resembling sane, setting up his approach to pass over the city. "How are our other flights doing?"

Lisa tabbed to the global tracking map. "Commander Warren's flight is over Minnesota, on track for Fort Dodge. Commander Brighton is approaching London from the Channel..." She looked out over the horizon of the city spread out around them, "What time do you think it is over there?"

"If I remember right, they're six hours ahead of Chicago, so it should be about midnight there..."

■ ■ ■

With a baseball game occupying the field at the park, Steele was going to have to make use of the bike trail across the street from his parent's home. Landing gear extended, anti-gravity holding the fighter in a hover, he maneuvered the Reaper over the small parcel around the trail, lowering it

359

gently in between the trees, the task made more complicated by the ARC system's ability to reflect its surroundings. "How are we on the right?" he asked, watching the outline of the left wingtip clear a heavy branch.

"Good to go."

Jack felt the ground and released the actuator for the anti-gravity, the Reaper settling on its legs. He sighed with relief as he pulled the canopy release, flicking systems off one-by-one with his free hand. The canopy motored back with a hum, a breeze flowing into the cockpit. "Mmm, smell that?"

"The flowers or the bar-b-que?" grinned Lisa.

"Yeah... all of it... Smells like *home."*

Dropping his helmet on his seat, he admired the trees along the house as he climbed down the ladder to the grass. He remembered planting those trees as saplings; they stood nearly forty feet tall now, a canopy of leaves that extended over the house and the street, a haven of shade.

"Hey, get out of the way?" griped Lisa, standing on the ladder.

"Huh?" Jack stepped aside, "Sorry," he mumbled, "I was just taking a trip back in time."

"What are you looking at?"

"I was just thinking about the trees..." he pointed. "When I was seven, Tommy Brooker and I planted them as saplings. That was a couple of years before his mom was committed..."

Opening a small panel on the side of the Reaper, Lisa closed the canopy and retracted the ladder, leaving the ARC system active. "I think you mentioned that once, she went crazy or something?"

"Yeah," he replied, heading across the street. "The rest of his family moved away after that, I never saw him again."

"They left her behind?"

He shrugged, "As far as I know..." Climbing the front stairs he glanced over at his sister, "Ready?"

■ ■ ■

Commander Derrik Brighton peered out of the shuttle's cockpit windshield from between the air crew's seats, watching London pass beneath them. Off the stubby right wing flew Commander Dar Sloan's Cyclone, rolling brown-outs following below the two craft like the wake of a ship in the water.

360

"C'mon c'mon, I feel like a sitting duck up here, Brighton... everybody in the city knows we're here," came Sloan's voice over the comm. *"Find a damn spot..."*

"Just ahead," pointed Derrik to the pilot of the shuttle.

"The oval thing?"

"No, that's the stadium. Just past that... the open square surrounded by trees. See it?" he pointed again.

"Yep got it... What is it?"

"Vauxhall Park. Should be fairly quiet this time of night. Enough trees to hide us..."

The pilot surveyed the lights of the skyline and moving vehicles on the streets, "Commander, I don't know what time it is here, but there isn't anything down there that even *resembles* quiet."

Derrik gave the pilot a look of derision, "Just land the damn ship..."

Easing down below the treetops into the park's grass clearing, the shuttle and Cyclone crabbed sideways on anti-gravity towards opposite sides of the field, concealing themselves under the overhanging limbs of the trees.

The side door of the shuttle popped open, a couple inches from the hull before articulating a zero-clearance swing up and over the top of the hull. The landing gear squatted to allow its occupants to step out with little more than a short jump. Marine Warrant Officer Dale Alaroot and Corporal Dunnom were the first to exit, another Marine staying inside with the aircrew.

"Clear," commented Alaroot as he scanned the clearing. He adjusted the sling of his Pulsar carbine, a light non-lethal defensive weapon. Without a moon and no lights in the park, Dale could barely see the Cyclone sitting under the trees across the park, its canopy standing open. Headlights of cars passing the park on Lambeth Road flickered through the trees and bushes. "OK, Commander Brighton, stay on comms, let us know if you need us..."

Derrik Brighton, unarmed and dressed in clothing resembling something civilian, hopped to the ground, "See you gents in a bit. Stay out of trouble, eh?" He nodded curtly, trotting leisurely off towards Lambeth Road.

As the Commander's form headed for the busy road, dissolving in the dark, It suddenly occurred to Dar Sloane, the neighborhood was behind where they sat. "TESS, connect me with Dale Alaroot..."

On the other side of the small park, a holo-screen popped up above Dale's TESS. "Is your comm not working Commander?"

"It's working fine, Mr. Alaroot. This is for your ears only..."

Dale stepped away from the shuttle, "Go ahead Commander."

"The neighborhood is behind us..."

"Yes..."

"Commander Brighton just went in the opposite direction toward the River. I don't remember seeing anything in that direction that looked like residences..."

Without the same view of their approach from the back of the shuttle as the pilots, Dale had to trust Dar Sloan's judgment. "Yeah that does sound rather off..."

"Can you catch up to him? Keep an eye on him? But don't let him see you..."

"Aye, sir." Dale Alaroot unshouldered his carbine, handing it to Corporal Dunnom and began stripping off his gear and light armor, tossing it through the door of the shuttle. "Dunnom, you guys stay with the bird," he ordered, tucking a Pulsar pistol into his waistband, covering it with his tunic. "Stay off the comm unless it's an emergency..." he added, sprinting off in the same direction as Brighton had disappeared moments earlier.

While the park itself remained quiet it was difficult to feel properly concealed with vehicle and foot traffic passing just outside the park's ivy-covered wrought iron fence. Not having experienced planetary atmosphere in almost two years, Commander Sloan drew it into his lungs, trying to identify the range of scents. Flowers, trees, *nothing beats the fresh air produced by trees...* Perfume of two women walking past, food cooking somewhere... It was funny how much you missed the small things in space. Able to see over the barrier from his vantage point, he watched a vehicle work its way into a parking spot on the street. The ping as the holo-screen of his TESS popped into view sounded loud in his helmet, and his reflex to cover the hologram hovering above his wrist with his free hand was unaffected by his attempt. He grabbed the frame and placed it below the console so the glow couldn't be seen outside the cockpit. "Dale?" he whispered.

"Yeah," came a whisper. "There's a large multi-residential building just outside the park, but he passed it and headed for the river. Everything over here looks like businesses, maybe offices. He just went into a large glass and concrete building that backs up against the water... looks like some kind of complex. It's got walls and steel gates all around it. It does not look to be open to just anyone, but he was able to gain entry..."

"Is there any indication of what kind of business it is?"

362

"No sir... I don't get the sense that this a business... there are several communication towers on the roof. I tried asking someone who passed by but they looked at me like I was speaking Aleurian."

Dar Sloane closed his eyes, *dammit.* "As far as they're concerned, Dale, you might as well be. They don't off-world here; they don't have translator technology..." Dar could hear the Marine groan in exasperation... "It's alright Dale, just..."

The sudden ear piercing squeal in Dar's earpiece had him clawing at his helmet to get it off, the sound dying to a whimper before it trailed off completely. He reached into his helmet to pull on his ear and relieve the tension in his jaw, gingerly running his finger around the piece to see if there was any blood, his ear ringing.

"What in the Lord's name was that..?" gasped Dale.

Sloane looked down at the holo-screen, "You heard that too?"

"Fuck, I almost passed out. Nearly tore my ear off trying to get this damn thing out of my ear."

Commander Sloane keyed the mic on his comm, "All units, check in..." Each man checked in. Except Commander Brighton. Sloane turned back to his TESS, "I don't know Mr. Alaroot, I don't like it. Do me a favor, have your TESS record the building, we'll see if we can identify it later."

"Aye sir."

■ ■ ■

Jack Steele reached for the bell a second time, the movement of the doorknob interrupting his action. An unfamiliar man with thinning hair in his mid forties opened the door, "Hello... may I help you?"

Jack and Lisa exchanged glances. "Who are *you?*" blurted Lisa unceremoniously.

The man's eyes shifted from Lisa to Jack then back again, *"Who are you?"* he countered.

"Who is it George?" A woman about the same age appeared at his side, peering past his shoulder.

"I don't know yet..."

Jack tried to look past the people in the doorway to see the interior of the house, "My name is Jack Steele, this is my sister, Lisa. We're looking for our parents..." The man shifted his body to block Jack's view. "My parents are Kyle and Lynette Steele..."

"Nobody here by that name," replied the man, swinging the door, blocked by the toe of Jack's boot in the door frame. "Move your foot," said the man pushing on the door.

"Mister I grew up in this house, my parents bought it shortly after I was born..."

The man continued to push on the door to no effect, "This is our house, we bought it a

year ago, now move your foot..."

"Where did our parents go?!" shouted Lisa.

"I don't know, we never met them. The house was empty when we bought it..."

The wife was kicking at Jack's foot but it wasn't budging. "Let me come in, I just need to take a quick look around..."

"I'm calling the police!" shrilled the woman.

Jack pursed his lips, having had enough, shouldered explosively into the door, flinging the owner against the back wall of the foyer. The wife froze mid stride, divided between heading for the phone and helping her husband. Jack glanced at the man before walking past, Lisa right behind her brother, giving the man an evil glare. Steele paused, picking up a cordless phone off the arm of a couch, handing it to the woman with a wicked smirk, "Go ahead, call. They'll get here in ten minutes... Five minutes after you're both dead and I'm gone." She stared at him wide-eyed. He didn't really mean it but he hoped they believed it. "Or you can just sit and relax while I just check something. And then we'll be gone and you can go back to your life." He got a deer in the headlights look from both of them.

"Sound fair?" They nodded in unison. "Good." He turned to Lisa, "Keep an eye on them, I'll be right back."

Lisa stood with her hands on her hips, her jacket swept behind her hands, revealing her flight suit and the hybrid 1911 hanging in its shoulder holster, as she watched them intensely.

Like all smart homeowners, Kyle Steele had created several special places in the house to hide things and Jack needed just a few minutes to check them for any indication of what might have happened. If something was left behind it might mean they had to leave in a hurry, or that someone that was doing much what *he* was doing today, had missed something. Or maybe his parents had thought to leave a clue...

Dammit. Nothing. He strolled back to his sister in the living room, "No joy."

"How did you buy this house?" asked Lisa.

"From a realtor... Like we said, the house was empty when we looked at it," replied the man, sticking to the established story. "We never met anyone but the realtor."

"The realtor never mentioned why the house was empty?"

"No... Not really..."

"Not *really?*" Steele stepped forward with a piercing glare, the man's expression changing to something approaching terror. "Exactly what does *not really* mean? That's a yes or no question..."

"He, he, he, might have mentioned they needed to move... or something," stammered the man.

"Or something." Steele's eyes narrowed, "You... are a very bad liar."

"I swear, that's all we know..."

"Sure," nodded Jack, a wicked smirk returning, "all liars say that..." He looked at the wife, "Give me the name and phone number of the realtor..." She stared at him cow-eyed. *"Now!"* he shouted, making her jump into action. In a few mere seconds she returned with two business cards, handing them to him with a shaking hand. "Had that handy, didja?" he sneered, taking the phone she was still clutching in her hand.

"That card," she pointed, "was our realtor. The other card was for the realtor representing the house."

Steele dialed the house realtor first. *"I'm sorry, the number you have dialed is no longer in service. Nothing more is known..."* He hung up and dialed the number on the other realtor's card. It answered with an open line, an occasional click and a beep. He hung it up and tossed the phone on the couch, eying the homeowners, tucking the cards away into a pocket of his flight jacket.

"Interesting..." he pinched his bottom lip. "One doesn't exist and the other goes nowhere. Or maybe somewhere it shouldn't. In either case, your line seems to be bugged. Or maybe you already know that." His eyes scanned the corners of the room, air vents, lamps, furniture. "You can let them know Admiral Jack Steele is back, *and he's not fucking happy!"* he shouted, heading for the door. Lisa passed him, heading down the stairs and he turned back, looking over his shoulder, "If you really don't know what's going on here, I would suggest getting out of the house before they get here. And don't come back. Ever."

"I have to ask," pointed the man, eying the gold wings on the leather jacket and the gold pips on its collar. "Are you a pilot or something?"

It was Steele's first real smile, "Or something." He turned and ran down the front steps, "Lisa check the next door neighbors, I'll check the one's behind, see if they know anything."

■ ■ ■

Talking to the neighbor directly behind his parent's house who had been on vacation when the Steele's mysteriously disappeared, he found it odd that Kyle or Lynette had not contacted him and his wife either before or after their move. Jack assured him that while he couldn't explain it, it was probably best that way. They invited him in but the blue flashing lights flying down the street told Jack it was time to say goodbye. Jack cleared the porch railing, jumping to the grass with the neighbor standing in the doorway looking dumbfounded.

"Take care!" he yelled, sprinting off. "TESS, get me Lisa!"

"Jack?"

"Lisa, we have Chicago PD coming! Get to the Reaper!"

"I'm here. Climbing the ladder now. I don't hear anything..."

"Bastards went Code 3 *silent...*"

From her vantage point atop the Reaper, she watched him sprinting toward her, a blue and white police cruiser, lights flashing, sliding around the corner behind him, tires squealing. Another unit was flying up the intersecting street to her left. "I'm getting in the front seat..."

"I'll make it," he panted, pounding down the sidewalk.

"No you won't, they're going to cut you off!"

In a full stretch run past his parent's house, a blue and white police cruiser, lights flashing, screamed to a stop as he reached the curb, blocking his path to the Reaper across the street, the other car behind him skidding to a stop. Out of the corner of his eye he could see several more, stacked up, racing up the street to assist, a parade of flashing blue lights. He leapt, feet first, sliding across the hood of the Crown Vic blocking his path like he was stealing home plate, landing on his feet, still in a run.

"Freeze! *Freeze!"* chorused the voices behind him.

Steele tromped to a stop an arm's reach from the outline of the invisible ladder, the Reaper's ARC system still operating. As he turned around slowly, hands up casually at shoulder height, the smell of hot engines and burnt rubber passed his face in a warm wash of familiar odors. Across the street the couple occupying his parents house stood shoulder-to-shoulder on the front porch looking smug. He surveyed the faces of the officers, guns drawn, the other cars pulling up, yet more officers piling out. "Don't you move mister, you stay right there..."

Steele remained stone calm despite his hard run, fighting to control his breathing. "Take it easy guys... just a big misunderstanding..."

An officer from one car and a sergeant from another cleared the front of their vehicles, their guns trained on him. "Turn around, slowly. Face away from me," commanded the officer. "On your knees... keep your hands above your head."

Jack was wary of his jacket exposing his shoulder holster if he reached too high. "Can't we talk about this?" he stalled, standing firm.

"Mister I'm going to taze you if you don't..."

"Jack?!" queried the sergeant, his eyes narrowing, looking over the sights of his firearm. "Jack Steele? Is that you?"

Steele's gaze shifted to the sergeant, his artificial eye studying the familiar but aged face, recognition suddenly coalescing in his brain, a smile breaking across his face, "Bobby?" The sergeant smiled, his firearm dropping in unison with Steele's hands. "Bobby Fortuno... holy shit! What's it been, about ten years?"

"At least that..."

"How's Sonja?"

Bobby Fortuno holstered his weapon, "Divorced..."

"Hey Sarge..?"

Bobby Fortuno waved off the inquiry.

Jack Grimaced, "Ahh geez, Bobby, I'm sorry to hear that..." He nodded, "Me too. How are the girls?"

"In college, doing well," shrugged the sergeant, walking up casually. "Put em away boys..." he called over his shoulder. "What's going on here Jack? What happened?"

I've been... away. "

"Away?" asked Bobby suspiciously.

"Traveling," he clarified. "So I haven't seen my parents for about a year. I showed up to see them and they're gone... moved away."

"Man, that's rough. I thought I recognized the house. Were you on the outs with them or anything?"

Jack shook his head, "No, I moved to Florida and I just travel a lot..."

Bobby had been studying Steele closely and something seemed out of place but he was trying to decide how to broach the subject. Running out of options he decided blunt was easiest. "Jack, no offense or anything, but it's eighty-five degrees and you're wearing a leather flight jacket and some kind of, I don't know... what the hell are you wearing?"

"It's a flight suit Bobby, I'm a pilot..."

"Yeah, I remember when you started flying... But I've never seen a civilian pilot wearing something like that..." he indicated the flight suit. He reached up and touched the pips on the collar of the jacket suspiciously. "Looks like a lot of brass..."

"I'm a military pilot..."

Bobby looked at him curiously, not sure what to think, too many things not coming together in his head. He *wanted* to believe Steele...

Jack could see and feel the uncertainty. "Bobby, we've known each other for nearly twenty years. We went on double dates, we went through the academy together, we rode a squad car together..."

Steele's earpiece chirped, *"Jack,"* came Lisa's voice in a whisper. Looking up he could see the two SUVs coming towards them up the street. *"Six occupants each, heavy equipment, armored vehicles..."* she whispered in his ear.

"Bobby, do any of your patrol vehicles carry six men?"

He realized Steele was looking past him and looked over his shoulder, "No."

"Bobby I know you're not sure what's going on, but I *really* need you to trust me on this, things are about to get *really messy...*"

"What the hell is going on Jack?" he slid his firearm out of its holster.

Jack dropped to a crouch, pulling on Bobby by the shoulder, "Get your men to *hard* cover, if they've got long guns, they'll need them." He pulled the hybrid 1911 from its holster and Bobby Fortuno shot him an angry look.

"You're holding? *Jack..!*"

Steele pointed at the officers, *"Now, Bobby! Now!"*

The SUVs, one black, one white, skidded to a stop facing away from each other in a 'Y', six heavily armed men piling out of each vehicle, taking cover behind their armored bodies. "We're here for Mister Steele! You local boys can be on your way, we'll take it from here!"

Bobby shot Steele another angry glance, incredulous, "Who are these guys and what the hell did you..."

Steele's TESS chimed, the holographic screen popping into view above his wrist, the smiling face of his wife, Alité, Queen of Veloria, smiling at him. "Hello my husband, how is your trip going? Well I hope..."

Bobby Fortuno's eyes nearly popped out of his head, "What the Sam hell..." he breathed.

Steele faced the holographic screen so she could see the sergeant crouched next to him, "Alité, this is an old friend of mine, Bobby Fortuno. Bobby, this is my wife, Alité Galaýa-Steele, Queen of Veloria." Bobby nodded blankly as she spoke to him in a language he couldn't understand. "Listen, honey... I've got a bit of a situation here, can I call you back in a little while?"

"Of course. Please be careful, my sweet." The screen winked out, the hologram dissolving.

"What. The *fuck*. Was *that*? What... What..."

"You've got a choice!" yelled one of the men concealed behind the SUVs. *"You can give him to us, or we're going to take him! You've got 20 seconds."*

"Sarge, we can't get a signal on our radios..." called one of the officers. "We can't call for backup!"

"Pull your guys back," said Jack.

"Nothing doing..."

"Bobby, this is going to get bloody, I don't want to see any of your guys get hurt."

"I suppose you're going to handle this all by yourself," he replied sarcastically. "Who are these guys? Why do they want you?"

"CIA, NSA, maybe contractors. I' don't know..."

"What?! What the hell are you into?"

"You have five seconds left!"

"Bobby, do you believe in UFOs?"

"I... I... what? I don't know, what does that have to do with..."

Jack keyed the mic on his earpiece, "Lisa, ARC off, weapons hot. If they shoot..."

"Got it," she interrupted, her gloved fingers flipping off the Automatic Reflective Camouflage system. The dark, menacing Reaper, shimmered in the sunlight as it slowly became visible, solid in its stealthy alien glory.

The question in his mind of who Jack was talking to, vanished, Bobby's mouth hanging open in disbelief, as did almost everyone else. The first ones to recover from their astonishment were the men behind the SUVs seeing the Reaper as the prized *golden goose,* worth more than Steele himself. *"Time's up! Take it boys!"*

Time slowed for Steele as fully automatic fire erupted from the SUVs, cutting into the police cars, the rounds passing through and kicking up divots of dirt and grass on the other side. At a serious firepower disadvantage, the police fired back from behind the hard cover of their cruiser's engines, vehicle wheels and oak trees lining the sidewalk. Their handguns were no match for the suppressive fire from the tactical team, some of who peeled out to the trees along the curb to increase their angular advantage. The air was filled with smoke, noise, splinters of wood and glass flying like hail.

Lisa Steele's hand on the flight stick, the articulated turret under the nose followed her gaze, steered by her right eye in relation to the pipper on the HUD. She squeezed the gun trigger and the Cryo Gauss Guns pumped out chain-linked super-frozen spikes of specially designed steel alloy, a metallic clatter as the guns cycled the spikes in the loading tray from the cryo tank. The spikes shattered, exploding like grenades as they passed through the armored SUVs.

Raking the two trucks with a short burst, produced baseball-sized holes, the engine blocks exploding, first one then the other, shredding both trucks, lifting them several feet off the ground, the front wheels and tires blown off, sailing through the air in flames. The gutted wreckage crashed to the ground, a shower of glass and plastic flying out in all directions, a fireball erupting with a roar as one of the gas tanks split open on the pavement. "The Reaper cometh, *bitches!"* screamed Lisa.

The men closest to the SUVs lay scattered in pieces, their body parts shredded and strewn across pavement, grass and sidewalk. Steele took the opportunity to advance quickly on the right side of the street, shooting on the move. The first man, slow on recovery as he raised his weapon, took a charged particle projectile from Steele's 1911 in the chest, the round punching through the ballistic trauma plate of his vest, driving pieces of it through his body, tearing out a section of his spine, physically taking him off his feet. A small portion of a second man's face peeked out from the trunk of a hefty oak tree and Jack's artificial eye targeted him, drawing a red outline around his calculated position. Steele squeezed off two rounds, passing through the side of the tree, shearing off a two-by-four sized section of the trunk and taking the man's head off in the process, a sloppy red mush running down the trunk of the oak, a gory pink mist drifting through the air. Bobby's officers rushed the stunned survivors on the other side of the street, taking two of the men in custody.

Bobby eased up next to Jack who was standing over a man laying in the street past the burning wreckage with no legs below his knees. Still alive. But just barely. "Who do you work for?" asked Steele, emotionless." He crouched down, "C'mon, buddy. You've gotta know you're not going to make it, nobody will know... just tell me." The man opened his mouth to talk and blood bubbled out, gurgling, running down the side of his face. Steele stood up, "May God have mercy on your soul." He turned and headed back towards the Reaper, sliding the 1911 back in its shoulder holster. A flaming tire had crashed through the living room window of his parent's old house and by the looks of it, the house was going to suffer in a big way, flames licking out and up under the eaves. He couldn't help but smile to himself. The neighbor on the other side of the street had a seat from one of the SUVs sitting on the peak of his roof like someone had placed it there on purpose.

"Hold on a minute Jack, where do you think you're going?"

Steele looked over at Bobby walking at his side, "To look for my parents."

"Jack I can't just let you go... you're a material witness and participant in..." he looked over his shoulder at the burning carnage, "*a war zone.*"

Stopping at the nose of the Reaper, Jack turned and casually draped his arm on the barrel of one of the Cryo Gauss Guns like he was leaning out the window of a car. Fire engine sirens wailed in the distance. "Bob," he said calmly, "I know there's a lot to take in here..."

"Ain't that the truth..."

"But you've got to trust me, there are dark forces at work here..." Bobby Fortuno eyed him with a critical gaze. "Not like devils and sorcery," waved Jack, "but bad people doing evil things."

"No shit, Sherlock..."

"What I'm saying is, it's good versus evil. Evil has infiltrated our way of life and it surrounds us. It must be stopped. You can't fix it, you can't change its mind. You have to end it when and where you find it. Sometimes you have to do bad things to do the right thing."

Bobby waved his hands "Who do you think you are? Captain America or something?"

Jack walked around to the ladder, his helmet dropping over the side into his hands. He turned it around and pulled it over his head. "No man, that's the guy with the shield," he joked, indicating the Reaper with his head as he sealed his helmet to his flight suit. "I got me this. And a few other things...."

Lisa stood up and climbed over the console to the back half of the cockpit, "Hiya Bobby," she waved.

He blinked hard, doing a double take, "Lisa?" He looked at Jack who was halfway up the ladder, "Little Lisa?" he asked, holding his hand at waist height.

"Yep," confirmed Jack, climbing into the cockpit.

"That's me!" She dropped into the rear seat, nearly out of sight.

Fire engines had arrived, their crews disembarking, covering the wreckage with chemical extinguishers, running and hooking up hoses to tackle the former Steele residence which was nearly engulfed, the occupants standing on the lawn looking on in dismay.

"Wait a minute Jack, wait... What am I gonna say about all of this?"

"Blame it on me..."

"Again, *no shit Sherlock.* It's going to look pretty bad that I let you go!"

"I promise, It's all going to make sense soon... I'm going to drag this planet, kicking and screaming if I have to, into the 25ᵗʰ century."

"Man, you are *really* not making sense," Bobby waved in despair. "You are talking like you're from outer space or something..."

Steele silently tapped his nose with a gloved finger and pointed at his friend indicating he'd finally gotten it, *on the nose.* "You and your guys have cell phones... take pictures, take video." Steele was progressing through his checklist as he chatted, glancing over the side, "Here's what you say, Bob; *Forces of unknown origin attacked Admiral Jack Steele, envoy and commander of the United Federation of Worlds, Task Force Lancer, endangering your officers and the general public in the process. With great risk to your own safety, you and your officers ended it. Admiral Steele slipped away in the confusion, unhurt. His wife, Alité Galaýa-Steele, Queen of Veloria, sends her sincere appreciation for your assistance...*"

"Aw *c'mon Jack!*" shouted Bobby, throwing his hat on the ground, "You're fucking killing me here, *I* don't even believe that crap! Internal Affairs is gonna ream me on this!"

Steele pulled on the canopy lever, the long canopy motoring forward. "Keep an eye on the network news Bobby, you'll be OK. *I promise.*" The Reaper became buoyant, a blue glow under her landing feet. "Pictures!" shouted Steele before the canopy dropped into place, hissing as the seal made contact.

The black alien craft rose, nearly silently, in full view of firemen, policemen and neighbors who had congregated to see what was going on, their upturned faces watching the event. It appeared to simply float, the landing feet retracting, disappearing into the hull. The turret under the nose rotated back and forth with the movements of the pilot who paused to salute, along with the co-pilot, to the people on the ground. A news helicopter who had been doing a traffic report over the nearby expressway, deviated to get a look at what they thought was a strange aircraft, circling it, the cameraman recording it and the bizarre scene below it.

■ ■ ■

Steele looked over his shoulder, "Where is he?"

"He's trying to keep up with us."

"Dammit, I don't want to light em up and suck him into a vortex..." He nudged the throttle a little higher, releasing the anti-gravity actuator, reaching forward and flipping it off, the Reaper in standard flight. He lifted the nose a little, the ship accelerating smoothly, gradually.

"He's falling back..."

Steele watched the helicopter's signal on his sensors; at a mile and increasing he throttled up smoothly. At five miles he gave the throttle a hard nudge, the rotor craft quickly dropping off the edge of the screen as the Reaper thundered across the sky.

It was dark by the time they crossed over the Gulf of Mexico, the Reaper dropping down over the water to fly under the radar. "What's the plan, Jack?"

"I want to check my house, see if mom and dad came down here."

"I figured that. I mean are we just parking this thing on the grass or what?"

"I think we can get it up against the house on the beach side without anyone seeing it..."

Six hundred miles an hour seemed slow in comparison to the Reaper's real ability, but at fifty feet off the surface of the water it seemed faster than it was. Lisa was watching the same high definition full color sensor screen as Jack, and when the outline that popped up as *unidentified* registered in her head she couldn't help but shout, *"Sailboat! Sailboat! Sail..."*

Jack leaned the Reaper over, jinking hard, kicking the rudder to pass around it, the twin masts of the schooner flashing past them on the left. "He needs to watch where he's going," Jack commented coolly, "people are flying here..."

"Sure, because he's got, like, the whole ocean to boat around in..." shot Lisa sarcastically.

Steele throttled back and toggled on the anti-gravity, letting the Reaper slow on it's own, coasting over the inky black water, waves rolling along just a few feet below them.

"Hey , um, none of my business, but weren't you supposed to comm someone back?"

Steele felt a jolt of electricity through his spine, "Oh *crap!* I forgot."

"Smooth move..."

"TESS, Alité Galaýa Steele."

TESS' screen popped up above his wrist and he moved it in front of him, "Acquiring nodes and relays, stand by." TESS' face retreated to the upper right corner to make room for the comm screen, the Velorian crest hovering above a plain blue-gray background.

"Hello my husband." The video came a moment before the video feed, Alité appearing dressed in a white nightgown. "I was beginning to think you forgot me."

"No, no, we were just a little busy..."

"You *forgot,"* she teased pointing at him.

"Yeah," he admitted sullenly, "sorry."

"It's alright. Now you can talk to me while I climb in bed," she cooed. "All alone in this big bed, what ever shall I do?" she breathed seductively.

"Oh, yippee," mumbled Lisa from the back seat, "just shoot me now."

"Who is there with you?" asked Alité attempting to see through the comm screen.

"Hi," waved Lisa, over her brother's shoulder, the top of her helmet and face mask visible.

"Sister Lisa," said Alité sounding relieved. "Are you two flying?"

"One of us is," complained Lisa.

"Yes," Jack interjected, interrupting the over-the-shoulder conversation. "We're heading to the beach house. Mom and Dad weren't in their home, they've moved and I need to contact a few friends, see if we can locate them."

Alité sat Indian style on her bed, pulling her nightgown around her, "Do you think they are in trouble?"

Jack shook his head, "I don't know. But I intend to find out."

"Bring them home, Jack, Colton needs a grand-papa and a grand-mama."

"I promise. How are things going there?"

"Going well. Lots of rebuilding. A group of volunteers started working on the palace. I think there's a lot of guilt over what happened... But people are working together again, in all sorts of ways."

"That's very positive. Any signs of the troublemakers?"

"The Peacekeepers have done a wonderful job. With the help of the UFW military I seriously doubt there are any left. The base has been very busy and ships come and go pretty regularly. We have approved UFW military leaves on a limited basis. The beach seems to be very popular, we set up an air shuttle to get them back and forth."

They chatted for a bit longer until the Florida shoreline appeared ahead. He assured her he would talk to her again as soon as he could. As the beach approached, Steele pulled the throttle into the negative, firing the breaking thrusters. Suspended on anti-gravity the Reaper drifting smoothly up over the sand toward the house. Swinging the tail, the ship coasted sideways up to the darkened house, the starboard wing hanging over the deck on the back of the house. A splintering crunch made him jump as he countered their drift with the stick, "What the hell was that?"

"I think you just took out the deck railing with the tail..."

"Crap."

"Yeah. Don't scratch my bird, dufus." She toggled the landing gear, the system whining, extending. "Gear down, set to auto leveling. Go ahead and set her down."

CHAPTER THIRTY

EARTH, NORTH AMERICA : *STRANGE SIGHTINGS*

"Good morning, I'm John Griff on the anchor desk..."

"And I'm Amy Halloran."

"And this is a *Channel 4, Special News Bulletin...*" continued the news anchor. "Violence broke out on the north side of Chicago late yesterday afternoon, turning a normally quiet neighborhood into a deadly war zone. Rolling brown-outs were reported across the north side of the city, preceding the altercation between police and a group of well-armed, unknown assailants. It is still not known what prompted the assault or what the goal of the men happened to be. An intense gun battle ensued and several police officers were wounded with non life-threatening injuries. They were treated and released from local area hospitals. Only two of the estimated dozen or so assailants survived the pitched battle and are currently in police custody."

"Channel 4's News Chopper One was in the area, John," interjected Amy Halloran, "and captured some startling footage, not only of the scene but what was *leaving* the scene... We have Channel 4's, Chopper One pilot, Tom Bridge here in the studio with us; we'll let him narrate his footage. Tom..?"

A helicopter video feed appeared on the screen. "Thank you Amy. We were doing the traffic report over the I90 – 94 interchange when smoke caught the attention of our cameraman and he spotted this object floating over the scene. As you can see, from this distance it looks very much like a flat disc-like object, such as what most people describe when seeing an unidentified flying object... But as you can see, when we get closer..."

"Oh my..."

"Yes Amy, startling isn't it? You can see wings, a cockpit..."

"The tails appear to be upside down..."

"Yes John, that's one of the first things we noticed too," continued the pilot. "Inverted twin tails. As you can see, we were able to get within less than a hundred feet from the craft and made eye contact with the flight crew inside..."

"Weren't you afraid, Tom?"

"Indeed we were, Amy, my heart was really pumping. From here our cameraman gets a shot of the scene below, the fire trucks putting water on the blaze, but we really wanted to concentrate on this unusual craft. As you can see it doesn't seem to have any means of staying aloft, no rotors no VTOL jets, just this unusual blue glow underneath..."

"It looks like it's turning now, Tom."

"Yes it is Amy, it rotates around and starts to leave the scene. We keep up with it a bit here..."

"How fast were you going?"

"Our Bell 407, will do just about 150mph and that's what we're doing right at this point when it appears the pilot waves at us and it starts to pull away... then it does this..."

Amy Halloran jumped in her seat, *"Oh my!* It just *disappears!* Do you have any idea how fast it was going?"

"Faster than anything we've got, Amy..." The video feed of the event dropped back to the shot of the news anchors at their desk.

"Thank you Tom," the news anchor nodded, "some amazing footage you got for us there... scary stuff indeed." John Griff switched his view to a different camera. "In an astounding coincidence of similar news, the BBC had this to say about events in London late last night..." the video switched to a view of a BBC news feed.

"I'm Terrance Watershaum, and *this* is the ... BBC. Londoners experienced brief rolling blackouts last night across large portions of the city. Since we are just entering summer, it begs the question, is this the new normal? Are these the power shortages we were promised coming early? How truly bad is our power grid? These and many other questions remain unanswered. Hopefully the mayor's *reward* for a plan to produce fresh new technologies will *reward* us with some answers to this looming problem." He turned to another camera. "In other news, amateur video footage taken last night shows two unidentified flying vehicles taking off from Vauxhall Park at approximately 2am. Witnesses report hearing little to no sound, but a strange blue glow was visible underneath both of the craft. In a strange coincidence, a blackout seemed to accompany the appearance of the two craft. The BBC is still awaiting confirmation from local police on what type of craft this might be. Could these strange craft and the blackouts be connected? This reporter remains dubious at best..."

The BBC video feed cut back to the Channel 4 newscast, John Griff paging to a new note appearing on his digital prompter, "This just in, in reference to the events on Chicago's northwest side; an unnamed source in the Chicago Police Department said, off the record; *That at great risk to their own safety, the police intervened, stopping a vicious attack against Admiral Jack Steele, envoy and commander of the United Federation of Worlds, Task Force Lancer."* He looked at his co-anchor, his face an unspoken question mark. "What do you think that means, Amy?"

"John, I think that means we'll be interrupting local programming throughout the day with up to the minute information as we get it..."

■ ■ ■

"Fuck me!" Agent Doug Mooreland jumped up off the sofa in astonishment, prompting the other members of his team to come running from all corners of *The Barn.*

"What the hell, Doug?"

Mooreland pointed at the screen, "Our friend Steele is back...!"

"How can you be sure?"

"I just saw..."

"Wait; hold on," interrupted Mercedes Huang, grabbing up the remote and turning up the sound, "What's he saying now..?"

Channel 4's anchorman John Griff continued his report, "In other news; our viewers in Nevada and Utah who may be accustomed to seeing green lights in the sky, may not be seeing them for a while, as NASA was handed a stunning setback of their Astral Body Defense System development. Designed to protect the planet against space junk and the possibility of dangerous asteroids hitting our planet, two of their units were damaged during testing. Details have not been released and foul play is not suspected, though this amateur video we've obtained from a viewer in Utah, clearly shows a beam of an intense pink light..."

"I do believe that is magenta, John."

"Thank you, Amy..."

Agent Huang thumbed the remote's mute button. "Two of Zenith's systems were damaged in testing? That's not possible!"

"Why is it not possible?

Because, Lou, Zenith is *fully operational,"* she replied. "And they operate completely independent from one another. If they've been damaged, it was not an accident. That pink beam cannot be produced by Zenith, only green.

378

Which leaves one alternative, they were shooting at something... *and it shot back."*

"Holy shit..." breathed Doug Mooreland, pacing. "We need to move fast..."

"Where are we going?"

"Fort Myers Beach. Steele's. First we need info; Lou, find out who got butchered in Chicago. Huang, find out what Zenith was targeting before they got their asses handed to them. Gene, get me more info on the London sighting, Steele can't have been two places at once." He clapped his hands, "Let's go people! The rest of you, get the gear ready and the trucks loaded..."

■ ■ ■

Dr. Michelle Fabry's eyes widened as she watched the Channel 4, Special News Bulletin while she readied herself for work, pouring her morning coffee into her travel mug. Nearly jumping out of her skin when the phone rang, she sloshed coffee across the counter. "Dammit..." The paper towel roll spun out of control, dumping twice what she needed and she didn't bother tearing it off, throwing the wad on the spill before reaching for the phone. "Hello?"

"Are you watching this?"

"The Channel 4 thing?"

"Yeah," replied David. "Now *that* is a UFO..."

Conscious of who might be listening she didn't confirm or deny what she saw. "I'm going to be late if I don't finish getting ready, David. I'll see you at work..."

"Got it."

■ ■ ■

Running to the bathroom in obvious discomfort, the intelligence officer from NIOC left his coffee on the table in the employees' break room of Green Bank Observatory, leaving Michelle Fabry's team alone to chat unfettered. Dr. Fabry looked over at Katie standing at the sink, who had an accomplished little smirk on her face. *"Katie... what did you do?"*

She held up a little bottle of eye drops, sliding it back into her pocket, "A couple drops in his coffee. I saw it in a movie... I guess it really works!"

379

Michelle cracked a smile, "Something tells me you enjoyed that a little too much."

"He had it coming..."

Minus the mapping data on Harding-Konos 452, overnight Sean had uploaded everything they had on the UFO sighting from the rescued thumb drive to the Deep Web, sending out invitations and links to every observatory in the English-speaking world as well as NASA, SETI, media outlets and web news outlets. Scrubbed of digital notations, no one would know the source, so whether it would be viewed as serious or not was anyone's guess but it was pretty convincing. This morning's news of multiple close-up sightings, whether they were connected or not, lent a lot of credibility to it. What they hoped to accomplish was beyond credit or discovery, it seemed the right thing to do, something that people needed to see and be aware of.

The intelligence officer from NIOC wobbled back into the break room looking a little pale, all conversation stopping, not that he'd notice at this point. As he reached for the coffee he'd left on the table his stomach roiled and he turned, quickly heading back to the restroom with a groan.

"I almost feel bad for him," commented Michelle, catching Katie's eye. *"Almost."* Katie giggled, something that sounded innocently cherubic yet sinister somehow, and headed for the front office to prepare for the day's facility tours.

David checked the corridor to the restrooms, "What do we do if we catch something today, Mitch?" he whispered.

Dr. Fabry took a bite of her doughnut, "If the babysitter is around, nothing we can do but follow their protocol. If he's still... *under the weather,* record it on the thumb drives, keep it off the system..."

■ ▨ ▨

The intelligence officer from NIOC was still asleep on the couch in Michelle Fabry's office when David spotted one of the ships in synchronous orbit over southern North America. *"Mitch..."*

"I see it." From the next console she glanced over her shoulder up at the second level, her office door still closed as were the curtains. "Go off-system." She eyed the readouts of data, "I only see one..."

"That's all there is," whispered Sean.

"The others have to be somewhere... keep scanning."

"It's beautiful, isn't it?" observed Samantha, staring at the screen.

"Something sinister about it though," commented Sean.

"My God," breathed Michelle, "I'd give anything to see it up close."

"I was thinking about that news clip," began David, "What do you suppose they meant about the whole; *United Federation of Worlds* part? Do you think that thing in Chicago's linked with this?"

"I wish I knew for sure, but it seems like too much of a coincidence not to be."

"Maybe we should send it a signal."

Michelle gave David a sideways look, unsure if he was serious or not. "NIOC?" she reminded him, knowing they would detect any communications.

■ ■ ■

For Chase Holt and Dan Murphy, stopping at the rendezvous point and waiting in the blazing Nevada sun all day until Jesse arrived later the next evening to pick them up was not an option. Especially when DOE Security teams were hunting for them. They rode all the way back to the motel, staying off the roads, getting back just before dawn. Exhausted, they slept most of the day away, waking up briefly to eat, review their files and deal with damaged equipment and injuries.

Most of it was a blur. Dressed in shorts and a t-shirt, Chase limped from the motel cabin to the motor home, his cactus assaulted leg salved and bandaged, the smell of bacon wafting in the dry desert air causing his stomach to rumble. He hoped it was for their breakfast not just from the restaurant, that would be a cruel tease. Allie and DOG were smart enough to stay in the air conditioning, unwilling to traverse the short distance to the RV even for the promise of bacon.

Chase slid into the dinette next to Dan but the baseball-sized bruise in the middle of his back prevented him from leaning against the seat comfortably.

"How's your leg?" asked Rain, pouring Chase and Dan coffee.

"It stopped burning, thanks. What was that stuff you put on it?"

"Something my grandmama taught me. You probably don't want to know what's in it."

Chase blew the steam off his coffee, "That's OK, I'm good not knowing what's in it." He took a cautious sip, "Where's Jesse?"

"He went to get fuel for the bikes," said Kathy, loading two plates with steaming eggs, bacon and hash browns. "How's your back?"

"Still sore. Like I got hit with a hammer. Did you get everything uploaded last night?"

"Yep, just like you showed me," she replied, sliding the plates across the table.

Chase dribbled some Tabasco sauce on his eggs, "Good girl." He took an entire strip of bacon and crammed it into his mouth, "I hope Jesse's not getting gas thinking we're going back out there again..."

Dan peppered his eggs, "I wanted to see if we could view the damage from that explosion..."

Chase shot him a *what the fuck* look ,"Oh, *hell no!*" he objected. "We go out there again we'll either get caught or get dead. Their security is going to double if not triple after what we saw. And you can bet they're going to have a *major* attitude after missing us the first time. They'll be shooting first, asking questions later." Dan didn't respond, simply taking it in, eating silently without looking up. Rain watched him closely. "Look Dan," said Chase, "I know you think you've got a score to settle for Caroline, but use your head, man..." he pointed a strip of bacon at Rain, "you've got this lovely woman here who obviously cares about you, are you ready to abandon her?"

Surprising everyone, Jesse stuck his head through the RV's door chattering like a chipmunk, "Are you guys listening to the news? Are you listening? You should be listening..." He backed out momentarily, looking up at the RV's roof. "Antenna's up, turn on the TV! *Turn on the TV!* It was all over the radio, people were even talking about it at the gas station..."

■ ■ ■

At TESS's insistence, Jack rolled his legs off the couch in his once familiar living room and sat up, his face in his hands rubbing his eyes. After living on ship for over two years the space seemed large, as personal spaces go. The fact that the cargo shuttle had come down in the middle of the night, the crew clearing out most of his personal effects made it seem even larger. The yellow tape and IRS property confiscation notice that was plastered across the front door lay crumpled on the floor where he'd tossed it. *The government claiming something that wasn't theirs. Go figure. Where did it end..?* Using the laptop from his zombie survival room and a wifi signal from a neighbor's house he watched hours of news video on the internet, hoping to understand the state of current affairs. He was to say the least, more than a little concerned. In some cases, horrified.

It made him sad and angry that he would likely never come back here again; to a place he built and loved. A place he'd called home. A country, *his country*, that seemed to be turning its back on its citizens, terrorism running rampant unchecked by a leadership that failed to lead, a world sliding into anarchy and turmoil. How would it end? Did it have to slide into oblivion or could it be turned around? If it could recover before a collapse, what would it take? Pictures of Veloria's capital city in ruins ran through his mind, seeing the same thing for Chicago, New York and Los Angeles... played out worldwide. Would a nudge into the 25th Century make a difference? He might be able to help with that...

Lisa wandered out of the guest room, "You awake?"

"Yeah, I'm in here," he called.

"Did you sleep out here?"

He shrugged, "Just felt right."

"So what's on the agenda this morning?"

"I need to take a ride over to Chase Holt's house, see if he's heard from mom and dad. I can't believe they just up and disappeared. Unless..."

"Unless what?"

He shook his head, "Nothing..."

She cut him off as he headed for the garage, "Don't nothing me," she shook her finger at him, "what are you thinking?"

Jack reached for the door to the garage, "Maybe they had help..."

"I feel an *or*, or a *but* in there somewhere."

"Maybe they had help because they needed it, *or*, maybe it wasn't their decision." He swung the door open, stepping into the garage, shafts of light streaming though the line of glass block in the east wall. Grabbing a corner of the cloth tarp that covered the entire car he began dragging it off of the Shelby Cobra roadster he'd built what seemed a lifetime ago.

"You're going to take *that?* Way to blend in, Jack. Why don't you take my SUV?"

"Beeecause, I want something with enough power to get out of its own way?" He tugged hard, the tarp sliding off the glassy blue body into a heap on the floor, the pearl white rally stripes gleaming in the muted light. Connected to the zombie room's solar power system, he lifted the fiberglass hood and plucked the charger clips from the battery and hung them on a wall

hook. He eased the hood down and turned the latches, locking it in place. Without power to the whole house, they rolled the aluminum overhead door up manually. "Don't be wandering around, stay in the house..."

Rumbling with a naturally lumpy idle, the 427 Cobra rolled back down the driveway into the street, the side pipes burbling, Steele checking the five point harness before shifting into gear. Lisa pulled the strap on the garage door, giving her brother a final nod before rolling it down till it bounced on the concrete.

He let the clutch out a little too fast and the tires hopped with a chatter as the rear end swung around. Feathering the clutch to settle her down, he smiled to himself, she sounded happy to be awake. He was going to have to shake off the rust or she was going to run away from him. The familiar and welcome sensation of the street, feeling it through the roadster, spoke to him.

Traffic on Estero Boulevard, the main beach drive, was light and he swung the Cobra left from the side street without much of a pause, producing a happy little fishtail, heading toward the San Carlos bridge, garnering a few dirty looks. The hefty V8 cleared its throat, singing its sweet big-block harmony as he shifted gears...

■ ■ ■

Agent Doug Mooreland turned around in the passenger seat of the lead SUV, as it whistled down the interstate, two others following behind in close convoy. "Talk to me, Huang, what did you find?"

Sitting behind him, Agent Mercedes Huang flipped open her lapbook, "This is what Zenith was shooting at, in synchronous orbit over the southwest United States..." she turned the lapbook around for him to see the picture of a space ship against a star studded sky, the moon peeking from behind it. "This is the view from Zenith at Area 51. No idea who approved the shoot order, but the report I managed to access said the first shot was a direct hit with no apparent effect. During Zenith's recharge the target returned fire. Zenith at Dugway never reached full charge before it was hit. Both units are completely destroyed."

"Jesus..." Doug took it and examined it, some of the color leaving his face, a flashback of the ship on Fort Myers Beach running through his head like a newsreel; the exact place they were heading now. He handed it back without speaking, his chest tightening.

Mercedes Huang continued, "Lou found the info on Chicago, they weren't our people, they were contractors..."

Doug looked somewhat relieved, "Thank God. But what the hell were they doing there? Were they rogue?"

"Looks like the Agency put a price on Steele's head..."

"*What?*" Mooreland looked like he was about to go apoplectic. "Who issued that bit of insanity?"

"Deputy Director. Three million," she replied coolly.

Doug was grinding his teeth, " Fucking two-faced son of a bitch..."

"And you know the kind of money and resources some of these contractor companies have, Doug. In some cases their equipment is as good as ours. They intercepted a call from Steele's parents' old residence..."

"What do you mean *old* residence..?"

"Records show the family vacated the house several months ago and the house was sold by an independent realtor on their behalf. The realtor had power of attorney to complete the transaction. The family moving in assumed the old phone number, something about it being a condition of the sale..."

Doug stared at her blankly, further stunned by this revolution. "How long has the Agency been aware of this?"

Mercedes tilted her head in sympathy, "Looks like the Chicago team knew fairly early on. They weren't exactly sitting on the house but the maneuver was rather quick and took them by surprise. *Not* surprising, is they make no assumption of the current location of the Steeles."

Doug was holding his head like he was trying to keep it from exploding. "This is fucking nuts..." His eyes narrowed, "Did the Deputy Director know?"

"There's no indication of that."

Doug rubbed his brow line to release the sudden tension threatening to blow his eyeballs out of his head, "Who gives a realtor power of attorney? That doesn't make any sense... signing your financial rights away to someone you don't know? Who can you possibly trust like that?"

Mercedes chewed on her lower lip, "CIA? FBI maybe? Witness protection program? Didn't I read in one of the files, Steele's old man had friends in the FBI?"

"*Black Two to Black One...*"

Doug spun around in his seat and snatched up the mic, "Go ahead Lou."

"Doug, we just got a sensor hit on Chase Holt's place."

Moorland took a quick glance around, realizing they had just come down off the interstate, heading toward the beach. "Lou, we're going to Holt's. You're with me. Black Three, continue on to Steele's house..."

■ ■ ■

When Steele saw the yellow crime tape on not only Chase Holt's house, but the house right before it, his heart sank. He could vaguely remember the faces of two girls who lived there but for the life of him couldn't remember their names. He idled the Cobra past Holt's and backed it into a neighbor's driveway, leaving it mostly obscured by an Oleander hedge with vibrant pink flowers. He hoped the homeowners had already left for work.

The same IRS notice was plastered on Holt's front door as at his own house, raising his ire, but he resisted the urge to tear it down. He left the tape and notice intact, making his way around the back of the house. While planning a device for entry through the back of the house he made note that the two Jet Skis were missing from the dock... and there were bullet holes in the dock posts. He swept the open yards around him and saw a number of strikes on the far seawall and surrounding pilings. His heart quickened.

Expecting heavy resistance, Steele quickly realized the sliding glass doors were unsecured. Stepping quietly into the kitchen he drew the hybrid 1911 from its shoulder holster, holding it at low ready as he eased cautiously through the house. The place was a shambles of wanton senseless destruction. It hadn't been robbed, it had been assaulted.

In the bedroom he opened the AC vent and reached inside, punching in the code on the hidden keypad, to check Chase's zombie closet, reviewing the inventory before resealing it. Chase departed in a hurry with two, *go bags.* But he'd left long guns and ammo behind. Since the entire money stash was missing, Jack assumed his friend expected an extended absence. Dirty old shoes and clothes lay at the foot of the bed indicating a possible quick change.

In the garage sat a severely disabled pickup truck... which might explain the fight out back if he used the Jet Skis for a quick exit. Skis... *plural.* He walked out to the living room, his eyes scanning the destruction there, a burn mark on the carpet. Smoke? Flash bang? At least he hadn't found any blood. He walked to the side window and looked across at the other house with the yellow tape, that was the other half of the story over there. Maybe he'd find something...

The nose of a black SUV appeared, barely visible, parked at the curb about four or five houses past the one he was looking at. Steele pulled back into the shadows as he watched and waited. No sense in panicking if it was just a neighbor with a black... *Shit. OK, time to panic...*

"Jack..?" TESS' holo-screen appeared above his wrist at the same time as the inquiry in his ear, making him jump. He watched the men in black gear, fan out.

"What?!"

■ ■ ■

Lisa's heart almost jumped into her mouth when she saw the man in the black tactical gear with FBI across his back stroll out past the corner of the house into view, looking at the Gulf Of Mexico as she stared out the living room window at the very same thing. If he continued around the house toward the deck he would walk into the nose of the Reaper sitting there with the ARC system active. Another man walked up next to him and they both turned in the opposite direction heading back toward the front door. She bolted down the hall to the zombie room, activating the command module. "All dogs go to heaven..."

"Hello Lisa Steele, command code accepted."

A clank in the back wall started the process of the door opening, at the same time she realized the laptop was sitting on the floor next to the couch in the living room where Jack had left it. And her leather flight jacket was on the kitchen counter. *"Shit,"* she hissed, sprinting back out into the house.

She scooped up the laptop like a football and as she passed the entry foyer the doorknob rotated, a flash of heat rushing across her body. She slammed into the counter with a wince as she yanked her leather off its marble surface, hustling back up the corridor, closing the office door behind her. She latched it and jumped though the zombie room door, palming the closing mechanism button on the wall. The room was empty now, cleaned out by the shuttle's moving crew, leaving nothing of value behind. She really wanted a bottle of water. "TESS get me Jack."

"Yes, Lisa. Connected."

"Jack..?"

"What?"

"I've got a little problem here! FBI... they're coming in!"

"Get in the Reaper and take off, I've got a bit of a problem myself..."

387

"I'm trapped in this fucking zombie room again!"

"Oh for the love of... Do you have the laptop?"

"Yes."

"Hook it up to the camera system, everything should still have solar power. Wait for them to move out then get your ass out of there."

"OK, got it."

"But take the laptop with you... I gotta go!"

■ ■ ■

They were coming through the front and going around the back, leaving Steele one exit, the side door of the garage. He jammed a wooden spoon between the sliding glass doors and headed for the garage, quickly understanding why they hadn't covered it; it was deadbolted without a key. "Dammit Chase," he breathed. He didn't have time to kick or force it, they would converge on it before he could get it open. It had to be an instant open. Stepping back he drew the 1911 and pumped two quick rounds into the door handle and deadbolt, an entire section of the door disappearing in a shower of sparks and splinters, the door swinging open freely. Ears ringing, Steele tucked the 1911 away and sprinted for the Oleander hedge toward the front of the neighbor's house without looking back, diving over the shoulder height hedgerow, a flurry of pink petals drifting through the air. He rolled, scrambled to his feet and jumped over the door into the Cobra, sliding down into the seat behind the wheel and cranking the key, the 427 rumbling to life.

He managed to get the lap belt on as a pair of arms appeared through the bushes grabbing him by the arm and shoulder, attempting to drag him out of the seat. Startled he popped the clutch and the engine coughed to a stall, half dragging the agent with the FBI patch through the bushes. The arm wrapping around Steele's neck, pinned him back against the rollbar and he strained to reach the key in the dash. He managed to turn it with his fingertips and the engine whined once then twice, the agent doing his best to choke him out. *Cmon baby...* he pleaded silently. The third try succeeding in starting the big power plant, roaring to life with a wicked snarl. As his vision started to gray, another body in black tactical gear appeared around the hedgerow. Steele popped the clutch again, this time mashing the accelerator, producing a roar and smoke as the meaty rear tires spun on the driveway pavers, the rear end swinging as he steered it into the street, the tires chattering on the change of pavement as he feathered the clutch to let them bite. The Cobra dragged the agent through the hedges, bouncing the other off the front fender before snapping back, flinging the agent off over the trunk like a ragdoll.

The little blue and white monster screamed down the street, tires smoking, breathing fire from the sidepipes.

■ ■ ■

Everyone else was in a full out run for the SUVs but the best Lou could do was hobble at a quick pace, having barely survived his stint as a slingshot projectile.

The SUV slid to a stop next to him, a door flinging open, hands reaching out and dragging him into the back seat. *"Go! Go! Go!"* The driver stomped on the accelerator, the door slamming shut of its own weight, as he wheeled the heavy SUV around, over the sidewalk and grass, the big tires tearing up the lawn before dropping back down over the curb, back on the street.

"I almost had him..." groaned Lou.

"You weren't even close." Doug picked up the mic, "Black Three, *Black Three!*"

"Black Three, go ahead..."

"This is Black One, We're on Steele! Lock on to our transponder, we're in pursuit..."

"On our way, Black One."

Doug had to brace himself for the turn, the SUV's tires howling. "Get us some air support!"

■ ■ ■

Steele wasn't sure what was worse, weaving through a dogfight, or weaving through traffic. The neighborhood was tight and full of dead end streets. One bad choice and he was screwed. Street signs and houses whipped past in a blur and he didn't recognize the main thoroughfare, Coronado Parkway, until he was crossing it, slamming on the brakes, smoke pouring off all four tires as he skidded to a stop. Dropping the Cobra in reverse the wheels hopped as he powered backwards into the intersection, the two black SUVs growing rapidly in his rear view mirror. He yanked and released the handbrake swinging the nose around with a snap of the wheel, popping it back into first gear, the car fishtailing up the street toward Cape Coral Parkway where he could take a bridge over the Caloosahatchee River.

389

Having to weave through residential traffic the SUVs caught up swiftly. He was faster but he didn't have the option to jump curbs or obstacles, his car was too low, built for racing not off-roading. One of the SUVs jumped the landscaped median, weaving between palm trees to reach the unused oncoming lanes in an attempt to outpace him and cut him off. Ahead the traffic came to a stop.

TESS chirped in his ear, "Admiral, I have tapped into the global positioning satellite system; turn right at the next street." Steele pulled hard, breaking and downshifting, sliding the Cobra around the corner, the tires screaming and smoking, swinging wide to avoid cars pulling in and out of a corner mini mart, drifting up the street sideways before the car snapped straight again, the engine snarling, the sidepipes popping as he shifted.

In the rearview mirror he watched the first truck jump the curb and run the sidewalk before dropping into the street again. He was too busy weaving past slower cars to see more, the speedometer sweeping up toward 100 mph. Catching air over an intersecting street the Cobra landed squarely, a shower of sparks fanning out behind it as it flashed between crossing cars, threading the needle.

"Turn left," chirped TESS, "it will take you to the Parkway to cross the bridge..." Downshifting and standing on the brakes he slid into the next intersection sideways, breaking to the left, popping the clutch to power up the street, the rearview momentarily free of big black SUVs.

He jumped into traffic on Cape Coral Parkway near the bridge heading over the river and breathed a little easier though he didn't completely let up, maintaining a speed considerably greater than the traffic, making his way through easily but more cautiously, continually checking his mirrors. It appeared he'd succeeded in losing them, whoever they were... Maybe they were FBI, maybe they weren't, he wasn't going to stop and ask for IDs.

"Jack?" TESS' hologram appeared above his wrist but he didn't so much as glance away from the traffic or the road, constantly moving and jogging around slower traffic.

"Lisa?"

"I'm clear, I'm airborne. I don't know what you did but they left here in a hurry. You OK?"

"I'm good. You got the laptop?"

"Yep. My TESS has your position, where do you want to meet? You probably don't want to come back here..."

"Right. I'm almost across the river now, let me think about that for a minute..." He checked his mirrors and slowed for traffic ahead. "Ooh, I know, there's a little airfield off Route 41... Where Stephen Miles used to keep his..."

The Cobra's hood and left fender erupted in dust and debris as shreds and strands of fiberglass blew over the windshield, a string of jagged holes appearing in front of him, the windshield spidering as bullets blew through it on an angle across the passenger side, punching holes through the seat next to him. Time slowed down as the left tire exploded, shredding, chunks of rubber tearing through the fender, flying up over the hood and windshield, yanking on the car and pulling it toward the center divider. Steele fought with the Cobra as it swung hard left, correcting stiffly, careening off the center concrete wall with a spray of disintegrating fiberglass and sparks, the image of two armed men in black and a black SUV parked on the other side of the wall flashing past, watching him go by.

Steele yanked on the wheel, steering away from the wall and downshifting, stomped on the accelerator, the fender tearing away with an agonizing crackle, the engine working hard to produce power, spewing its life's oil across the pavement, fuel spraying across the engine block and running through the holes in the torn hood, spattering what was left of the windshield.

There was a flash as it all ignited at once, angry red and orange flames reaching up around the body on the left, licking up through the right fender and through the holes in the shredded hood. She was done. His baby was gone. He let the wheel go and she drifted back to the wall, grinding along the concrete, leaving pieces of herself behind before she came to rest. Feeling the heat through the aluminum racing tub, the floor carpet began to smoke as he unbuckled, flinging the straps clear. Black smoke billowed up from underneath as the tires caught and the oil burned, the sickening sweetness of the flaming fiberglass, painfully gagging. He climbed over the passenger door, nuggets of glass spilling across the pavement like diamonds glittering on the asphalt. He ignored the voices calling for him to stop, and staggered, running across the roadway, a little wobbly at first as he gained his legs back and the adrenalin flooding his body pushed him forward.

■ ■ ■

Lisa saw it all, reflected in her brothers face on her TESS's screen even though he never looked at his unit, the video and audio feed displaying the chaos, unabated. Amidst the fury he didn't or couldn't respond to her calls.

The two TESS units synched, she was tracking his movements, accurate to within five feet as she doubled back from the airport, covering the ten mile span in the blink of an eye.

Thunder exploded in the crystal clear blue sky with a flash of lightning as the Reaper arrived above the scene at little more than treetop level, the ARC system shutdown revealing the angry black Reaper screaming over, overshooting, swinging flatly around in level flight, sliding sideways in an arc, front turret sweeping the chaos below.

The news helicopter arriving on the scene nearly dropped into the trees from the turbulence created when the black ship appeared, recovering over the golf course, keeping its distance from the alien craft.

Lisa swept in low over the golf course where Jack was headed, never turning her back on the chaos. The roof of the black SUV on the other side of the bridge popped open, two halves of a circle splitting down the middle, a minigun turret appearing between the protective halves, her threat screen instantly alerting her of it presence. She tapped the right rudder pedal, the maneuvering jets swinging the nose to bring her nose turret to bear, the gun pipper settling over the target. "Don't you do it asshole..."

The operator with the minigun spun the barrels up and a stream of fire lanced up at her, the shields absorbing the rather small rounds, the sound not unlike rain on the roof of a car. She flipped the safety clear and blipped the trigger, the Cryo Gauss Guns firing three rounds, the turret's chain feed clacking quickly as the concrete wall exploded around the truck, cratering it with holes the size of garbage can lids, the third passing through the truck, blowing it apart, splitting it in half, adding to the flaming wreckage on the bridge.

Having lost sight of her brother she coasted the Reaper backwards, watching the remaining operators dashing across the road and down the gentle grass slope towards the golf course. Blue and red lights converged on the insanity below from all directions, but it was the chirping of the markers on the threat screen that caught her attention. One low and slow appearing well inside her range, *helicopter*, and four high and fast... *Dammit, fighters.* She needed Jack up and out as fast as possible. Two black SUVs were pushing their way through traffic across the bridge from her left and the helicopter was coming in low on her right, over the strip mall south of the golf course.

■ ■ ■

The landscaped island between the greens, which would unfairly be called *the rough*, was a welcome sight with its stand of palm trees, Steele's lungs screaming for a rest after their recent scorching. An icy cold drink, a shady cabana, and a beach would be better, but this wasn't a vacation after all...

He cleared the sculpted hedges and when he landed, his left leg collapsed underneath him, sending him crashing to his hands and knees in a roll. The searing hot poker of pain in his thigh told him something was more than just a little wrong as he rolled on his back, pulling the hybrid 1911 from its shoulder holster. He didn't want to look but hazarded a glance while scrambling awkwardly behind the closest palm tree, a massive Canary Island Date Palm. It wasn't the best cover, palm trees being rather soft and porous, but it was the best he had available. The exit hole in his thigh was about the size of his thumb. He was right, looking made it worse. *He shouldn't have looked.*

"*Son of a bitch,*" he breathed through clenched teeth. "These assholes are really starting to get on my last nerve..."

"*Jack! Jack... where are you?*"

"Under the trees. I'm hit, I can't run any farther."

"*How bad?*"

"Bad enough, I don't have anything to stop the bleeding..."

"*I'll land, there's a med kit in the Reaper...*"

"NO! Stay up there... no sense in both of us getting nabbed. We're not handing them that bird."

"*Your twelve o'clock, Jack!*"

On one elbow, Steele rolled from concealment, his artificial eye zooming in, his gun coming up and the sights lining up instantly, squeezing off one round, the agent running at him with the submachine gun dropping backwards off his feet, a spray of blood exploding through his back, his tactical armor useless. A glance to his right and he could see the black helicopter past the Reaper, a team fast-roping down at the far end of the golf course. "Chopper on your right!"

"*I see it.*"

Steele saw the glint of sunlight on the gold canopy before he heard them, a pair of F-22 Raptors coming down, head on with Lisa's Reaper. Then he noticed the two higher up. *"Lisa!* You're being set up! *Get out of here!"*

"I see them, I'm not blind..."

"Lisa they're going to pass you, the two above will drop on you from behind... *Get out of here!"*

"On the left!" she shouted.

Steele saw the nose of the Reaper swing, the turret rotating, the Cryo Gauss Guns thundering a short burst, the rounds passing over him, a vacuum of air imploding, the palm trees swaying. By the time he rolled to look to his left, a flaming black SUV sailed into the air in mangled chunks, vehicle-sized craters disfiguring the once-manicured green. He covered his head, a rain of dirt, sand and grass falling around him, the second SUV nose-dived into a hole, crushing it's front end less than a hundred feet away.

The two low F-22s swept in low, a high pitched scream turning into rolling thunder as they passed overhead, their gold canopies gleaming in the sunlight. They began an upward sweep. Steele figured they didn't fire because of the neighborhood beyond the golf course. The flights would switch places; the high flight would come down and do the first pass the low flight go high and turn back for their run. In that direction collateral damage would be the bridge or the river. He searched the sky over his shoulder, he couldn't see the other two, but the color of his vision was fading, "You're a sitting duck, Lisa... get moving..." he said drowsily.

■ ■ ■

Lisa was watching her scope as well as everything surrounding her, the multitude of vehicles, lights, people, her brother... She eyed the threat indicator, the chirping becoming more insistent as the top flight of F-22s descended on her position. She didn't want to have to shoot them down, but she would if they forced her to. Completely out of visual sight, the gun pipper was already locked onto the first jet, another marker locked onto his wingman. She could kill them with her guns at this distance easily. The other two were notations on the screen, still facing away from her. When they turned in her direction the computer would lock them in too.

She could see the reflection of their cockpits as they dove in, the target marker displaying their speed at 1200 miles per hour. She was going to have to time this just right... Cranking the anti-gravity actuator on the throttle while pulling the handle into the negative, catapulted the Raptor upward and back, leaving only empty space for the F-22's twenty millimeter cannon shells. It suddenly disappeared from view altogether, dissolving as Lisa activated the ARC system.

■ ■ ■

Major Less McArthur, 43rd Fighter Squadron, 325th Fighter Wing out of Tyndall Air Force Base, got the order; *"Shoot it down."*

The Major looked out over his wing, his wingman falling back for their gun pass. He keyed his mic. "Yellow Jackets, we're cleared for guns only. Guns only. How do you copy?" Each member of the flight acknowledged. He flexed his gloved fingers around the flight stick, "Lead, is beginning the first run..."

"Copy Lead, second element in position for cleanup..."

The Major lined up on the flat black craft, hanging motionless, the targeting pipper pickling the target with an indicator and lock tone, a targeting solution showing him where to shoot. The air around his Raptor compressed, a sonic boom trailing behind him and his wingman as they punched through Mach 1, approaching Mach 2. He released the safety with his thumb and squeezed the trigger, "Guns guns guns..." the 20 millimeter Gatling on the right side of his plane mounted in the wing root spun up, producing a quick *bbbrrraaattt* sound as the rounds lanced downward. The target shot straight upward prompting him to quickly release the trigger, the short burst drawing a dirty line on the green velvet of the golf course below. His eyes followed the ship upward as it disappeared before his very eyes, dissolving in thin air. "What the fu..." He pulled back on the stick, leveling off, flashing over the bridge and began to climb, heading back to altitude, grunting through the G forces.

"Mac, where the hell did it go?"

Major McArthur craned his neck, looking around, "Damned if I know... What the hell was that thing?" He checked his radar, the screen blank, his electronics showing static. "I just lost avionics..." He looked back, relieved to see his wingman still in formation. "Hello? Yellow Jacket Lead; can anyone hear me?"

■ ■ ■

Covered in sand and bits of grass that was still floating down, Steele rolled over at the sound of footfalls running up behind him, the muzzle of his 1911 leading the way, a figure in black rushing towards him. His eye zoomed in, the sights lining up, his vision blurry, forcing him to squint. The woman in black tactical gear dropped a duffel at her feet, her hands going up.

"Don't shoot! I'm unarmed..." She nodded towards the bag with the red cross on it, "I'm a medic."

He nodded sedately, his gun hand and the 1911 dropping slowly to his stomach as he lay on his back, "Fine..."

She snatched up the bag and moving swiftly, dropped to her knees at his side, unzipping the bag as she eyed the pool of blood soaking into the grass. "Damn, you've lost a lot of blood..."

He looked up at her face, as she concentrated on stopping the bleeding. "Looks like you lost some too," he waved, indicating the laceration across her forehead. "How'd you get that?"

"We'll share war stories later, we need to get you out of here..." she said looking around, people closing in from across the golf course. "Are you Jack Steele?"

"That would be me..." he replied slowly, "Admiral Jack Steele, United Federation of Worlds, citizen of these United States of Amer... "

"Oh good! You found him..."

Steele turned his head, focusing on the man walking up behind the woman who was doing her best to keep him from bleeding to death. The man's face was covered in blood and some of his gear was missing, his tactical uniform looking burnt and tattered, his bare right arm blistered and blackened. A handgun hung from his left hand. "Geez," said Jack slowly, "you should probably sit down, you don't look so good..."

Doug Mooreland waved his gun,"Get out of the way Mercy, I'm just going to finish him off. Fuck it. I'm tired of all this. Pete is dead because of him, most of my team is gone, he's ruined my life..."

"Sit down, Doug," she said without looking back, "you're in shock..."

"Nah, I'm fine. C'mon, move Mercy... *Move!*"

Hidden by her position over his body, she slid the 1911 out from under Steele's hand, keeping it hidden against her body, "OK fine, Doug. You want to throw it all away? Go ahead, be a dumbass..." As she turned, the muzzle appeared between her arm and body underneath her armpit, clearing as she twisted, squeezing off two rounds producing a three foot flame, the first round low, exploding through his pelvis, his body crumpling, collapsing backward as the second passed through his ballistic vest under the sternum and came out through his shoulder taking the arm with it. He was dead before he hit the grass. She turned back around and looked down at the gun, "What the hell is this thing?"

"That is a custom made, .45 caliber, charged particle blaster..." Steele annunciated slowly, taking it out of her hand and with some effort, sliding it into its shoulder holster. His head rolled to the other side following the noise, a team of officers running in their direction. "Uh, oh... they don't look too happy. I think somebody's in trouble..."

CHAPTER THIRTY ONE

FLORIDA, FORT MYERS: *MERCY ME*

Sheriff Frank Naywood couldn't believe what he was seeing, a war zone over his municipal golf course, pyres of fire and smoke on the bridge and fairway. He had to believe it had something to do with the whole *Steele-Holt-Murphy* thing. And that pissed him off to no end that it had boomeranged back into his jurisdiction again.

Standing on the top of his patrol car in the parking lot near the clubhouse at the far end of the course, he stared at the scene through binoculars, having witnessed the run on the black object by the F-22s from Tyndall Air Force Base. The departure of the black object seemed to have an adverse effect on electricity and electronics over a fairly sizable area, the news chopper having to put down on the putting green near the pro shop, narrowly avoiding a crash. He wondered if that's why two of the F-22s departed, leaving the other two patrolling at altitude.

Radio contact with the SWAT team was spotty at best but he was fairly certain they were going to reach the man on the island between the fairways. He hoped they'd get there safely before that *thing* returned.

FBI Agent Phil Cooper climbed up on the trunk of the Sheriff's car, holding his hand out for the binoculars, "May I?"

Frank handed them over, "Glad you could make it."

"What did I miss?"

"Not sure I could accurately describe it, Mr. Cooper. You may have to watch the news footage. I know I'm going to have to..."

"There's two people up there now."

Naywood nodded, "There were two, then three, now two again. The newest arrival to the meeting got shot... I'm seeing FBI on their gear, are they your people?"

"Nope. SWAT team is closing in..."

Frank Naywood stuck his hand out, "Let me see?"

Phil Cooper handed back the binoculars, "Why didn't your team drive in?"

Naywood was watching the SWAT team's advance through the binoculars, "Because that *thing;* whatever it was, doesn't seem to like vehicles very much..."

What could only be described as an absolutely massive formation of multicolored ball lightning, appeared over the river on the far side of the bridge, almost fluid tendrils of light reaching out and dancing in all directions, skipping across the water, feeling for the edge of the bridge, gingerly touching the tops of the tall palms lined along the river.

Phil Cooper's mouth dropped open, "Frank... to the right..."

The Sheriff turned the binoculars on it, "What in God's name..."

The clear blue sky split with deafening thunder and a ring of lightning, like the hand of God reaching downward, the Earth shaking, a downward blast of hurricane force wind, palm trees instantly shedding palm fronds, a brief rain falling from the clear sky as a result of the severely compressed air, the phenomenon suddenly producing a dark shape casting a massive shadow across the golf course.

■ ■ ■

"GOD jump complete in: three, two, one... and we're clear..."

Commander Brian Carter had his hands full in the command chair of the Revenge, Maria in the first officer's seat. "Tactical, shield status?"

"Commander; coming up now... all port, topside, bow and stern zones at one-hundred percent. Starboard and belly zones zero for recovery, that side..."

Brian nodded, "Helm, maintain anti-grav, no legs, descend to ramp contact height."

"Aye sir, descending."

"All guns manned and armed?"

"Aye, sir. Commander, we have air threats inbound."

Brian turned to Maria, "Lieutenant?"

"Aye, Commander." She keyed her mic, "Revenge to R1, copy?"

"Reaper One, go ahead."

"Fuel and weapons status?"

"Eighty percent fuel, plenty of ordnance."

Maria smiled a knowing little smile, the response from Lisa positive and full of confidence, "You've got no back seater, can you still chase off a few bogies?"

"Roger, Revenge. Weapons clear?"

Brian turned to Maria shaking his head, "No. Only if it's absolutely necessary."

■ ■ ■

The SWAT team blown to the ground, Mercedes Huang threw herself over Steele's body, trying to maintain the elevation of his IV bag, palm fronds dropping across her back, the air filled with static electricity. When the wind subsided she sat back up, the debris falling away, the sky above them obscured by something long and dark, a heavy shadow cast over them. She stared up at it, her mouth hanging open.

Steele looked up at the belly of the Revenge off to their left, floating motionless a hundred feet off the fairway. "Oh, I think my ride's here..."

Mercedes continued to stare up in amazement, "This thing is *yours?"*

"Uh, huh. But you should see the *big one...*"

"Big one..?" she squeaked.

The ship seemed to simply sink as it dropped closer to the ground, Mercedes aware of a strange electric tingling crawling across her entire body. With a metallic clang and a rolling sound, a large armor panel popped outward on the side of the hull and it slid upwards, almost flush with the hull, revealing a reinforced door behind it, swinging inward with a hydraulic hiss, creating a sizable black opening. The ship halted its descent a few feet from the ground, a ramp extending from the belly...

■ ■ ■

"Reaper, copy." Hovering on anti-gravity over the golf course at three-hundred feet with her ARC system active, halfway between the Revenge and the clubhouse, Lisa kept everyone below in an electronics blackout. She toggled the system off, activating her shields, startling almost everyone with her sudden appearance. She rotated the anti-gravity actuator, sailing flatly upwards, her engines thumping as she throttled up, shooting off. "TESS?"

"Yes, Lisa?"

Lisa grabbed the holographic screen and placed it where she could keep an eye in it. "See if you can locate the radio frequency used by the military jets."

"I will only be able to locate it if they are actually transmitting..."

"Then let's give them something to talk about." Lisa adjusted her sensors, locking a missile to a Raptor about fifty miles away.

"Searching for signals," noted TESS.

"I'm being painted, I'm being painted..! He's got a lock on me...!"

"Aggressor at fifty miles and closing..."

"Tyndall Control to Yellow Jackets, you are clear to engage! Take it out!"

"Good TESS, that's the one. Can we transmit on that?"

"Yes Lisa."

Lisa punched the throttle a little, pulling it back almost in the same motion, her speed exceeding Mach 2, shooting past the two approaching F-22s underneath them, then curling the Reaper into a climb to bleed off the speed, finishing a half loop putting her twenty-thousand feet above them and fifty miles behind them. She canceled her missile lock. "Yellow Jackets, this is the black craft you have engaged, can you hear me?"

"Unidentified craft, this is Captain Luke Speek, 43rd Fighter Squadron, identify yourself. You are in American airspace, you are ordered to depart our nation's airspace or be shot down."

Lisa activated her ARC system and keyed her mic, "Captain, this is Ensign Lisa Steele, United Federation of Worlds, Task Force Lancer. That ship below you is the Revenge and we are here to pick up our man, we will be out of your hair momentarily..." Eight new markers were inbound on Lisa's scope from the panhandle of Florida at Mach 1; she could see them the moment they left the ground.

"United Federation of... What?"

ARC system on, nearly invisible, Hecken Noer's special coating confounded radar signals, allowed Lisa to ease in behind the F-22s, flying a close chevron formation, the nose of her Reaper in between their wingtips. *"Worlds.* United Federation of *Worlds.* In case you haven't noticed, these ships aren't from around here... And when I say that, I mean *planet.* This is by your definition, a *UFO."* She toggled off the ARC system, the Reaper appearing in between them. "See, can you do this..?"

"Break! Break! Break!" They rolled outward, splitting, winging over in full afterburner, curling away from the black ship in opposite directions.

Lisa took the Reaper to Mach 2 to intercept the new threats that were descending on the Revenge, the air thundering behind her. She keyed her mic, "Do not engage us, gentlemen," she warned sternly, "it will not end well for you..."

■ ■ ■

Armed with Pulsar carbines, the UFW Space Marines waited at the door in full combat armor for the go signal. Sergeant Draza Mac checked their gear as he walked through the group, "This is not an assault, boys, let's not shoot anybody unless we have to..." there was some lighthearted grumbling and gaffes. "We're here to scoop up the Admiral. So let's, stay on mission. Got it?!"

"Aah*Woo!"* they replied in unison, a five-hundred year old UFW Space Marine battle cry, an ingrained tradition based on the attack call used by the Jalezian Timber Wolf.

"This is a highly volatile and hostile situation, that's why we're going in with the heavy armor. I know it's slow and heavy, but we're not going very far..."

■ ■ ■

Mercedes Huang liked to think of herself as an enlightened person; worldly, traveled, knowledgeable, intelligent, privy to some of the most important secrets and technology her government had to protect. But as unprepared as she was to absorb what she was seeing, failing to fully comprehend that the ship she was looking at was indeed a real alien UFO, she was equally unprepared for the appearance of Space Marines... vastly different from what she saw on the videos Doug showed her at the Barn... *The Barn,* they had left it just a couple hours ago, *it seemed like a week...*

Emerging from the black opening in the side of the ship, figures emerged, tromping heavily down the ramp, fully armored like bipedal tanks, no human features of any kind visible through the gold visors to indicate what they might be. Were they robots? Androids? "Aah*Woo!"* they chanted, dropping to the grass, eight of them spreading out in a tactical combat formation, strange looking weapons in their hands. The whole thing looking like something out of a Hollywood movie... fantastical, surreal, dreamlike.

Her blood ran cold with the realization it was all too real, all too frightening. Although she didn't realize it, she was shaking like a leaf, flooded with adrenalin, wanting to run, filled with dread, speechless, nearly frozen with fear. Two of the mechanical men tromped over to them and she tried to scoot back, her breath halting, her heart hammering. But she found her wrist locked in a vice-like grip. Looking down she realized Steele was

402

looking up at her, clutching her arm, "It's OK," was all he said. It wasn't so much *what* he said, but the *way* he said it... warm, calm, relaxed.

"Litter! We need a litter!" called one of the two Marines over his shoulder.

"No time," said the other, handing his long gun to his partner. He dropped to a knee, "How are you doing Admiral?" His voice was mechanical through the armor's external speaker.

"Better now, Sergeant Mac."

Draza Mac eyed the body laying in the grass behind Mercedes, "Looks like your handiwork..."

"My gun, her shooting..."

Mercedes' eyes darted from one to the other, curiously listening to the exchange, only understanding Steele.

"Let's get you to the infirmary, sir." Draza Mac slid his armored arms as gently as possible under Steele's body, lifting him almost effortlessly, the suit's power assist doing most of the work. Mercedes Huang rose with them, still clutched by the wrist in Steele's grasp, still holding the IV bag. "What about her?" asked the Sergeant.

"She comes with..."

Thunder rolled in the clear blue sky prompting Draza Mac to look up, "Time to go," he commented, "we have company coming..." The Sergeant caught movement from past the armless corpse laying in the grass, just below the rise in the rolling green, spinning his body to protect the Admiral with his armor, the rattle of a silenced submachine gun cut short by a return volley from several Pulsar carbines, the blue-white beams lancing out, electricity crackling, the security team hitting the target several times.

"Target is down..."

Steele lost his grip and Mercedes tumbled to the ground in Draza Mac's violent maneuver. She lay crumpled where she fell, motionless, the IV bag still clutched in her hand. "Lou, you fucking asshole..." she gurgled, spitting blood, her world going black.

■ ■ ■

After yesterday's startling news report, both Chase and Dan had been at a loss of what to say or do. Could it have been a hoax of some kind? A government false flag operation? To what end? It was stunning. If Jack were indeed back, what was he doing? It didn't make a whole lot of sense. But they did come to the conclusion that Steele may have had something to do with the events at Area 51 and Dugway. It seemed as likely an explanation as anything else they could come up with.

For the time being, working on the dirt bikes seemed the only thing to do at this point, having taken quite a beating from their last ride. The wide canopy attached to the side of the motor home gave a shady place to work, the dry desert breeze waffling the fabric above them while they worked.

"Man I can't even sweat," complained Dan Murphy, rag in hand. "It dries as soon as I perspire."

"Reminds me of the sandbox," mumbled Chase.

Reclined in the hammock, Jesse watched Dan try to clean the dust off the various nooks and crannies of his dirt bike, "You're wasting your time, Dan..."

Dan threw his hands up, "I know I know. I'm bored, I don't know what else to do... we haven't heard a peep from the Commandery..."

"Chase!" Karen trotted up from their cabin, his laptop under her arm. She dropped to her knees beside him; laying the laptop on the seat of the dirt bike he was working on and opening its screen. "There's a message for you here on the comms board, posted at three in the morning last night... From *Starwalker & WonderDog...*"

"Who? *Starwalker & Wonderdog...*" they said together. They stared at each other for a moment, his eyes widening.

Chase Holt flicked his attention to Dan then back to Karen, "Noooo, it couldn't be... Could it? No, it *has* to be a coincidence..." His hands greasy he pointed at the laptop, "Open the message."

"I can't, it's passworded..."

"Nobody does that on our comms board," he frowned, grabbing up a rag and wiping his hands on the towel to clean them off. He typed in several different attempts, failing all. *"Starwalker & Wonderdog..."* he said slowly, "I wonder if it's this simple..." typing in; *Jack & Fritz.* The message popped open on the screen. "Son of a bitch, it *is* him..."

"What does it say?" asked Karen, leaning in.

"Say's he's looking for his mom and dad; he'll stop by in the morning to say hi..." He went from kneeling to sitting in the sand, staring at the screen, "His parents live in *Chicago...*"

"Yesterday's news..." breathed Karen.

"Yeah," he mumbled in a trance, imagining his house wrapped in crime tape. *Where would Steele go from there?*

Dancing Rain came running out of the cabin waving her arms, "Hurry, you need to *see this..!"*

■ ■ ■

"Good morning, I'm John Griff..."

"And I'm Amy Halloran."

"And this is a *Channel 4, Breaking News Special...*" continued the news anchor. John Griff looked intensely into the camera, "We're interrupting your regularly scheduled program to bring you this very important breaking news. A little over twenty-four hours ago we brought you coverage of the sudden deadly violence that broke out on the north side of Chicago and this very strange unidentified flying craft at the scene..." The screen split, the video coverage playing on one half of the screen. "Well today that same craft is seen here, in the Fort Myers area, along the Gulf of Mexico." The video on the split screen played nearly live coverage, edited with elements from viewer contributions.

The camera switched to Amy Halloran. "It started early this morning with a high speed vehicle chase through the neighborhoods of Cape Coral, originating at this home; owned by a man named Chase Holt." The split screen showed the house, then the route the chase took. "Authorities pursued the vehicle, later found to belong to this man; Jack Steele, of Fort Myers Beach." The video showed a picture of the wrecked and burning Cobra on the bridge, a DMV picture of Jack appeared on the screen.

Anchorman John Griff continued, "Authorities used force to stop the vehicle here as it came down the bridge into Fort Myers, the driver exiting the crashed vehicle and running onto the municipal golf course..."

"A very dangerous situation, John."

"Yes it is Amy. It was there, over the golf course, that the mysterious flying craft appeared again, exchanging fire with authorities..."

The video and news broadcast continued, the footage from the news chopper continuing to roll, playing back all the events including its own near-disaster. The spectacular appearance of the much larger ship sat everyone in the cabin back, dumfounded. Except for Dan Murphy, he'd seen it before. He'd *lived* it before. He picked up the television remote and muted the sound. "That's not the same ship... As the one on the beach, I mean."

Chase raised an eyebrow, "How can you tell?"

"It's... different. The shape. And this one's even black in the daylight... the other one was more of a dark gray or dark silver."

"What does this all mean?" asked Karen.

Dan pointed at the laptop, "I think it means you'd better answer Steele's message." He hit the mute button again returning the sound to the end of the news bulletin.

The anchorman looked into the camera, "At a news conference in Washington just a few minutes ago, the President was asked by reporters about the significance of the appearance of these strange craft. He was quoted as saying; *This is the first I'm hearing about it, you guys know as much as I do.*"

"He doesn't seem to know much, does he, John..."

"No he doesn't, Amy."

■ ■ ■

"This would be a whole lot easier if I could shoot them..." breathed Lisa, looking out over the open water of the Gulf of Mexico.

"Only if you are forced to protect yourself or the Revenge," TESS reminded her.

"I know, I know..." She leaned the Reaper over gently, angling in on the two flights of four F-22s approaching from Tyndall, on their flank, the ARC system active. About two thousand feet of altitude separated the two flights and she intended to pass between and ahead of them. Reaching forward, her gloved fingers pipped on her ordnance stores screen, making some selections, "Three should be enough to make an impression..." she mused, flagging the items for atmospheric use. She adjusted throttle, dropping the Reaper to below Mach 1, allowing the ship's skin to cool, reducing the chance of it being visible. Flying with shields didn't allow the skin to heat up, but then again you were fully visible. She never found out why the ARC system and shields couldn't be used together, she wasn't about to experiment on her own, either.

The flights had all switched channels for security, their previous selection compromised, but TESS had been able to locate the new frequency. Lisa had been listening in and what she heard was disturbing. All flights had been cleared to attack and shoot down either the Reaper or the Revenge by any means necessary. Collateral damage was anticipated and acceptable.

406

Four more fighter aircraft appeared on Lisa's sensor sweep as they left the ground from Naval Air Station Key West, an AWACS from MacDill Air Force Base in Tampa and four more from Homestead Air Force Base.

Lisa switched to her UFW frequency, "Reaper One to Revenge... status?"

"Recovering the Admiral now, R1. Stand by..."

"Can you step it up, Revenge? It's starting to look like a convention up here and my dance card is overflowing..."

She quickly switched back to the USAF frequency, clicking her mic, *"Currahee!"* she shouted, thumbing the decoy release with her left thumb as she passed in front of the flights of F-22s.

The free-flight drones she configured and armed, appeared seemingly out of thin air, fired from dispensing racks through launch tubes in the Reaper's belly, momentarily disturbing the reflective camouflage. Rocket-propelled with oscillating fins, they flew erratically, flashing visible and IR strobes with low grade lasers, an assortment of jamming electronics cycling on and off, confusing and disrupting targeting systems.

Hearing the reactions on their radio chatter she realized the ploy had the desired effect, the markers on her screen separating into pairs and breaking in various directions. She throttled up, climbing straight up, rolling over and button-hooking back toward the Fort Myers area.

"Revenge to R1, extraction complete. Repeat, extraction complete. Heading to exit route. Proceed to rendezvous, best course."

"Copy that." The *exit route,* coordinates in the center of the Gulf... Draw a line from Tampa to Tampico, Mexico, and another from New Orleans to Merida in the Yucatan. The intersecting point was the exit coordinate.

All civilian air traffic either diverted, canceled or forced to land, her sensors were empty of clutter allowing Lisa to concentrate on what mattered; aircraft with the capability to shoot her down. And covering the Revenge, of course. This is where someone in the rear seat would be helpful. *Two sets of eyes on the sensors were better than one...*

■ ■ ■

Yellow Jacket Three and Four were the remaining element of Captain Luke Speek's original flight of F-22s, he and his wingman in Yellow Jacket One and Two having had to return to Tyndall without avionics.

Having experienced the hijack of their military channels twice already, Three and Four had gone dark, and they were hunting. Rotating radio frequencies and brief, cryptic messages, simple microphone clicks and sign language, Captain Alan Scott communicated to his wingman he was getting a radar profile as they flew at supercruise, just below Mach 2. Descending, trading superior altitude for speed, they closed gradually, the computer working on a lock and missile firing solution. Captain Scott had no illusions of getting close enough for guns, the *thing* was too fast for that. But he fully expected the AIM-120 AMRAAM's Mach 4 speed would be sufficient to catch it if they were close enough. He couldn't think of anything that could outrun it, except *maybe* an SR-71 Blackbird. The problem was, he needed to close to a distance that would allow the AMRAAM to catch the target before it ran out of fuel, the outside range being just under sixty miles.

At twenty-four miles a solid growl in Scott's headset matched the diamond appearing over the target box floating on his HUD, the word *SHOOT* blinking at him. *Come to daddy, bitch...* "Fox Three, Fox Three..." His gloved thumb squeezed the firing button on his flight stick, the center bay doors on the belly of the jet opening, the AVEL, *AMRAAM Vertical Ejection Launcher,* flinging an AIM-120 clear of the fuselage, the doors closing again, the whole process taking less than two seconds, it's solid rocket engine lighting, streaking away, accelerating to Mach 4.

A matching missile left his wingman's F-22, closely pacing his own and he watched them close in on the target. The chase was on and he throttled to full afterburner, his wingman hanging tightly on his wing. Captain Scott selected another missile from his weapons stores...

"Scott, I have visual..."

As they closed, it appeared so suddenly, just a spec at this distance, Alan Scott momentarily dismissed it. "I see it..." As his thumb hovered over the fire button there was a blue flicker then a giant comet tail as the *thing* appeared to take an instant ninety degree deviation straight upward. "She's going vertical..."

Scott pulled, grunting through the intense Gs, his wingman falling back but staying with him. "It's fucking accelerating," he grunted, the nose of his F-22 pointing straight up. "Mach 3... Mach 4... Mach 5... Mach 6... Jesus, it's gone..." He pulled the Raptor on its back at fifty-five-thousand feet, brought it level and rolled it upright looking up through the canopy, his eyes searching for something. Anything. Throttling back he dropped one wing in a gentle sweeping turn heading back toward Florida.

Having lost their target lock and no new target to engage, the two AIM-20 *Slammers* ran out of fuel, their solid rocket engines shutting down, the missiles falling into the Gulf of Mexico and sinking in about seven-thousand feet of water.

"Yellow Jacket Three and Four, returning to base... we lost it."

"Tyndall Control, understood. AWACS reports departure of craft velocity as hypersonic at nearly Mach 10. Can you confirm?"

"It was above Mach 6 when we lost it, Tyndall Control... Going vertical." He blinked hard and shook his head in disbelief, "Never seen anything like it," he breathed. "I need a beer..."

CHAPTER THIRTY TWO

UFW REVENGE, EARTH ORBIT: *SPIES LIKE US*

The docking arms locked the Reaper in place with a metallic *kachunk*, the seal between the Reaper and Revenge complete, a series of lights above Lisa Steele winking green one-by-one. The belly access doors split open and she pulled her canopy release, the canopy glass motoring backwards as she wrestled with her helmet. Hands reached in from above, clearing her belts and umbilical cords.

"Welcome back, Ensign..."

"Yeah, yeah," she chattered, tossing her helmet up, "how's my brother?"

"Brother?"

"The Admiral, the Admiral, How is he?" she insisted, climbing up and out of the cockpit with a helping hand from the puzzled crewman.

"Oh..."

"Oh? What oh?" she interrupted.

"Oh, I didn't know he was... your brother?"

"Are you *new* around here?"

"Not really ma'am... I just never met him..." Seeing her agitation he acquiesced to her nervous pressure, "I heard he was fine," he added, trying to calm her, "he should be in recovery..."

Lisa sprinted off, heading for the infirmary, tromping to a stop and looking over her shoulder, "What about the woman? The one who came in with him?"

The crewman shook his head, "I'm not sure ma'am, but I don't think she made it..."

Lisa didn't wait for the elevator, dashing up the stairs two decks, running into Maria in the corridor.

"Hold on, Hold on..." Maria physically caught her, hauling her in to a stop. "He's OK..." she insisted, placing herself in front of Lisa, forcing her to focus eye-to-eye. "He's fine... look at me, *he's fine."*

"What about the woman who came in with him? Somebody said she didn't make it... She saved his life..."

"I know. She's alive," replied Maria calmly. "They're stabilizing her before they do surgery." She steered Lisa back the way she came, "Let's get you something to eat, and you can tell me what happened down there while he wakes up..."

As hungry as she was, Lisa picked at her food, concentrating on relaying the events for Maria who was debriefing her as gently as she could.

"Uh, Ensign? Lieutenant?" The deck hand that had assisted Lisa gave a clumsy salute, a bundle under his arm. "Sorry to interrupt, but we found this strapped into your rear seat..." he handed her flight jacket to her, bundled around Jack's zombie room laptop. "Thought you might need it..."

"Thank you..." Lisa accepted it, unwrapping the leather jacket to find the laptop intact. She glanced at him a little sheepishly, "Sorry if I was a little short with..."

"Forget it," he interrupted, brushing it off. "I understand."

■ ■ ■

Jack, completely awake and alert, was sitting up when Lisa and Maria entered, Fritz laying on the bed at his feet. The doctor, CABL M7, *Computer Assisted Biological Lifeform*, was reviewing the patient vitals on the holo-screen above the bed, making notes simply by pointing at the information quadrant and dictating his orders. His artificial right eye, designed for microsurgery, looked like a camera lens, whirring quietly as it focused. "You can return to duty tomorrow, but only with a TRS brace, *Tissue Regeneration Stimulator*," he pointed at the Admiral, "But *no* flying. Of *any kind*. For *any reason... I mean it.*"

Steele held up his hands in surrender, "OK, Doc, I get it. When do you think I can fly again?"

"When it's healed..."

"How long do you think that will be..?"

"It will heal when it heals."

Steele propped himself up on one elbow, "How's our guest?"

"We have her in a torpedo, in an induced coma..."

Jack frowned, "A *torpedo?*"

CABL M7 did something that resembled an awkward shrug, "A nickname. It's an MPOT, a *Magnetic Pressurized Oxygen Tube*. It aids in healing and tissue regeneration." He held his arm up as a demonstration, "It appears she had her arm elevated in this manner. The projectile entered above her protective gear under her arm here," he pointed at his armpit. "It broke a rib, went through her lung and stopped against her spine." He put his arm down. "Since the projectile was flatly deformed and appeared to lack substantive power, I surmised it was likely a ricochet off the Sergeant's armor. Had it not, it would have surely killed her. As it is we had to reconstruct her lung and the vertebrae is cracked with surrounding tissue trauma..."

"Is she paralyzed?"

"No Admiral, I don't think so. But we have everything aligned and she must remain still for a while. The bone adhesive will become bone in time, but it needs time to harden." He turned to leave and paused, "Do you know her name? I don't have anything to put on her files..."

Jack stared blankly for a moment, searching his mind, "I don't remember..."

Maria had walked past the curtain on the other side of the room, peering down at the woman laying on the gel foam pad inside the clear half-tube, a curved stasis field completing the open top of the tube. The stasis field distorted the view so she squatted to look through the curved glass side. "Mercedes Huang..." she said, standing up. "Mercy to her friends."

Lisa moved to the side of the MPOT, staring through the glass, "You *know* her?"

Maria stepped back out into Jack's view followed by Lisa. "Yep. We went through Quantico together. Haven't seen or heard from her in seven or eight years..."

"Her vest said FBI," offered Jack, "I remember that much."

"Mmm," nodded Maria, "same place to train, but she's CIA. We graduated in the same class. Last I heard, she was working with military intelligence over in the Middle East."

"Then what the hell is she doing with the FBI?"

"Judging by what Lisa's been telling me, that wasn't FBI..."

"Then who was it?"

"Don't know. You killed them all." She reached over Fritz and patted Jack's foot through the hospital linens, "Nice going by the way." She thumbed over at the MPOT hidden by the curtain, "She'll be the only one who can tell us."

Steele ran his fingers through his hair in exasperation, "Y'know, I know they're kind of necessary and all, but I really hate spies..."

"Yeah, thanks for the love..."

"Sorry, but you people bring it on yourselves."

"You people? Are you being racist?" she joked, thickening her Latin accent on purpose.

"You *spies,"* he hissed.

Maria moved to the side of the bed, "Scootch over, scootch scootch..." She climbed up, sitting next to him, Lisa standing on the other side looking on. "TESS?"

"Yes, Maria?"

TESS' holo-screen popped up and Maria grabbed it, making it much larger, moving it further away for them all to see. "That brings us to our next problem..."

Steele cupped his hands over his face, "Do I really want to know?"

"I think you do," she replied.

"OK," he sighed, his hands dropping to his lap.

A series of nighttime pictures of a very large building fronting along the water next to a bridge came up on the screen. It was concrete, steel and glass, semi-modern with an institutional flair to it. It looked like an office building but had an abundance of cameras and walls that looked more than decorative, hinted at something else. Something about the cars on the street looked odd but he couldn't put his finger on it... *Until* he noticed the double-decker bus in the background. Then it hit him, they were all driving on the opposite side of the street. "London?"

"Good guess... do you know the building?"

Steele shook his head, butterflies gathering in his stomach, "No, should I?"

"It's MI6 Headquarters in London. SIS, *Secret Intelligence Service...* The British version of the CIA."

"How do you know that?"

"Because *our* company had a listening post in an office right across the street. I've been there, standing right in the spot this picture was taken from."

"So we're talking about Derrik, now..."

"MmmHmm," she affirmed. "Dar Sloane and Dale Alaroot were on Derrik's landing detail. Something aroused their suspicions and Dale was able to track Derrik to MI6 and watched him enter the building. In Dale's words; *like he owned the place."*

"Holy crap..." he groaned, giving Maria the evil eye. "You lived with him, I thought you said you would have noticed something."

"Yeaah, weelll... I guess he's better than I am."

413

The evil eye transformed into something more mischievous, "Were you like the *worst* spy *ever*, or something?"

Lisa looked away, "Ouch."

Maria raised an eyebrow, "No. Fuck you very much." She had to bite her tongue to keep from laughing. "So... what do you want to do about it?"

Jack leaned back against his pillows, "*Dammit*. I didn't really expect it to be someone from our original circle..."

Maria's face scrunched into a frown, "What the hell? You had no issues throwing *me* into the brig, but when it's *one of the boys...*" She folded her arms in defiance, "And then you left me there..." she grumbled.

Jack raised his hands, "For the *gazillionth* time, I'm *sorry*. Are you going to start throwing cups and flatware again?" From reflex of thought he reached up and touched the spot on his forehead where she had caught him with a coffee cup.

"I've grown out of throwing things," she replied smugly, "I prefer *shooting* things now..." She tapped on TESS' holographic screen, "So? What are we going to do?"

"Mmm, nothing tonight. We'll take a ride over there tomorrow... Have you told anyone else?"

"No one else knows but Dar Sloane and Dale Alaroot. They didn't even tell the other members of the landing detail."

"Good, keep it that way. Then we can..."

"Aren't you forgetting something?" interrupted Lisa, emphasizing with mock sign language; *"You. Can't. Fly.* How do you plan on getting over there?"

"I won't be *flying*, I'll be *riding*." He started laughing, "OK I can't even say it with a straight face..."

■ ■ ■

Unable to sleep, Chase Holt lay in bed half-watching the news replay on the one o'clock news, hoping there would be some new footage or reporting angle. It was all the same rehashed stuff, the newscasters simply massaging it a different way. Chase wondered why this event had been different from the others, the government making no effort to deny, debunk or remove the telecasts like they did with Caroline Murphy's news special. Too many witnesses? It happened in broad daylight and thousands of people saw it. Or perhaps the administration decided it was the perfect diversion from the

414

latest crisis on the Mexican border. His eyelids were heavy but his mind refused to shut down. He almost missed the chime tone from his laptop sitting on the night stand, debating if he should look or leave it till morning. He glanced over at Karen sleeping next to him and reached over cautiously to lift the laptop without shifting on the bed.

Venturing into the Deep Web he logged into the message board, a marker showing the new message that had pinged his notifier;

From: Starwalker & Wonderdog. Plans didn't go well today, you may have heard about it. Picked up a little lead condition, but the dark side paid dearly. Returned topside, will recover fully. Ma & Pa invisible? Need to locate. Brotherly assistance requested.

To avoid trigger-words warranting a closer look by NSA software, it was common to creatively hide words and meanings. Just because it was harder to find you on the Deep Web didn't mean you could use it as an excuse to be stupid or careless. Chase typed back a message confirming his understanding, and that he would inquire about his parents though he had no idea where to start. He added a question about how Jack was able to reach the web.

From: Starwalker & Wonderdog. Borrow sat lite.

Chase laughed out loud, "Son of a bitch is hijacking a satellite signal from space..."

Karen rolled over, "Huh?"

"Sorry baby, didn't mean to wake you. Go back to sleep, I'll tell you in the morning." He laid the laptop on the end table, finally feeling like he could nod off.

■ ■ ■

Steele was almost dressed by the time Lisa and Maria came to collect him, a nurse having to help him with his boots. Finished tucking and straightening, he strapped the hybrid 1911 around his waist and draped his leather flight jacket over his arm.

"Take your cane Admiral," said the nurse intercepting him at the infirmary door.

He closed his eyes momentarily, "I don't *need* the cane."

She pointed at the armor-like device strapped around his wounded thigh, "I know it feels snug, but the stimulator will not provide enough support... you need to keep your full weight off the leg. The Doctor will not be happy

415

if he has to readdress work he's already done." She held out the cane, "He can always order a hoverchair if you'd prefer..." Jack made a face of derision and took the cane without a word. "He *is* allowing you to transport over to the Conquest..."

"And I appreciate that," said Jack leaving the room. "Considering it's *my* Task Force..."

"What's that, Admiral?"

Steele cleared his throat, "Nothing..."

■ ▦ ▩

Having pulled the Conquest and Westwind out of the Moon's shadow and into formation with the Revenge in Earth's synchronous orbit, making them geostationary, put them all in full view of anyone with a telescope in North or South America, day or night. After yesterday's adventure, Steele thought it best to display his hand. It also made the shuttle ride over to the Conquest rather short, making the doctor much more comfortable about letting him travel.

Climbing in and out of the shuttle was a bit awkward, more than a little uncomfortable sitting in the contoured seats, the tissue regeneration stimulator clamshelled around his thigh hindering a comfortable seated position. He was glad to be out and vertical but the walk from the flight bay to the bridge was longer than he remembered it being. Of course he'd never paid much attention to it before... Thank God for elevators to take them up five decks.

Steele dropped himself gingerly onto the sofa so he could keep his leg extended on a soft, level surface, leaning back against the armrest. "Holy crap, that feels good," he sighed. Fritz plopped himself down at his human's free hand, nosing for a pat and getting a scratch behind the ears.

"You lost a lot of blood yesterday, you have a right to be tired," Lisa commented, leaning against the holo-chart table. "Did they check your dipstick this morning?"

"Funny," he said flatly.

Maria sat behind his desk, "I've got breakfast coming up; you're probably hungry, I know I am..." She leaned forward, "So what's the plan?"

I talked to Dale Alaroot before we left, his security detail will wait until Derrik gets here before he posts... I don't want him preparing his head, I want him off-guard."

"He's MI6, Jack, I don't think that's necessarily much of an advantage... Think James Bond."

Steele shrugged, "Maybe, but I'll take what I can get. I also don't want him jumping a bird and rabbiting to the surface where we could lose him..."

■ ■ ■

Commander Derrik Brighton strode through the bridge doors and waited at-ease to be noticed, saluting to Captain Ryan when he caught his attention. "Commander Brighton, reporting as requested..."

"I believe that was the Admiral," directed the Captain, pointing towards the Admiral's office.

"Thank you, sir." Derrik saluted, turned on his heel and headed for the door, which slid open with a hiss. He stepped inside and saluted, "Admiral."

Jack returned the salute, "Derrik, good to see you. How was your visit?"

The Commander stepped forward to shake Steele's hand, "Not as eventful as yours, I hear. Are you alright?" he motioned to the TRS on Steele's thigh.

Steele surmised the answer was deflection disguised as courtesy. "Oh, I'm fine." He waved to a chair, "Have a seat, make yourself comfortable. We just ate but there's plenty left. Have you eaten yet?" He glanced at his sister, "Lisa, make a plate for the Commander..."

"Oh that's not necessary," interjected the Commander, sitting comfortably in a chair across the desk from Maria. "I've eaten. Thank you though." He indicated Steele's leg, "So what happened out there?"

It felt like a clear misdirection, an attempt to steer the conversation and Steele knew Commander Brighton sensed there was something amiss. "A major clusterfuck happened. Trying to find my parents and the government getting in the way. Same as always," shrugged Jack. "Does Great Britain have those same issues, Derrik? Did you encounter this kind of stuff going to see your parents?"

His earpiece tweeted, Dale Alaroot's voice in his ear, "Security detail posted, Admiral."

"Just my mother, Admiral," corrected Derrik. "No, our visit had no issues. I don't think the British are quite as paranoid as you Americans..."

It was impressive to note that the details were so programmed in, he corrected Steele without hesitation or thought. But what Jack found odd, was that while he was being casual and friendly, Derrik maintained military protocol. "Well I'm glad you had a chance to see your mom, was she

417

surprised?" Steele watched for facial tells but saw nothing he could latch onto. His overall impression was the Commander was suspicious but his calm and controlled demeanor made it difficult to read. He was too calm, too controlled.

His earpiece tweeted, Dale Alaroot's voice in his ear again, "Search team found a Comm unit in Commander Brighton's quarters, Admiral. When we attempted to check the transmission logs it erased itself, destroying all data..."

Listening to Dale, Steele missed most of what the Commander had said but it didn't really matter. He feigned interest and nodded almost imperceptibly to Maria.

Maria enlarged her TESS' screen, turning it around to face the room and Derrik. She moved from her seat to the corner of the desk, flicking up the first photo. "Commander, can you tell me what building this is?"

Derrik raised an eyebrow, making a show of scrutinizing it, "It's terribly dark..."

Maria flipped to the next photo, and the next, "How about this one? Or this one?"

"Are they all of the same building? I can't really tell..." the Commander said innocently.

"We thought they might be your grandmother's building..." offered Jack.

"*Mother*. And now that you mention it..."

"Aww, *COME ON!*" exploded Maria. "Are you kidding me with this act?" She flicked the screen and it winked out. "That's MI6 Headquarters and you know it. You were seen entering and coming back out an hour later. So why don't you cut the shit before I beat..."

Derrik could see the personal hurt on her face. "I'm sorry, darling..."

"Don't you..!" she shook her finger at him. "Don't you *darling me,* you lying limey bastard, or I'll kick..."

"Don't *make* me have to get up," Steele warned her.

The Commander sat quietly for a moment, legs crossed casually at the knee, hands resting in his lap, completely calm, his eyes shifting from Maria to Jack and back. It was the calm of someone who practiced it. Measured. Calculated.

"We have your comm unit..." volunteered Jack. "Unfortunately, or should I say fortunately for you, it was rigged to destroy all of its data if it was discovered." There was a brief change in facial expression and if you didn't know what to look for it would have gone unnoticed. *Yeah, that got your attention didn't it...* Steele tapped on his TESS, the door from the bridge hissing as it opened, Marine Warrant Officer Dale Alaroot stepping into the room accompanied by Corporal Dunnom. "Mr. Brighton," Steele continued. "You have a limited opportunity here to explain yourself. I have a very short attention span for these types of things, and little love for all things *spy...*" Jack wondered if this was how the villain felt before 007 jumped up and killed everyone in the room to make his escape. *Bond, James Bond.* He shook it off, he wasn't the villain here... *Shut Up,* he told the little voice in his head.

Derrik Brighton took a deep breath, unhurried, deliberate. "I apologize for the deception Admiral; I assure you it was absolutely necessary and no affront to you personally or professionally." He reached into his uniform tunic...

Steele's hand dipped and emerged from under his leg, hybrid 1911 in hand, appearing from its hiding spot. "Slowly Mr. Brighton, don't do anything foolish..."

The Commander raised his hands, "I wouldn't think of it, sir." He pointed at his tunic, "May I retrieve my ID?" Steele nodded curtly and the Commander reached into his neckline, pulling the linkless serpentine chain around his neck, his clear, holographic military ID appearing, sliding it over his head and laying it on the desk next to Maria. He readjusted his position and crossed his legs at the knee, his hands resting in his lap as before. "It is true, I am with MI6, I have been for many years..." He paused, eying the Marines at the door, "What I'm about to tell you is all classified, Admiral..."

"They stay, Mr. Brighton. Get on with it."

"Very well," he acknowledged. "My position with MI6 is legitimate but it is my *cover...*" He pointed at the ID on the desk, looking at Maria, would you be so kind as to scan my ID please?"

Maria glanced at Jack and got an approving nod, passing the card near the reader, the computer pulling up his UFW military records and displaying them on the screen at the work station.

"Now a retinal scan..." added Derrik.

Maria picked up an e-Pad and held it out as he stared at the unit, the screen projecting a green bar passing slowly across his eyes. She sent the scan to the computer and a new screen popped up, overlaying the first. "Passcode?"

Derrik took the e-pad and typed in a lengthy series of information, hitting send. "Alright, it might take a while for it to verify and provide everything we need..."

"In the meantime?" asked Steele.

"In the meantime, I shall explain what the data will prove out." He leaned comfortably back in his chair. "My position with MI6, while useful, is not my true assignment; I get more information from them than I give... In fact, Derrik Brighton is not my real identity..." He looked at each person before continuing. "Like Professor Edgars, *who really is my Uncle by the way,* I was not born on Earth. I am an alien. My real identity is Major Durock Brithauz. I am a special agent with GIS... I came to Earth as a young man with Uncle when *he* had the position I have now."

Steele raised a dubious eyebrow, "GIS?"

"GIS; *Galactic Intelligence Service.* GIS works separately but in concert with MIS, *Military Intelligence Service.* While their scope is generally limited to military secrets, treason and military espionage, GIS has a much broader base covering smuggling, terrorism, espionage, governmental intelligence, infiltration, etc. There are places where our services overlap and we coordinate efforts, but for the most part we operate autonomous of one another."

"And Walt was a part of this GIS?"

"Yes, Admiral. Colonel Walter Edgars. He is retired, of course."

"Of course." Steele's face pinched in contemplation, his lips pressed tight. "And when did he retire, Mr. Brighton..?"

"On... Veloria..." he replied slowly.

Jack's eyes narrowed, boring holes into Brighton, or Brithauz, or whatever the hell his name was... The muzzle of the 1911 charged particle blaster found its way back toward the man sitting in the chair, "Are my wife and son *safe...?*"

"Absolutely!" Brighton replied without hesitation. "In fact, that's primarily why Uncle decided to retire. He felt it necessary to protect your family and the stability of Veloria. That entire region of space relies on the stability of Veloria. Being retired he knew he could not be reassigned, he could remain there. He felt with his expertise and connections he could spot any threats, neutralize them before they came into play. Just because he's retired does not mean he has lost his connections, influence or resources."

"We will be able to confirm this?"

"Yes, Admiral. The retirement was strategized and planned. It was intentional to secure the region and keep an eye on it. GIS *and* MIS both approved the decision. There's a lot of information flowing through that system, and with him there, they have eyes and ears they can trust."

Steele's mind was rolling history backwards, looking for something, anything, that he might have overlooked. "What about when we met?"

"Sir?"

"On the princess Hedonist. Was that an accident? Our meeting?"

"Completely a matter of fate, Admiral. Fortuitous I might add. Although..."

"Although what?" interrupted Jack.

"Although once we got to know you a bit, we realized you were someone who required watching. Your whole group in fact."

Steele frowned, "Why is that?"

"Because you had drive... a real homing instinct..."

"And that's somehow bad?"

The Commander shifted his weight, uncrossing and recrossing his legs in reverse. "In a spacefaring community you don't see that very much. When you can carry everything you own, family and belongings in a ship, home is where you are, where you go. People don't have the same attachment to *places*..."

Steele thought about that for a moment. "Hmm, like an RV. Nomadic travel."

"If you think about it, Admiral, that's exactly how humanity spread throughout the stars. It's how we got to where we are today. And your desire, your *group's* desire was a little out of the norm for us to see. We were ordered to keep an eye on you..."

"What the hell for?" interrupted Maria.

"We weren't sure. *They* were unsure, collectively, what you might be capable of, what you might do to achieve your goal. I think initially, Control was more curious than anything else. But then when you took the Ynosa from Captain Kidd and claimed it for yourselves, renaming it the Freedom, that shocked them. They were *very* concerned."

Steele pinched his lips, "Concerned how..."

"Concerned how effortlessly your group seemed to transition to violence, how willing others were to follow your leadership..."

"Might I remind you, Commander, you and your Uncle were right there being violent alongside us?"

"Derrik smiled, "I never said the operation was a *bad* idea Admiral... It seemed you had a good chance of success. Uncle and I wanted to do what we could to assure that success and to take down a wanted pirate in the process. Though to be honest, I found the execution of Kidd a little... savage."

Steele reached over and patted Fritz's head. "I think *we'd* have to disagree with you on that..."

"Very bad man," grumbled Fritz, articulating slowly.

"I will say," added Jack, thinking of Voorlak, "that my *conscience* and I had a discussion about that... While I am not proud of my actions, and initially felt regret, I don't know if put in the same situation today, I would react any differently. It feels to me like an instinctual defensive reaction when faced with pure evil. I have come to terms with it and I make no apologies, right or wrong..."

"There is absolutely no doubt," offered Derrik, "that Kidd was a completely horrendous waste of flesh. And whether he ever had a soul or not, is probably open for extensive debate. And I cannot even make the argument that he deserved better, because I can think of more deserving, hideous and gratuitous ways of killing him..."

"So what are you saying then?"

"It was the chilling way it seemed to come to you so easily. And *that's* what they were the *most* concerned about."

"And whose version of the events were they relying on to make that assessment?"

"Mine," admitted Derrik. "Because as you remember, Uncle was wounded and on his way to the infirmary during the event. Uncle did provide an addendum to the report of his observations and opinions, which carried considerable weight because of his experience and rank. Probably why they chose to continue observation and reassign us instead of the possible alternative."

Steel raised a questioning eyebrow, *"Possible alternative,* Commander?"

"We were originally headed to new assignments. Mine in Phi Lanka, Uncle was heading back to UFW Directorate on Tanzia. They reassigned us both to follow you and your crew... the best way to do that was to be a part of your crew." He looked down at his hands, wringing them together to release tension, a human moment, which he hadn't shown until this point. "Control wanted to be sure you weren't a Kidd in the making. Uncle was already convinced you weren't, I wasn't so sure... Power and control have a way of affecting people, eh? Even good people."

"I suppose... You haven't mentioned what the *alternative* was."

Derrik cleared his throat, looking Steele in the eyes, "It would have been relatively painless. And it would've looked like natural causes..." He sat back in his chair again, shifting his weight, "I'm glad time proved Uncle right."

"That makes two of us," retorted Jack. "So what are you still doing here then? Still observing? Still judging?"

Maria was seeing information from GIS Control filling her screen. "Jack, you probably need to see this... Forwarding this to your TESS."

"Incoming information, Admiral," announced TESS, her screen popping up. Jack grabbed a corner and enlarged it, the information flowing in:

GIS Control, K-Star Sector Command
Major Durock Brithauz, AKA: Commander Derrik Brighton
Serial Number: Redacted
GIS Control Handler: Vetry B'nock
Current Attachment: Task Force Lancer, Carrier Conquest
Force Commander: Vice Admiral Jack Steele
Immediate Commander: Captain Paul Smiley
Current Assignment: Operation Magic Pawn

Accompanying the avalanche of information scrolling down the screen were photos, official agency seals and logos, past assignments, operations and accomplishments, personal information, medical records and contact information.

"Hmm, Operation Magic Pawn..." The information finally stopped, Steele examining it carefully. "OK," he waved, casually. "This is all very nice, very thorough. But because of past experience, let's just say I'm a skeptic. How could I confirm this..? I want to know what Magic Pawn is, and I'm assuming you're not going to tell me."

"You could call my handler, Vetry B'nock. She'd be able to..."

Steele shook his head and waved it off, "Na, I don't know her..." He looked at Maria, "Let's see if we can get Admiral Kelarez..."

"No, no," objected Derrik, "don't do that..."

"Why not?" asked Maria suspiciously.

"Because he won't know," countered the Commander. "Call Fleet Admiral Higdenberger, he's Chief of Staff of MIS and one of the Joint Chiefs of GIS. He'll be able to clear you and provide the information... I cannot."

"Can't or won't?" asked Jack.

CHAPTER THIRTY THREE

EARTH: *RETRIBUTION and the HOUSE OF CARDS*

The blue and green marble surrounded by black looked like a piece of shiny candy to Steele as he viewed it from the shuttle's slit windows. Funny how un-black it was out here, the Milky Way spread out behind it. He wondered, if it *was* a piece of candy, what flavor it would be...

It was a brief diversion to avoid thinking about what was really on his mind. *Operation Magic Pawn.* It was so disturbing he wanted it to be a bad dream as opposed to reality. He *wished* it was a bad dream, it was much closer to a nightmare. Of staggering proportions. Despicable, devious, evil, callous, showing a complete disregard for life or liberty, driven by immeasurable greed and an unquenchable thirst for power. Apocalyptic in scope. Nearly extinction level.

His eyes watered with anguish as he stared at that shining orb, it's seven billion inhabitants, most of which were completely innocent of their fate, clueless livestock living out their days in ignorant bliss. The Shepherd in the seat next to him set his head on Steele's thigh, looking up at his human with one real brown eye and one green eye that glowed softly in the dark interior of the shuttle. "What the hell are we gonna do buddy?" he breathed.

"Fix it."

No longer a simple dog's mind, Fritz was capable of human reasoning and intelligence. He was definitely smarter than many people Steele had met throughout his lifetime. But he wondered if the Shepherd knew how much was involved in those two simple words. If he could understand the width and breadth of the situation. He took a deep breath and stroked the top of the dog's head, "Yeah buddy, we'll fix it."

■ ■ ■

After completing the shuttle's shutdown, Lisa hustled across Revenge's bay, catching Fritz and her brother at the elevator, "You're walking better..." She held out his cane, "You forgot this..."

He took it without a word as the door swished open, stepping in, "Mm, thanks," he mumbled deep in thought.

The three of them stood silently as the elevator carried them up to the command deck, the car slowing, the door swishing back open again. "What the hell happened after the Admiral made us leave the room, Jack? What's going on? And Brighton, you just let him go back to duty... I don't get it. I can't believe you *trust* him..."

"He's a Brother..." said Jack quietly, heading for the infirmary.

"He's a Mason?"

Steele rubbed his face, "He's an Ancient Knight's Templar..."

"Like you..." she replied. It was more a statement than a question.

"No. I'm a *Knight's* Templar. He's an *Ancient* Knight's Templar..."

"What's the difference?" she frowned.

"About five-hundred-thousand years." His hands were shaking and he was sweating, something he hadn't been aware of until that moment.

"He's not that old..."

"No, of course not. But his order goes back that far... It appears all of Masonry does. It's freaking me out a bit." He wiped the perspiration off his forehead, "He spoke perfect Aramaic..."

"Is that a language? How did you know what it was..?"

"Not sure, something with the translator... I just knew. Aramic was the oldest form of language ever recorded on Earth, dating back to 700 B.C., it's what Jesus Christ spoke..."

"Whoa..." She gently steered her brother through the infirmary doors and to the first bed, easing him down, lifting his feet up. "You look a little pale, I'm going to go get the doctor."

■ ■ ■

Maria stood with Lisa near the bed, an IV bag dripping into Jack's arm as he slept, a small device near him blowing pure oxygen across his face. "Is he OK?"

Lisa nodded, "Doctor said he overdid it today. Didn't have enough fluids or food. His blood sugar was way low."

"Did he say what went on when we had to leave?"

Lisa leaned back against the wall, "Nothing about Operation Magic Pawn, which has me really worried. All he could say when he was falling asleep is we need to find mom and dad and get them out before the World burns..."

425

Maria's eyes went wide, "Before the World *burns*? What the hell does that mean?"

"I don't know but I'm scared. Even If I'm not going to live here anymore I don't want that..."

A scream of panic from another part of the infirmary cut her off, the two women sharing a curious glance. They both darted in the direction of the commotion, leaving Fritz laying on the bed at Jack's feet.

Still laying in the MPOT, a frightened Mercedes Huang was doing her best to fight off the nurse changing her dressings. The nurse, reaching in through the stasis field, tried to calm her to little effect.

Arriving together, Maria moved the nurse aside, "She doesn't understand you..." She slapped the button on the MPOT shutting off the translucent blue shimmer of the stasis field, reaching into the torpedo shaped capsule. "Mercedes! *Mercedes!*" She gripped her firmly by the shoulders, "Agent Huang! You're safe, *you are safe...*" Mercedes stopped struggling, her mouth open, no sound coming out. "You're alright..." Maria assured her. "Remember me? Maria Arroyo? Quantico..?" Maria could see a bright spot of recognition, "That's right, the Academy. Listen you've been shot. You're going to be alright but you need to let the nurse finish your dressing, OK?"

Mercedes nodded silently.

Maria held her hand, "I'll stay right here. We're going to turn the blue screen back on, it won't hurt you, it just holds the air in; like an oxygen tent." The blue screen wavered back into view, Maria still holding her hand. "See? You can reach through it," she added, lifting Mercedes trembling hand through the static, letting it ease back down.

"Am I on that *thing?*" Mercedes asked weakly.

"Yes, you're on the black ship. And yes, the nurse is an alien. The doctor is an alien too. You can't understand them yet, you don't have a translator. You'll get one soon."

"Steele?"

"He's here. You did a good job. Thank you for that..."

"The robot?"

"Robot?" frowned Maria. "Ahhh, the Marines. Those are armored suits. There was a man inside there, a Space Marine."

"Huh. Alien?"

"Yes, most are aliens. There are people from Earth out here too though."

They were looking at each other through the glass side of the tube, Mercedes' eyes wet, "Will I get to go home?"

Maria took a measured breath, looking into her eyes. "I seriously doubt it. Your mission is over, Mercy. It seems anyone who goes back is instantly a pariah. Look at Steele..."

"I wasn't with them, you know... Doug, the leader of the team, he was obsessed..."

"Who were they?"

"NSA."

Maria's head bobbed, "You still with the Company?"

"Yes. Director Miles thought if..."

Maria's eyes lit up, "Stephen Miles? Director of South American Operations for the CIA?"

■ ■ ■

"Is anybody there..? Hello? Can anybody hear me?"

Steele sat bolt upright in the muted light of the infirmary, the room quiet, the purified, ionized oxygen blowing past him in a gentle breeze. Checking his arm, he was free of the IV, his treatment complete. He blinked, the odd visions in his brain fading slowly. Disturbing visions of a bleak future...

"Hello? Please, can anyone hear me...?"

Originally unsure if he's actually heard the voice as opposed to dreaming it, he slid off the bed, shuffling in his socks, following the crying to the MPOT in another area of the infirmary. *"Ssshhhh,"* he urged, "I'm here..." He turned off the stasis field so she could see him, reaching in and holding her hand. "You OK?"

Mercedes looked up at him, "I'm sorry, I know it's stupid but I got scared. I hate this thing, I feel like I'm in a coffin..." Her eyes focused on his face. "You're *him.*"

"I'm me," he smiled. "Jack Steele. What's your name?"

"Mercy... Mercedes Huang."

"Welcome aboard the Revenge, Mercedes. And thank you for what you did out there, I probably owe you my life."

"I think that's a two way street, Mr. Steele. Or should I call you *Admiral?*"

"Jack is fine..."

"Is there any way I can be in a regular bed? This thing gives me the creeps, it's freaking me out."

"I'm sure there was a medical reason they put you in the MPOT, but let's check and see if you're stable enough to move..."

■ ▓ ■

"Jack? *Jack!*"

Steele moved away from Mercy's bed to where he could be seen from the infirmary doorway, "Back here!" He moved back to the bed where the nurse was finishing up a dressing change on Mercedes.

"Is that better for you?"

Mercedes eyes were wide, realizing she could understand the nurse. "Uh, huh... You don't speak my language..." she said slowly, "I know because I can hear the words. How come I understand you?"

"We taped a temporary translator disc to you here," replied the nurse, touching it behind Mercedes' ear. "Don't peel it off or it will stop working."

Lisa and Maria rounded the corner followed by Fritz. "Moved her to a full bed," observed Lisa, "she must be doing better?"

Steele shrugged, "She was getting a little claustrophobic."

"I don't blame her," commented Maria. She touched Mercy's foot through the linens, "How're you doing?" She got a lazy nod and a thumbs up, the nurse still hovering over her.

"Jack," Lisa pulled him away from the bed, "I've been posting notes all night with Chase," she indicated the laptop under her arm. "He thinks he knows where mom and dad are... but we need to hurry. the NSA has been hunting down the people who helped them. They know you're here and they want to get to them first. The realtor..?"

"Yeah, the one on the card?"

"Yeah, dead. The lawyer who did all the paperwork? Dead."

"They're obsessed, Jack," called Mercedes weakly. "They want the comm unit. Or more..."

Jack wheeled, stepping over to the bed, "The comm unit?"

Mercedes looked up at him, "Worldwide communications that can reach into deep space in something the size of a laptop? Whoever has them will control all communications on the planet and beyond... If they can get your parents, they figure they can bargain for something bigger..."

Steele took a controlling breath, "We'll see about that..."

"Jack," whispered Lisa. "The people that have been helping mom and dad are Knight's Templars."

Jack's eyes narrowed, "That would explain the trust level for the whole real estate and banking deal. The must have the money in a safe account somewhere off the grid."

"Just so you know," added Maria, grabbing his arm, looking over at Mercy, "she had nothing to do with it. She's CIA, she was assigned to infiltrate the teams and investigate their abuses in an effort to stop them."

"She saved my life, so I owe her the same consideration, but don't kid yourself," he growled, heading toward the front of the infirmary. "I'm betting they wanted the comm unit just as bad as the NSA."

■ ■ ■

Having watched Lisa launch in the Reaper from the control station in the cargo bay, he headed to the elevator past the Marines gearing up for the landing party. "Listen, Dale," he said, pausing, "I'm going to tell you the same thing I told Lisa and Sergeant Mac; I'm tired of playing nice with these assholes. Don't start trouble, but if they ask for it, don't hold back. Fuck 'em up."

"Understood." In heavy armor with his visor open, a light machine gun cradled in one arm, Dale Alaroot looked at Steele with a curious expression, "How come you're not flying, boss?"

"Would if I could, Dale. But passing out in flight would probably be a bad thing."

"Yeah, probably," agreed Alaroot. He set his armored hand on Steele's shoulder, the padded fingers resting heavily there, "It's OK, Admiral, we'll take care of it for you." He looked over his shoulder, five more Marines in heavy armor standing behind him, "Right boys?"

"Aah*Woo!*"

■ ■ ■

The Earth rushed toward the Revenge in its view-screen, filling it completely as it plunged downward. Steele dropped himself into an empty chair next to Maria sitting in the first officer's seat, flipping on the tactical screens, scrolling to the armaments and shields screens. "Where are we?"

"Sixty seconds to Gulf entry point." Brian shot him a sideways glance, "You sure you don't want the command chair, Jack?"

Steele shook his head. "No, I'm good over here. Your ship, your bridge." He activated TESS and pulled her holo-screen away, placing and sizing it where he could keep an eye on it. "TESS, connect to Lisa."

"Connected, Admiral."

Maria's fingers pipped across her keyboard, "All turrets manned and armed, shields at one-hundred-percent." She glanced over at Jack, "How's the leg?"

"It hurts, but it stopped throbbing like somebody was pounding on it with a hammer... So I'd call it an improvement." He pushed on the TRS clamshelled around his thigh, hoping to change the tingling sensation to something less irritating. It didn't.

With a momentary increase in felt-gravity, the view on the big screen swept from the sparkling water of the Gulf of Mexico to a level attitude with an actual horizon. "Twenty-five-thousand-feet," called the helmsman, adjusting the throttle. "Fifteen minutes to the waypoint."

Fifteen minutes from the middle of the Gulf to the lower corner of Nevada would put them at Mach 4 or 5. Hopefully twenty-five-thousand feet would be sufficient to prevent breaking every window below them on the way. Steele activated his mic, "Lisa, you running ARC on or off?"

"ARC is off, I'm running with shields. With you guys behind me, I figured what's the point?"

Steele smirked,"Copy that." He switched to a fleet command channel, "Revenge to Conquest Flight Control, status?"

Pappy's face appeared in a corner of TESS' screen. "All set, Admiral. Four flights of two, dispersed and standing by. They'll hopscotch around if necessary to stay local to you..."

"Thank you, ."

"Interceptors leaving the ground here, and here..." announced the EWO, *Electronic Warfare Officer,* icons appearing over the inset map on the big screen.

Steele paged to the map on his left command screen, highlighting the first icon with his finger, a wireframe diagram appearing of the aircraft in the flight, the summary blank and unnamed. He typed in; F-35 Lightning and the computer filled in the summary with knowledge taken from data sources all over the planet. The second flight were F-16's and the computer, already having encountered them before, had a complete summary. As he watched, the data changed; speed, altitude, flight plan, armament and ordnance, flight identification, call tag and current radio frequency. Stunned by the sudden abundance of information he glanced up, "EWO, where is all this flight information coming from?"

"I've intercepted data communications between a satellite, the ground and something called an AWACS..." she responded.

"Can you disrupt or disable those communications?"

"Aye sir. Would you like me to do that now?"

"Not at this time, I'll let you know. Can you provide me a screen of the AWACS communications?"

"Stand by, Admiral, creating a separate screen... under the communications tab... naming it... AWACS," her fingers pipped on her keyboard. "Ready, sir. You'll have text and audio."

Steele pulled up the screen, "Excellent. Nice work."

■ ■ ■

Lisa pulled the throttle back, dropping the Reaper's nose, letting its momentum and gravity take them down from altitude. "Revenge still with us?"

"Keeping pace, Skipper." Draza Mac looked out over the desert and rugged ridges. "Some real wide open territory down there..."

Lisa wrinkled her nose, "It can be pretty... in a rugged sort of way but if I had my druthers, it would be something with trees and water. Too many rattlesnakes and scorpions down there for my taste."

"You like it colder?"

"Lisa adjusted the throttle, slowing their approach to the waypoint, "Only for short visits. I grew up in the snow, it kinda wore out its welcome. I prefer something a little more tropical, nowadays."

Draza Mac tapped his sensor screen, "I have four new bogies coming off the ground to the west of us."

"Crap that's Area 51. Where are the others?"

"Seven-hundred miles behind us, I think we'll be long gone before they reach us. But these four are pretty close... Uh, oh. OK, I have four more. Different location a little south from the ones out of Area 51. This area's going to get hot pretty quick."

"There are military bases all around out here... Landing zone coming up..." announced Lisa, "Switching to ARC."

■ ■ ■

Having reached the coordinates, Brian leaned forward, concentrating on the big screen, "On the mark... Helm take us down." A series of live-feed video squares appeared along the bottom of the big screen, showing different angles on the ground and horizon around the ship. "Landing party ready for deployment?"

"Aye sir, and the Admiral is with them..."

Brian leaned back, and shot a glance past Maria, "Geez, I didn't even see him leave."

"Reaper off the port bow, ARC system active," called Maria. "We've got four, low and slow, coming from the Area 51 in the west. I'm reading two Blackhawks and two Apache gunships. Four F-16s coming in from the south. All gunners stay alert."

"Looks like we've got one vehicle on the ground... five people," noted Brian. "Ready gear for severely uneven terrain..."

"Aye, gear deploying, set for auto leveling. We won't set full weight, Commander; I'm adjusting anti-gravity for seventy-five percent."

Jack's voice cut in on the comm, *"EWO, jam the signals on that AWACS..."*

"Aye, Admiral," she replied, initiating the touch screen she had readied, "jamming active."

■ ■ ■

Standing there, stunned into inaction, Chase Holt was not aware his mouth was hanging open until the cloud of dust and grit that blew past them like hot wasteland entered his mouth, making him gag and turn away, the ground rumbling beneath their feet as the black ship settled to the desert floor less than a hundred feet away. The only person who seemed to be more excited than awed, was Dan Murphy, clapping his hands in approval, Dancing Rain hidden behind him.

Karen hid from the sandstorm behind the back door of the pickup truck and Jesse ducked behind the driver's door while Chase spit sand and grit out of his mouth, his back to the ship and drifting microdust.

Karen's wail hit Chase like an air raid siren and a quick glance told him she was truly terrified, peeking above the rear door glass, her eyes wide with terror. He spun on his heel, a squad of heavily armed mechanical men thundering down a short ramp into the sand, breaking left and right, their feet making a hollow metallic *clom, clom clom* as they ran, watching the desert in a semi-circle, scanning the horizon through their weapon sights. He was mesmerized by the fluidity of their motion and almost human gestures. He stepped around from in front of the driver's door to snatch her from where she stood, petrified like a statue, into his arms, holding her close, "It's alright..." although he wasn't so sure himself, his heart pounding in his ears with a deafening thrum. There was a lot of yelling and waving but he understood none of it, sounding metallic and distorted. Allie and DOG, Rain's Coyote/Wolf hybrid were out of the cab circling, barking at everything and nothing. There was a man standing at the top of the ramp yelling in what sounded like English, waving them in, but it was all such a blur when one of the machines jumped to its feet and tromped toward them, waving, pointing toward the ship.

There was no sound when the mechanical unit crouched behind the one approaching lost his weapon, the mangled thing flipping out of his hand in slow motion, something heavy hitting the truck to Chase's right. He caught the deformation of the driver's door out of his peripheral vision as an explosive splash of red and metallic *whang* cut through the pickup truck, exiting out the other side. He didn't have to look to know Jesse was dead, cut in half by the round.

A .50 caliber Barrett does that... Sound, smell, taste, heat, electricity, all came rushing in at once, military conditioning flooding forth, *"SNIIIPERRR!"* Snatching Karen around her waist he yanked her off her feet, sprinting for the ramp, looking over his shoulder at Dan and Rain. *"Move! Move! Move! Allieeee...!"*

The ship's main guns pummeled the ridgeline nearly a mile away as an Apache passed over the ship into view, the chaingun on the chin tracking the commotion on the ground. The armored unit that had run towards Chase and Karen spun on it's heel, planted it's feet and unleashed a long burst of fire on it, the gun sounding like a cross between a Gatling and a laser, the rounds punching holes through the armored helicopter which immediately began to smoke heavily, turning away and heading for open desert, a swirling ribbon of black marking its retreat.

Forming a shifting line of protective armor, the machines provided a wall to the ramp allowing Dan and Rain to run across the open toward the ship, each outside-end machine peeling off one-by-one as they moved back themselves.

The waist door closed and sealed, the Revenge lifted off the floor of the desert, a low-grade hum filling the bay, the deck rumbling underfoot. Ignoring the chatter, the crying women and the circling pack of dogs running about, Steele grabbed his stunned friend by the elbow, "Chase... *Chase!* Where are they? Where are we going?"

Chase blinked mechanically, pulling a paper map from his back pocket, pointing to his notes, "Just outside of Kingman, Arizona..."

Jack stepped away from the low din and cupped his hand over his ear, reading the coordinates to Brian on the bridge.

"Copy that, Jack. We'll be there in about ten minutes..."

Rain was on her knees wailing, Dan trying to console her, "What about Jesse?" she cried, "We need to go back for Jesse."

Still in his armor, Dale Alaroot dropped to one knee with a muffled clank, machine gun cradled across his body in one arm, his visor up, "I'm sorry for your friend ma'am, there's nothing we can do for him..."

She recoiled in fear, able to see the face peering out of the metal man, unable to understand him. Seeing this, Steele stepped back to the four humans huddled together, "He said he's sorry, but there's nothing we could do for him."

"What are they?" Rain whispered, her eyes shifting nervously from one Marine to the next.

"People in armored suits. They're Space Marines." He looked over at Dale, "You guys OK to do this one more time?"

Corporal Dunnom held up his mangled carbine, "I need another pea shooter..."

Dale Alaroot smiled, "Sure. That went too quick, we were just getting warmed up..." His face shifted to serious, "Sorry about the kid though, I don't think he was the target..."

After a few words with the Marines, Steele returned to the traumatized group. "Let's get you guys up to the infirmary and then..."

"Jack," urged Chase, "We need to go back, we left our packs and bags..."

"And our laptops," reminded Dan.

"Yeah..." continued Chase. "We have nearly twenty grand in cash in our gear bags. It's all we have to survive..."

Jack shook his head with an interrupting wave of his hand. "Guys, we're not going back. *You're* not going back..."

"We have work to do... a mission..." interrupted Dan.

"Getting killed isn't a great career choice, my Brother." He shifted his eyes around the group, "I know this is a lot to absorb. I know it's all foreign and weird..." He pointed at Fritz, Allie and DOG sitting in a row, watching their humans converse, "Take their example; remain calm. Try to take it in stride." He pulled TESS' holo-screen up to check the progress to the coordinates and closed it again, seeing the startled looks. "This will all make sense soon enough. I have to stay down here for the next jump off, but you need to go to the infirmary and get translator discs, it'll help you understand what's going on around here..."

"How do we find it? Are we just going to wander around?"

"Fritz will take you up there, just follow him..."

Chase frowned, "Are you serious?"

"Fritz, please take them up to the infirmary for translator discs," waved Jack.

The Shepard rose and strolled up to the group, rubbing Jack's leg and touching his hand with his nose as he passed. "Sure. OK, everybody follow me." He walked past, heading to the elevator, slowing to look over his shoulder, "C'mon, *follow me*. Stay together."

▪ ▪ ▪

The heat was staggering, a wind blowing across the desolate terrain like an unrelenting blast furnace. A range of purple mountains shrouded in heat waves stretched across the backdrop and flat-topped buttes jutted out of the desert floor. Kyle Steele stood next to a barrel cactus in jeans and a loose white t-shirt looking bronzed, nearly sunburned. His t-shirt flapping in the breeze, he scoured the horizon with binoculars, "Lynette... *Lynette!*"

The big helicopters were back again, but this time they weren't searching the desert in long sweeping patterns, they were headed straight for the house. For at least a week they had been searching the desert, the canyons, the ranches. He hustled back to the house, his aching knees preventing him from a real run. Past the large angular boulders bordering the rock garden, past the pool, over the deck, almost colliding with his wife as she strolled out through the french doors, dishtowel in hand.

"What on *Earth* are you shouting about?"

"Military helicopters." Kyle steered her back through the doors, into the modern adobe ranch house built partially into the side of a foothill, the only

435

structure for at least five miles. "They're headed here..." He pulled the cheap cell phone Phil Cooper had given him for emergencies out of his pocket and flipped it open, texting 911 to the only number programmed into the phone. He had taken to carrying with him wherever he went the day the helicopters first appeared. Jamming it back in his pocket as soon as the message sent successfully, he continued to steer her. "Pete? *C'mon Pete!* Where is..."

The Black Lab trotted out of the kitchen, his tail swaying, looking up at Kyle, water bowl drool running down his chin.

"What do we do?"

"Storm shelter..." he replied, guiding her through the house across the Mexican tile floors, Pete following closely behind.

"You know how I hate that thing. Have you cleaned out all the scorpions yet?"

"Yes, yes..." he said tediously, passing a native Indian totem pole carved into one of the house's main support posts. Once in the dual purpose, man cave - office, he pulled on the wall-sized media center and it swung smoothly away from the wall, mounted to a door, suspended mere millimeters from the surface of the floor. Ushering her in, Kyle pulled the heavy vault door closed behind them and turned the manual locking wheel, sending the pistons into the surrounding steel and concrete frame.

"I always feel like I'm going to suffocate in here," complained Lynette looking around the darkened concrete room lined with shelves of food and water, bunk beds lining another wall. Pete walked around sniffing the floor, inspecting each and every corner.

Kyle didn't offer a reply, flipping on a switch, lighting the windowless but sizable room. At twenty-five feet by thirty feet, it was comfortable, holding enough food and water for several months. At the back of the house, tucked completely into the hill and sitting on bedrock, the room remained a constant seventy degrees, the previous owners having used it as a wine cellar. Air vents hidden above them at the top of the hill in the low trees, scrub and rocks, provided filtered, fresh air. Kyle had added a coax cable and a camouflaged Ham Radio antenna rigged to the trunk of one of the trees, its top hidden in the leaves. He moved to the small desk and flipped on the Ham Radio...

■ ■ ■

Marine Warrant Office Dale Alaroot locked the heavy armored torso to the frame tabs sticking out of the waist, the legs and torso now powered as the system connections linked up. "Boss are you sure you want to do this? I told you we'd handle it for you..."

"I know..."

"What changed your mind?"

Steele shrugged inside the suit, the armored shoulders moving up and down, "I don't know Dale, it just feels like something I should do."

Dale held up Steele's TRS brace, "You sure you're not going to need this thing?"

"I'd wear it but it doesn't fit in here..."

Dale hung it on an empty armor rack, "The suits *are* pretty snug. I'm glad we had one that fit you... But don't make me regret taking you along, I don't want to catch flack from Doc..."

"Let me worry about Doc. He said I couldn't fly, he didn't say I couldn't walk."

"Or shoot?"

"Right, or shoot."

Dale locked Steele's helmet in place, "Systems and HUD up?"

Jack scanned the information on the heads-up display that positioned itself in front of his eyes no matter which way his head moved, visor up or down. "It's a lot like our flight helmets. Yep, everything seems to be good." He accepted the carbine, attaching the sling to his shoulder mount. He noticed when he looked at the other Marines, a *No Shoot* and *X* appeared over their target outline. *Nice.*

"Bridge to Admiral Steele, sixty seconds to ground. We have targets on the ground and in the air. Sending images to your TESS."

TESS' holographic screen appeared above his armored wrist, live video of three desert camouflaged helicopters, one on the ground, two in the air, men moving about and two desert camouflaged armored vehicles on the dirt road, a Humvee and an MRAP.

"If they engage us, shoot them down," he ordered.

"Aye, sir."

A red light near the ship's door frame winked to yellow, "Popping seal!" yelled a deck hand.

■ ■ ■

With the ARC system on, Lisa eased up within a hundred feet of one of the helicopters hovering a football field's distance from the house on overwatch, swinging her nose to bear on the cockpit from an angle, the pilot in the crosshairs of her gun pipper. "Mac, where did those F-16s go?"

"One of the security flights from the Conquest is running them ragged. There are two other flights in the area, F-35s and they're busy too. We have one flight in reserve about ten miles from here."

The Revenge came screaming in from her left, behind the helicopters, skimming the undulating dessert terrain, a massive cloud of dust behind her. Her nose reared up as she came to a hover, settling level and descending to the sand, an armor plate on her waist popping open and sliding up the side of the hull, revealing the reinforced door within. Lisa saw the moment the pilot she was watching noticed the intrusion and she switched the ARC system off, the Reaper slowly appearing like glitter in the sun, toggling her shields on, the hum of her shield generator whining up.

"Door gunner just woke up..."

"I see him." The pilot's head whipped around on the gunner's call and the surprise on his face quickly turned to determination. She shook her head in an exaggerated no, "Don't do it buddy..."

The door gunner let loose, the heavy machine gun rounds splashing on the shields as the pilot swung the nose."

"He has rocket pods..."

Lisa squeezed the trigger, the turret's Cryo Gauss Guns rattling a burst of frozen exploding metal spikes through the armored skin, heavy Lexan cockpit perspex and pilot, who completely disappeared in an obscene splash of red slop. It blew the gunner out of the helicopter door and he hung unconscious in his harness as the mangled bird dropped out of the sky and crushed itself into the desert below, creating a miniature sandstorm.

She watched a little too long, seeing the Marines drop down the Revenge's ramp to the sand, passing into the dust storm, fire and smoke. The clattering of hammer blows on the Reaper's hull illicited a simultaneous slew of profanities as she cranked the anti-gravity actuator, vaulting her ship straight up out of the line of fire, nudging the throttle.

"Break! Break!" The Reaper leaned over and the artificial gravity generator struggled to keep up with the demand when Lisa punched the throttle, pilot and EWO grunting under the pressure. "Firing decoys," gasped Draza Mac. The missile detonated harmlessly near the second decoy, Lisa pulling the throttle back into the negative, sliding the Reaper flatly around over twenty miles away from their starting point. She bought the nose around and the moment the gun pipper passed over the computer's outline of the chopper she squeezed the trigger, the ammo chain feed rattling as the guns chattered, rewarded by an instant fireball. "Prick..." she hissed, easing the throttle back up. "Damage?"

"Shield loss was momentary, all systems running normally."

■ ■ ■

In response to being fired upon, the Revenge's defensive miniguns were clattering away as the hull door opened, cutting the helicopter that was sitting on the ground in half. It fell apart like someone had sawed it into pieces. Stepping out onto the ramp was a dicey proposition as a rain of helicopter parts fell from the sky, a smoking fuselage slamming into the ground a hundred feet away with a crushing thud. Debris and sand splashed against Steele as he tromped down to the rocky sand, his visor down, the helmet's visual pickups allowing him to see through the blowing smoke and debris.

What looked like soldiers in full desert gear poured out of the house and had already positioned themselves outside their vehicles along the gravel road to the house. Small arms fire erupted from multiple angles, forcing the armored UFW Marines to engage with brutal superior force.

Jack dropped to a knee, prompting his thigh to scream at him, reminding him how much of a bad idea it was. His armor deflected hits like hail on steel but some felt heavier than others, producing substantially more noise and feel. He wondered how much the armor could take. Sighting in, he hit one, two, three, with short controlled bursts, keeping his eyes and muzzle moving. The Marines swept right, out toward the large boulders of the rock garden. He moved to his feet, concentrating his fire on the men along the road.

The *whack* in the center of his chest was almost deafening inside the armor, pitching him over backwards and taking his breath away.

"Man down... Man..."

"I'm OK! I'm OK..." he called. With a groan he rolled to his side to right himself, seeing a streak of fire pass to his right, taking a marine off his feet and carrying him through the air, his armor exploding out the back, the rocket powered projectile designed for antitank use, dooming him instantly.

439

Jesus! That was either an RPG or a LAW rocket... "Reaper where are you? *LISA!*"

A Marine medic in full armor trucked across the sand and slid on his knees to his fallen squad mate, hooking a tether to his armor, jumping back to his feet, and like a tow truck on a race track, bolted for the ramp, dragging him out of the fight.

"Lining up... heads down..." called Lisa.

Another streak of fire passed from the vehicles on the road, smacking into a boulder with a jarring explosion, the boulder splitting down the middle, a sphere of shrapnel and granite spraying in all directions, pelting Jack's suit with a hailstorm of metal and stone, Marines tumbling left and right to get clear.

"LISAAA!"

Steele saw the streak of black as it screamed over the house, the nose turret growling angrily, blue-white flames cutting a wide trench in the road, right through both vehicles. The up-armored Humvee blew apart like a cheap soda can, flaming tires flying outwards, airborne, bouncing, rolling across the desert, its wreckage sitting where it dropped, twisted beyond recognition. The MRAP fared better but not by much, the body bloating as the explosion inside was contained by the mangled armor, smoke billowing out of the window openings, the fractured bulletproof glass laying in the sand along the road, the turret missing, blown clear, laying in the scrub brush somewhere out of sight.

The Marines pressed around the house and Jack moved across the open, firing on the move. Catching a sparkle of light in the brush on the other side of the road, his artificial eye zoomed-in without prompting or conscious thought, identifying a sniper with a .50 caliber Barrett searching for a target. Jack tromped to a stop, sighted and squeezed the trigger, holding it until he was rewarded with something that resembled an exploding bowl of spaghetti and red sauce painting the sand and rocks.

Back on the move he hustled to the rear of the house nearly running into a soldier coming out of the patio doors. A 9mm pistol in hand he backed away, plinking Steele's armor. "Pew, pew, pew," laughed Jack, his voice sounding evil and metallic outside the armor. He lunged forward and swatted the handgun out of the soldier's hand, snagging him by his tactical vest. "Today is your lucky day, I'm not going to kill you," he sneered, dragging him backwards out the patio doors to the deck. He flung him bodily through the

440

air into the pool, the suit's power assist providing him greatly magnified strength. "Somebody keep an eye on that one."

"Aye, sir."

Jack scanned the area, Marines pressing toward the road beyond the vehicle wreckage, "Dale, where are you?"

"On your six, boss."

Steele reentered the house not sure what he was looking for, when a soldier emerged from another room, a fully automatic 12 gauge shotgun in his hands. Steele brought the muzzle of his carbine to bear and it clicked, the charge-pack empty. Dale danced to one side to get a shot but Steele had already dropped his carbine and charged, hands outstretched, the carbine dropping across his body, hanging from its sling, banging against the armored suit.

Backpedaling, the soldier fired and held the trigger down, the rounds thumping out past Jack's shoulder as he swept the muzzle wide, blowing pictures off the wall, destroying the flat screen TV, killing plants, crystal figurines and a Navajo wall rug. Driving him bodily backwards with the force of a small, angry locomotive, their momentum stopped in a wood splintering, bone crushing collision with the totem pole, the eagle's beak blasting through the soldier's spine, impaling him there. Steele backed away and the soldier hung there, his eyes vacant, the shotgun dropping to the Mexican tile with a clatter, blood running down the totem forming a pool at the base.

Steele collected his carbine and purposefully ejected the spent charge-pack from its receiver, letting it bounce across the floor, slapping a full one in place. "Search the house, they have to be here somewhere..."

▪ ▪ ▪

"Boss! Got something back here..."

Steele followed Dale's voice to the entertainment room, "Whatcha got?"

Dale pointed at the far wall with the entertainment center against it, "Use your thermal..."

"Steele closed his visor and brought up his thermal vision, seeing a section of the wall considerably cooler than the rest. He went over and moved items on the shelves, reaching behind and tapping on the surface, "Its metal..." He checked the rest of the wall, which was concrete. "This has to be a door..."

t."

.vy, I don't think they'd hear it..."
Admiral Steele."

"We're seeing a radio signal transmitting from this area. Low tech but we can still work with it..."

"Can you send it to my TESS?"

"Aye, routing the signal."

TESS's holo-screen popped up, her face appearing in the corner. "What would you like me to do with this Admiral?"

"I want to receive and send. Can you do that?"

"I will have to lower my signal standards..." she said sarcastically.

Steele exchanged a curious glance with Dale. "Just *do it* please..."

"Very well..."

■ ■ ■

As the mechanism rotated the door's locking pistons scraped metal on metal before clearing the frame. Swinging open slowly, heavily, the entertainment center and big screen TV moved with it. Jack waited patiently, resisting the urge to pull it open, Dale Alaroot standing behind him.

The muzzle of a shotgun preceded the person holding it, emerging from the dimly lit room, Kyle Steele squinting in the brighter light. Lynette hesitated, a flash of fear crossing her features and Pete stomped stiffly out to Kyle's side, his sizable Black Lab bulk hackled in protection mode, giving a low guttural growl, his teeth showing.

"Boss, is your visor up or down?" Dale almost whispered.

Steele shook his head mentally, "Thanks," he replied, reaching up slowly and touching the release, the gold reflective shield sliding up out of sight, revealing his smiling face, his eyes moist at having found them, safe and sound. "Hi guys..!"

■ ■ ■

Steele wasn't sure what he was more upset about; that the soldiers were a private corporate army or that he'd lost a Marine, a good man, Corporal Dunnom.

442

The armored suits were an outstanding design, a composite metal skin *grown* molecule-by-molecule in a special process, lined with a bioelectrical conductive encapsulated gel. When your muscles moved, the gel read the bioelectric impulses and told the suit what to do. The gel kept the occupant's temperature regulated and provided a distribution of force quotient to minimize the transfer of kinetic energy from exterior impacts to the wearer. The only drawback Steele could see was they were heavy and considerably slower than a man, unencumbered, on foot. You'd lose a footrace in one of these things. But if that footrace was though a firefight, slow and alive was better than fast and dead.

But the suits were not meant or designed to defeat something like an antitank weapon... Dunnom was dead before he hit the ground. Hell, he was dead before the projectile exited the back of his armor, cut in half then juiced by the explosive pressure created inside the suit. The upside, if there was one, was that he probably never saw it coming and he never felt a thing, the event of his death measured in hundredths of a second.

Examining the empty armor suit hanging on its rack, he rubbed his hand over the dent the .50 caliber round put in the armor he was wearing, the bullet's copper jacket permanently fused to the armor, a smooth, burnished, golden plasma burn on the surface. He reflexively rubbed the softball sized bruise on his chest. At the time, he hadn't even noticed that the impact had blacked out half of the suit's HUD. It was probably why he had run out of ammunition in his carbine's charge-pack without noticing.

His thoughts went to the private corporate army. So many of them, and in some cases, so little oversight. And depending on the company and its integrity, so little ethics or control.

ChekMate Solutions was one of those on the lower side of the quality scale, a private security and communications company run by a couple of former special operators who broke away from another company. They had never been in the real military and hadn't the discipline required of true leaders. A minor Department of Defense contractor, they were someone to do the dirty work for the government, giving them culpable deniability... *They went rogue, hoping to get the technology for themselves...*

Yeah sure. More likely they were working on a government-paid bonus plan if they *secured the package* to complete the mission. A politically correct way of issuing a *bounty*. There are plenty of legitimate uses for defense contractors; hunting American citizens on their own soil isn't one of them.

And some people might like to think Steele went too far when he used the information he received from the small handful of survivors to track down and illustrate that point. By destroying everything that company owned, a veritable operational military base and training center in the Arizona desert. Helicopters, trucks, Humvees, MRAPs, warehouse, hangars, office buildings, barracks, runway... all while their personnel stood out in the field in their underwear, watching a live demonstration on the topic of *scorched Earth*.

Maria and Derrik contributed their spy skills and hacked ChekMate's bank account, clearing it of all funds. A news story the next morning talked about the generous anonymous donation of ten-million dollars to the Injured Warriors Foundation. There were others less famous, or perhaps less publicized, but the money all went to places that could do better things with it.

Some talking heads in the news called it *retribution*, others called it a step too far, too violent, an invasion. It depended on the station and which way they leaned, left or right. As far as Steele was concerned, when someone tries to kill you or your family, you don't hold hands with them and sing kumbaya. You kill them. And you do it in such a way as to convince anyone who might think to follow in their footsteps, that treading that path would be an unwise and unhealthy choice, with permanent life altering or life ending consequences. Fine, let them sing kumbaya like a bunch of sheep, he preferred the Battle Hymn of the Republic.

Not wanting to ignore the government's participation in this massively aggressive fiasco, Steele struggled with a course of action that wouldn't ultimately boomerang back onto the American people, either in a loss of security or a loss of tax dollars to pay for replacement of... *whatever*. He considered a little visit to Eagle Mountain, Utah and the NSA's Camp Williams intrusive data collection center. But mired in all the deceitful things they do there, were also things that helped prevent terrorism. Though he had to admit that margin might be pretty slim.

The thought had come to mind about erasing the UN presence from American soil, which would probably bring joy to millions of Americans, but he expected the government would just spend more tax money to replace the building.

With great power comes great responsibility... for the government, its agencies, its leaders, *and him.* Just because he *could* doesn't mean he should. Even though he *really really* wanted to.

Steele wished the government and its agencies had as much restraint, but there was a cancer at its core, eating at it from the inside. The designed checks and balances had been eroded, lines of conduct blurred, power corrupted. He remembered discussing that very thing with Boney in his kitchen; *power corrupts, and absolute power corrupts absolutely.* And in the case where that power is corrupted with evil from the very beginning, enemy operatives embedded in key positions, the results would be catastrophic if left unchecked. He saw the resulting magnitude of chaos on Veloria first-hand. Government and infrastructure wiped out, millions dead... he shook the images of the tattered, starved, forlorn citizens, emaciated slave-miners and advanced cities turned to rubble, out of his mind.

With a far larger population, the loss of life would be catastrophic on Earth, the survivors subjected to the free market slavery trade. The entirety of Earth's culture, art, music, religion and history would most certainly be wiped from existence.

The conversation with Chase Holt, Dan Murphy and a member of the Commandery about the Knights Templars and the Commandery's network was both informative and impressive. Jack had been completely unaware they were as capable and intricately prepared as they had proven to be. Their ability to move, hide and protect his parents had shown substantial resource, stunning imagination and major sacrifice. Would they have the manpower and ingenuity to provide stability and guidance to a nation, a *world*, needing leadership? Time would tell.

He sure as hell hoped so...

EPILOGUE

TASK FORCE LANCER, UFW CONQUEST: *OPERATION MAGIC PAWN*

Reflecting on it, Operation Magic Pawn was going to create one hell of a mess... And it more than irritated him, *it infuriated him,* when he learned the entire scope of the operation. When he learned *HE* was the Magic Pawn. When he learned that the operation had been planned long before he was awarded his Admiralty. That Derrik Brighton had known from the very beginning of the plan's inception. The entire thing blindsided him, and that pissed him off even more.

Was it a *necessary* operation? Looking back at Veloria and seeing how bad Earth was at this moment, he'd have to agree. But this was not going to go smoothly, not by any stretch of the imagination. And he didn't want to have to be the one to execute it. But there he was, the *Magic Pawn.*

It had been an exhausting two weeks of intelligence gathering, espionage, secret meetings, and even a few abductions. Some with the assistance of a few choice agencies, some without. Derrik's connection with MI6 and the British had been very helpful, as was Kyle Steele's friend, FBI Agent Phil Cooper. Knowing the FBI was ahead in the game, gave Maria leverage to convince her old boss at the CIA, Director Stephen Miles, to cooperate. With the CIA and MI6 involved, they used their combined connections to reach out to their counterparts in Australia, Israel, Germany, France and Canada to bring them to the proverbial table.

To bring a planet and its civilization to its knees, requires destroying its key pillars of freedom to initiate the collapse. It may take years, decades, and in some cases, centuries to create a permanent fall. Primarily because the people who enjoy freedom, guard it carefully, jealously, vehemently, courageously. But time and complacency are their greatest enemies. Plainly said, previous evils are forgotten from one generation to another and the enemies of freedom are, if nothing else, patient. Patience, infiltration and slow incremental changes from within, are the key tools, because an outright attack like that of the Nazis in WWII is too obvious and meets determined resistance.

Dressed in the guise of safety and security, people remain blind and deaf to craftily designed, silent, incremental losses even when they're occurring all around.

Judging by all of the indicators set forth by the Galactic Intelligence and Military Intelligence Services, Earth's collapse was close at hand, far closer than many realized. With unrest, conflict and fires burning all over the world, Steele found it impossible to ignore and was baffled by the self-imposed blindness.

■ ■ ■

Looking less like a grunt and more like an officer in his dress uniform, Marine Warrant Officer Dale Alaroot stuck his head into the armory, "Admiral, they're ready... We've got all the satellites locked in, waiting for our transmission."

"Are the new members of our task force in formation?"

"Yes Admiral. The Archer and Westwind are on our flanks, the missile destroyer, Dark Star is running escort off our stern with the troop transport and the supply ships, the Revenge is on point."

Steele took a deep breath and smoothed his uniform, "Alright, Dale, let's do this..."

"You nervous, boss?"

"I'd be lying if I said no... I've never talked to an entire planet before..." They headed out of the armory, down the corridor toward the flight deck. "Has Lisa given them the timeline of events?"

"History from the day your group disappeared, yes sir. Miss Lisa did a fine job too."

The flight deck was uncommonly well lit, rows of chairs overflowing with people, a wide unobstructed aisle down the center from front to back, standing room only, nearly three-hundred people in attendance including the commanding officer of each ship in the task force. Armed Space Marines in dress uniforms dotted the sides of the group, standing unobtrusively off in the shadows to prevent anyone from wandering away and getting into something restricted. Fighter craft sat in the launch racks and pilots milled about beyond the area set up for the conclave.

Making his way to the podium set up near the bay's forward bulkhead, the logos of the Conquest and squadrons painted there, faded away as the temporary holo-screen wavered to life, obscuring the art. Oohs and ahhs washed across the crowd as the live image of Earth came to clarity, giving the perception that the wall had disappeared and you could walk right out into space. Fleet and command officers sat in rows on either side of the podium.

"Attention! Vice Admiral on deck!" The UFW officers stood and saluted smartly, Steele returning a sharp snap. The officers returned to their seats.

Acknowledging friends and family with a nod, Steele looked out at the throng of news crews, dignitaries and staff from different countries, ambassadors, a few congressmen and senators braving the visit, not to mention the intelligence operatives and military representatives. As much as he didn't like the idea, if this was to succeed, he was going to need the intelligence communities' cooperation and participation. The silhouette of a man in a long, hooded cloak stood in the shadows near a launch rack, looking over the shoulder of a Marine Sentry. *Voorlak.* In hindsight Jack thought he'd felt his presence. It made him smile inwardly, not having seen the old man in quite a while. He wondered if this is what he had meant about being special, chosen. *There you are old man, I thought you'd forgotten me...*

"My prodigy? No. I've been around here and there. The queen of Veloria sends her love..."

Steele looked out over the audience and the television cameras, "Good evening ladies and gentlemen, I am Vice Admiral, Jack Steele, welcome aboard the UFW carrier, Conquest. I thank you all for being here with us... even if a few of you needed a little more, *encouragement,* than others." There was some light, polite laughter. "I'm sure you won't regret being here tonight..." He looked into the cameras, "Oh, and a quick thanks to my friend, Sargent Bobby Fortuno on the Chicago PD, he was very helpful during my recent visit there." He looked over his shoulder at the image of the blue and green marble, the moon peeking out from behind it. "Quite beautiful, isn't she?" He looked back at the group, the cameras broadcasting live on nearly every television channel on the planet below, as well as every comm on the ships in the task force. "It could just as easily look like this..." The image morphed into a lifeless desert planet, swirling winds blowing angry red and gray clouds of dust into the thin atmosphere over its endless badlands. "Or this one..." The picture morphed again, to what the Task Force encountered in the Gedhepp System, the fifth planet merely dust and pieces floating in space. The gasps in the audience were what he'd hoped for.

An impeccably dressed attractive blond woman with piercing blue eyes raised her hand from the third row, "Admiral, is that real or are we looking at computer generated images?"

"And you are..?"

"Dr. Michelle Fabry, Director of Green Bank National Radio Observatory."

"These are real images, Doctor, of real planets that this task force has visited en-route to Earth." It switched back to the image of Earth. "They used to look like this..." He glanced down at the notes on his e-Pad. "Abraham Lincoln said; *'America will never be destroyed from the outside. If we lose our freedoms it will be because we destroyed ourselves.'" He looked back up* "I think the same thing can be said for Earth itself. The deaths of these planets aren't a result of natural progression or natural disaster... There have been no apocalyptic volcanic occurrences, no rogue asteroids... These planets were killed. *Murdered.* Intentional extinction level events caused by *man."*

Steele stepped out from behind the small podium, needing to walk, his leg stiff. "Let me tell you a little story about a planet called Veloria, I'll keep this short and sweet. It's a smaller planet than we have here, beautiful, clean, a much smaller population, but advanced, spacefaring people. Immigrants from another planet. Their government was a Royal Oligarchy, but very benevolent. The government did what it could to help its people. As in any society, there were malcontents, outcasts, intentionally jobless, homeless. It is a problem that is not unique to Earth. Instead of letting things work themselves out naturally, they constantly tried to placate those who didn't contribute and produce by taking from those who did. As you can imagine, as a spacefaring society, this information goes a lot further than physical borders. And more malcontents arrived for free support. This was quite a burden on the government and the citizenry who produced." He held his hand up in the air, "Anybody recognize this scenario yet..?" He saw many hands and satisfied with the response, dropped his.

"But the far more insidious reason some of these people were there for; to intentionally destabilize the government and the economy. More than one person of like mind worked their way into the government and provided flawed ideas and guidance, corrupting the system. The end result was a collapse of society, the government and its infrastructure. The reason? Power and resources." He ticked them off on his fingers; "If you control the

449

resources, you can control the *people*. If you control the *people*, you can control the *planet*..."

"So they want our resources?" asked a voice.

Steele nodded. "Yes, Earth holds enormous wealth; water, metals, diamonds, oil, gas, food, slaves..."

"I'm sorry Admiral," interrupted a man with a distinctly British accent, "I just don't see that happening on Earth..."

Steele laughed out loud, a laugh of derision. "Then you're sleeping. Wake up, it's already happening! The plan is almost seventy percent complete! And believe me when I say the last thirty percent will go *very* quickly." He pointed at the man, "You have neighborhoods in London your citizens can't walk in because of the invasive immigrant population that runs the neighborhoods with Sharia law. And you *let* them! So don't tell me this *can't* happen, it *IS* happening. And you looking away and saying it isn't so, won't make it go away." Steele regained his composure. "It's happening all over the World and your governments are letting it. Have you thought to ask why? Because a compliant citizenry is a live, working population. It's still useful."

He got closer to the British man, his voice low, foreboding, still heard by everyone in the group. "The *really scary* part? They're not the *truly dangerous* ones..."

"Who should we be looking at then, Admiral?" asked a female reporter for a major network in the second row.

"The ones who *look* like they belong, but *sound* like the enemies of free people..." replied Steele.

"I'm not sure I understand, Admiral."

"In general; stark hypocrites in positions of power and money. People who propose something grandly beneficent, while in the same breath trying to convince you that giving up your freedoms is worth the reward; tangible or intangible, like safety and security."

"That's a lot of people..." said someone from the crowd.

"Yes it is..." agreed Steele. "Commander Brighton..." called Jack.

Derrik Brighton stood from his seat to the right of the podium, "Yes Admiral."

"Folks, this is Commander Derrik Brighton. He moved to London with his uncle at the age of eighteen. He served and flew with the RAF before joining MI6... He looks like you and me, anyone else you'd meet on the street, wouldn't you agree?"

A wave of nods passed over the crowd, Steele remaining stoic, "His real name is Colonel Durock Brithauz and he is with the GIS, *Galactic Intelligence Service*. Some of you may remember his uncle, Professor Walter Edgars. He famously taught history and anthropology at Cambridge University. Walter Edgars also worked for the GIS. The Galactic Intelligence Service is our equivalent of the CIA, MI6, etcetera."

"So... you're an alien, eh?" asked a man with a Canadian accent in the front row.

"Correct," replied Derrik. "I was not born on Earth. Though my physiology is the same as yours." He sat back down.

"How can your physiology be the same?" asked the Canadian.

"Because, all of humanity across the Universe," explained Steele, "has come from the same place, moved and transplanted over and over again, across the stars for thousands of years. You will see some differences here and there, adaptations for new environments... Like our Lieutenant Myomerr over there..." he indicated Myomerr sitting elegantly with her legs crossed at the knee, who smiled and waved, her feline fangs showing.

"So... that's... not a costume or something..." a cameraman stuttered.

Steele smiled crookedly, glad the broadcast was live and direct so no editing or tampering could be made. "No. And herein lies the danger. Anyone that looks like they belong here on Earth, good or bad, can blend in quickly once they learn the language. They're smarter than you, have more experience than you, and are more advanced than you. And please believe me when I say, they walk among you, and have been for a long time, in nearly all walks of life, good and bad."

"Can you name someone we might know?"

Steele ticked a few on his fingers, "Einstein, Nicola Tesla, Houdini, Amelia Earhart..."

There was a wave of muttering before it quieted down again. "Was she really lost? Amelia Earhart, I mean..."

Steele shook his head, "No. She was rescued."

There was another wave of muttering before it quieted down again. "Anyone bad?"

"Hitler, Heinrich Himmler, Joseph Stalin, Pol Pot... there are hundreds, but we're not here to talk about the dead ones..."

He walked back to the podium. "We're here to talk about the live ones. The evil ones. While investigating the overthrow on Veloria we came across a list of people that were part of the movement involved in the criminal

451

activities of Planetary Subversion, an extremely serious crime in the eyes of the Galactic Courts. It exceeds almost all other crimes because of its ability to cause widespread destruction up to and including planetary extinction level events. Over the last several months, the GIS has continued the investigation after our Task Force mission there was complete. The results produced a much wider list of subversives and criminal ties on a number of planets. One of those planets is Earth."

A wave of nervous chatter swept the audience.

"The investigation is ongoing and continues as we speak. The names of known subversives on Earth are in the e-RIPs you've been issued." He waved his hand, "You may activate them now, just press the red button on the side." The little *electronic-Report In Progress* devices were no bigger than the average watch, producing a scrollable, re-sizable holographic screen. "The e-RIPs will provide you up-to-date information on the capture or elimination of the alien criminals on the list, as well as additions if more discoveries are made. And I don't want you to forget; these people are alien criminal offenders with ties to a vast intergalactic empire of illegal sins. They are here to commit high crimes, treason and despicable acts of piracy. Should anyone have delusions about aiding or abetting someone on that list, they become guilty of collusion and will be tried in the same Galactic Court as those on the list."

"This list has *hundreds* of names on it..." said a reporter in the front row. "Are these *all* aliens?"

Commander Derrik Brighton rose from his seat, "I might be able to answer that more completely..." He got a nod from Steele and continued, "At last count there were four-hundred-twenty-seven names on the list. The GIS and MIS estimate that approximately seventy percent of those names are alien operatives, the balance being known collaborators. This additional information was provided by MI6 and the CIA."

The reporter held up his e-RIP, "Is this all the aliens on the planet?"

"No sir. We are not concerned with aliens involved in a society as working, contributing members."

"Good Lord! How many of them *are* there?"

"I'm sorry, we are not at liberty to discuss that..." replied Derrik.

"How do we know this is the truth?" asked someone from the center somewhere.

"Yeah, how do we know this isn't all a ruse to get us to give up all these people?" asked a reporter near the front, waving his e-RIP.

Steele pursed his lips in thought. "Hmm, well I suppose if I was a member of the media who has been asleep at his job for the last decade or so while the world burned, I might also be skeptical of real news and events that contradicts nearly everything I've been telling people for years. And maybe instead of taking a real look at what's going on around the world, and admitting I hadn't done my job, I'd just dismiss the fact that there's a space armada circling my planet that can turn it into this... Nearly overnight," he added, switching the holo-screen to the lifeless desert planet, producing a gasp from the audience. He left it there for a moment. "Fortunately, my job is to save it, not destroy it." He flicked the holo-screen to the fifth planet in the Gedhepp System, "We determined the demise of this planet was a direct result of strip mining..."

"What happened to its inhabitants?" asked Dr. Michelle Fabry.

"That is another concern, Doctor," admitted Jack. "Human trafficking and slaving is common with these criminals. They have little respect for life. It is a simple commodity to be used, bought and sold." He returned the holo-screen to the blue marble. "Perhaps a better question might be what's in it for me?"

"What would your answer be, Admiral?"

Jack leaned forward, his elbows on the podium, "That no matter *where* I go, no matter *what* I do, *this* is where I was born. *This* is my home. I am an American by birth and I will not stand by while terrorists I have the power to stop, destroy my home. We were too late for Veloria and they have a long recovery in front of them. I don't want to see the same thing happen here. The mission of the GIS, *our mission,* is to find and arrest these people... We can do it without you, by force, or with you. We would *prefer* your participation. Helping us, means helping yourselves." He straightened his posture. "And working with us has its benefits..."

"Like what?"

Steele let a knowing smirk escape, "Like a space station that doesn't look like it was cobbled together with remnants from an Erector set and a handful of Tinker Toys, large enough to have its own gravity, sophisticated enough to accept and deliver trade goods to and from the surface and elsewhere about the stars. A station with a mall, nightclubs, recreation, spa and resort. Then of course there's medical technology that takes Earth out of the Stone Age. Communications that don't require tin cups and a wire. Advanced alternate forms of energy... Oh, and of course there's the whole traveling in space thing," he added with a casual wave of his hand. He found the collective, wide-eyed, silent, deer in the headlights look, satisfying. "Ultimately, Earth could take a leap into the twenty-fifth century in extremely short order. The United Federation of Worlds is extending membership in the Federation, to Earth, with all the benefits that holds, upon completion of this operation."

Steele let that sink in and it was quiet for a while, the audience reading through the list of names and photos, low waves of chatter rolling through the audience.

"Muammar Gaddafi's on the list, he's dead now..."

Steele looked over his shoulder at Maria who had an e-Pad in her lap. She nodded as she silently updated the file, a wave of chirps washing over the audience as the e-Rips updated themselves. "If there are more names on that list that are out of date, please let us know so we can make it as accurate as possible," commented Jack.

"The president," someone whispered, "the *president's* on the list..."

Another whisperer answered the first, "So is Vladimir Pu..."

"She's on the list..!" interrupted a man on the far left, standing up, excitedly pointing at a woman in a suit sitting a few seats away.

Steele shielded his eyes from the lights for a moment, his artificial eye zooming in, recognizing the senator from California. "Ahh, Madame Senator..." he smiled, "It appears we have our first arrest!" He waved a Marine in her direction.

"This is absurd!" she shouted, "I am a United States Senator! Unhand me!" she shouted as he drew her out of her seat by the arm. "I have diplomatic immunity!" The Marine scanned the back of her neck with something the size of a cell phone, the device chirping as it passed near the translator disk imbedded under her skin. The area filled with chirps as the sea of e-RIPs automatically updated, people clapping.

"No lady. You don't," countered Steele.

"You will address me as *Senator!*" she screamed, staring at Steele. "I have worked long and hard for that position!"

"And you've come full circle," replied Steele. "You have achieved the arguably unenviable position as prisoner of the United Federation of Worlds, Galactic Intelligence Service, for the crime of planetary subversion. You will be further addressed as prisoner 5.1.18.20.8-001," he replied calmly. "You will want to commit that number to memory." The Marine took her into custody and guided her through the crowded rows of occupied chairs. Steele pointed toward the brig, "Take our guest to the Polarized Molecular CryoFreeze Suspended Animation Lab...."

The Senator's face morphed from indignant arrogance to mortified terror. "You can't do this to me!" she screamed. "You don't have jurisdiction here! This isn't a UFW territory..!"

"You're going to *freeze* her?" asked a stunned reporter in the front row.

"Steele laughed, "No, sorry, a little space humor there. Sounded pretty convincing though, right?" Polite laughter spread across the audience. "Did you see what you immediately focused on though?" he continued. "You were more concerned about what would happen to her than what she is guilty of. She so much as admitted her guilt when she stated the UFW has no territory here. How would she know anything about the UFW?"

"Does it? Have jurisdiction here?"

"Yes it does..."

"What will happen to her if she is convicted?" came a voice from several rows back.

Steele ran his fingers through his hair, "Most likely death by Molecular Evaporation..." A confused chatter and laughter circulated through the crowd. Jack rubbed his forehead, "Um, no. Sorry, that time I was serious. She's one of the top conspirators, death is the most likely sentence. "I am told it is painless and instantaneous," he shrugged. "But for someone who has conspired to literally destroy a planet and all of its inhabitants, can you really say she deserves anything less? Remember we're talking about *seven billion* people, here..."

"I have a question," asked a man in uniform standing on the other side, holding up his e-RIP. "Why have you included the press and media in this process?"

"General," acknowledged Steele with a nod. "You mean why not just let the military and intelligence community handle it? Because I think you'll find some of *their* names included on that list. And because every man, woman and child needs to know what evil these criminals have planned for them. They have a *right* to know. They need to wake up and see what's happening around them. Give them the opportunity to be part of the solution... Give them a chance and a reason to fight for their survival. Maybe some of them have aspirations to be more, travel, explore, join us in space, ensure the freedom of other worlds like ours..." He stepped around the podium and closer to the audience and cameras, "I'm not going to lie to you, we don't expect this to be easy, but we will help you every step of the way."

The impeccably dressed blond with the blue eyes rose from her seat, "Dr. Michelle Fabry, Director of Green Bank National Radio Observatory..."

"I remember, Doctor. What's your question?"

She looked nervous, uncertain but determined, "I can't speak for the rest of my team because they're not here, but um, I'd like a chance to conduct research from out here. If that's possible?"

Steele smiled warmly, "I think we can make that happen for you..."

Flashing red lights and the overhead lighting of the flight deck dimming to pre-launch parameters preceded the blaring alarm klaxon. *"Red Alert! All hands to battle stations! All hands to battle stations!"*

TESS units throughout the command staff lit up, their holographic screens popping up over their wearers as they jumped to their feet. Steele's TESS displayed a video inset from the bridge of each of combat ships in the Task Force. He tapped the Revenge, "Mr. Ragnaar, report."

"Surface launch, Admiral. Sensors identify it as a *Taepodong 2.*"

Captain Paul Smiley appeared at Jack's elbow, "That's a North Korean ICBM."

Steele glanced sideways at his CAG officer, "That crazy little bastard's on the list," he indicated the e-RIP in the palm of his hand. He looked back at TESS' screen trying to ignore the commotion of the clearly frightened audience. "What's the target, Mr. Ragnaar?"

"Trajectory calculations put the impact in Washington D.C., Admiral. Stand by..." The Lieutenant turned away briefly before turning back, "We've detected another launch..."

"That little prick has lost his mind..." interrupted Jack.

"No sir, about six thousand miles from there. A desert country. Iran..?"

"Another crazy bastard on the list," interjected Paul.

"What's the target, Lieutenant?"

"Calculations put the impact near the Mediterranean Sea, Admiral. Tel Aviv..."

"Evil hides best in the shadows, preferring to work in the darkness.
It withers and dies when exposed to the bright light of truth for all to see."
~ Vice Admiral Jack Steele

THE END - *FOR NOW...*

Thank you for reading about the Wings of Steele universe, I hope you enjoyed the adventure as much as I did creating it for you. As an independent author and publisher, readers like you are the reason I am able to continue writing & creating.

If you enjoyed this book, please leave a review on your favorite retailer's website and Goodreads. Even a short review can make a world of difference for authors like me - it really does help.

If you're hooked on Jack Steele and his universe, join my mailing list at www.wingsofsteele.com for updates on new volumes, cool giveaways, and other neat stuff!

-

Books in the series...
Book 1 - **WINGS of STEELE - Destination Unknown**
Book 2 - **WINGS of STEELE - Flight of Freedom**
Book 3 - **WINGS of STEELE - Revenge and Retribution**
Book 4 - **WINGS of STEELE – Dark Cover**
Book 5 - **WINGS of STEELE - Resurrection**

ABOUT THE AUTHOR

Jeff Burger was born and grew up in Chicago, Illinois, moving to the Gulf Coast of Florida at the age of 28, where he still lives today with his German Shepherd, Jax. Jeff returns to Chicago on a regular basis to visit family and friends.

Originally drawn to law enforcement like his father and uncle, Jeff's extremely creative nature drove him toward a rewarding career in photography, illustration, design, marketing and advertising.

Jeff's choice in career and life in Florida have offered some truly unique experiences which he continues to enjoy. A certified firearms Instructor, Jeff has worked with civilians, Military Personnel and Law Enforcement Officers from many agencies. This has afforded him the opportunity to regularly handle and become proficient with firearms of all types, new and vintage, from all over the world.

An affinity for aircraft and flying have provided many opportunities to fly with talented civilian and military pilots in a wide selection of fixed wing and rotary aircraft. While Jeff finds jets to be supremely exciting, nothing beats the sublime sound or primal feeling of a piston-driven Rolls Royce Merlin V12 in a vintage P51 Mustang.

For more information about the author, additional Wings of Steele content, events, future novels, or to join my mailing list, please visit:

www.wingsofsteele.com

Made in the USA
Coppell, TX
09 June 2021